THE SILENCE BEFORE THUNDER

Kathy Shuker was born in nor
working as a physiotherapist,
work as a freelance artist in c
full-time, she lives in
The Silence Before T

G000065985

To find out more about Kathy and her other novels, please visit:
www.kathyshuker.co.uk

Also by Kathy Shuker

Deep Water, Thin Ice

Silent Faces, Painted Ghosts

That Still and Whispering Place

THE SILENCE
BEFORE THUNDER

Kathy Shuker

Published by Shuker Publishing

All enquiries to kathyshuker@kathyshuker.co.uk

ISBN: 978-0-9932257-7-2

Cover design by Lawston Design

To Dave
for always being there

Chapter 1

An argument always leaves an echo. Vincent had gone, slamming the study door behind him, but the row was still in the room, a tangible thing.

Eleanor heard the front door bang and turned away, feeling infinitely weary. The box file containing the manuscript he had brought was still there, insolently balanced on top of a pile of other papers, as if claiming superiority.

'No, I want you to read it,' he had insisted. 'Keep it. When you get down from your high horse, you'll see how good it is. OK, so I should have asked you first.' He'd held up his hands in mock defeat, looking anything but apologetic. 'Mea culpa. But you did promise to let me do another adaptation sometime if the story seemed right. I took you at your word.'

'I promised nothing of the kind.'

'For God's sake, Eleanor. After all the work I've put in, you could at least have the decency to read it.'

The row had escalated; it had become unpleasant. And now the manuscript sat there, taunting her. It was probably good - Vincent was a fine playwright when he wasn't dissipated - but he wasn't to be trusted. The last time she had agreed to let him adapt one of her novels for the stage he had changed the script at the last minute, removing elements she thought essential to the narrative and introducing a new character she disliked. She wasn't going to be tricked like that

1

again. He was her cousin and always tried to play the 'family' card but their bonds weren't that strong; she wasn't going to compromise her work for him.

Fretful, she began to pace up and down. The study was a long, bright room with patio doors to the rear garden and a single large window to the front where she now paused to look out.

It was seven o'clock in the evening on a late Friday in June and a golden glow still illuminated the grounds. The house stood on a small coastal headland in Devon, Eleanor's own private land, which fell away down rocky cliffs and through woods to the sea. An old rambling farmhouse had stood on the site when she'd first bought it but permission had been granted to raze it and build a new house on its footprint. The old farmyard was still there though. Shrubs, paths and trees separated it from the house but Eleanor could imagine what she could not see: the paved courtyard with a long run of low converted outhouses on either side, each now a small apartment; the old barn, tidied up and fitted out with a stage, heating, lights and seating.

The annual summer writing workshops were about to begin and all the old familiar faces would be gathering there to act as tutors, probably bickering as usual over which apartment they had been given. No doubt there would be the same comparisons of royalties and advances and the same complaints about how hard it was to make a living from writing. There would be camaraderie and stories of their youth, retold and endlessly embellished, but there'd be the old rivalries and petty squabbles too. She had heard it all before. She must have known most of them for more than thirty-five years, since they had all been students more or less. She was fifty-six already. Where had the time gone?

2

There was a brief knock at the half open door and she turned as a man walked in, tall, erect and greying at the temples. It was Lawrence, her personal assistant. His office was just along the hall and he lived in an annexe attached to the other side of the house. She glanced at the clock on the wall. They were both working late.

'I thought I heard Vincent leave,' he said. 'Problems?'

'Just Vincent being Vincent.'

'Had he been drinking?'

She managed an ironic smile. 'He said he's a changed man. He's found God. It clearly hasn't helped his temper but he goes to church on Sundays, he says, and only drinks in moderation.'

'And pigs might fly. Anyway, I thought you'd want to know that I've checked them all in now. Vincent's in one. Imogen and Mari are in two. Frank Marwell's in four and Louisa Dunnell's in five.'

Something clutched in the pit of her stomach. 'Thank you.'

She could see the familiar tensing of his shoulders and the frustration in the lines of his face, knew only too well what was coming.

'They all take advantage of you,' he said coldly. 'Every year. You don't owe them anything, Eleanor. There's no need for them all to be here yet. Some of them don't have workshops planned for another week or even two.'

'We've been through this before, Lawrence. They use the spare time for their own writing and they like to meet and catch up. We all go back a long way. You should know that. They were your friends too.' Had she emphasised the 'were'? She hadn't intended to.

'They always argue.'

3

'Friends do that too.'

He sighed and wouldn't quite meet her eye. 'Anyway, Mari's already left to take part in a poetry weekend in Exeter.' He hesitated. 'And Frank's gone with her. He's speaking at the same event.'

'I see.'

'Frank and Louisa have got engaged,' he blurted out.

It wasn't like Lawrence to lack control so presumably it was an expression of his annoyance: he intended to shock her.

'I know.' She vaguely indicated an envelope and its contents spewed out onto the desk beside her computer.

'He told you? By letter?'

'Frank? No. Frank didn't tell me. A friend did.' Lawrence was expecting some reaction, anger perhaps, something he could feed off. She refused to give one. 'Look, there's no need for you to do any more tonight, Lawrence. It's late. You should go. It's the weekend.'

'You seem on edge. I don't mind staying around if you'd like some company.' He offered a conciliatory smile. 'We've got a game of chess to finish.'

'I know, but not tonight...thanks.'

Still he didn't move, looking at her with an aggressive lift of the chin, then he turned abruptly and walked out of her study and down the hall, leaving something unsaid.

She waited for him to be gone and listened for the sound of the distant door closing, thought she heard it then turned back to the window.

So Frank and Louisa had arrived. Louisa was the only newcomer, the only one who didn't have that shared history. This was her second summer of running workshops and already she and Frank were a couple. They had been allocated separate rooms but that had been before anyone knew. It didn't

4

take much imagination to see how that would play out. Was Frank planning to tell her? When exactly?

She turned away and walked back to her desk where she picked up the cutting a friend had sent her from a poetry magazine. Headed *Engagement of poet Frank Marwell to novelist Louisa Dunnell,* there was a photograph of the two of them, standing in his study, his arm around her waist. It didn't matter how many times she looked at it, she felt the same slow chill, as if her body was shutting down. It shocked her that he was able to keep things from her like that, especially after all the years they had spent together... How naïve she had been.

In a fit of anger and impotence, she screwed the cutting up in her hand, squeezing it tight, crushing it, then threw it across the room. She paced again, taking deep breaths, regaining control, chiding herself for being childish. She retrieved the ball of paper, flattened it out and folded it in half then glanced along the bookshelves for somewhere to put it. This wasn't the moment to throw it away; she needed time to process it. It was what she did. She kept things, putting them out of sight but to hand, available if she felt the need to look at them again.

A few minutes later, phone in hand, she left the study for the tranquillity of her sitting room. She badly needed a drink. She poured herself a large gin and tonic and stood by the patio doors, looking out over the garden: a paved terrace and a broad expanse of lawn leading the eye to a shrubbery, descending treetops and a purple-blue haze of sea.

The phone rang and she turned quickly, grabbing it from the top of the drinks cabinet, checking the screen avidly. Lifting her head, straightening her shoulders, she paused to collect herself before answering.

'Joselyn,' she said simply. Her niece.

5

'Hello Eleanor.'

'Long time, no see.'

'I know. How are you?'

'Oh I'm OK.'

There was a heavy pause. When Jo spoke again, her voice seemed to have shrunk.

'I'm sorry. I was in the wrong.'

Eleanor was silent.

'I'm ringing to apologise, Eleanor. I messed up. Big time.'

'Yes darling, I know. I'm sorry too.' Eleanor hesitated. She wanted to have this conversation but not right now. 'Are you all right Jo?' she asked, genuinely concerned.

'Yes, I'm fine. I've broken up with Richard.'

'Ah. Good.'

Another silence.

'Look, is this a bad time to call?' said Jo. 'Because if it is...'

'No. No, of course not. I'm glad to hear from you. I am really. It's just...'

'I was out of line.' Jo's voice was higher pitched than usual, squeezed with tension. 'I mean, I know I've made some bum choices in the past but I thought he was going to be different. How wrong can you be? We even got engaged. Then I was too proud and too stupid to admit my mistake.'

'Richard didn't like me, did he, thought I was a bad influence on you?'

'Yes, that pretty much sums it up.'

'But then I didn't like him either. He's a pompous prig.'

'You said.'

'Is that what started the row? I can't remember now.'

'It doesn't matter. I said some awful things too. In any case, you were right: he is pompous *and* narrow-minded. And

I've missed you. So much. Can you forgive me?'

'Of course. Don't be silly. I didn't handle it very well. I've missed you too. You know, Jo, some men are like an addiction. You can't bear to be without them but you can't live with them either. Still, I'm sure you're hurting. You should go out and see friends. Travel. You work too much. Life's too short...'

Eleanor stopped abruptly and allowed the silence to lengthen.

'Eleanor? Are you...?'

'Normally I'd say come and stay,' Eleanor cut across her, 'but it's bad timing. The summer workshops are about to start and all the crew have descended again. You know what it's like.'

'Sure. And I'd love to see you, but I've recently got a rescue cat. Sidney. I've got to stay here to let him settle in.'

'Really, Jo, you should be going out, not babysitting a cat.'

'I suppose. Are you writing at the moment?'

'Yes, off and on. The usual. Look, I must go. I am glad you called though. Remember, you've got through worse than this. You're tougher than you think. And Jo?'

'Yes?'

'Be yourself. Don't try to be someone else to please anyone. If they don't love you for the way you are, they're not worth bothering with.'

'OK,' Jo said slowly. 'Thanks for being so forgiving. Love you. Speak soon.'

Eleanor closed the call but continued to hold the phone. An image of the young Jo came into her head: her niece, barely ten years old, turning up at Eleanor's first house along the coast near Dartmouth, standing on the doorstep with a small suitcase in her hand, eyes bright with pent-up emotion but with

7

a gritty thrust to her jaw. Eleanor pushed the image away and the memories that came with it. Jo was thirty-five or maybe thirty-six now. She was smart and able but kept too much bottled-up inside. And she kept confusing intense, self-absorbed men with dependability and strength. Eleanor blamed her sister, Jo's mother. She might be dead but Candida could still be blamed. Even the way she'd died had been part of the problem.

She checked her phone for messages, put it down and opened the patio doors. Cloud had developed in the west, dulling the light and misting the air. Knocking back the last of her drink, she went back to the cabinet and refilled her glass, took another large mouthful of gin and wished she was better at taking her own advice than giving it.

A break appeared in the clouds and suddenly a low shaft of sunshine cut through the treetops and lit up the patio. Eleanor drifted outside with her drink then glanced at her watch again, stopped, and came back for her phone. A few minutes later she walked off the patio and into the green of the garden. She wandered and lost track of time. She was sitting on the bench on the lower terrace and the sun was creeping low to the horizon when she heard the creak of the hinges on the side garden gate and turned her head, surprised. A figure appeared and paused, framed by the rose archway.

*

For several minutes after the call ended, Jo sat holding the phone, staring into mid-air. It had taken her days to pluck up the courage to make that call. It was eighteen months since the row with Eleanor - the only real row they'd ever had - and it had long since ceased to be important. When had she first realised her mistake? It was impossible to say now but she had persisted in the relationship with Richard for far too long, trying to persuade herself that it would work out. At least she had finally seen sense. Though to estrange Eleanor like that, after all she had done for her, was unforgivable.

The bundle of grey and white fur on the table beside her laptop got up, stretched and came across to her, stepping down onto her lap, rubbing his head against her hand, purring, coaxing her to stroke him. She put the phone down and reluctantly rubbed his head.

'Hello Sidney.'

Her friend, Trish, had insisted she get a cat - 'to help you get over that man'. Trish sometimes helped out at a nearby cat shelter.

'We've got some lovely cats who badly need a home,' she'd said.

'I don't want a cat. I'm busy. And I don't like cats. They're temperamental. Temperament's the last thing I need right now.'

'Of course you like cats. They're not all temperamental. And you're busy doing what exactly? Sitting at home all day at your computer, editing other people's books? It doesn't stop you having a cat, Jo. The company would do you good. Stop you navel-gazing.'

'I'm not navel-gazing.'

'Yes you are.'

Trish had insisted on taking Jo to see the cats and Sidney had come to her, stalking across the room to curl himself round her legs, demanding her attention. He had been abused: his tail had been cut off, one ear had been damaged and he'd been starving and nearly dead when he was rescued. 'He never goes to anyone,' the girl on duty had said, eyes wide, slack-jawed. 'He's normally too nervous.'

That had been three weeks ago. And now here he was, in Jo's little Edwardian terraced house in Sussex, cautiously exploring and claiming it as his own. He hadn't been temperamental so far, it was true; he was affectionate and timid and stayed close. Too close: she kept falling over him. But she still wasn't convinced. And Trish, recently made redundant, had gone off to France, helping someone do up a house in the Dordogne. Clever girl, Jo thought wryly. Sidney was not her problem.

Jo swivelled in the chair to look at a photograph on the wooden mantelpiece, a picture she had only recently put back on display. In it she and her aunt stood side by side on the beach below Eleanor's home, both with trousers rolled up above their knees. It was Eleanor's private beach, small and pebbly but a magical haven all the same. They had found a dead crab on the shingle and were holding it up, posing for the camera, looking absurdly proud and pulling silly faces, as if they'd just fished it out of the sea themselves. Jo had been maybe fourteen, staying over for the summer as she often did. Frank had probably taken the picture. He and Eleanor had been an item, off and on, for as long as Jo could remember.

She regarded the photo wistfully. They had shared some fun times. Eleanor was strong-willed and a little eccentric with a taste for eye-catching hats, but she was a no-nonsense sort of person and generous to a fault. Jo turned to look at the photograph on the other end of the mantelpiece: her mother. Candida had never worn a hat, though she did sometimes wear jewellery in her hair. Or flowers. Jo stared at it a moment then turned away. Putting Sidney back on the table, she returned to her computer and tried to work but odd sentences from the phone call kept coming back to her. She had formed the strong impression that her aunt had been waiting for a call from

10

someone else when she rang and that she had been disappointed. That was hardly surprising in the circumstances but there had been something odd about her behaviour nonetheless. Even for Eleanor.

*

Lying in bed the next morning, still inhabiting the half-world between sleep and wakefulness, Jo could hear rain drumming against the window. Sidney won't go out then, she thought dully; he didn't like rain. Her thoughts drifted to Eleanor again. Was it raining in Devon too? She remembered standing in her aunt's garden as a child, getting wet, shocked and fascinated at the suddenness of a rain shower that had blown in off the sea. She had been living with her mother then in a flat in Greenwich, East London. The weather there was equable and changed subtly and slowly. It was muggy. She wasn't used to the freshness, wind and sudden mood swings of the southwest.

Once more the previous night's phone conversation played through her head. Maybe her aunt was more cross than she had seemed. It wasn't like Eleanor not to want her to visit. Jo had stayed over during the writing workshops before and there had never been an issue of accommodation. The tutors all stayed in the yard apartments and Lawrence did most of the day to day organising. But Eleanor hadn't sounded cross, nor was she one to shy away from confrontation. If she was angry, she told you straight.

Sidney mewed pitifully outside her bedroom door. Unaccountably ill at ease, Jo gave in and got up.

It was late morning when the house phone rang and Jo was working at the computer again, Sidney curled up nearby. He opened one eye as she got up to answer it.

11

'Joselyn? It's Lawrence. You know, Eleanor's PA?'

Lawrence never rang her and her heart skipped a beat.

'Yes. I know. Is something the matter? Is Eleanor all right?'

'I realise you haven't bothered with your aunt lately but I thought you'd want to know all the same.'

His tone was offensive. She tried to ignore it.

'Know what? I spoke to Eleanor just last night actually.'

'Really? You'll forgive me if I sound surprised. How was she?'

'Fine. Why?' She started to feel clammy. 'What is it Lawrence? Go on, tell me.'

'Bad news, I'm afraid. Eleanor's had a fall...in the garden. She's seriously hurt but she is at least alive.'

'What do you mean: she's alive? A fall? I don't understand. What sort of fall?'

'From the cliff steps. You know, the ones down to the private beach? There's a hell of a drop there. It's a miracle she didn't tumble all the way down the cliff. I found her this morning, half way down on a sort of sloping shelf. There's some greenery there - perhaps you remember?'

He paused, making her wait.

'Yes, yes, I remember. And?'

'She'd got caught up in a bramble bush. I couldn't reach her but she was unconscious and in a terrible state when the emergency people finally got to her. It took them ages to bring her up.'

Jo started pacing up and down, phone rammed to her ear. 'How did it happen?'

'No-one knows. She was still unconscious when they took her to hospital.'

'Where?'

'Plymouth. She's in surgery now. They did say there was a chance she mightn't make it so I thought you should know.'

Jo stopped pacing, frozen. Her mouth felt like blotting paper. She tried to lick her lips but had no saliva. This was some kind of horrific nightmare, unreal, and she couldn't take it in.

'I'll come,' she managed to get out. 'I'll come, Lawrence. Now. Straight away.' She looked round wildly, thoughts pell-mell, unable to fix on anything.

'There's no point rushing Joselyn. You can't help her at the moment. She's in the hands of the doctors and they said it could take some time.'

'No, no, of course. I need to plan.' She glanced at her watch: it was eleven-forty. 'Damn, I've got Sidney to sort out.'

'Who's Sidney?'

'It's a long story. I'll think of something.'

'Can you give me your mobile number? I couldn't find it.'

She said it, thoughts dazed.

'Lawrence, how could this have happened? Eleanor isn't ill is she? She's never had any problems with the paths or the steps before.'

'I don't know. They'll do tests, they said, once they've got her stable.'

She got the impression he was hiding something. And then it came.

'The thing is, Joselyn, it's been suggested that she might have jumped.'

'No way. Eleanor jump? No.' She wanted to laugh but couldn't quite. 'I don't believe it.'

The phone went dead. Jo stared at it, still shaking her head.

'No...no. I don't believe that.'

Chapter 2

Frank and Mari pulled out of the remaining weekend events in Exeter as soon as news of Eleanor's fall came through, and Frank drove them back to the estate. Imogen had made the phone call but had been unable to supply any meaningful information other than that Eleanor was seriously injured. Their return journey was painful: long tortured silences broken only by wild speculation as to what could have happened. Mari was upset but Frank felt in a strange kind of limbo, numbed, and couldn't wait to get back, desperate to get more news.

He parked the car and they made straight for the den. 'The den' was a communal living space at the end of one of the blocks around the courtyard, created when the outhouses were converted into apartments. Casually furnished with a couple of sofas and armchairs, a large dining table and a television, it also boasted a run of kitchen units along one wall and some basic cooking equipment.

'Ah, a common room,' Vincent had remarked in his sonorous voice when he'd first seen it. There had been a disdainful curl of the lip. 'Ideal. We can play at being students again - but with better meals, obviously.'

But Frank had christened it 'the den' and the name had stuck. Over the years it had seen parties, games and film nights as well as trial readings, meetings and the inevitable rows. It was the place the tutors always converged when anything

14

significant happened and it was where they convened now, late on the Saturday afternoon, still struggling to process the news. As soon as Frank entered, Louisa got up and went to his side, putting her arms round him, seeking solace. He gave her a brief, comforting hug.

'There's a load of press people hanging round the gates,' he said irritably to the room in general. 'That didn't taken them long, did it? How the hell did they find out?'

'Strange how much more interesting writers are when they're not writing, isn't it?' said Vincent. 'Books and plays disappear without trace but a good fall generates a lot of publicity. I should try it sometime.'

Imogen tutted. 'Don't be flippant, Vincent.'

'It's an awful thing,' said Louisa. 'What on earth could have happened? I mean, she's not unsteady or anything is she? And she's not that old.'

Frank saw the glances thrown their way and winced inwardly. Louisa was forty-two, more than twelve years younger than anyone else in the room and it wasn't the first time she had obliquely drawn attention to the fact.

'No, Louisa, she's not that old,' said Imogen dryly, wedging the handle of her stick over the back of one of the easy chairs and lowering herself into it. 'Nor, like me, does she have a gammy hip.' She bestowed a withering gaze on Louisa, looking her soft, generous figure up and down. 'And Eleanor is trim, fit and active and looks after herself. Sadly, we can't all say the same, can we?'

'What are you…?'

'What do we know exactly?' interposed Frank, nudging Louisa back towards the sofa again and sitting beside her.

'Not a lot really,' said Imogen. 'Lawrence was as tight-lipped as usual. You always have to work so hard to get anything out of him and yet you know he's just dying to tell you. Eventually he said maybe she'd slipped from the steps down to the beach. There's no hand-rail on the right at the top as you go down, he said. I can't remember; it's been a while since I saw them.' She looked across at Frank for corroboration. 'Is that true?'

Frank felt Louisa stiffen against him. Anything which emphasised his former attachment to Eleanor still seemed to bother her.

'Yes,' he said. 'There's a hand-rail on the left but nothing on the right till four or five steps down, where they get steeper.'

'Well she was lucky not to kill herself,' Imogen continued. 'A bramble bush stopped her from going right over, but she'd had some awful knock to her head on the way down apparently.'

'How horrible.' Mari shuddered. 'Poor Eleanor.'

'Perhaps it was raining and the steps were wet,' Vincent suggested from his seat at the table.

'Was it raining last night?' Mari turned to Frank, frowning. 'Was it raining in Exeter?'

He shrugged. 'I don't know. We were inside most of the evening, weren't we?'

'I don't know either.' Louisa spoke defensively, as if someone had pointedly asked her. 'I was tired and stayed in my room. But it seems a bit strange to go down to the beach in the evening by yourself, especially if it's raining.'

'Ah but Eleanor doesn't behave like other mortals.' Vincent flicked an arch glance from Louisa to her companion. 'Does she Frank?'

Frank ignored him. 'So how is she, Imogen? Did Lawrence say?'

'She's been taken to hospital and is having surgery. That's all he'd say. Well…' She looked from Frank to Louisa and back. '…there was something else.'

'What?'

'He'd got the feeling that the police thought she might have jumped. They'd found out that she'd just heard about your engagement.'

A strained silence filled the room. Looks were exchanged.

'Oh really,' said Louisa. 'That's not fair. You can't all go blaming it on me.'

'I didn't hear anyone blame you.' Vincent stretched his legs out and crossed one ankle over the other. 'In any case, as the Good Book says, no-one is without sin. Though there's nothing the press would like more than an attempted suicide.'

'Shut up Vincent.' Frank put his arm round Louisa and squeezed her. 'Of course it's not your fault, darling. Lawrence is just being a bastard, spreading gossip. He likes to get in our heads and mess with us. Don't let him get to you.'

'Well, it's horrible to think she might have tried to kill herself, whatever the reason,' said Mari. 'I hope it's not true.' She glanced nervously at the others, not quite managing to include Louisa. 'After all, she's not alone, is she? She's got us. And didn't you say that Jo was coming down, Immy?'

'Yes. Lawrence rang her. She's coming today sometime. After what happened to Candida, the poor girl'll find it all quite difficult I imagine.'

'Candida?' repeated Louisa, looking around their faces. 'Who's Candida and what happened to her?'

No-one replied but they all looked at Frank.

'I'll tell you later,' he said.

*

17

Arriving at the main entrance to the estate, Jo registered the cordon of journalists and photographers but resolutely ignored them. There was a policewoman standing there too, saying something to them, gesturing with one hand as she talked. Jo tapped the code Lawrence had given her into the security pad by the gates and waited, eyes fixed ahead of her as they slowly swung back to admit her.

There had been none of this security when she first used to visit her aunt. Right from the publication of her first political thriller, Eleanor's books had sold well but she hadn't had the sudden, meteoric success that her older sister, Candida, had enjoyed. Rather she had stayed largely under the radar, writing, publishing and gradually increasing her readership. It was a new publishing deal and the sale of film rights to a particularly successful title which had enabled her to buy the once tumbledown estate she now lived on. It was only later, when the film had made the book a household name, that Eleanor had become obliged to secure her grounds: too many people came looking for her. Even so, the security seemed half-hearted, a token gesture, insufficient to keep out the keen fanatic. But there had been no recent blockbuster film adaptations to keep her name in the public consciousness. Eleanor had never taken her fame that seriously anyway.

'Meaningless,' she had said once. 'Just a great gaping hole waiting for you to fall right into if you're daft enough.'

Jo followed the winding drive, passed the car park and barn on her right, and wound round the back of the old yard to draw up on the hardstanding by a run of garages, just shy of the large cream-rendered house. She switched off the engine and turned in her seat to look at the cat carrier in the back. Sidney, who had yowled pathetically for the first half of the journey, had been silent now for a couple of hours. With the killing of the engine, his face appeared at the grill, eyes wide and accusing. She reached an arm back to put her fingers to the mesh to reassure him.

'We're here Sidney. I'll let you out soon.'

The driver's door opened and she quickly turned back. Lawrence had yanked it open and now stood there, tall and imposing, like a hotel porter - or maybe a palace guard - waiting, silent. He had presumably been watching for her.

'Hello Lawrence.' She got out, offering a smile.

'Joselyn. I hope you had a good journey.'

'Jo. Please call me Jo. Is there any news? I left my number with the hospital but I've heard nothing. I don't know if my message got through to the right place.'

'I've just rung. Apparently Eleanor's out of surgery and stable.'

'Thank God.'

'She's on ITU, on a ventilator, I believe.'

'That's something, I suppose, but it sounds frightening.' She glanced at her watch: nearly six o'clock. 'I'd better sort Sidney out and then get over there.'

'Who's Sidney?'

She opened the rear door and pulled out the carrier, holding it up so that Lawrence could see. Sidney peered out at him balefully and emitted a pathetic cry.

'Sidney's my cat.'

'You've got to be joking.' He looked into the carrier with distaste. 'You brought him here? I'm not fond of cats. In any case, that's unwise. He's sure to get lost or run away.'

'I'm not pretending it's ideal, Lawrence, but I didn't have a choice. He's not long out of a cat shelter; I couldn't take him back. We'll just have to take care not to let him out of the house until he's used to the place.' She grabbed her handbag

19

from inside the car and pushed the door to. 'I'd better get to the hospital.'

'There's no rush. You can't help her and she is stable. Charlotte's left a salad for you in the fridge. She came up to the house as soon as she heard the news and insisted on preparing it specially.' He was already moving to the back of the car. 'I suppose you have other luggage?'

'Yes...thanks. There's a suitcase in the boot and a bag of things for Sidney. And my laptop and briefcase. Oh, and there's a litter tray too and a bag of litter but it's OK, I'll come back for those.'

Lawrence lifted the boot lid. Jo turned away, thoughts elsewhere, and carried Sidney into the house.

It hadn't changed. Why would it have? A surge of emotion caught her off guard as a disconcerting mix of memories, both good and bad, assailed her. Distracted, she put Sidney's carrier down in the hallway and walked into the sitting room. It was one of the rooms she remembered best, a large, rectangular room, awash with the artefacts and mementoes of Eleanor's life and travels: colourful rugs and throws, paintings, sculpture and wooden carvings from places she had visited; an eclectic pile of books waiting to be read, and a variety of magazines tumbling over the lower shelf of the coffee table. At the further end a small table was set up with a chess board, a chair either side. Nearby stood a huge world globe on a stand and, against a far wall, an upright piano.

The room should have been oppressive but wasn't. There was a white stone fireplace in the wall to her left with three small sofas positioned around it, a broad window in the opposite wall facing northwest towards the village below, and, the eye-catching highlight of the room, the wide patio doors which gave onto the garden. Jo walked to stand in front of them. Between and over treetops, there was a bewitching and ever-changing view of the sea. She had spent hours here when she was younger. Eleanor used to make up stories about the people on the boats which passed by, sometimes close in, sometimes miles away: tankers and freighters, yachts big and small. The young Joselyn had been entranced.

'What do you want me to do with these?'

Jo turned, abruptly brought back to the present. Lawrence was standing in the doorway holding up the litter tray and the bag of litter, both at arm's length.

'I thought perhaps in the conservatory,' she replied. 'The floor'll be easy to clean in there if he spills any.'

Lawrence offered a pained expression but said nothing and disappeared. Jo went back out into the hall where he had left her other luggage. She pulled a cloth out of Sidney's bag and began rubbing it over the door frames all the way along the hallway, then back in the sitting room, over some of the furniture.

'What are you doing?' Lawrence was watching her again. He was unnerving. For a big man, he moved remarkably silently. She had always suspected that he was on his best behaviour around Eleanor. But Eleanor wasn't there.

'I'm putting Sidney's smell around so it feels like home. The rescue staff recommend it. You rub the cloth over his coat first.'

'Well, when you've finished desecrating Eleanor's house, you'll find your meal in the kitchen. I assumed you'd use the same bedroom as when you used to come here.' There was just the faintest hint of emphasis on the 'used to come' and he paused, allowing the negative tone to hang in the air. 'I'll put your case there.'

He left and she heard him climbing the stairs.

Jo picked up the carrier and took it to the conservatory where she put it down and opened the door. Sidney hesitated and slowly emerged. He stretched, then stalked deliberately around the room before sniffing at the litter tray and relieving himself in it.

It was a start. She put down food and water for him and left him washing himself while she went in search of her salad. Charlotte, Eleanor's housekeeper, was a force to be reckoned with; it was wise not to offend her.

*

Jo sat on the plastic chair by the side of her aunt's bed, holding Eleanor's limp fingers. The ventilator made a rhythmic click and pumping sound and the cardiac monitor beeped with comforting regularity. Even so, the place was intimidating. The Intensive Therapy Unit felt like an operating theatre with beds: it was alien and sterile and inhuman. The smell of antiseptic hung in the air. Eleanor's head had been shaved and a soft dressing had been taped over her craniotomy. She looked achingly exposed and vulnerable, her usually animated body flaccid and, but for the profuse cuts and bruises that were visible, frighteningly pale. The ventilator was attached to a thick tube which had been put down her throat and other wires and tubes dangled from her body like so many marionette strings. Jo struggled to keep looking but couldn't bear not to keep watching her aunt's face, just in case she opened her eyes, just in case anything happened. Anything at all.

The surgeons had done the craniotomy to relieve the pressure on her brain, she had been told. The fall from the terrace had fractured a couple of her ribs and caused massive bruising. It had also fractured her skull and caused some bleeding and swelling on the brain.

'Will she recover?' Jo had asked, aware that she simply craved reassurance, certain they would tell her nothing.

'I'm afraid it really is too soon to say what the prognosis is. We won't know for a while. We'll take her off the ventilator as soon as she can breathe for herself.' There had been an unvoiced 'if' in the surgeon's explanation and a second's hesitation before he'd added, gently, 'You do need to be prepared for the worst, I'm afraid. Her condition could still go either way.'

'Do you think she's ill? Is that why she fell?'

'We're running tests and we'll do more. It's early days.'

Jo sat and watched and waited. Her eyes stung from staring, first at the road to get here, now at Eleanor's pallid face. From unshed tears too.

Click, sigh.

'Who suggested she might have jumped?' she had asked Lawrence before leaving.

'The police - from their preliminary enquiries, they said.'

'I don't believe it.'

'So you said, but I suppose they must have their reasons. They said there was no sign of an intruder or a burglary gone wrong. Nothing appeared to have been taken. They want to interview you too. I told them you were arriving today and gave them your number.'

An interview. What could she tell them? She knew nothing about it. And she didn't want Eleanor to be ill, but better that, surely, than that she had tried to kill herself. If she was ill, maybe it could be treated, maybe... There were too many maybes.

Click, sigh.

Jo's eyes stayed fixed on Eleanor's face. It was hard to see the person she knew under all these tubes and wires but she seemed to have aged since their last meeting. Guilt gnawed at her. She should have been there, in her aunt's life. The phone call from the Friday night kept circulating in her mind. Eleanor hadn't sounded herself. Was that from illness or because of something else, something that was bothering her?

'You should have told me,' she leaned forward and hissed to Eleanor's blank face. 'This is me, remember? Jo. I mean I know I've let you down lately, but why didn't you tell me, Eleanor?'

Alerted by her manner, a nurse came and stood nearby, glancing over the bed and her patient, incorporating Jo in her cool assessment. Jo straightened up, silent again. Apparently satisfied, the nurse moved away.

Click, sigh.

The lead weight of guilt swelled and grew a little more. She wasn't likely to tell you, said the voice in her head. You hadn't bothered with her for ages. You can't claim back the relationship you used to have with her, just because of one phone call.

'You should go home and get some rest.'

Jo jumped. The ward sister had come to stand just behind her.

'Thanks, but I'm fine,' said Jo.

'Your aunt's stable. And we need to see to her anyway. I understand you've had a long day. You can wait outside if you want but if you give me your number, I'll make sure the night staff let you know if there's any change. You're staying at your aunt's house aren't you?' She began to move away. 'Oh, I nearly forgot. A police officer's just arrived to see you. She said she'd wait outside.'

'Right. Thanks.'

She had been given permission to escape and was

shamefully relieved. She made for the exit to the corridor.

The officer - a tall woman with a quick smile - drew a notebook out of her pocket as soon as Jo introduced herself. After a polite expression of sympathy, she got straight to the point.

'Miss Lambe, when did you last speak to your aunt?'

'Last night…on the phone. I rang her.'

'Did you ring for any particular reason?'

'No-o. Yes. I hadn't been in touch for a while so I wanted to, you know, catch up.' A half-truth.

The officer nodded, scribbling in her notebook. 'How did she sound, your aunt?' She looked up. 'I mean, was she her usual self or was she agitated in any way?'

'She was…' What was she? Jo was an editor so she lived and breathed words. It felt important to choose the right one so there could be no misunderstanding and 'agitated' didn't fit the bill. '…I'd say she was preoccupied. She said she had a lot on her mind. The workshops, I imagine.'

'She didn't mention anything else?'

'No.'

'We understand that someone she used to be in a relationship with has recently become engaged to someone else. Do you think that would have troubled her?'

Jo frowned yet half smiled at the absurdity of it. 'You don't mean Frank?'

The officer flicked back through her notepad. 'Yes, Frank Marwell.' She fixed her penetrating gaze back on Jo. 'That surprises you?'

Jo paused, the smile gone, taking a second to gather her thoughts, keeping her expression as neutral as possible. She hadn't heard about this engagement. Soon after her last visit to Devon, Eleanor had told her in a phone conversation that she and Frank were 'having a rest'. The euphemism had been used a couple of times before and Jo had given it little thought. Their relationship had always been stormy. But then, after a succession of ever more sporadic emails and calls when Frank hadn't been mentioned again, she and Eleanor had had that row and lost touch completely. Clearly the 'rest' had been permanent this time. That was hard to take on board.

'It's a while since Eleanor and Frank Marwell were a couple,' she told the officer. 'Apart from the workshops, I don't think they see much of each other.'

'And her work? Someone suggested that she was having problems with her current book. Did she mention it?'

'Who said that?'

'Did she mention it?'

'Not specifically, I don't think.' Jo tried to remember what Eleanor had said exactly but, put on the spot, couldn't recall. 'I'm not sure.'

'Did she suffer from depression?'

'No.' Jo almost laughed at the suggestion.

'She had consumed a lot of alcohol.'

'So it could have been an accident?'

'It's one possibility.'

'She's not the sort of person to let things get her down. You don't know her. She's not like that.'

A non-committal nod. 'No, well we haven't found any evidence to suggest that anyone else was involved.'

The police officer finished writing notes, thanked Jo and left. A couple of minutes later, Jo followed her out and drove away.

Back at the house, Sidney gave her a rapturous greeting, curling round her and purring loudly. She picked him up, rubbing his head.

'That's a nice welcome, Sidney. You're not so bad, are you?'

She became aware of the presence of Lawrence at the end of the hallway. His annexe was accessed through an enclosed passage from a door near the kitchen. She wondered if it was possible to lock that door from this side. She wondered if she dared.

'How is Eleanor?' he asked.

'She's just the same. There's no change. She doesn't seem to be conscious of anything.'

He nodded. 'They won't let me see her yet,' he said coolly. 'Only family at the moment.'

'Oh.' She felt a rare pang of sympathy for him. 'I'm sorry. But she doesn't know anyone's there anyway.'

'It doesn't matter. Someone has to be here to keep everything running.'

He was about to turn away.

'Lawrence? I hadn't heard that Frank had got engaged to someone else. Who is it?'

He paused and held her gaze in that way he had, stonily, rarely blinking, like a lizard.

'Louisa Dunnell. She's one of the tutors here. Ran her first course last year.'

'Is that when they met?'

'I couldn't say.'

She frowned. 'Lawrence, was it you who told the police that Eleanor was having problems with her current book?'

'They were asking questions about any issues that were troubling her.'

'I see. And was she?'

'You think I tell lies?'

'I find it hard to imagine Eleanor being so distraught over

27

her writing that she'd walk off the side of a cliff.'

'That, of course, is an entirely different question.' He wished her a brief 'goodnight', already walking away, and disappeared back to his own quarters.

He hadn't answered her. But Lawrence had always been a man of few words. She had once complained about it to Eleanor and her aunt had laughed.

'There's the pot calling the kettle black,' she'd said.

Jo made herself a mug of tea and went upstairs to her old room, Sidney close at her heels. The house was silent and empty and she sat on the bed, stroking Sidney, keeping him close. Tiredness and pent up emotion finally got the better of her and the tears flowed, dripping onto the cat's fur faster than she could wipe them away. Drained and exhausted, she fell asleep in the end with the cat on the bed beside her, haunted by dreams of Eleanor in her hospital bed and the constant click, sigh of the ventilator.

Chapter 3

A road ran alongside the public beach at Petterton Mill Cove, a low stone wall and a narrow pavement separating it from the sandy shore. On the other side of the road stood a convenience store and a coffee shop called Millie's. The café was double-fronted, bright and cheery and had tables outside in the summer, looking out to the bay. Matthew Croft had bought the café the previous autumn. Millie had been the wife of the previous owner who had kept her name over the door even after her death, unwilling to separate her from the place which had been such a big part of her life. Matthew hadn't changed the name either, though he had no particular reason for not doing so; he simply hadn't bothered.

On the Sunday morning only a handful of tables were occupied, one of them on the pavement outside. Matthew was wiping the nozzles down on the espresso machine when he heard the door open and turned to see a couple approaching the counter. The man was wiry with a stubbled chin and a slightly curling thatch of white-grey hair. The woman looked younger; she was pretty and curvaceous with an open, smiley face and a toss of blonde hair. She walked with a short, bustling step.

'I thought he was never going to let us leave,' she was saying to her companion in the kind of voice that carried. 'All those questions, Frank. I've never been interviewed by the police before. What was he trying to get at? I mean, why would any of us know anything about it?'

'He was just doing his job,' the man replied calmly. 'Don't fret over it. It's done with now.'

They reached the counter and paused, looking up at the list of available drinks written on the board on the wall. Matthew picked up the biro next to the pad by the till.

'Morning,' he said. 'What can I get you?'

The woman smiled and made eye contact. 'A cappuccino.'

'Regular or large?' Matthew pointed to the cups behind him.

'Definitely large.' The smile broadened. 'With lots of chocolate on the top.'

'I'll have a filter, please,' said the man. 'Large.' He hesitated. 'Are you new here?'

Matthew's eyebrows lifted. 'Fairly. Does it show?'

The man grinned. 'I'm used to Gareth, that's all. He always used to be here.'

'He retired last year. I took the place over in the winter. I'm Matthew.'

'Frank. This is my fiancée, Louisa. Anyway, best of luck with it. It gets a bit crazy here in the season.'

'So I've heard.' Matthew heard the back door bang followed by voices in the kitchen. He listened for a second then forced himself to concentrate. 'Do you want milk with your filter?'

'Please. Cold.'

'Anything to eat?'

Louisa shook her head. 'No thanks.' She squeezed a smile sideways at Frank. 'Do we darling? Though after that ordeal, maybe I do need something. Yes, I'll have one of those caramel slices.'

Matthew wrote it down.

'We're staying up at Skymeet,' Louisa added. 'Frank's a poet and I write romance novels.' She paused as if expecting a response but Matthew didn't give one. 'We're going to be running the writing workshops...' She glanced across at her companion. '...or we were. But who knows now?' She looked enquiringly at Matthew. 'I suppose you've heard about the accident?'

'No-o. What accident?'

'I don't suppose it's common knowledge yet, darling,' Frank said quickly.

'No, but we weren't told not to say anything and it's bound to come out.'

She turned back to Matthew who hesitated, unsure if he should back off from this conversation or not. He still wasn't good at the sort of easy-going chat expected by most of his customers. In any case, he got the impression that this woman wasn't interested in conversation so much as simply having an audience. To prove the point, she paused and glanced round the room; there were only six people there.

'Do you know the writer who lives up at Skymeet?' she asked. 'Eleanor Lambe? She's had a fall. She's very poorly.'

Matthew did know Eleanor Lambe, the novelist who lived up on the headland. She had been into the shop for coffee and had made a point of consulting him about a couple of matters. He had seen her at meetings in the village hall too. She was approachable, not at all stand-offish, and direct to a fault. In his experience, too many people said one thing, smiling, while meaning something else completely. He rather liked her.

'What sort of fall?' he asked.

'Oh, awful. She went over the cliff. The police have been

31

asking all sorts of questions and the press are hanging around too. We decided to escape.' She glanced round the room again. 'I'm glad they haven't got here yet. Well, you know what they're like,' she protested to Frank as if he had disagreed with her.

The couple settled at a table near the window and Matthew prepared their drinks, took a caramel slice from the glazed cabinet and carried the order over on a tray. Returning to the counter, he walked straight through into the kitchen. Gail was there, making sandwiches for lunch-time. He had inherited Gail with the shop and she was worth her weight in gold. All the courses in the world couldn't prepare you for what it was really like to run a place like this. Gail, late twenties, calm, matter-of-fact and more experienced than her age suggested, had stopped him from making a lot of mistakes already. But it wasn't Gail he had come to see. His son, Harry, had come in through the back door from the yard. He was wearing sloppy jeans and a sweatshirt and a baseball cap with the peak at the back and Gail had just handed him a plate of hot buttered toast.

'Why on earth didn't you make toast at home?' Matthew demanded, his voice pitched low enough to avoid it carrying into the shop. 'We've got bread. Gail has better things to do than make your breakfast. I assume you've only just got up?'

'It's no problem,' Gail said quickly. 'I've nearly finished the sandwiches.'

Matthew glared at his son but let it drop, reluctant to involve the girl. He turned back into the shop and began aggressively wiping down the nozzles on the machines again and emptying out the coffee grounds into the plastic bin beneath. He watched Gail take the tray of sandwiches out to the chiller cabinet and start to unload them just as two young women got up from their table and left.

He returned to the kitchen. Harry was leaning against the units, shovelling the last piece of toast into his mouth.

'I thought we agreed you were going to work weekends to earn some money?' Matthew said tersely. 'You get through enough of the stuff. That was the bargain we made when we came here.'

'It was your idea to come here,' Harry said sullenly. 'I didn't ask to come.' He turned to put the empty plate down on the side. 'Anyway, I've arranged to go out today.'

'Where?'

'Just out.'

'Well, my pockets aren't bottomless young man. You need to earn money if you want to spend it.'

Harry said nothing, looking down, pushing the toe of one trainer against the instep of his other foot.

'And where were you last night? It was after midnight when you came in.'

'It was a clear night. I don't like staying in that house. It's too dark. It gives me the creeps.'

Gail returned and silently slipped past Matthew, putting the dishes from the recently vacated table to clean. Harry took the opportunity to let himself out of the back door and leave. Matthew sighed heavily. He had tried both the stick and the carrot and nothing seemed to make any difference. Harry was out of his control. He couldn't even hold a conversation with him.

Gail glanced across and offered a sympathetic smile.

'He's fifteen, Matthew. It's normal, especially after what he's been through.'

Matthew heard the shop door open and went back to the counter, his thoughts shifting to the news from up on the headland. Skymeet. It was an odd name to give a house. He wondered how Eleanor was. Preparing the new drinks order, he glanced across at the two writers who were now speaking in quieter tones, the man resting his hand on the woman's arm. He couldn't quite place the dynamic between them. Still it had nothing to do with him.

A few minutes later, they'd gone and he went across to clear their table and wipe it.

*

Jo rubbed her thumb over the back of Eleanor's hand in a movement that had already become automatic. The cardiac monitor still bleeped regularly; the ventilator clicked and sighed. Eleanor, turned on her left side, was as immobile and unresponsive as ever. But she wasn't any worse so at least that was something. It'll take time, Jo kept telling herself. Be patient.

She had been there all day, sitting in that plastic chair, escaping to the hospital café downstairs when staff needed access to her aunt, walking outside a few minutes to get some fresh air. She was exhausted, wrung out. Talk to her, the doctor had suggested that morning; she might hear you. So Jo had tried to think of something to say for hours now, off and on. It wasn't easy. She had talked about Sidney, at greater length than she could have imagined, and work, and the way she'd redecorated bits of the house since Richard had left, rearranged things, made it feel more like hers again. She was trying to keep it light and happy, avoid anything controversial or upsetting. Perhaps she should go further back. She leaned forward now and spoke confidentially to Eleanor's impassive face.

'Eleanor, do you remember the first time you took me to

see a pantomime? Mum was ill and we went to see *Cinderella* together. Do you remember how you shouted "behind you" louder than anyone else and stood up every time, pointing? A woman behind us told you to sit down. "Behave yourself," she said, as if you were one of the children. You told her to get into the spirit of the thing. We did laugh afterwards.'

Jo studied Eleanor's face. Nothing. Not the slightest response. She glanced around to see where the nurses were and cast about for something else.

'What about that time we went on a trip to Paris, just you and me? You must remember that. We visited the galleries and drank ridiculously expensive coffee on the Champs Elysées and went on a boat on the river. And there was that man who approached us and you thought he looked suspicious and were telling him to leave us alone, trying to drag me away. "Go away," you kept saying in every language you could think of, and then you called him a pervert. You'd dropped a glove, do you remember, and he was just trying to give it back, poor man. He clearly understood English. He handed you the glove without speaking and nearly ran away. He's probably never picked up anything for anyone since.'

Jo ran a hand across her forehead which felt hot and taut. This one-sided conversation was tiring, embarrassing too in an open ward where her every word seemed to resonate and hang in the air for all to hear. She glanced at her watch: it was after five. She needed some rest. She got up and leaned over to plant a kiss on Eleanor's visible cheek, promised she would be back tomorrow, and left. The nurses would ring her if there was any change.

Back at the estate, drawing the car to a halt near the house, she noticed a man sitting on the bench seat beside the broad path leading through the shrubberies to the courtyard. As she

35

got out of the car he stood up and she went across to join him.

'Frank, I thought it was you but...'

'But you didn't remember me looking so old and grey?' He grinned, spread his arms wide and gave her a hug. 'How are you poppet?'

'I'm no more a poppet than you're old and grey.' She grinned back. 'Well grey maybe. But you haven't changed much.' It was true. He was of average height but his rangy frame made him look taller. And perhaps his hair was more white now than grey. Even so, but for a few more lines around the eyes, he hadn't really aged.

'Much?' he was saying. 'What do you mean much? Cheeky. I'm in my prime. Well, just edging past it, maybe.'

She laughed, then remembered Eleanor and her face fell.

'You know, of course,' she said.

'Yes.' He took her hand. 'Here, come and sit down with me for a minute. You can spare a minute?'

'I've got a cat who'll be desperate for his food,' she said. 'It's the main way to his heart, I've found.' She sat down anyway, savouring the sunshine and the fresh air and the brief sense of freedom.

'Tell me about Eleanor.'

'There's nothing to tell, Frank. I guess you know about her operation?' He nodded. 'She survived it, thank heavens, but she's...' Jo shook her head despondently, feeling her lower lip quiver. '...she's not there. She's on ITU, on a ventilator and drips and all sorts of stuff, and there's nothing happening. It's like she's left me.' Tears threatened and she bit her lip to hold them back.

Frank put his arm around her shoulder again and squeezed her. 'She'd expect you to be strong.'

'Yeah, I know. Strong. Right.' She rubbed a tear from the

corner of her eye. 'I'm OK.'

'I heard you'd left that publisher and were working freelance now.'

'I am. Luckily I've got a lot of work coming my way.'

'Good. You haven't been around for a while.'

'No.' She shook her head slowly. 'I'm not exactly proud of myself right now. Eleanor and I fell out - but I guess you knew that.'

He nodded.

'We spoke briefly for the first time in ages, just that evening before she fell.'

'Really? I'm glad. I know she missed you. She loves you very much, Jojo.' He hesitated. 'Did she say anything - only you know there are already rumours that maybe she jumped? I mean, was she...?' He shrugged. 'It doesn't bear thinking about.'

'She didn't say anything like that. It was all just normal stuff.'

'No. Well, look, I waited to see you for two reasons, well, three: I wanted to see you and know you were all right; I wanted to find out about Eleanor; and I wanted to tell you about tonight's meeting.'

'What meeting?'

'Exactly. I knew he wouldn't have told you. Lawrence has called us all together this evening in the den. He said he wanted to discuss "the summer". I thought perhaps you might want to be there too. In any case, the others would like to hear about Eleanor directly from you, I think.' He looked at her questioningly, eyebrows raised.

'You don't get on with Lawrence.' She said it as a statement. Frank had never said much in front of Eleanor - not after their first rows on the subject - but he had made his

37

aversion pretty clear to Jo over the years.

He dismissed the remark with a wave of his elegant hand. Frank had long, fine fingers which he used expressively and quite unconsciously. His hands always moved when he talked, emphasising, describing. And he was both eloquent and passionate, both of which made him a brilliant performer; if he was reciting his own poetry, he burned with it.

'I just thought you might want to know what he was planning,' he said. 'Don't you?'

She looked at him a moment, then nodded. 'Yes. Yes I would.'

Frank stood up, put out a hand and pulled her to her feet.

'Good. We'll see you at seven-thirty then.' He kept hold of her hand and waited for her to look into his face. 'Are you all right, Jojo?'

She produced a tired smile. 'Yes, Frank. I am. Thanks.'

He released her. 'Go and feed your cat then. I didn't know you had a cat. What's his name?'

'Sidney.'

He smiled and walked away and Jo watched him go. He wasn't handsome, Frank Marwell, not at all. But there was something magnetic about him all the same and he could be very, very kind. He had been so to her, many times. His relationship with Eleanor might have been stormy but it was easy to see how much it could hurt to know he was now engaged to someone else. And Jo had forgotten to congratulate him. She turned back to the house. Or was she being treacherous to Eleanor even by talking to him?

God, she was tired.

*

Jo arrived late to the meeting. She had eaten, then fallen asleep on the sofa with Sidney stretched contentedly across her and ended up running to try to get there on time. Reaching the big wooden door just before seven forty, she paused, catching her breath, steeling herself. She didn't want to do this. These people brought too much baggage with them. Baggage of their own. Baggage for her. Baggage for Eleanor too - though it was her aunt who had invited them here in the first place.

They had all known her mother, Candida, right from those early days when she was the 'emerging writer', 'the talented newcomer'. They had seen Jo grow from a baby. She had been the little girl they bought sweets and ice-cream for, the child they told stories to when she was tired and bored, waiting for her mother to take her home. They had all met when they were young, part of a group of writers and self-styled intellectuals who'd inhabited the coffee shops and public houses of Bloomsbury in London, talking and arguing into the small hours. Partying too. Jo knew about the parties; her mother had loved them. She wondered that these people had stayed friends all this time. Or were they? It wasn't her idea of friendship - there had always been friction between them.

A thunder of voices from the other side of the door brought her back to the present. Everyone seemed to be talking at once. Then Lawrence called for silence and banged on something, demanding their attention, and Jo took the opportunity to look through the tiny diamond window in the door.

Lawrence was standing somewhere by the television, out of her line of vision. The others, facing him, were a sea of mostly familiar faces, older than when she had seen them last but still recognisable. There was Imogen Pooley, short and squat with a round, intelligent face, a fantasy and young adult author. Sitting beside her on the sofa was her partner, Mari

Williams, slight and looking tearful. She was a poet and an historical novelist. At a slight remove, standing near the door, hands rammed in his pockets, was Vincent Pells with his customary bow-tie and red-face. He was a playwright and literary novelist. Further over, Frank was standing behind one of the armchairs, his hands on the shoulders of the only person in the room Jo didn't know: an attractive woman with shoulder-length blonde hair and a shuttered expression. That must be Louisa, his new fiancé.

Jo blew out a long breath, pushed the door open and went in.

'Jo,' exclaimed Mari. She jumped up and wrapped the young woman in a hug. 'You poor thing. Are you all right? We've been so worried about you.'

'I'm OK, thanks.'

Mari looked fixedly into Jo's face.

'You haven't come to tell us something dreadful about Eleanor, have you?'

'Mari, please?' intervened Lawrence. 'I'm sure Jo will tell us all the latest news about Eleanor if you would just sit down.'

'For God's sake,' muttered Imogen as Mari sheepishly returned to her seat. 'Who does he think he is?'

'Hello Joselyn. Bearing up there?' Vincent put a hand to her shoulder and squeezed it. 'Yes, do tell us how poor Eleanor is.'

She looked round the expectant faces. 'Eleanor's very ill but there's no change. She's on ITU, on a ventilator. She's not conscious. They did say that they might try her off the ventilator tomorrow and see how she copes.'

There was silence for a minute as this news sank in.

'Are they letting people visit her?' asked Mari. 'I'd love to see her.'

'Only family,' said Lawrence firmly.

'What, haven't they let you in, Lawrence?' said Frank dryly. 'How disappointing for you.'

'Please don't let's argue,' Mari interposed, in her quick, breathy voice, and looked round. 'We all need to stay strong for Eleanor.' She looked back at Jo. 'Can we send flowers?'

'She wouldn't see them at the moment, Mari. I'm sorry. And on ITU...'

'What are the doctors saying?' asked Imogen.

Jo shrugged. 'Not a lot. They say it's a wait and see job.'

'I hope we're still going to get paid,' said Vincent.

'Really, Vincent.' Imogen glared at him. 'This isn't the time to be thinking about that.'

'You might not need the money, but I do.' Vincent wandered across to a vacant armchair, descended into it and crossed his stick-like legs. 'I'm simply being practical. The first students have already arrived in the village. I saw some today and I'm supposed to be running a workshop tomorrow. It's too late to cancel. I just want to know if we'll be paid. That's not unreasonable, is it?'

'Some mightn't have come if they heard it on the news,' offered Louisa.

'I have fielded a number of phone calls,' said Lawrence, 'and, since you were all here already, I told the students for this week and next to keep to their original plans. As for the rest of the summer...' He paused, waiting to get their full attention. '...I've decided to get in touch with all the students to cancel and refund the money. It's the only thing to do in the circumstances.'

'Is it your decision to make?' Frank challenged.

'Well it's certainly not yours,' Lawrence spat back. 'Anyway, to answer Vincent's question, I am in a position to make sure you're paid for whatever workshops do run. Naturally, it won't be possible for you to stay on here after that. Oh, and please say nothing to the press. I know they're camped out at the gates. For Eleanor's sake we need to keep a lid on this. If they aren't fed, hopefully they'll lose interest.' He hesitated. 'This is not an opportunity for personal publicity,' he added, and turned as if to leave.

There was a rising swell of comment and dissent.

'Lawrence?'

Jo had been perched on the edge of a chair nearby but now stood up. The room fell silent again as everyone turned to look at her.

'Yes?' Lawrence stopped, turning back.

'Is that the right thing to do?'

'I'm sorry?'

'Isn't it too soon? To cancel all the workshops?' Jo hesitated, glancing uncertainly round the room. 'Eleanor planned and arranged these from the beginning. She didn't do it for herself but because she thought a lot of people would benefit; she thought she was giving something back. Her words, I remember, because she thinks she's been lucky. I don't think she makes much money from them. Does she?'

Lawrence cast an accusing glance around the room. 'No. Sometimes we barely break even.'

'The workshops have been very popular,' Jo said, 'and a lot of people will be disappointed if they're cancelled. But to be honest there's something even more important to me.'

The room was still silent, watching her.

'Eleanor is very ill, there's no denying that, but she's still alive. Maybe she can hear what's said - I don't know. But...' She hesitated. '...I think she'd want to know that everything was going along the way it was planned. Because it was important to her. I don't want to have to tell her that the workshops have been cancelled. It would feel like we've given up on her. Not now, anyway. It's too soon.'

She ran out of words, frowning, and waited. There was no immediate reaction, then Vincent began to clap and the others followed suit.

'Oh you're so right darling,' exclaimed Mari.

Frank winked at her, then stared at Lawrence, defying him to disagree. A muscle had begun to twitch in Lawrence's left cheek.

'If that's what you want, Jo, so be it. But you're being naive. There are issues here about which you know nothing.'

Lawrence stalked to the door, dismissive and stately. Jo wanted to follow him, to ask him what he meant but Mari was already at her side, giving her a hug and Lawrence had gone. Imogen levered herself up from the seat and joined them.

'Well said, Jo,' said Mari. 'Good for you.'

'Yes indeed,' agreed Imogen, patting her on the back. Her next remark was so quiet that Jo almost didn't hear it. 'But that's a powerful enemy you've just made.'

Chapter 4

Jo got up early on the Monday morning, unable to stay in bed, too many conflicting thoughts pounding through her head. Before going downstairs, she hesitated on the landing, then pushed back the door of Eleanor's bedroom and slipped inside. It was strange to be in Eleanor's house without her aunt's commanding presence and impossible not to feel an interloper.

The room was much as she remembered it: the pale decor, a lightweight patchwork quilt on the bed, a variety of framed watercolours on the few walls which didn't catch the sun. And there was Eleanor's handbag on the slipper chair by the door. With all the events of the weekend, it hadn't crossed Jo's mind before to wonder where it was. Eleanor kept everything in that bag. If Jo needed something as a child: sticking plasters, crayons, paper, a comb, sweets, a favourite toy, even a magnifying glass, Eleanor almost invariably produced it from her capacious handbag. Jo was fascinated by it, always wanting to look inside but never allowed. 'That's a magic handbag, isn't it, Aunt Eleanor? Do you keep big stuff in there too, like furniture? Or a bike? I'd love a bike.'

Jo glanced at it, fingering it open but reluctant to trespass further on Eleanor's private space. Her aunt was still alive, if only just; it felt ghoulish and intrusive to pick through her things. Still a feeling of unease, of things unexplained, made her look inside. She could see Eleanor's reading glasses case and a small notebook. No phone though. Jo frowned, and looked more thoroughly. There was an empty pocket at the side, the size for a phone, but it definitely wasn't there. Was that significant? Jo looked round the room. There was no sign of it anywhere. Perhaps it was downstairs. Or maybe Eleanor had taken it with her into the garden. She made a mental note to look outside later and went to give Sidney his breakfast.

It was still only eight twenty when she returned to the sitting room and sat on the floor, idly playing with Sidney, watching the clock. She wanted to speak to Lawrence as soon as he arrived and clear the air, but he was too quick for her and the next moment he was in the doorway, stealing the initiative.

'Joselyn? May I have a word?'

He didn't wait for a reply and walked in.

'I wanted to see you too, Lawrence.' She scrambled to her feet to face him and waved a hand vaguely towards the sofas. 'Shall we sit?'

He ignored her. Standing with legs apart, arms crossed aggressively in front of him, his body bristled with anger.

'What did you think you were doing last night? If you wanted to interfere, you might have had the courtesy to speak to me privately and not make me look ridiculous in front of the others.'

'If you'd had the courtesy to tell me in advance that you were planning to cancel, I would have explained how I felt then, without finding out about your meeting by chance.'

'Who told you about it?'

'Why didn't you want me to know?'

'I wasn't aware that you had any part in the running of this estate or the workshops. You haven't bothered with your aunt for years, but for a cursory message here and there. Who are you to come and tell me what I should and shouldn't do on

45

Eleanor's behalf?'

She felt the accusation as badly as he intended her to. But that was her affair with Eleanor, not his, and she refused to give ground.

'I'm her niece, her closest living relative. I've been away too long but my love and concern for Eleanor haven't changed. I have a right to express my opinion and I believe I have a right to take some responsibility for what happens here until she can do it herself.'

He smiled grimly. 'You've decided to take over. How noble of you.'

'No.' She shook her head. 'No, that was never my intention. But I should be involved. I want to help.'

Their eyes met and locked. It felt absurd, like a childish game to see who would blink first.

'You're very out of touch,' he said, a shade less belligerently. 'You don't understand the half of what's going on here.'

'So tell me then. What are "these issues about which I know nothing" which you mentioned last night?'

'All right. Let's assume you genuinely care about her. What if you're actually making the situation worse? What makes you think she wants the workshops to continue? Eleanor's not been herself lately. You haven't been around to see. She's been having trouble with her writing, really struggling. It's been painful to watch. I had her agent, Jenny - you remember Jenny Huggins? - on the phone yesterday. She'd heard about the tragedy and wanted to know how Eleanor was and what was happening. She knows Eleanor was having problems; she's been having them for some time. The publishers are getting impatient because deadlines have come and gone. There's been a lot of pressure. The workshops are a distraction and just add to that pressure. They barely pay their way and she refuses to charge the tutors for their accommodation.

'And then this engagement. It was a shock for her. Can you imagine how much? Do you think she wants Frank and Louisa here all summer, in her own back yard, after that? Are you going to sit by her hospital bed and tell her you've arranged to keep them here, nice and close? How cosy for her.'

Jo was silent, frowning. She turned and sat down. Sidney immediately jumped up and insinuated himself onto her lap. She stroked him without thinking, then looked back up at Lawrence. He hadn't moved but something in his manner suggested that he thought he had won.

'You think she jumped?' she asked softly.

'I don't know. It's possible. Frank has hurt her a lot over the years. She hides a lot, you know. I've often thought she struggled more than she admitted. A person can only take so much. Maybe it finally got too much.'

'And you told the police that.'

'I believe I mentioned it.'

She nodded, then glanced at her watch, moved Sidney to the side and stood up again.

'I've got to go to the hospital. By the way, do you know where Eleanor's phone is?'

'No.' He glanced round the room. 'It'll be about I expect.'

'I can't find it.'

He shrugged the issue away. 'How long are you planning to keep this vigil?'

'I don't know. I'm taking one day at a time. I've brought some work with me. I'll fit it in as and when I can.'

'Well I have to plan ahead, so please rethink your stance on the workshops and let me know your decision later today.'

'That's too soon. I need to think about it.'

'What possible diff…?' He stopped himself, pressing his thin lips together. 'All right. Tomorrow then. And, if you insist on them going ahead, I shall expect your support and input. If any of the tutors were unable to run sessions for any reason, Eleanor would step in. I assume you'll do the same.' He raised one sardonic eyebrow then walked to the door, paused and turned. 'Eleanor was involved in planning a literary festival for the beginning of September too. It was a new venture suggested by someone down in the village, all absurdly last minute. Now there's the inevitable committee which spends hours debating the trivial. It was all too much, even for her. She got talked into trying to arrange speakers. I hope you're going to see sense and not try to keep her part in that going too. Oh, and maybe don't believe everything Frank tells you. Eleanor certainly didn't.'

Later, sitting beside Eleanor, waiting in vain for the twitch of an eyelid or the fleeting pressure of her hand, the argument reran through Jo's mind and she began to question her motives. Maybe she only wanted to keep the workshops going because of Lawrence's arrogance and proprietorial attitude. She hadn't thought of it as a power struggle before, but perhaps it was. Or maybe she was trying to prove to herself and everyone else that she did care about Eleanor and hadn't just abandoned her.

Perhaps Lawrence was right about Eleanor's state of mind. Jo had been away too long and could have misread the situation. She tried to recall their telephone conversation from the Friday night. Had there been any clues in it? 'Life's too short,' Eleanor had said at one point. Was that significant? But the Eleanor she knew had never been a quitter. It was one of the things Jo loved her for: Eleanor rose to meet problems. She never backed off.

But maybe jumping had been the final escape. If Eleanor had been drinking, perhaps with her mind clouded from alcohol, her resolve weakened, it had seemed like the best way out. Perhaps she was too tired of it all to continue. Jo hadn't allowed herself to believe it before but now she felt sick with regret and recrimination. Why hadn't she paid Eleanor more attention?

She looked down at her aunt's face and wished she could ask Eleanor what she wanted her to do but the blank, closed expression gave nothing away. That morning, the doctors had reduced her sedation in order to try her off the ventilator and she was now breathing unaided - constantly monitored by both nurses and the ITU doctor on duty - but she remained as still and silent as before. Jo was acutely disappointed. She had naively hoped that the reduced sedation would reveal a conscious Eleanor, the thinking, restless person Jo knew so well. But there was nothing.

The nurses moved in to see to Eleanor and Jo went in search of coffee.

*

Frank wandered down the footpath through the woods on the western slope of the headland and let himself out of the side gate. It was the only access point in the fenced estate other than the main gates and it too had a keypad lock. For security, Lawrence changed the codes every week though Frank wouldn't put it past the man to change them again without warning - just to spite them all.

He and Louisa had slept late and she had still been in bed when he left. A short winding walk downhill from here took him onto the road through the village, not far from the public beach. He liked the walk, always had. Even when he lived with

Eleanor, he had never got over the novelty of being able to stroll along the sea front in the freshness of a sunny morning. It was such a contrast from the noise and bustle and grimy streets round the flat in London where he still stayed intermittently. His relationship with Eleanor had always been elastic. They had both appreciated the space his occasional spells in London had given them. It made their relationship more special when they were together.

Eleanor. She kept intruding on his thoughts. He wondered how she was. A new romance didn't mean he didn't still care about her. Eleanor was part of his life and always would be. And now she was... He didn't want to think about it. He was desperately trying not to show his distress to Louisa. She wouldn't understand.

He reached the bottom of the path and turned left towards the sea, trying to regain his train of thought. Yes, he loved it here. Walking through the village, buying fresh rolls for breakfast from the shop, watching the waves lap the shore, smelling the salt air... He had written about it many times.

> Sparkle of sun on sea and stone,
> Gritty salt sand in your shoes.

But he didn't want the place to become too known, too popular or trendy. He wanted it to stay quaint and old-fashioned - like the beaches he remembered from his childhood, the way he and Eleanor both liked it. There she was again. But every time he thought of her now it was as if something was extracting all the air out of him.

He bought a broadsheet and one of the tabloids from the display just inside the door of the convenience store, paused by the bakery section to make his choices, then paid and left. He didn't look inside the papers until he was back in the apartment, sitting on one of the easy chairs at the back of the room, a coffee and a brioche on the cupboard to his right. He could hear water running: Louisa was in the shower. He opened the tabloid first and glanced over the headlines, turned the page and stopped short. There was a large photograph of Eleanor with the headline: *Mystery fall of famous author.*

'Oh shit,' he muttered.

He frowned, reading it through. It was garbage, a selective mix of quotes from the police and 'locals' and an insight from 'a friend'.

'Where the hell do they get this stuff?' he exclaimed, and tossed it on the floor in disgust, just as Louisa emerged from the shower room, wrapped in a bath towel.

'Mm,' he said, approvingly, as she came towards him. 'Are you joining me for breakfast then?' He reached out a hand as she got close. 'Are you sure that towel's tucked in tight enough?'

He nearly managed to get hold of it but she giggled and pulled away, ducking to pick up the strewn newspaper.

'Something annoyed you, darling?' She perched on the armchair nearby, fussing the pages back into position.

'There's a rubbish article about Eleanor in there. One minute it's making her out to be a party girl and virtual alcoholic, barely able to stay upright, the next she's a depressive recluse with financial worries. God knows where they got it from. All innuendo and hearsay. And made up. Though Vincent's likely to be one source, the bugger.'

He felt the anger build inside him again and tried to quell it, looking away, taking a bite of his brioche.

Louisa opened the paper and read the article. Her eyebrows lifted.

'They haven't painted a very pretty picture, I must say.

51

And she had been drinking. Oh dear. How sad that her life should be reduced to this.'

She got up, dumped the newspaper on the bed and grabbed a croissant and a paper napkin before sitting down again. Frank was aware of her eyes on him, looking up through her lashes as she tore the croissant in two, examining his face.

'Does it bother you?' she asked eventually.

'What, the article? No. It goes with being famous, doesn't it? Eleanor's had negative press before. She used to laugh it off.'

'Really? It looks like it bothers you. Perhaps you don't find it as easy to laugh off as she does. She's quite tough, isn't she?' When he didn't reply, she added, 'Perhaps it's being here. Is it too difficult for you, being at Skymeet with all the old associations?'

There it was again, the unasked question about his affections. She kept needling at him, worrying over his attitude to his old lover. Louisa was so insecure. He hadn't realised until they'd arrived here just how much. She seemed haunted by the idea that he might still want Eleanor, however many times he denied it and told her he loved her.

'No, I'm fine here,' he said. 'It's years since Eleanor and I were an item. You know that. I mean, the circumstances are awful of course but…' He shrugged then reached out a hand to touch her bare arm. 'It's tough on you though. I think maybe we shouldn't have come here this year after all.'

She swallowed the last of her croissant, got up and came to perch on his lap. 'No, it's good that we did. It was important for you that we faced her sooner rather than later. She needed to see us together, didn't she? So she understood.' She shrugged her naked shoulders, making her towel start to slip. 'It just didn't work out the way we thought. But we can't let her come between us, even when she's in a hospital bed.'

'She's not going to do that, Louisa. You keep talking about her as if she wouldn't accept it. But Eleanor had moved on too, you know.'

'Are you sure? If the gossip is true, it doesn't seem that way.'

He didn't answer but brushed a croissant flake from her cheek and kissed her on the mouth. Then he bent forward to bury his head in her chest, pushing away all thoughts of Eleanor, comatose in her hospital bed.

Louisa arched her neck back and giggled again as he pulled the towel down.

*

As usual, it was late afternoon when Jo got back to the house. Already the number of journalists hanging around outside the gates had dwindled. Hopefully they would soon leave altogether.

Sidney curled round her legs, purring, as soon as she walked through the door, hampering further movement. She picked him up and took him through to the kitchen. Charlotte was still there, her broad backside incongruously perched on a tiny stool. She turned as Jo walked in.

'Good. I was hoping to see you.' Charlotte eyed up the cat in Jo's arms. 'Ah yes, Sidney. Thank you for the note. We've been getting acquainted.'

'Thank you for keeping an eye on him.' Jo put him down. 'Has he been any trouble?'

'He cried a bit early on, missing you no doubt, but he seems to have got used to me now. Doesn't appear to like Lawrence though.'

'That would be mutual then. Lawrence doesn't like him,

either.'

There was a brief, tense silence. The air was thick with unspoken accusation. It was more than ten years since Charlotte had come to work for Eleanor. She came up from the village every weekday, cleaning, cooking, managing all the household issues which Eleanor never quite got around to. The two women were of an age but very different. Charlotte had no interest in books; she loved eighties pop music, television soaps and cookery programmes. Eleanor listened to classical music and occasionally jazz and she watched crime dramas and witty sitcoms. They often argued, exchanging vitriolic insults, and Charlotte had handed her notice in more than once, but she was still here. They were perversely devoted to each other. Now she was regarding Jo reproachfully.

Jo offered an olive branch. 'How are you, Charlotte? It's been ages but that's my fault, I know. I was wrong to stay away. There's no excuse.'

'Yes, well,' Charlotte allowed grudgingly, 'we've all done things we're not proud of, I dare say. But I can't pretend your aunt hasn't missed you. Not that the old bat would ever admit to it.'

'How has she been, Charlotte?'

'How do you think she's been? All by herself since she finished with that man. You staying away like she had a contagious disease.'

'Was she depressed, do you think?'

'Depressed?' Charlotte gave a shake of the head. 'No. Not the type.'

'I guess anyone can get depressed though.'

'Maybe. But she just gets on with things.' She hesitated. 'Though she did seem distracted on Friday, now you mention it. Not that you should believe that rubbish in the newspapers.

I think she lost her footing and slipped. I've told her a thousand times that she should fence that terrace off properly and the steps but would she listen? "It'd spoil the atmosphere of the place," she said. "I want to keep it natural." Natural indeed. Stuff and nonsense - and now look.' She sniffed, adopting a careless expression. 'And how is her ladyship today?'

'Unconscious still, but breathing for herself at least.'

She grunted and prised herself off the stool. 'Well I'm off. I've left you a lasagne to eat this evening. No doubt you're not eating properly...' She tutted. '...just like her when she's writing. You look awful, I must say.'

'I blame myself, Charlotte,' Jo blurted out, desperate to say it to someone. 'It's my fault and now look what's happened.'

Charlotte hesitated then took Jo's hand. 'Now there's no point getting yourself in a state about it. She's a strong-willed woman, your aunt. Stubborn as hell. She's not going to go anywhere without having her own say in the matter, you can be sure of that.' She patted Jo's hand and let it go, turning for the door. 'By the way, Lawrence has gone but said to tell you he has to know by tomorrow - whatever that means.'

Charlotte left and Jo put her fingers to her eyes, pressing them gently, then massaged her temples, easing the tension out. She hadn't made a decision. She was beginning to wonder if it was her decision to make after all. Just at this moment she doubted everything. There was no way she could fill in for Eleanor if that was needed, tutoring a writing workshop or doing anything else her aunt usually did. Lawrence knew that too; that's why he'd said it.

She wandered down the hallway to Eleanor's study. It was more Eleanor's private sanctuary than anywhere else in the house. The room held its familiar clutter. Eleanor kept everything: every book and notebook, every interesting article or photograph of people or places. When Jo had suggested dryly - years ago - that half of it could be thrown away with no loss, her aunt had claimed it as a virtue. It was astonishing, she claimed, how often she found something which proved to be invaluable for her research, or memory-jogging, or inspiration. And this place housed her mental map, she had said, waving an expansive hand to embrace the room. 'It's all in here, somewhere.'

Her mental map. So would anything here give Jo an insight into what Eleanor would want her to do? She glanced over the overstuffed bookshelves, finding her eyes drawn to familiar titles, books she had read when she used to stay here, others her aunt had let her take away. It felt like a lifetime ago. There were all the classic novels of English literature and below them the complete works of Shakespeare. There were shelves of modern and contemporary fiction and an astonishing array of arcane reference material. And countless volumes of poetry, old and new, just out of reach. Jo rolled the library steps over and climbed up, pulling one off the shelf, the most successful of Frank's anthologies and her particular favourite, *Now and Then*. Flicking through the pages, a piece of folded paper fell out onto the floor.

Jo climbed down and unfolded it. *Engagement of poet Frank Marwell to novelist Louisa Dunnell* was the title above a photograph of the couple and a short article. It wasn't hard to see what Eleanor had made of it. The paper was all crinkled, as if she had tried to crush it in her fist. After a moment's hesitation, Jo folded it back up, replaced it in the book and put it back on the shelf. That had been Eleanor's decision. It could stay there.

She turned away. On the desk at the centre of the room

Eleanor's laptop sat open in front of her chair while the rest of the desk was strewn with loose sheets of notes, open books and pieces of notepaper with odd jottings on them.

Jo sat in Eleanor's chair and allowed her gaze to wander, her mind barely noticing what she was looking at. Then one of the notes caught her eye.

Fest Committee, Monday 26, 7.30. V Hall.

Monday 26. That was today. A meeting about the literary festival presumably. Jo glanced at her watch. She would go.

*

Matthew left the house and walked to the end of the lane near the beach. It was a sunny evening with a clear, almost cloudless sky and he paused; there was plenty of time before the meeting started. He glanced round and up towards the playing field higher up the village though it wasn't visible from where he stood.

Harry was there, supposedly meeting up with 'a mate', though, as far as Matthew could tell, Harry struggled to make many friends.

'Name?' Matthew had pressed.

'Clive.'

'I haven't heard that name before. Who is he?'

'Yes, you have. He's at school.'

'And where are you going?'

'Aw come on dad, give it a rest.'

'I want to know.'

'Just around.'

'Harry?'

'OK, so there's going to be a barbie on the playing field tonight.'

'And anyone can go?'

'Clive knows the guy whose birthday it is.'

'Barbecues are usually held on the beach here.'

'The tide's too high.'

'I see. OK. But no alcohol, right? And home by eleven, latest. You've got school tomorrow. What about your homework?'

'Done it.'

'Good.' If it was true. Matthew hesitated. 'Do you need money?'

He had given Harry a ten pound note but was already regretting it. What would the kid spend it on? But was he safer not having money? The lad would be sixteen soon so he had to give him a bit of slack, didn't he? And when Harry had been taking drugs back at their old home, he had managed to get them from somewhere even when he'd had no money, and being in debt for drugs seemed an even worse scenario. Matthew regularly tried to look into his son's eyes, checking his pupils to see if he had been taking anything, or watched his movements and listened for any change in his speech. He'd seen no sign recently and hoped the issue had been caught in time. Sophie would have known if there was a problem, but Sophie wasn't here. And if she had been here, there wouldn't have been a problem.

He carried on walking, following the turn of the lane at the end of the beach and heading up to the village hall. Most of the committee were already there. He took a seat at the table and sat back, wishing it over. With Eleanor Lambe in hospital, he expected the festival to be a non-event anyway; they'd have to cancel it. The chairperson, Nancy Turner might be running the committee but Eleanor had been the motor behind it. And Nancy was unusually late. Minutes slipped by and the volume of chatter swelled.

Then Nancy walked in alongside a young woman with a guarded expression and a swing of dark, bobbed hair. She wasn't one of the committee.

'Evening everyone,' said Nancy. 'Sorry I'm late. We were talking.' She smiled at her companion. 'Can I introduce Joselyn to you? She's Eleanor Lambe's niece from Sussex. She's also the daughter of Candida Lambe, the novelist. Anyway, she's staying up at Skymeet since this terrible accident - I'm sure you've all heard about it. I bumped into her outside and she has the latest news about her aunt. Jo?'

The young woman stayed on her feet and talked briefly about her aunt's condition. She was obliged to field a few questions which she did succinctly but without giving any more away, then sat down opposite Matthew. He formed the impression that a great deal was being left unsaid.

'Jo is here to find out more about the festival,' said Nancy, 'by proxy, you might say, for her aunt. She herself is a book editor and no stranger to the publishing world.'

'So the festival is going ahead?' Matthew asked.

'I think it would be premature to cancel at this moment,' said Nancy. 'We've got so far with planning it already and money has been spent. Eleanor had already booked a number of speakers - I was just discussing that with Jo actually. The caterers are booked too. It's my opinion we should go ahead and keep the situation under review.' There was a general muttering of agreement. She glanced back up the table at Jo. 'Unless we hear otherwise.' She embraced them all with a regal smile. 'Shall we put it to a vote?'

The vote went with Nancy. It always did.

Matthew sat back and resigned himself to a long evening. He had been enlisted because in his previous job he had been a computer programmer and they needed his expertise to create a website for the festival, an event which they hoped would be the first of many. The evening dragged. Without Eleanor, they skirted over the issue of speakers but discussed programmes, posters and tickets, banners and bunting, sponsorship money and advertising revenue. It had been decided that a concert would close events on the Saturday night, something inclusive to a wide audience, and someone had been tasked with getting local performers involved and organising it. Matthew barely heard a half of it and had to keep stifling a yawn. Occasionally his gaze roamed to the woman opposite. She looked pale and drawn but seemed to be listening intently, her eyes flicking from one speaker to another. He wondered that she could find it so interesting.

It was twenty past nine by the time the meeting closed. Matthew noticed Joselyn slip quickly away before anyone could speak to her and it wasn't long till he followed suit, glad to leave.

The sun was setting and the light danced with pink and gold. With the cove facing west, the sunsets here could be magical. Matthew kept his gaze on the sky and headed for the slipway then down onto the sand, wishing he'd brought his camera. He knew from experience that his phone wouldn't do it justice. The tide had turned and, though water still covered the beach, a strip at the top rarely got wet. He stopped and rested his back against the wall, waiting in the half light. The sun was still a pale golden orb, low in the sky, lightly touched with a wisp of violet cloud drifting along the horizon line. He could just pick out the tiny silhouette of a ship way out in the channel.

Then he realised he wasn't alone. Joselyn was there too. Unmistakeable - the bob of her hair was distinctive. She was sitting down on the sand almost touching distance away, her knees drawn up, hugging them, watching the sea.

'Hi,' he said, after a moment's hesitation.

She turned her head briefly. 'Hi.'

The sun slid closer to the horizon and deepened into apricot. The sky around it was softest pink and the clouds burned purple. Matthew wondered if he should speak. He glanced down at the girl again; she seemed wrapped up in a world of her own. Maybe if he spoke she would think he was coming on to her and he didn't want that.

He stayed silent and watched the sun drop, watched the way the colours intensified, the pinks to reds, the apricot to a flaming orange, and the whole bowl of the cove: the sand, the water and the rocky sides, lit up like a cauldron of fire.

'Flirting, fondling, melting, melding,
Steeps the sun in the skymeet sea.
It's a fury of fire and flames and passion,
Or is it rejection and a broken heart bleeds?'

Matthew turned his head. The young woman had said the lines out loud. He wondered if she had intended to.

'That's beautiful,' he said.

'Oh they're not my words,' she said hastily, getting to her feet. 'Frank Marwell wrote them.'

'Right.' The name rang a vague bell. 'So is that where the name Skymeet comes from?'

'Yes.' She turned her head to look at him. Her face reflected the fiery glow from the sea and rocks. 'Frank has a way with words. Words are like pictures, after all.'

He stared at her and swallowed hard. 'I suppose so.'

She turned her face away, looking back to the sea. Already the fire was extinguishing, the red glow deadening and

61

mutating to purple and grey.

'I'm sorry about your aunt,' said Matthew. 'Nice lady.'

She turned again, frowning. 'I'm sorry, I can't remember your name.'

'Matthew.'

'I'm Jo. Do you know her, Matthew? I mean, to talk to?'

'A little. She comes into my café sometimes and always makes time to speak. She asked me to be on the committee in fact.'

'Did she? Nancy implied that the festival was her idea but I got the impression tonight that my aunt was the prime mover.'

He produced a wry grin. 'Nancy claims credit for a lot of things but your aunt had the original idea. I remember her talking to me about it. What's your point?'

'Oh nothing. I've just caught someone out in a lie. Which makes me wonder what else he's been lying about. And why.'

It was too dark now to see her expression clearly.

'Thank you,' she said. 'You've helped me to a decision.'

She left and he shrugged her remark away. Trudging home, he glanced automatically up the hill towards the playing field but didn't dare go up to check on the boy; he risked damaging the precarious peace they had established.

He didn't expect to think of Jo again but several times her remark came back into his head that night. *Words are like pictures*. Sophie used to say that.

Chapter 5

Tuesday morning dawned grey and overcast. Cloud had pushed in overnight and a light mizzle hung in the air. Jo walked to the edge of the paving on the eastern terrace and tentatively stepped onto the shallow grassy slope beyond, looking down. From here, all she could see was the cliff rising from the other side of the beach. There was a line of large angular stones placed at intervals near her feet, markers that the ground would soon fall away, the coarse grass, gravel and wild flowers giving way to bare stone and an abrupt and dangerous drop to the rocky shore below. A couple of shrubs grew there too, softening the edge. Jo was twelve when Eleanor had taken on this estate and on her first visit she'd been sternly warned not to go close to the edge. She was no fool; she had paid attention.

Now she took another couple of steps as far as she dared and peered over. Way down, she could see waves lapping on the far side of Eleanor's personal beach and could smell the salt. It was just after eight o'clock and the tide was in. It really was private down there, barely visible except from certain places in the garden. If she looked to her right she could see, beyond the undulating headland and treetops further on, a glimpse of the sea horizon. Eleanor walked in the gardens most evenings - or used to - and would pause occasionally to enjoy a particular plant or flower or savour a view. And she liked it down on this terrace. There was a favoured wooden seat and several huge terracotta pots accommodated cordyllines and phormiums. It was a sheltered spot and had a Mediterranean feel.

To Jo's left, tucked into the angle between the rocky headland and the rear wall of the cove, were the wooden steps which led down to the beach. There was a handrail close in against the cliff wall on the left and a single wooden post on the right. The first few steps were shallow and easy, then they turned a little, following the line of the rock, becoming steeper. Years ago a rail had been added to the lower section on the right.

Jo glanced back along the terrace then down to those first few steps. Eleanor had fallen from somewhere around here though it was hard to understand how she could have slipped from the terrace. She would have had to go beyond the marker stones and then some. Perhaps she was trying to see something in particular on the beach and slipped on damp stone?

Jo crossed to the beach steps. It was more likely that Eleanor had slipped from here, near the top. The steps were very steep, more like a ladder; Eleanor, like most people, turned and descended them backwards. Perhaps in turning, she had lost her footing and so ended up in that thicket of now cut and crumpled brambles down there on the tiny ledge, a miraculous escape from certain death on the rocks below. Unless, of course, she had chosen to do it. If she'd wanted to fall, she could have done it from almost anywhere. Jo shook her head; she couldn't believe it. She didn't want to believe it.

She turned away and jumped as a figure moved out from under the rose arch nearby. The arch broke a line of clematis covered trellis and led into the next 'room' of the garden and ultimately out to the front.

'Vincent,' she exclaimed. 'What are you doing here? If you want to see Lawrence, I imagine he's still in the annexe.'

'I'm sure he is. He has no life really. But it was you I came to see. I'm sorry if I gave you a fright.'

Now she understood. He was in the garden to avoid bumping into Lawrence who rarely strayed into the main garden but was often in the house. And with all the shrubs and hedging to the side of the property it was possible to reach the gate to the private gardens without being seen. In any case, Lawrence's apartment had its own small fenced garden which was a secluded fortress in itself.

Vincent came closer, smiling in that way he had as if he possessed some secret knowledge, still wearing his trademark bow-tie and waistcoat.

'What is it?' she asked.

She had never felt comfortable with him. A little older than Eleanor, Vincent had been closer, if anything, to her mother. She had seen him at parties, drunk. She had seen him after parties, flat out on the floor, bristle-faced and dishevelled. He used to carry sweets in his trouser pocket, the old-fashioned kind you bought loose in a white paper bag. God knows where he got them from. As a child she would take one when offered but pretend to keep it for later. She couldn't bear to think of it coming out of his pocket.

'Is this where it happened?' he said now, moving across to cautiously look over the cliff. He shuddered theatrically and backed away.

'What is it, Vincent?' she repeated.

He smiled genially. 'Well, Joss darling, I wondered if you'd come across a little manuscript of mine? In Eleanor's study, I expect. That's where she was when I gave it to her anyway.'

65

'No, but I haven't really looked through her study,' she said coolly. 'It's not my business. Anyway, I have had other things on my mind.'

'Of course, dear. I understand. Only it's rather an exciting little venture we were going to do together - a play I've written based on Eleanor's novel, *Mr Ridge Might Know*. You must remember the one? It's come out rather well. But, since Eleanor isn't in a position to look at it at the moment, I thought I'd have it back. I've got a producer lined up, you see.'

She considered his studiously casual manner. Eleanor was a loner when it came to her work and she had never been of a mind with Vincent; it was a stretch of the imagination to see them working together.

'Really?' she said. 'And Eleanor agreed to this, you say?'

'Certainly. She was looking forward to seeing it on stage. It's such a tragedy, what's happened. The Lord moves in mysterious ways.'

'Indeed. Still, it wouldn't be appropriate for you to do anything about the play until Eleanor's better, would it? I'm sure there needs to be an agreement in writing for such a venture - unless you've already got one?'

He looked surprised. Clearly, he'd thought she would be a soft touch, Candida's little girl.

'No, Eleanor didn't bother with things like that, not between friends.'

'Really? I'd have to check that then.' She began to move back towards the house. 'Must go, Vincent. I need to get off to the hospital.' On an afterthought, she stopped and faced him again. 'By the way, I remember Eleanor telling me that these gardens at the back were off limits to everyone during the workshops. She wanted to keep some privacy. It was important to her.'

66

'Yes, but I'm family, Joselyn.'

'I believe we should keep to the rules Eleanor set, don't you?' she said pleasantly. 'That's the way I want it while she's not here. Can't afford exceptions, I'm afraid.'

'I really don't think you should go throwing your weight about, Joselyn.' He came closer. Too close, the smile now thin and fixed. 'You might overbalance. Look what happened to poor old Eleanor.'

Her eyes narrowed. 'What do you mean by that?'

'Oh my dear, it's just an observation.'

He left through the arch again and was soon out of sight.

'Slimeball,' she muttered, and glanced round one last time.

There was no sign of Eleanor's phone here either. It probably fell and smashed on the rocks below. She headed back to the house. She planned to see Lawrence before she left and tell him her decision: she would keep the workshops and festival running, just as Eleanor had intended.

*

Eleanor continued to breathe for herself. They said she was stable. Day to day, Jo saw no perceptible change, which was presumably what they meant. The results of the tests had come back and showed no hidden illness. On the Wednesday, the doctors said she could be moved to the neurosurgical ward when a suitable bed was available and when Jo turned up at the hospital on the Thursday morning, her aunt was already there, in a side room off the main ward, close to the nurses' station. She still had the feeding tube down her nose and the drip in her arm but there was no cardiac monitor now. The room was eerily silent. Was this progress or had they just decided they couldn't do any more for her? Jo felt a twinge of apprehension. All around her, she sensed the negativity of other people's expectations. Someone had to stay positive and focussed.

She sat in the chair at the side of the bed and studied Eleanor's face. The bruises were already starting to turn yellow; the scratches had healed over; shiny white bristles had begun to peak through her scalp. Jo cast about for something new to say.

'When your hair grows back we'll have to get the hairdresser in to do your colour, Eleanor. Will you go for something different this time? I know you like to change it now and then and this is a great opportunity.'

Why was she talking to her as if she were stupid? If Eleanor could hear her, she must be screaming inside.

'Better to be here, on an ordinary ward, isn't it?' Jo remarked brightly. 'A bit more going on.' A patient call bell started its insistent beeping at the nurses' station. Drawn curtains covered the window out to the ward passage but footsteps and the squeal of wheels could regularly be heard passing by. A man was shouting unintelligibly and insistently from one of the main wards. 'Maybe not so great for sleeping at night,' she added. 'But think what material you might get for a novel.'

She dropped her voice and murmured to herself. 'Or maybe you think it's some sort of hell.'

Arriving back at Skymeet, she sought out Lawrence in his office and told him about Eleanor's move.

'I was wondering if she would be better in a private hospital now. It's very noisy there and she's such a private person. And I'm concerned about journalists tracking her down. The nurses promised me they'd keep an eye out at visiting times but they've got enough to do.'

'I doubt it'll be a problem,' he replied dismissively, barely looking up. 'The press seem to have lost interest already, haven't you noticed? She's not a movie star, after all. Anyway, these side wards are pretty secluded. They can close the door, can't they? Eleanor doesn't like special treatment or fuss; she's a big supporter of the NHS.'

'I know. So am I and the staff have been wonderful. But she seems kind of lost there and I'm scared she'll be forgotten. She could afford to be moved, couldn't she?'

Finally he pulled his gaze from his computer screen and rested it languidly on her.

'Eleanor's not as wealthy as you seem to think. Sales of books aren't what they were, you know. These are tough times. Anyway, a lot of Eleanor's money is tied up - invested - and interest rates are abysmal these days. Private care is bloody expensive. Whatever, I think you're worrying unnecessarily.'

'Still, I'd like to see her accounts, Lawrence. Can you arrange that?'

'Why?'

'Is there a problem with that?'

'She has an accountant to organise most of it. He keeps all the records.'

'Perhaps I'll go to see him then. Can you give me his name?'

'Of course. But he won't show you. The accounts are confidential. You'd need to go to court if you want to take control of your aunt's financial affairs and jump through all sorts of hoops. And, even if the criteria are met, I believe it takes ages.' He paused, still regarding her coolly. 'And perhaps would be inappropriate at this time.'

He was good at this, Jo had to admit: stone-walling, keeping her at arm's length.

'So what happens about Eleanor's household bills?' she persisted. 'How does she pay the gardeners for instance?'

'By Direct Debit. Most of the bills are paid that way. I get cash out for small items and one-offs. Why?'

'You've got her debit card then? I'd assumed it was in her handbag in her bedroom. I've been thinking I ought to start sorting things out.'

'There's nothing to sort out. Eleanor opened a current account in our joint names so I could use it too. We both have a card. She thought it made life easier that way.' He raised his eyebrows patronisingly. 'I have it all under control.'

I'll bet you do, she thought.

'Eleanor can have visitors now,' she said, meeting his steely gaze. 'Perhaps you should go and see her in her new ward and experience just how secluded she is.'

*

Frank stood at the end of the bed and surveyed the room: the bedside locker with an array of cards and a vase of flowers on it; the cot sides to the bed; the disgusting pink mouthwash in a plastic tumbler on the movable table, pushed to one side. And Eleanor: the tube rammed up her nose, the drip in her arm, the catheter showing under the edge of the covers, draining urine into a bag hooked on the side of the bed.

It was nearly a week since her fall. Jo had come to the den the night before to tell them all that her aunt had been moved and could now receive visitors. She had warned them about the tubes and Eleanor's continuing unresponsiveness. Even so, what he saw now shocked him. She was very white. Deathly. She was breathing for herself, lying half-turned onto one side but she didn't look good and nothing like the woman he knew. Perhaps it was the shaved head. And the multi-coloured

70

bruising. Or her flaccidity. Even when she had been asleep, she had never been like this: limp-limbed, mouth sagging, vulnerable. He didn't want to look at her yet couldn't pull his eyes away.

A nurse passed the open door, paused and stepped inside.

'There's a chair behind the door,' she said kindly. 'Do sit with her if you like. Let her know you're here.'

'Thanks.' She started to move away and he stepped after her. 'Excuse me? Do you think she can hear me? Is there anything...?' He shrugged, reluctant to say it.

'She might hear you. Try talking to her.'

He grabbed the chair, pushed the door to, and sat by the bed on the side Eleanor was facing. He opened his mouth to speak then closed it again. What do you say to someone you've had a love affair with when it's all over? Especially now, in a situation like this. He was a man of words - they were his life and his means of support - but this was different. His words had all deserted him.

'Ellie?' he murmured.

He reached out a hand and took hers. It was cold. He had to force himself to keep holding it.

'Ellie? It's Frank.'

This was harder than he had expected. He frowned and released a deep sigh, odd scenes of the past flicking through his brain. Laughter, passion, rows. Once she had started throwing things at him when they were arguing; he had thrown things back. They had both apologised, both suddenly spent with anger and full of remorse. They had laughed about it. Soon after they'd made love on the sitting room floor, wildly, violently, as if they had so much to prove.

And was it all come to this: this hospital bed and her life ebbing away? The tube rammed up her nose came from a machine at the side of the bed which seemed to be administering something white into her. Of course she couldn't eat. She couldn't do anything. His eyes explored every inch of her face. The years had dropped off her somehow and, now he looked at her properly, he thought she looked surprisingly beautiful, serenely smooth-skinned, the neat lines of her facial bones clearly etched. He remembered saying once that she should cut her hair really short - like Mari - because she had the bone structure for it. He'd got hold of her hair, pulled it back off her face and pushed her to the mirror.

'See,' he'd said. 'Look at those cheek bones. You could carry it off. Don't be so conventional.'

'Me? Conventional?' she'd said in disgust, shaking him off. 'How dare you?'

She was though. The rest of it was just an act. He knew her better than anyone. She had never forgiven him for not asking her to marry him. 'It would have been nice to have been asked,' she had said once, 'to show you cared that much.'

'How would that prove anything?' he'd retaliated.

'It's a promise. A commitment. You're scared of them. But life's meaningless without them.'

Why couldn't she see? He had been committed in his own way. So much of his poetry had been written for her. He cared. So why did she drive him away, always being so contrary? And now this.

It was true that he had asked Louisa to marry him, after just a few short months. But Louisa was...different. She needed him in a way Eleanor never had and he liked that. He wanted to be needed. Eleanor was so bloody independent. And pig-headed. It always had to be on her terms.

He sighed. What an unholy mess.

'Oh Ellie,' he murmured. 'I'm so sorry. I should...'

The nurse appeared in the doorway; a second one stood behind her.

'Sorry to disturb you but we need to turn her,' the first nurse said.

'That's fine. I have to go anyway.'

Frank gave Eleanor's hand a last squeeze and made his escape. He couldn't afford to spend too long there. It was important Louisa didn't find out he had been sitting holding the hand of his ex-lover.

*

It was July already and Jo's first full weekend at the house since Eleanor's fall. Without the presence of Charlotte and Lawrence, the house felt cavernous, sepulchral. Sidney's company was a pleasant distraction but Jo hungered for conversation or sound or activity, anything to break the silent monotony. Even arguing with Lawrence would be better than nothing. She had spent most of the day with Eleanor, had been there while Imogen and Mari had called in for a few minutes, bringing flowers and chatting awkwardly then looking desperate to get away. Otherwise it had been the usual vigil of inconsequential remarks and silence.

She wandered to the piano at the back of the sitting room, lifted the lid and ran her fingers in a scale up the keys. The notes vibrated listlessly in the air and only emphasised the stillness. She closed the lid again and glanced back towards the patio doors and the sunshine beyond. A few minutes later, in shorts, T-shirt and canvas shoes, she was in the garden, carefully negotiating the steps down to the beach.

It was a tiny cove with a shore of pebbles and shells and a heavy deposit of seaweed at the top where flies now swarmed and settled in the sun. Private and peaceful, Jo had loved it here from her first visit, an oasis of calm after her life at home with her mother. She released a slow breath, trying to unwind, glancing round. There was no sign of Eleanor's phone. But if it had fallen onto the rocks it would have broken up and been washed away on the tide. She looked closer towards the rocks near the cliff. There was a cigarette butt there though. That was odd. Eleanor hadn't smoked in decades and Frank had given it up years ago too.

She glanced back up the cliff, frowning, then walked slowly out to where the sea lapped the shore, disturbing a pied wagtail which fluttered to bob further along the beach. The tide was still ebbing but couldn't have far to go. Waves edged and hissed over a fine gritty sand which was only visible for a short while either side of low tide.

Her thoughts drifted. All those times she had come here to visit and her mother had never come. The sisters didn't get on. Candida would drive her here, but drop her off by the gate. Her mother had once visited the other house Eleanor lived in, the one near Dartmouth, but that time she'd had no choice. Jo, still little more than a child, had taken money from her mother's secret savings pot and spent all her saved pocket money to bolt there and was refusing to go home. In any case, Eleanor had summoned her. The two sisters had fought one of their more spectacular arguments while Jo listened outside the door.

'It's hardly surprising she doesn't want to go home, Candida,' she had heard Eleanor say. 'I gather your latest lover has wandering hands. Jo was terrified. Beyond terrified: repulsed, disgusted, ashamed… Luckily she had the sense to get away and she had somewhere to go. But what the hell were you thinking: letting a man like that near your daughter?'

'I didn't know, did I? I didn't know he was doing anything

to her. I didn't.'

'Perhaps if you spent more time thinking about her and less about yourself, you'd have noticed.'

'Thank you for the instruction in mothering, Eleanor,' Candida retorted witheringly. 'Of course, you're such an expert. How many children is it you've had? Oh, that's right: *none*. If you'd actually had any children, you'd know how difficult it is to have any social life of your own, let alone a love life.'

'Is that your excuse? Because you seem to manage just fine. Jo has told me about the parties.'

There'd been a pause from her mother, a regrouping.

'She exaggerates,' said Candida. 'Look, Eleanor, I promise I'll be more careful in future. I've already kicked him out. It won't happen again.'

'You're bloody right it won't happen again. If it does I swear I'll tell Social Services myself and she can come and live here permanently.'

Driving Jo home, Candida had apologised extravagantly. She always apologised when she made a mistake and she always meant it. And no man came near Jo again. But nothing else changed much. Her mother's life was like a car with the brakes gone: it went too fast and bounced and bucked as it bowled along until it finally crashed.

Now a gull mewed overhead, breaking Jo's reverie, and she looked up, shielding her eyes against the sun. She needed to buy some sunglasses; she hadn't thought to pack any. A movement at the edge of her vision caught her attention, over to her right by the headland, and she turned her head, struggling to focus. That part of the beach was in shade.

A youth had been standing, or maybe sitting, over on the lowest rocks below the cliff face, watching her. Now he'd started picking his way over the rocks away from her.

'Hey,' she shouted, walking towards him. 'Wait a minute. I want to speak to you.'

He hesitated, looking round, furtive.

She shouted again and he stayed where he was as she approached, standing a little straighter, lifting his chin defiantly. He was younger than she had first thought, wearing baggy shorts, a reversed baseball cap and huge trainers, all of which looked too big for him. Close up, he looked forlorn, not a man but not a child either.

'I haven't done nothing,' he mumbled.

'You mean you haven't done anything.'

'That's what I said.'

She let it go. 'This beach is private. It belongs to my aunt. How did you get here?' She glanced round but could see no boat or surfboard.

'I swam.'

'Uhuh. Dressed like that?'

'What difference does it make?'

'Because if you came through the estate…' She pointed up towards the gardens and house. '…and down onto the beach that way, I'd want to know what you were doing up there and how you got in.'

'I didn't.' He was defensive now. 'Some rocks broke off from the cliffs in the storms a few months ago. You can climb round from the other beach when the tide gets low enough. Other people don't know that.'

'I see.' She nodded thoughtfully. 'Sounds like a risky thing to do though. Especially if the cliff's unstable.'

'I'm careful.'

The tide had turned and a penetrating wave had the lad jumping down onto a flat rock higher up the beach and Jo scurrying back up the shingle to avoid getting wet. The boy saw an empty crab shell in a rock pool and bent over to pick it up. A way to avoid looking at her.

'OK so why?' said Jo. 'Why do you climb all the way round the headland to this private beach when there's a great beach with more sand on the other side?' He didn't reply. 'Just to show you can?'

He shrugged but still didn't answer, examining the crab shell more minutely.

'Where are you from?'

He frowned and looked up sharply. 'What d'you mean?'

'Are you on holiday here?'

'No. I live in the village.'

'I see. And do your parents know you come here?'

He flicked her a malevolent look and scoffed. 'Yeah, right. Anyway, there's only my dad. I suppose you're going to tell him, aren't you? Hey, why not - I'm always in trouble with him anyway.'

She shrugged. 'If you don't do any harm, I'd have no reason to tell him. How old are you?'

He hesitated, watching her warily. 'Seventeen,' he said eventually. He raised his eyebrows with a cheeky grin. 'How old are you?'

She had to smile then. 'Thirty-six.'

He looked her up and down but didn't comment and turned and threw the crab shell back into the pool.

'So can I keep coming here?' he said, not looking at her. 'It's not like you use it much, after all. And I like it 'cause it's quiet.'

'That's because it's private.'

'People shouldn't own beaches,' he said sullenly. 'They should belong to everyone.'

'Maybe. But if my aunt didn't own this beach, you wouldn't want to come here because it wouldn't be quiet.' She paused and when he didn't speak, she prompted, 'Would it?'

'S'pose not.'

She relented, unable to be cross with him. He was just a kid. There was no way he was seventeen. And he looked harmless - lonely more than anything else.

'I'm Jo,' she said. 'You?'

'Harry.'

'OK Harry, so, yes, you can come again, but only to the beach. And just you. No friends. My aunt's not well at the moment. I don't want her to come home to find her special place has been spoiled for her. Whatever you might think, she's worked damn hard for this.'

He stared down into the rock pool, saying nothing.

'Agreed?'

'Yeah, yeah, I get it. Don't go on.' He looked at her sidelong. 'She fell, didn't she?'

'My aunt? Yes. Why?'

He shrugged, then began studying the rock pool again and edging around it and away from her.

She left him to it and climbed back up towards the house, pausing at the top of the steps and looking down again to where Eleanor had been stuck in the brambles. There was something about it that didn't fit.

Chapter 6

The alarm on his phone woke Matthew with a start. The night before he had stayed up reading in bed for too long as usual, trying to wear his mind out. Even when he'd finally slept he had done so fitfully, checking the time two or three times during the night. He had become resigned to this routine. Then he'd drifted into a light sleep not long before the alarm was due and now lay there sweating in the bed.

Sophie had just come to him again in a dream. Vivid, whole, as healthy as when they had first met, she had talked with him and laughed with him, made plans and teased. They had been on an excursion together with Harry, Matthew driving, Sophie and Harry in the back singing a succession of children's songs. Bizarrely, Harry had been the same age he was now but it hadn't mattered in the dream. He was happy: happy singing children's songs; happy to be with his mother; maybe even happy to be with his father.

And for several minutes after Matthew woke, he thought it was true. It had been so real, he could still hear Sophie's voice, could smell her perfume. Even now, if he just reached over in the bed, he felt sure he could touch her...

But reality washed through him bringing the familiar pain and longing. He covered his face, wanting to hold Sophie still in his head yet desperate to make the pain go away. He couldn't do both. He couldn't do either, it seemed. He had lost count of how often this had happened. How long was this going to go on for? Wasn't it bad enough to lose her once, but to keep doing it over and over again like this? He couldn't stand it.

'Why, Sophie?' he said angrily. 'Bloody hell. Why? Why leave me then keep coming back to haunt me?

He had spoken too loudly and immediately listened for Harry but heard nothing. Did Harry dream about his mother like this? Matthew wouldn't know. Harry had become a closed book since Sophie had died.

He sat up and threw himself out of bed, needing to move, to distract himself somehow. It was Sunday and he would have to open the shop later but there was plenty of time to go out first. Quickly washing and dressing, he trod as silently down the stairs as the creaking boards would allow and let himself out of the tiny cottage.

Their house was on the end of a thatched terrace, a short walk from the rear of the coffee shop. Harry was right: it was dark. The small windows, low ceilings and overhang of thatch only exacerbated the cottage's gloomy position at the northern end of the terrace. Exiting through the back door and moving round to the lane at the front, Matthew found himself squinting as he walked into the sunshine. The lane hugged the side of a stream which ran down through the village to the shore. He turned right towards the sea and headed for the coastal path.

It was still early and there were few people out, mostly dog-walkers. He reluctantly exchanged a brief greeting with those he recognised and kept moving. Reaching the footpath up the headland to the north of the cove, he pounded briskly up it, then did the same with the steps, savouring the physical effort, feeling the blood pumping through his body. He was breathless by the time he reached the top but kept going, seeking out the highest point and the spectacular view it afforded. He hoped he would have it to himself at this time in the morning and he did. He took a step onto the soft, spongy grass nearer the scrubby edge of the cliff and looked out and round as his breathing settled.

This was one of his favourite places: crisp, clean air and a stunning panorama. To the northwest the coastal path wound along the clifftop and away out of sight. In the far distance he could see South Rock, the next village along, and the suggestion of its shoreline. To the south and east, below him, was the bowl-shaped sandy beach of Petterton Mill Cove and, on the other side, the wooded headland which sheltered Eleanor Lambe's home. Gazing down to the straggle of village buildings reaching up the valley, Matthew could see someone slowly laying out the beach gear in front of the convenience store. A single car navigated the road winding down through the village and looped round and up into the small car park above the beach. A herring gull, wings outstretched, wheeled and hung on air currents out over the sea.

This is why he had brought Harry here: the peace, the simplicity, the quietness. If the lad couldn't sort his problems out here, where could he? As soon as Matthew had seen the advert for the coffee shop, he had known. And once he'd looked into the place and found out that Eleanor Lambe lived in the village, that had clinched it. It felt like fate. Sophie had been a big reader and Ms Lambe had been one of her favourite authors. Sophie. You see, he couldn't get away from her because he kept chasing her. His shoulders sagged. It was wrong to get angry with Sophie because he was the one who wouldn't let her go. He was destined to go round in circles like this forever.

With an effort he pushed her out of his head and thought

of Harry again. Most kids would kill to live somewhere like this, wouldn't they? OK, so he didn't like the house but this was a place to be outdoors and the house was only a rental that came with the shop, a convenience for the time being.

But maybe it was his own fault. It wasn't working out the way he'd hoped. Before they'd come here, he had planned beach cricket and cooking together and walks like they used to do with Sophie. But he was finding the coffee shop too all-consuming. It was busy and more demanding than he'd expected. Gail was wonderful of course and there was Freddie too - a lad of twenty-one. Freddie had a ponytail, a ring through one eyebrow and a line in bizarre jokes but he was genial, polite and hard-working. They were a good team, but Matthew wasn't good at delegating. The café was his responsibility; he felt he had to be there. But he felt guilty for not being around for his son too - though when he did have time with Harry they barely spoke.

'Take some time off,' Sophie said in his head. 'It would do you both good. Stop being a martyr.'

'Easy for you to say,' he replied. 'I'm trying to juggle a hundred balls here - without your help.'

'You're hiding, using the shop as an excuse.'

'Oh, you're so clever these days. You should try what I have to do.'

He had a lot of these silent conversations with Sophie. It upset him that they were always so cross. When she was alive it had never been like that.

He sighed and began the walk back down the hill towards the village and work.

*

'Why didn't you tell me?' hissed Louisa.

'Because I didn't want to upset you. I was scared you'd read something into it that wasn't there, that's all.' Frank glanced towards the counter, aware that Matthew was not far away, making their coffees. Why had she waited until they'd come out for a Sunday morning walk to challenge him about his visit to Eleanor? He hated arguing in public.

'Why?' she pressed. 'Because you don't feel you can talk to me? Because I'm too blinkered in my thinking? And how come Imogen knew when I didn't?'

'Because I bumped into her when I got back, that's all. She could smell the disinfectant on me. You know - that stuff you have to squeeze onto your hands when you go into a ward. Hospitals leave a smell on you anyway. Bloody Imogen, misses nothing.'

'Don't blame Imogen.'

Matthew brought their drinks over and they immediately fell silent while he put them on the table and withdrew.

'Oh, I have a right to blame Imogen,' muttered Frank. 'I asked her to keep it to herself and she said she would. So much for her promises. Perhaps I should warn Mari she's not to be trusted.'

'Don't. Mari's devoted to Imogen. They're planning to get married.'

'Exactly my point.'

Louisa tipped a sachet of sugar into her coffee and stirred it round, her unhappy gaze fixed on the cup.

'So why did you go?' she said, not looking at him.

'Because we used to be close. Because she's had a terrible accident. Is it really so surprising? Come on, darling, please understand, it has nothing to do with us.' He reached out and took her free hand, dropping his voice. 'I'm in love with you. I was just paying a brief visit to someone I used to know well

83

who's very ill and probably dying. It may be the last time I see her.'

Louisa frowned. 'I suppose that could be true.' She freed her hand from his but seemed to relax a little and sat back, cradling her cup and saucer, looking across at him solicitously. 'I'd hate to think you hadn't had a chance to see her before she went. I'm sorry, Frank. That was thoughtless of me. But still, you should have told me beforehand. I could have come with you. You know, made it easier for you.' She smiled and he melted as he usually did. He loved her smile: it was broad and cheerful and guileless and made her eyes crinkle. And he hated to upset her.

'I didn't stay long,' he said. 'It wasn't so hard; it's been a while now. But thanks anyway. Now let's talk about something else. Shall we walk over to South Halcombe and have lunch there?'

*

For Jo, Saturday rolled imperceptibly into Sunday which rolled into Monday. There had been no change in Eleanor. There was no evidence that she was even aware that anyone was with her and Jo finally accepted that there was going to be no quick fix, no fairy-tale recovery. In the darkest recesses of her mind, she began to doubt if there would be a recovery at all but refused to go there. Already wrung out, physically and emotionally, she was going to have to settle in for the long haul and pace herself. She adjusted her daily pattern, working on her editing commissions at the house in the morning, visiting Eleanor in the afternoon.

Eleanor's study was the obvious place to work but it wasn't a comfortable thing to do, pushing her aunt's laptop to the back of the desk, shifting papers and notebooks out of the way. She had strayed in here a few times as an inquisitive child and her aunt would invariably find her and ask her what she was doing. The study was the one room Eleanor had always liked to keep to herself.

But now it was Lawrence who was keeping track of Jo's movements. On the Monday morning she had been at Eleanor's desk barely half an hour when he pushed back the half-open door and stood in the doorway.

'Is there something in particular you're looking for in here?' he demanded.

'No. Should there be?'

His eyes quickly scanned the room before he replied.

'No-o. But I thought if you were, I could help.' He finally registered her computer and books and his eyebrows rose. 'You're working?'

'Indeed.' She bit back a sarcastic response. Better not to antagonise Lawrence unnecessarily. 'Charlotte said you were planning to see Eleanor over the weekend.'

The housekeeper had made the remark casually when she'd arrived that morning while Jo was still in the kitchen. Though, as if she'd spoken out of turn, she had seemed reluctant to say anything more on the subject.

Lawrence regarded her dispassionately. 'Yes. I went last night.'

'How was she?'

'Just as you described,' he said crisply, and left.

He's a cold fish, thought Jo.

It was later that morning when, mug of coffee in hand, she finally allowed herself to pick through the papers she had moved. She found one headed *Lit Fest* with a list of possible speakers, some of whom had ticks and TBC written by their names. Inevitably, Eleanor's own name was at the top. Since the meeting in the hall, Jo hadn't given the festival much thought and had no idea how she would fulfil her rash promise to Nancy to step into Eleanor's shoes. But this would help. She recognised all the names on it and had even met some of them. They were a mix of fiction and non-fiction authors including one politician, Brian Hunwin, a close friend of Eleanor's and a retired Member of Parliament. At the bottom of the list were the names of the course tutors too, all except Vincent and all ticked. Interesting. Why had Vincent been excluded?

She checked through the other papers for anything similar but all she found, buried under the mound of paper, was a small digital recorder. Eleanor had used a variety of these devices over the years to record her writing thoughts. She carried one round with her everywhere.

Jo picked it up, considered it thoughtfully, then trod softly to the door and closed it, turning the handle as silently as she could. Back in the heart of the room, she switched it on and hit 'play'. Eleanor's voice spoke to her as loudly and clearly as if she were in the room.

'Chapter four needs to start with a flashback to '84. What Donald decides to do has to be seen to result from his experiences at that time.'

She quickly reduced the volume. The date stamp for the recording was the Friday morning, the same day Jo had rung, the same day Eleanor had fallen. And there were other recordings - similar snatches of thought, all made within the previous week.

Jo stopped the recording. There had been footsteps in the hallway and she was convinced that Lawrence was standing the other side of the door, listening. She found herself holding her breath, waiting. The steps eventually moved away and she breathed again, then slipped the recorder into her bag. It seemed important not to leave it there.

Back at the desk, Eleanor's voice still echoed in her head. She didn't sound like someone gripped by writer's block. Nor did she sound anything other than her usual determined, forthright self. Jo sat, staring blindly at her computer screen for some minutes, then began searching the drawers of Eleanor's desk. There were all the usual stationery items: pens and pencils, new notebooks and adhesives and paper clips; old filled notebooks too, some going way back. But Eleanor used to keep an address book. She said modern technology was great but paper and pens didn't break down or go off-line. Yes, here it was, in the middle drawer. Jo found the page where Eleanor's agent was listed, programmed the mobile number into her phone and promptly left the house, walking down the slope to the parking bays where she got in her car. Lawrence couldn't eavesdrop here. She glanced round, then called the number.

'Hello, yes?'

'Jenny? It's Jo here, Joselyn Lambe, Eleanor's niece. Have you got a minute?'

'Jo? Oh yes, Jo. How are you? I haven't seen you in…oh ages. How's poor Eleanor? I've been meaning to come down but it's been hellish busy. Lawrence said she wouldn't know me anyway.'

'I'm afraid that's true at the moment. But Jenny, I wanted to ask you something.'

'Of course.'

'How was Eleanor's latest book coming on? Did she have problems with it? I gather she'd missed a few deadlines already.'

Jenny laughed. 'Eleanor always misses deadlines. Though she did have a bad patch with the latest book a while back. She seemed to be over the hump the last time we spoke. She'd got into that excited phase. I guessed it was coming together. Why do you ask?'

'Oh, you know…I'm trying to talk to Eleanor as much as possible but it gets hard to know what to say. I didn't want to say anything about her work in case it upset her.'

'Oh no, she loves her work. I mean, she hates it too - you know what writers are like.'

Jo hesitated. 'Have her books not been selling well lately? Is she not as popular as she used to be?'

'Eleanor Lambe is one of the foremost writers of our age,' said Jenny smoothly, as if doing a press briefing. 'Her political thrillers are edgy, pacy and above all smart. They're popular the world over.'

'Jenny, please. You don't have to tell me how clever she is. I know that. But is she struggling to sell?'

'No. Well, not exactly,' she said coolly. 'The margins have got tighter lately but certainly she's selling. Maybe not as much as we'd like. There are fashions in writers - well, you know that - but compared to most writers, she's doing very well.'

'I see. Well good.'

Jenny's voice softened. 'Look I'm really sorry Eleanor's in such a bad way. I will try and get down there soon. I'd like to see her.'

Jo closed the call but continued to sit in the car. The unease that she kept shrugging off had closed in again and thickened. There had been no writer's block. Sales were OK. Lawrence kept lying to her.

*

Eleanor was going backwards. She was running a temperature

and had developed a chest infection, incubated silently and insidiously over the preceding days, not uncommon in patients who are very static, the nurse told Jo.

'You are treating it?' Jo demanded, frightened they would think there was no point. Would they do that? Not without asking her surely?

'She's on antibiotics,' the nurse patiently replied. 'And the doctors are reviewing her regularly. She's comfortable.'

Comfortable. What a ubiquitous word that was in hospitals; it seemed to cover every conceivable condition.

Sitting again on the hard plastic chair, holding Eleanor's clammy hand, Jo felt a chill fear spreading through her. Her aunt's face looked paler than ever and yet there was a tiny unnatural spot of colour high in each cheek. Her slow decline was beginning to feel inevitable.

'Eleanor,' she almost shouted, patting the hand roughly. 'Eleanor, come on, wake up. It's about time you got up and about, you lazy bones. That's what you used to tell me when I stayed in bed. Do you remember? So come on. Let's see some activity.'

There was no reaction.

'You'd have laughed last night, Eleanor. I took Sidney out on a lead. You know: my cat? The rescue people said I should wait two weeks before letting him out but I thought at least he could get used to the gardens and get some fresh air. Sidney thought it was a game to start with and kept trying to catch the lead in his paws. Everyone we saw looked at me as though I was mad and Vincent was very sarcastic. Not that he's in any position to talk.'

Nothing. Eleanor was breathing too fast, Jo could see that. The afternoon dragged. By the end of it, she didn't know whether to go or to stay.

'We'll call you if she gets worse,' a nurse assured her. 'Of course we will.'

For four days, there was no change. On the Saturday morning, when Jo rang the ward, she was told that Eleanor's temperature had come down a little. When she saw her on the Sunday, her skin was no longer clammy and the red spots had gone. Her breathing had slowed. Jo silently thanked a God to whom she spoke only rarely and settled in her customary seat. It felt like a huge weight had been lifted off her. She could have cried.

'You had me scared there, Eleanor,' she berated the blank face before her. 'Don't you dare do that again.'

Jo rubbed the cool hand. There again, maybe the antibiotics had simply bought a little more time, a reprieve. It was too soon to feel relief.

'You've got to wake up, Eleanor,' she hissed, frustrated and scared. 'Please. Come on, wake up. And tell me what happened. Come on.'

For days, she had tried to talk brightly about nothing in particular so that Eleanor would feel positive. It hadn't worked. Perhaps she needed a different tack. How could she get into that head and get some reaction? The magazine cutting secreted away in the poetry book loomed into her mind. It had been crushed in a fit of emotion, then meticulously straightened out again.

Jo leaned forward, speaking close to Eleanor's ear.

'People are gossiping, Eleanor. I know you don't care about gossip. "Sticks and stones", you used to say. But they're saying that it was Frank's engagement that made you walk off the cliff and it's not true, is it? I'm waiting for you to wake up and put these rumours to bed. You don't want people to think you'd hurt yourself over Frank, do you? I wouldn't want anyone to say that about me over Richard.'

Jo straightened up and watched and waited. There was still nothing. She sat back and closed her eyes. She didn't know what else to try.

*

It was late on the Sunday evening when Eleanor became aware of a sound. Something had woken her, she was sure, but, eyes still closed, all she could make out was the sound and she couldn't identify it. The world was very dark around her and yet there seemed to be some lightness somewhere too. Now the sound was beginning to resolve into something identifiable. A woman's voice…maybe. But still nothing made any sense - the sounds were too jumbled - and now the sound was moving away again.

Ugh, there was something horrible in her nose. She tried wriggling it but the irritation wouldn't go away. Damn. Double damn. How disgusting.

She wanted to open her eyes but nothing happened; her eyelids felt too heavy. So very heavy, weighted down with lead. Anyway, the voice had gone now and she couldn't be bothered to try and open her eyes any more. A deep wave of the darkness was overwhelming her and it was too hard to try and fight it so she gave in and slipped back.

Chapter 7

There was a bright light searing Eleanor's eyelids, burning through to her retinae. And something in her body hurt. She couldn't pinpoint where. In fact, now she thought about it, lots of things hurt, too many to care about. The light grew dimmer. She was drifting again and she was glad. She wanted to sleep, to slip back into the darkness. It was easier; it was comfortable and safe and it was too much effort not to go there.

'Eleanor? Eleanor?'

Eleanor heard the voice but took a minute to understand what it was. It was quite close. And it seemed familiar. She tried to open her eyes but they felt sticky. It wasn't important after all. Nothing mattered except the darkness, that sweet, velvety blackness where she could rest.

'Aunt Eleanor? I'm sure I saw your eyes move. Eleanor? Can you hear me? Squeeze my hand if you can hear me. Come on, you can do it. Eleanor?'

Eleanor became aware that there was pressure on part of her. Yes, that might be her hand. Which hand, she wasn't sure. Was someone holding it? A woman? It sounded like someone who knew her. She thought about trying to squeeze the woman's hand and maybe she had. It felt like she had. She didn't care much but she'd love a drink. She would ask for one. There. She'd asked. She was sure her lips had moved but nothing was happening. No-one gave her a drink. That woman was saying something to her again but none of it mattered because she was going to sleep. She had to sleep.

*

'We've been doing some tests and your aunt can clearly hear,' the doctor told Jo, 'though we can't formally test the range of her hearing yet. She can see too. Her eyes follow movement but again we're not sure what her vision is like. I understand she wears glasses just for reading, is that right?'

'Yes. Should I bring them in?'

The doctor looked tired, the way she felt, but he managed a weak smile.

'Maybe soon. I don't think she'll be reading just yet. She's coming up quite quickly now but there's still a long way to go. Fortunately she seems to be swallowing all right so we're going to try her with fluids. She has some motor function but of course she's very weak and quite uncoordinated. That might improve - it's too soon to say - but there are things she may need to relearn; simple things some of them. We'll get the physio working with her.'

A nurse touched him on the arm and gave him something to sign. He glanced at it and scrawled his name, saying something in a low voice. He looked as though his mind had already moved on to something else and he was impatient to be away. Jo had so many questions she wanted to ask him, many of them barely formed in her mind, just abstract concerns which had no real shape as yet. The doctor offered another brief smile and was about to turn away.

'Do you think she understands what's happened to her,' Jo said quickly. 'Does she know where she is?'

His eyes narrowed for a minute. She could sense him planning carefully what to say, what not to say.

'As you've probably heard, she's managing some speech though most of it is incoherent. But it does seem to be getting better. It's too soon to know how much brain damage there might have been and what functions might be impaired long term. Undoubtedly there's quite a lot of confusion there. Her memory might be an issue. Try to give her as much stimulation as you can.'

He walked away but the words *brain damage* lingered in Jo's head. She had known all along that damage, possibly permanent, might be a result of the fall but hearing it said like that felt brutal. She walked back into the little side room where Eleanor was now sitting propped up in a chair, supported on all sides by pillows. Jo had brought a radio in for her aunt to listen to when she was alone and someone had been in and switched it on, turning it to a commercial station where a strident DJ's voice was reading out a succession of tweets. Then music began to thump out and Jo fiddled with the tuning to change the station. When Eleanor listened to the radio, it was always Radio 4. She switched the radio off and went round to sit by the bed. Her aunt's mouth dragged on one side; a trail of saliva ran from the side of it and down her chin. Jo pulled a tissue from the box on the locker and wiped it up.

It was Thursday, the thirteenth of July, nearly three weeks since Eleanor had fallen on the cliff. Since the first fluttering of her eyelids that Jo had seen on the Monday, the change in her aunt had been remarkable in many ways. That night she had gripped the nurse's hand; by the morning she had tried to pull the tube out of her nose and had managed to kick one foot out from under the bedclothes; by the afternoon her eyes were frequently open and she was making noises and getting agitated because she clearly wanted to say something but no-one could make out what.

Still clutching the tissue, Jo sat back down in the chair she had recently vacated.

Eleanor's hair had grown about half a centimetre. The bruises had largely faded. Even the surgical wound on her scalp had healed over and was rapidly looking less livid and submerging into the hedgehog-like growth. The dressing had long since gone. Jo watched her aunt avidly. Her eyes were closed at the moment, her breathing regular; she looked peaceful, as if she was sleeping. The touch to her chin hadn't woken her. *Try to give her as much stimulation as you can.* She reached forward, took Eleanor's left hand, squeezed it gently then patted it with her other hand. Immediately her aunt's eyes opened.

Jo smiled. 'Hi Eleanor. How're you doing?'

The hazel eyes fixed on her. They looked much darker now against the luminous white of her hair and the pallor of her skin. Jo felt herself examined as if she were an alien from another universe.

'You know me,' she said brightly. 'It's Joselyn. Your niece. Jo.' Was that the faintest flicker of recognition? It was hard to be sure. 'You're in hospital, Eleanor,' she said for the umpteenth time. 'You had a fall in the garden at home - knocked yourself out. Cracked a couple of ribs too. What did you think you were doing...' Jo squeezed her aunt's hand again, adopting a flippant tone. '...trying to nose dive down the cliff? You gave us all a fright.'

Eleanor was watching Jo's lips intently as she spoke. Did that mean she understood? Or was she struggling to follow? Her aunt's eyelids started to droop again and Jo leaned back in the chair, drained. Thrilled and relieved to see her aunt awake, still the journey ahead looked long, its outcome uncertain. Foolishly, she had been hoping - if not admitting it to herself -

that when Eleanor woke up, she would be her old self again. She had also hoped that Eleanor would be able to tell her how she came to fall, but that seemed unlikely now.

*

It had started to rain, one of those bouncing, stair rod showers that suggested that someone, not far away, was suffering a thunderstorm. It was dark in the den and somebody had flicked the lights on which only served to exaggerate how dismal it was. There was an uneasy feeling in the air too, the proximity of the storm perhaps or maybe an intangible tension in the room. Frank wasn't sure which.

It was five past eight in the evening and Jo had just come down from the house to see them, ducking into the room not long before the heavens opened. He and Mari were playing whist; Imogen and Vincent were watching the television - having argued at some length about which station to put on - and Louisa was sitting reading, though her attention regularly appeared to wander. Frank would catch her at times, her gaze settling on each of them in turn.

'Come and join us,' he'd said to her, indicating the vacant chair by the table, but she had smiled weakly and shaken her head.

Now Jo stood near the doorway, apologising for disturbing them. Imogen muted the television and they all turned to look at her.

'I'm glad to catch you all,' she said. 'Only I thought you might like to know the latest on Eleanor. She's woken up and after a few days of, well, ups and downs, she's definitely conscious now.'

'That's wonderful,' said Mari.

'Marvellous,' agreed Imogen.

Vincent turned his head, his manner studiously casual. 'Can she remember what happened?'

'I'm afraid she's not making much sense yet.' Jo paused, frowning. It struck Frank just how pinched and pale she looked. 'I'm not sure she remembers anything much, or even who I am, but it's early days. Anyway, I thought you'd want to know. She tires very quickly though so visiting needs to be restricted.'

'Still, I think this calls for a drink,' said Imogen, pushing herself to her feet. 'Will you have one, Jo?'

Jo thanked her but declined and turned to leave. Frank got up and moved quickly, meeting her by the door.

'It's hammering down out there,' he said. 'Stay and have a drink. You look done in.'

She produced a weary smile. 'I am. But I think I need an early night. Thanks all the same.'

'Wait.'

He put a hand to her arm, staying her, glancing back into the room. Imogen and Mari were in the kitchen, pouring drinks, and Louisa was deep in conversation with Vincent. Frank turned back to Jo and dropped his voice.

'I was hoping to see you. It's not easy for me to go and see Eleanor in the circumstances. Will you keep in touch, let me know how she's doing? This is my phone number.' He slipped her a small piece of paper. 'Perhaps we could have coffee sometime soon?'

She glanced across at Louisa and reluctantly pocketed the paper then fixed him with an earnest expression. 'I don't know what to say, Frank. It's difficult for all of us, isn't it? I found the cutting Eleanor saw about your engagement. It clearly upset her. I don't want to get caught in the middle here. My first loyalty is to Eleanor. You do understand?'

He nodded and let her go, and she slipped out into the rain. Turning back, Frank saw Vincent move away from Louisa, heading for the kitchen, and a drink no doubt.

Frank walked back to his seat at the table, pausing by the sofa to rest his hand briefly on Louisa's shoulder.

'Everything all right?' he asked.

She tipped her head back to look at him and smiled. 'Of course.' She returned to her book but there was a look in her eyes he couldn't place. He couldn't read her. There had been a spell, when he and Eleanor had been at their best together, when they had always known what each other was thinking, like two violin strings, resonant with each other. They had joked about it, how they didn't need to talk, how they kept finishing each other's sentences. Or perhaps it was an illusion. Every couple wants to think that they're made for each other, that they're two halves of a whole.

The volume on the television went back up and Frank played cards with Mari for another twenty minutes. He had his back to the room and didn't notice that Louisa had left until they finished and he got up from the table.

'When did Louisa go?' he said.

Imogen shrugged. She had picked up a magazine and was buried in its pages. Frank went outside. The rain had stopped but water still lay in pools on the stone slabs and dripped from the shrubs and trees. There was no sign of Louisa. It unnerved him that she could slip out like that without him realising, but he was prone to let his mind wander. Snatches of poetry stalked his brain and he was often only too happy to let them catch him.

He went to the apartment he was sharing with Louisa - it was theoretically hers - and let himself in. There was no light on and he was about to go out again when he saw her sitting

98

on the side of the bed in the fading light.

'Louisa? Are you all right?'

She didn't reply and he crossed to sit beside her on the bed, putting his arm round her shoulders.

'What's the matter?' he asked softly.

'Nothing.'

'There must be something. To sit here like this. It's almost dark.'

He pulled her closer, put his other arm around her and rocked her gently. She had been like this when he first knew her: vulnerable and reflective. Her mother had not long died and she'd been grieving. Her softness and vulnerability was one of the things he loved about her. Sometimes now though she seemed like a different person: challenging, teasing, temperamental.

She tilted her head up and fixed him with sad eyes. 'You seem to get on very well with Mari.'

He laughed, taken aback. 'Everyone gets on well with Mari. You know what she's like.'

'Yes, but she's especially fond of you. I can see it in her eyes. And she's very pretty.'

'Louisa, that's absurd. You can't be jealous of Mari. She's gay. She and Imogen are a happy couple.'

'She used to be married to a man though, didn't she? Imogen told me. Imogen worries that she still...you know...wants a man in her life.'

'No.' He shook his head. 'In any case I don't want her.'

She leant into him and he hugged her hard.

'What did Vincent want?' he said softly.

'Want? Nothing.'

'But you were talking.'

'Oh, we were just wondering about Eleanor. Why did you

want to see Joselyn?'

'I felt sorry for her. She looked so worn out. I've known her since she was a skinny kid.'

He stroked her hair. She had lovely hair: thick and glossy.

'Do you think Eleanor is going to pull through?' she muttered into his rugby shirt.

'I dunno. She doesn't sound good but...' He shrugged.

Louisa eased herself from his hold and stared into his face, a little too long, as if trying to read his innermost thoughts. 'I wish we hadn't come here this year, Frank, don't you? It was a silly idea.'

So she'd changed her mind again. She kept doing this.

'You shouldn't let Eleanor's fall upset you so. All we did was get engaged. Where's the harm in that? What Eleanor did or didn't do isn't our fault. We'll just do the work we've agreed to do and leave. It'll be OK.'

She reached up and kissed him, passionate suddenly, greedy even. Frank responded but part of his brain wondered what was bothering her. A spark of suspicion had started to form deep in his head, a smouldering, singeing glow which, once ignited, refused to be damped down. And it had too many implications. He couldn't bring himself to ask her about it.

*

Jo thought it would get easier but it didn't. Eleanor awake but not really Eleanor - an incoherent stranger who stared blankly at her - was a reality she struggled to come to terms with. The words *brain damage* regularly crossed her mind, accusing and reproachful.

At five-thirty on the Sunday, having sat with Eleanor all afternoon, alternately talking to her and reading out items from the newspaper, Jo went home. Sidney was now free to go out by himself and came running as soon as she called his name. He didn't seem to stray far from the grounds and when she bent to pick him up his coat was warm from the sun. It was hot today. The gloom and storms of the week had been replaced with blue sky and the odd wispy white cloud. She fed Sidney, then wandered down to the sitting room and threw herself on the sofa, trying to relax. A few minutes later she gave up, changed into a sun dress, shut Sidney inside and descended the steps to the beach and the lapping therapy of the waves.

Harry was there again, sitting on the rock where he had been before, reversed baseball cap on, facing out to sea, lost in his own world. She was surprised to feel so pleased to see him.

'Hi Harry.'

He turned at her approach, sliding quickly down off the rock onto the pebbles. Today he was wearing flip-flops. It amazed her that he could climb over rocks in them. He was holding his phone, and pulled the earphone out of his right ear, watching her with a wary expression.

'What is it now? he demanded.

She shrugged and smiled. 'It? It's nothing. I just came down to hang out on the beach and I said hi.'

'Oh.' He hesitated. 'Hi.'

He looked away awkwardly to where the tide had recently turned and each wave was slowly eating up a little more of the shore.

'Seen anything interesting today?' she asked. 'I've sometimes seen dolphins out in the bay. Of course there's the whale that's been in Start Bay this summer. I don't suppose it's made it over this far.'

He turned to look at her, eyes narrowed, as if trying to work out if she was making fun of him. He shook his head. 'I haven't seen nothing.'

101

'Anything.' She grinned. 'Sorry. Grammar police. I'm a bit compulsive about stuff like that. Used to drive my boyfriend crazy.'

He looked at her but didn't respond, and she walked away down towards the sea, bending over, searching the pebbles. Finding a suitably flat one, she skimmed it over the water, counting the number of times it skipped before falling in. Four. She bent to choose another stone and heard the crunch of Harry's feet getting closer. She straightened, pulled her right arm back, twisting and bending to get the right angle. Frank had taught her to do this, years ago, patiently showing her how to hold the stone and how to use her wrist to flick it. This one skipped five times.

'Not bad,' Harry admitted grudgingly.

She glanced across at him. The phone and earphone had been rammed into a pocket of his baggy shorts, the wire still dangling, and he already had a stone in hand.

'OK, so you do better.'

He leaned over and threw it, then raised his hands in the air. 'Six,' he exulted.

'I'm out of practice.' She threw again. It managed six skips too, then a vigorous wave caught her by surprise and had her scurrying backwards, too late, her feet getting washed in brine.

'Ugh.' She shook her feet off; her canvas shoes were soaked.

'Hey, you're on the beach,' taunted Harry. 'Going in the sea's what it's all about.' With youthful bravado, he paddled into the next wave, water sloshing around his knees, and looked round at her. 'Anyway, the stone'll go further from in here. I dare you.' He grinned provocatively, then turned back to face the sea, waiting for a wave to swell and pass, jigging up onto his toes to stop it rising too high. He released his stone. It kept on skipping.

'Yeah.' He pumped his fist in the air. 'Seven. I'm the best. Oh shit.'

He put his hand to his pocket then peered down desperately into the water. 'Shit, shit, shit.'

'What's the matter?' She waded into the water to join him. 'What are you looking for?'

'My phone. It fell out of my pocket. Shit.'

She began hunting too, but the incoming tide was getting stronger and each wave, foaming and eddying, made it difficult to see. Then a wave sucked back and, for a moment in the shallower water, the sun reflected off something. Jo reached down and grabbed it.

'I've got it.'

'Here.' He held out his hand and almost snatched it from her. 'It's probably buggered now. Shit.'

'Harry? Look out.'

It was too late. While he had been desperately poking at the phone, he'd turned with his back to the sea and the next wave had reared up impressively. He was caught off balance as it thundered in and he stumbled and fell to his knees in the water. He got up again, still clutching the phone but was soaked through.

Jo grabbed him by the arm. 'Come on,' she said, hauling him out of the water. 'We'd better go up and get you dry.' She pointed towards the house, invisible from where they stood.

'I'm fine.' He shook her off, still staring at the phone, trying to get it to work.

'No, you're not. You're wet through. Come on. There's no-one else at the house now.'

He glanced up and she could see him start to shiver. That

water was cold.

'Well OK,' he muttered.

She let them both in through the kitchen door, tossed him the only small towel the kitchen possessed and went upstairs. A couple of minutes later she returned with a hand towel and a huge bath towel and thrust them at him. Sidney stood at the end of the hallway, watching Harry suspiciously.

'Here. There's a cloakroom through that door. Take your clothes off and wrap this round you. And here's an oversized T-shirt of mine. It should fit. I'll put your clothes in the tumble dryer.'

When he emerged a few minutes later, the bath towel was neatly in place, the T-shirt hanging off his bony shoulders but the cap was still on his head. In one hand he held the phone, in the other he held his clothes, his underpants carefully hidden between the bundled up shorts and T-shirt.

'Go in there...' She pointed towards the sitting room, then held out her hand for the clothes. '...while I sort those out and get us a drink.'

In the utility room she tossed the garments in the dryer. They were all cotton and would probably have dried as quickly hanging on the line outside but that might draw attention. Lawrence didn't have a window onto the main garden but it was amazing the things he noticed. She grabbed two bottles of ginger beer from the fridge and a couple of packets of crisps and headed back up the hallway.

Harry was standing staring at the chess board. He'd abandoned the phone on the glass-topped coffee table and taken off the baseball cap. His hair stuck out in tufts.

'Do you play?' she asked him.

'Yeah.' He sounded surprisingly keen. 'You?'

'Badly. My aunt taught me but I don't play much. That's

Eleanor's last game.'

He nodded, studying the positions of the pieces. 'Who did she play? Herself? That's what I usually do.'

'Maybe she does too, but usually she plays against Lawrence, her PA.'

'Was she white or black?'

'I don't know. But she probably wouldn't mind if we finished it.'

Eleanor's hedgehog hair and staring eyes came into her head. Jo wished she would mind. Eleanor wanting and able to play chess again was unimaginable at this moment. In any case, it was a good way to occupy Harry till his clothes dried.

So they sat and played, drinking ginger beer and eating crisps. Harry took black and he was good. Very good. She was beaten hands down. By the time they'd finished, Sidney had slipped into the room and was watching from a safe distance.

'Another game?' he suggested.

'No, thanks. I'm no challenge for you and I'm not sure I can cope with any more failure. Where did you learn to play like that?'

He shrugged. 'My dad taught me. And there used to be a chess club at my old school.'

'Where was that?'

'A small town near Cambridge.'

'Do you play with your dad then? You probably beat him, huh?'

'Nah. He never has time any more.'

She nodded and glanced at her watch. It was after seven.

'I'd better check on your clothes. Speaking of your dad, he'll be wondering where you are. Shouldn't you ring him? You can use my phone.'

'No need.' He got up and went back to the coffee table to

retrieve his own, staring with a dejected expression at its blank screen.

'I guess salt water's the worst,' said Jo doubtfully. She had no idea how or if it could be made to work again. 'Is it new?'

'No. It's worse. It's old but it had important stuff on it.'

He looked upset. It was possible tears threatened.

'Important, like photos?'

He looked up at her, surprised. 'Yeah.' He fixed back down on the empty screen. 'Photos of mum. She bought this for me.'

'Oh. I see.' She paused, uncertain. 'What happened to your mum, Harry?'

He didn't reply immediately and she began to think he wouldn't. Then he swallowed hard. 'She got cancer and died. Nearly two years ago.'

'I am sorry.' She paused. 'I lost my mum when I was sixteen and I still remember how difficult it was. Still is sometimes.'

He looked back at her then, studying her face to check she was being genuine.

'Have you got photos of her anywhere else?' she asked. 'Saved to a memory stick maybe.'

'A few.'

'Your dad must have some too, right?'

Harry gave that now characteristic shrug.

'Yeah, some. But he doesn't like me looking at them and he never does. I found a box with photos of her in just after we moved and he went ballistic because I put a couple of the framed ones around the place. He won't have them up in the house. There's just one in my room. He won't talk about her either. It's as if mum never existed.'

She didn't know what to say. 'Do you talk about her?' she ventured.

'Who to?'

'To him, I suppose.'

'Yeah, right. Like I told you, he doesn't want to know.'

'Why not?'

'I don't know,' he said belligerently. 'Maybe he's glad she's dead. You ask him. No, don't or he'll know I've been here. Look my clothes'll be dry by now. I've gotta go.'

She went to the utility room and came back with his clothes, still warm and still slightly damp. He disappeared in the direction of the cloakroom and, when he came back, he had slicked his hair back and the swagger had returned. He picked up his cap and pulled it on.

'I'll let you out of the gate,' she said, heading for the door.

'I can climb over the fence.'

'Well, that's very clever of you but I'd rather you went through the gate.'

She went with him down the path, Harry always a step or two behind her, flip-flops slapping and scuffing. Once through the gate he paused and turned to face her.

'You know everyone says that aunt of yours jumped?'

'She fell, Harry. Slipped. The rest is just gossip.'

He stood, staring at the ground.

'The thing is...well...y'know, she might have been pushed.' The shrug again. 'Just sayin'.'

'Why do you say that? Hey, Harry? Wait a minute.'

But he'd gone, quickly slip-slapping away down the path and out of sight.

Chapter 8

The nurse had left the radio on in the little side ward and Eleanor turned her head, regarding it with distaste. It was on the bedside cabinet on the other side of the bed from where she sat in an armchair, propped up with pillows. The movable table had been pushed in front of her, its two-pronged supports carefully straddling the chair legs, precluding her movement. The station the radio was tuned to was playing a succession of up-tempo chart hits, interspersed with chat from the DJ, a man who seemed to pride himself on speaking as quickly as possible. And he laughed at his own jokes. At least, Eleanor assumed they were jokes: she struggled to register what he was saying and didn't want to know anyway. It was simply an irritating noise, twittering constantly into her head when what she really wanted to do was think. She wanted to understand what was going on here. She wanted to order her thoughts, organise them into some recognisable sequence but they stayed obstinately all over the place, random, fragmented, snapshots of events and people which never quite surfaced properly before they had gone again.

Now and then, bits seemed lucid. She had had a fall - she understood that now - and she was in hospital. But what kind of fall and where, she couldn't remember. There was a lot she couldn't remember. Nor did this feel like her body or her brain; she wasn't in control of them and it was driving her crazy. And no-one seemed to understand…anything: how much she was trying; the things she kept telling them; the things she kept asking for. They kept looking at her blankly, asking her to say it again, looking at times concerned, at other times irritated. Well she was irritated too.

And why did her sister, Candida, keep coming to see her? They had never got on. Well, maybe when they were little. Yes, they'd been fine then. But not since. Candida hated me, she thought. Or did she say it out loud? It wasn't always easy to tell.

There was no-one there to hear anyway. The radio still twittered away on the cabinet on the other side of the bed. Candida had probably brought her that radio; she was in a conspiracy with the nurses, no doubt. Eleanor pushed at the table but couldn't get it to move. She grabbed the plastic tumbler from the table and launched it towards the radio. Her co-ordination was all wrong and, disappointingly, it didn't connect. In fact, it went nowhere near but the feeder top came off and it did throw water in a pleasing trajectory, all over the curtain at the window to the corridor before ricocheting off the glass and falling with a clatter to the floor.

A nurse appeared in the doorway, looking fraught.

'If you want someone to come you should press the buzzer, Eleanor,' she said firmly, coming up to her and showing her once more the red call button which had been placed on the side of her lap.

Eleanor waved an angry finger towards the radio. 'Poff.'

'Sorry. Say that again.'

Again the angry finger. 'Poff,' she shouted.

'You don't want the radio on?'

'Yesh,' said Eleanor, shaking her head.

She might have been pushed. Harry's words reverberated through Jo's head all that Sunday night and continued to do so through Monday. She wasn't sure why they had shocked her so. The same dark thought had lurked, unwanted and unacknowledged, at the back of her own mind ever since the news of Eleanor's fall. But, short of a gut feeling - more of a fear - she had seen no reason to entertain it. Nor had the police, apparently. Why had Harry said it? Did he know something - or was he just trying to be cute? Or maybe it was a plea for attention, a need to be important - but then why, having got her attention, rush away like that? Whatever the reason, it had left her feeling deeply uneasy.

She had been at the hospital with Eleanor all afternoon as usual. Her aunt was being difficult. She was talking now but little of it made sense and she was getting increasingly frustrated and cross. The previous day she had hit one of the nurses. This afternoon she had thrown her plastic beaker of tea at Jo who had taken evasive action, getting sprayed with the lukewarm liquid when the beaker hit the bed end and the lid came off. But for a tea-stained T-shirt, no harm had been done, but it was upsetting all the same. And Eleanor kept confusing Jo with Candida which she found unsettling. All her life she had worked hard not to be her mother; this was a cruel muddle.

'I'm not Candida,' Jo had insisted repeatedly. 'I'm her daughter, Joselyn. Jo. You remember me? I came to live with you when mum died.'

She had been met with stony silence and an obstinate set to the mouth, like a toddler who refuses to eat its dinner.

'Can you remember your accident, Eleanor?' Jo asked too, in vain hopes of shedding more light on it, her only response a glare. Eleanor had never been like this. It was as if a malicious spirit had taken hold of her body.

Home now, Jo was prowling the estate, looking out for Harry. It was six thirty on the Monday evening and low tide had occurred more than an hour previously. If you ignored the danger warnings and managed to get between the swathes of bamboo planted along the rear cliff edge beyond the shrubberies, it was the quickest way to see the parts of the beach where Harry usually hung out, short of actually going down there. But he wasn't there. Maybe he was just messing with her, voicing what a lot of people had thought but not dared to say. But why would anyone want to push Eleanor off the cliff anyway?

Jo eased her way back through a gap in the bamboo, returned through the side gate into Eleanor's private gardens, and walked to the lower terrace and the top of the beach steps. She looked down over the edge to where Eleanor had fallen, then, glancing round to be sure no-one was watching, bent over and picked up a handful of small stones.

With her left hand firmly gripping the handrail, she moved to the second step down. This was where you would be most likely to slip from onto the cliff; it sat level with the edge of the rock while the others had been fitted and shaped into a slight recess. She dropped one of the stones on the rock near her feet and watched it fall. It rolled, jumped, rolled again, then sped down and away over the edge to the beach below. It hadn't gone anywhere near where Eleanor was found. She dropped a second and a third stone with the same result.

Returning to the terrace, she went as near to the edge as she dared and again threw a stone, landing it on the slope just beyond where she stood. It rolled and bounced and scurried down, bounced again, and missed the place Eleanor was found by a foot or more before rolling off the cliff. The second stone tumbled close to where her aunt was found and trickled into the bramble. A third fell even closer. She had known all along that there was something wrong about the theory of Eleanor falling from the steps. But Eleanor was not a stone and it wasn't proof of anything, except that she almost certainly fell from the terrace. Jo needed to think this through and she needed something more concrete. If she could only find out if Harry truly knew something.

*

A new girl had started working part time at Millie's - Sam, a university student on her summer break who lived locally. She had worked there the previous summer and came highly recommended by Gail. The coffee shop was getting seriously busy now and another girl called Cheryl was going to help out at weekends.

'Are you sure we need this many people?' Matthew queried, concerned about the wage bill, another aspect of running his own business that preoccupied him. He always worried about money. Sophie had regularly teased him about it.

'Definitely,' said Gail. 'You think it's busy now? Wait till the schools break up next week. We'll be crawling up the walls.'

Matthew did think it was busy now. It had been October when he'd come down to see the place before buying and it had been quiet then. Mid-morning to mid-afternoon these days were hectic. Gareth hadn't told him it would be like this. Or maybe he hadn't listened. He had been too full of his own ideas and plans and his desperation to do something about Harry.

It was Harry's sixteenth birthday before long and the night

before the lad had asked for a drum kit. Matthew laughed, thinking it a joke. It wasn't but neither was it going to happen, not when they lived in a tiny end-terrace in the middle of the village. And Matthew had looked them up online and they were bloody expensive. But he had no idea what else might please the boy.

'You talk to Harry sometimes, don't you Gail,' he said on the Wednesday morning, sidling into the kitchen before the place got too crowded. She was making sandwiches as usual.

'Ye-es.' She looked at him with an odd expression.

'What do you think he might like for his birthday? You know, for a treat?'

She frowned, pausing from spreading butter on a baguette. 'Why don't you ask him?'

'Well yes. But I thought he might have said something to you. I was thinking of a surprise, I suppose.'

She wrinkled up her nose. 'He didn't have his phone with him when I saw him yesterday - you know he's always listening to something on that? When I asked about it, he said it was broken. I guess he might like a new one.'

'He didn't tell me. How did it get broken?'

'He didn't say and I didn't ask.'

She turned back to her sandwiches.

'OK. Thanks.' He went back behind the counter of the shop.

A broken phone? That was all he needed. How had that happened and why hadn't Harry said something about it?

Then he saw Joselyn walk in. It was mid-morning, mid-week and he was surprised to see her. She dropped a shirt over the back of a chair at an empty table and came to the counter. Matthew acknowledged her with a nod but Freddie was already there, offering his lopsided smile and taking the order.

113

She looked preoccupied. Maybe her aunt had got worse. He watched her walk back to her table and sit, looking out towards the beach. There were several boats drawn up and tethered on the sand and someone was pulling one down to the water's edge ready for launching. A couple of wind surfers swung and sailed out in the bay.

A family came in with two young children who spent ages at the counter, unable to decide what they wanted. A group of young teenagers arrived behind them, joking and nudging; they had either skived off school or finished some exams. A couple came in. The queue at the counter grew; the sound of chatter in the room swelled. For half an hour Matthew, Freddie and Sam never stopped, making drinks, waiting on tables, clearing dishes.

Then, as quickly as the rush had started, it calmed down again. Matthew made a point of clearing the two empty coffee cups from the table next to Jo's. She was staring, unfocussed, out of the window.

'Hi,' he said. 'How's your aunt?'

She visibly jumped. 'Oh, hi. Sorry, er, yes, she's improving slowly, thank you.'

'Good.' There it was again: the hedged answer. 'Don't see you down here much.'

She smiled, wanly, he thought. 'No. I should be working but I needed a break.'

He wiped a cloth over the neighbouring table. 'Perhaps I'll see you Friday.'

'Friday?' She frowned. 'What's happening on Friday? I thought the meeting was next week.'

He straightened up. 'It is. But I'm coming up to Skymeet on Friday. Lawrence invited me to discuss what we'd put on the website.' She looked at him blankly. 'Didn't you know that

114

Richard Medlar had pulled out of doing the publicity for the festival? An illness in the family apparently. Lawrence Felton offered to do it and he thought we ought to liaise. He thinks that publicity and the website go hand in hand and I suppose he's right.'

Jo frowned at him. 'No, I didn't know. But I'm glad you told me. What time's this meeting on Friday?'

'Four o'clock. I gather there's a lock on the gate but he told me the code.' Jo's expression had darkened. 'That's OK, isn't it?'

'Yes, yes, fine.' She stood up to go. 'Yes, I'll see you then. Thanks, Matthew.'

He watched her go, then realised that she had left her shirt behind and took it off the back of the chair, folding it loosely into his hand. He made no effort to run after her. It wasn't till he turned to go back to the counter that he saw Freddie watching him. Freddie grinned.

*

It was two minutes to four on the Friday afternoon when Matthew emerged from the woods on the Skymeet estate and walked up to the house, carrier bag in hand. Before ringing the bell, he glanced round, his first chance to see Eleanor Lambe's private domain. From where he stood high, dense shrubberies masked much of the grounds but the scale of them, and the extent of the garages and hardstanding over to his right, suggested the sheer size of the place. Impressive. He turned. The house, too, looked big though not perhaps as huge as he had expected. He was about to ring the bell when the door opened.

Lawrence smiled at him. 'Matthew, you're punctual. Come in.'

He was shown into a large, bright sitting room where Lawrence offered tea or coffee, then went in search of the housekeeper to make it. There was no sign of Jo. He registered a minor disappointment. The room was nice though. He had expected something minimalist and pale, the sort of coastal house interior featured in the glossy magazines that Sophie used to buy. But this room was all colour and artefact, painting and photograph. He supposed it fitted Eleanor Lambe's personality - what little he had seen of it. His attention was drawn by a photograph on a cupboard to the side and he picked it up to study more closely. Two young women side by side, not quite touching. One was saying something; the other was gazing steadily yet diffidently at the camera. That gaze reminded him of Jo. The other woman had to be Eleanor.

Lawrence returned and a small woman with short brown hair and an accusing expression appeared soon after bearing a tray of tea things. She set it down and disappeared, saying nothing. There were only two cups and saucers. Lawrence poured the tea and offered the plate of biscuits.

'Thanks.' Matthew gestured to the carrier bag lying beside him on the sofa. 'Is Jo around? She left a shirt behind at the café the other day.'

'She's out. I'll see she gets it though.' Lawrence paused, sitting back, cradling his cup and saucer. 'So Jo's been to Millie's then.'

Was it a question? It was hard to tell.

'Yes.'

Lawrence nodded, his expression impassive. 'I suppose you met her at the festival meetings. Has she said much about what happened? With Miss Lambe, I mean.'

'Not really. She's not a big talker.'

'I'm glad. We don't want to excite the press again, not

with that anyway.'

Lawrence swiftly changed the subject. They had just begun to discuss the kind of audience most likely to come to a literary event in a small coastal village and how best to target them when they heard the front door open and then footsteps. Lawrence immediately stopped talking and looked round, frozen. A moment later Jo walked in.

'I see you decided not to use your office for this meeting, Lawrence,' she said, tossing her handbag down on the empty sofa. 'Interesting that you chose Eleanor's sitting room. Sorry I'm late. Have I missed much?'

'Not really.' Matthew smiled. 'I've brought your shirt.' He patted the bag. 'You left it in the café the other day.'

'Oh, that's where it was. Thank you.'

She smiled back. He didn't think he had seen her really smile before. What a difference: she lit up. Matthew looked down at his teacup guiltily, then across at Lawrence who seemed momentarily lost for words.

'I'll get Charlotte to make more tea,' said Lawrence, rising to his feet.

'Don't bother. I'm sure Charlotte's got enough to do.' Jo dropped onto the sofa. 'So, where are we at? I've been ringing some of the people Eleanor listed as speakers. Some are already pencilled in but I managed to get two more to definitely commit this morning.' She mentioned their names. 'High profile people like that should help the publicity effort.'

'Great,' said Matthew, finding renewed enthusiasm. 'Could you write me a brief resume about each of them? I want to put something about all the speakers on the website with links. I need photos too.'

'I'll arrange it.'

For over an hour they thrashed out ideas, making notes on

things to do and people to contact. Matthew had already taken photos around the village for the website and showed them on his tablet; they discussed others he might take. It was a quarter past five when Lawrence got to his feet and thanked Matthew for coming, prompting Matthew to get up too.

'Yes,' said Jo. 'That was useful.' She glanced at the clock on the wall. 'Have you got time to stay for a few minutes, Matthew? I wondered if you'd like to see the garden? My aunt's very proud of it.'

'Ye-es, I'd like that.'

She stood. 'I'll see you Monday then, Lawrence. Have a good weekend.'

Dismissed, Lawrence hesitated, nodded curtly and left, pulling the door to behind him. Jo waited, listening, then crossed to open one of the patio doors. Immediately a bundle of grey fur appeared by her feet and she bent to stroke him.

'This is Sidney. He's a rescue cat and rather wary of people. Are you all right with cats?'

'So long as he doesn't scratch.'

'Only people he doesn't like.' She grinned. 'I'm joking. Come and have a look outside.'

They walked out onto the patio but she waited to speak until they were safely out of earshot.

'I just wanted to thank you for taking all that in your stride.'

He smiled, momentarily fixed by the steadiness of her gaze. It was resolute, stubborn even, and drew him in. And her eyes were a deep blue-green, like the sea.

He collected himself. 'I suppose you mean your determination to show you aren't going to be pushed around?'

She gave a rueful smile. 'Was it that obvious? Sorry, I didn't mean you to get caught up in our petty power struggle.

118

Lawrence planned this meeting assuming I'd be at the hospital. Fortunately I was able to rearrange things. Knowing about it also forced me to do something about organising the speakers; with so much else on my mind, I'd kind of let it ride. Thank you for that.'

'But what's going on here? Why would Lawrence exclude you?'

She shrugged. 'It's nothing. I didn't see my aunt for a while so now he resents me being here, taking over, as he sees it. You can see his point of view.'

She wandered a few steps towards the gap in the wall separating the patio from the lawn beyond. As usual, he felt she was telling half a story.

'Maybe,' he said, drawing level with her. 'But it's also obvious that Lawrence is someone who has to be in control. I've worked with people like that.'

She turned her head, looking at him curiously, as if seeing him for the first time.

'You're right. He does. That's exactly it.'

He felt himself being examined. He wondered what she saw.

'I'd better be going,' he said. 'I need to check back in at the shop before it closes. And I've got a son at home. A single dad, you see. Well, I hope he's at home anyway. His school broke up today but he's a wanderer at the best of times. Drives me mad sometimes, trying to keep track of him.'

He turned back to the house, keen to leave now. He was talking too much.

Jo walked with him. 'How old is he?'

'Fifteen. Sixteen in a few weeks.'

She seemed on the point of asking something else but choked it back and they returned to the sitting room.

119

'I noticed that photo over there earlier.' He nodded towards it. 'Is that your mother with Eleanor?'

Barely a glance at the photo. 'Yes.'

'It had to be. It's the way she's looking at the camera. It's so like you.'

She looked uncomfortable. 'Let me see you out.'

At the sitting room door, Matthew paused, stopping her from opening it.

'Lawrence's animosity seems very personal,' he said quietly. 'Be careful.'

Her expression clouded but she said nothing and he left, wishing he had never made that 'single dad' remark and wondering why he had. He didn't want sympathy. He didn't want anything.

Chapter 9

'Were you able to get your phone working?' asked Jo.

Harry looked disconsolate and shook his head.

'Maybe an IT guy could rescue the photos though?'

He didn't answer. It was Saturday morning and finally the boy was back on the beach.

'It might be possible,' she said. 'A laptop died on me once and a computer geek I know managed to get a lot of the files off it. The laptop was toast mind you, but still...' She shrugged.

He looked at her speculatively. 'You think this friend of yours could get the photos off my phone?'

'Oh no. I'm sorry, Harry. Really. That's kind of difficult. She's the sister of my ex-boyfriend and I'm not her favourite person, if you know what I mean.'

'Whatever. It doesn't matter.'

He picked up a stone and skimmed it half-heartedly over the water. Five skips.

'I'm getting a new phone for my birthday,' he mumbled. 'It was kind of a deal. Dad went ballistic when he found out about the old one. Anyone'd think I did it on purpose.'

'I guess new phones are pretty expensive. And maybe he was upset about the photos too.'

'Nah. I told you, he's not interested in photos of mum.'

A yacht came into sight round the headland and they both

turned and watched its apparently effortless progress across the bay.

'Harry, does your dad run Millie's?'

He looked into her face, brows furrowed, and glared.

'Yes. His bright idea for a new life. Why?'

'Nothing. It's just that I've met him a couple of times - we're both involved with the literary festival in September.'

'You've been talking about me, haven't you? You said you wouldn't tell him.'

'No. I never mentioned you. It was something he said which made the connection for me.'

'Oh.' He wandered away and sat down on his favourite rock, pulling a small digital radio out of the pocket of his shorts and ramming the earphone in his ear.

Jo sat down nearby. 'When is your birthday?'

'September fourth.' He restlessly bounced his leg up and down on the ball of his foot. 'I'll be sixteen.' He flicked her a furtive look. 'I was just kidding when I said I was seventeen.'

She nodded, straight-faced. 'You know when I said I was thirty-six?'

He turned his head then, curious. 'Yeah?'

'I wasn't...kidding, that is.' She grinned and he did too, fleetingly, then began to nod his head to the music on his radio, staring out to sea.

Loneliness was etched all over him, a grieving child - he seemed little more - desperately trying to cocoon himself in his own private world because everything around him had crumbled to ashes. She was cross with Matthew, the more so because she thought she liked the man and felt obscurely betrayed. Why was he shutting the boy out like this, refusing to talk about his mother? Had the relationship been that bad?

'What was your mum like, Harry?'

122

He turned to look at her. 'Why?'

She shrugged. 'I think about my mum still, often late at night. She used to read to me some nights before I went to sleep. Other times she seemed to forget I was even there.' She paused. 'It's not easy to talk about her. Isn't that weird? But she had a great laugh. And when you were with her…' She smiled ruefully. '…somehow you thought everything would work out. No idea why.'

'Do you miss her?'

'Yes. Living with her was really difficult at times but…' She pursed up her lips and sighed. '…she was my mum and I loved her. Yes, I miss her. Sometimes. But not like at the beginning. It's got easier.'

He nodded, still bouncing one foot up and down.

'My mum was an English teacher. She loved books and poetry. She used to quote poetry sometimes. I hated that.' An agonised expression contorted his face. 'And whenever she had time to herself, she was always reading.'

He paused, pulling the earphone out of his ear as if this required his full concentration. Jo could make out the heavy pulse of a bass beat from the earpiece even from where she sat.

'And she liked walking. And taking picnics. There were always sausage rolls.' He smiled. 'She used to take us on these ridiculous hikes. Wore us all out but they were fun.'

'Why sausage rolls - because she liked them or because you do?'

'Because I do.'

He stopped talking and began to chew on his lip, looking away.

They sat in silence, watching a herring gull strut towards them across the beach. After a couple of minutes it moved off, disinterested, when it realised they weren't eating.

'How did she die, your mum?' Harry asked suddenly. 'Was she ill?'

Jo turned to look at him. 'No. Mum was at a party on someone's boat. A big fancy yacht with a load of different decks. She fell overboard. She liked to party, you see, and she'd been drinking.'

'You mean she drowned - just like that.'

He made it sound so simple. For years she had thought about that night, relived it in her imagination a hundred different ways, wondered how it had come to that and if she could have prevented it. She didn't find it simple at all.

'She couldn't swim,' said Jo. 'It wasn't until the party was packing up and the last people were going to bed that someone noticed she might be missing. They couldn't find her on board. So they raised the alarm but no-one knew how long she'd been gone. Divers went in to look for her.'

Harry stared at her, mouth open. 'That sucks.'

'Tell me about it.'

'What about your dad? Was he at the party too?'

'I never knew my dad. It's the reason I'm so close to my aunt. Eleanor gave me a home and lots of love when I needed it. That's why I'm looking out for her now.'

He nodded, frowning.

'Harry, the last time we met you said maybe my aunt had been pushed. Why did you say that?'

He refused to meet her eye. 'Forget it. It was a dumb thing to say.'

'No, come on. You must have had a reason.'

He flicked a bit of sand off his leg. 'It was just a thought I had.'

'But what made you think it? Were you here the night she fell?'

124

Harry stood up suddenly, ramming the radio in his pocket again, and walking to the water's edge. He bent to pick up a couple of stones and skimmed one across the water. Jo went to join him.

'It's important, Harry. I wouldn't ask otherwise.'

'I don't want to get into trouble.'

'Of course not. Why should you?'

He didn't answer and continued to mechanically bend and throw.

'You promise you won't tell anyone if I tell you?' He wouldn't look at her.

She hesitated. 'I'm not sure I can.'

He turned his head then and glared at her. 'I won't say unless you promise.'

She hesitated. 'OK, I promise.'

He threw another stone. 'I did see something that night. That is, I saw someone.'

'Who?'

'I don't know.'

'What do you mean?'

'I mean I don't know,' he repeated crossly. 'I couldn't see them clearly. 'Cause I was down here, looking up. It's not that easy to see who it is up there. People are like dark…like…'

'Silhouettes?' offered Jo.

'Exactly. And I was trying not to be seen. I kept ducking out of the way.'

'OK. So what did you see exactly?'

'I saw your aunt. I recognised her 'cause of the way she stands. I've seen her before. She's not very big is she but she sort of stands very straight.'

He demonstrated, pulling his shoulders back, lifting his head. He had caught Eleanor's posture perfectly.

'And then there was some other guy there too, talking to her.'

'A man then?'

'I'm not sure. As soon as I saw there was someone else, I thought they might come down here so I kept back and tried to listen.'

'Could you hear what they were saying?'

'No. It sounded like an argument but I could only hear your aunt and no words, just sounds. The other person was further away and sort of moving around. They were quiet, then got louder, then quieter again to almost nothing which was kind of worse. It felt…like…menacing. Like that silence you get before a big thunderclap, you know - that sort of charged vacuum, and you're just waiting…?'

There was an uneasy fear in his eyes. It was infectious.

'So what happened then?'

'I dunno. I left. The tide was low enough for me to get round so I was outta here.'

'You didn't see my aunt fall?'

'I've just told you, haven't I?' he said belligerently.

'OK, OK. You didn't see her. What time was this, Harry?'

He pursed up his lips and shrugged again. 'Dunno. Can't remember.'

He threw another couple of stones aggressively along the water and they fell disappointingly short, lacking his usual finesse. He was still hiding something, she was sure.

'You should tell this to the police,' she said eventually.

Again the accusing stare. 'You promised you wouldn't tell.'

'I won't. But you should. If someone tried to kill Eleanor, they should know. Whoever it was might try again.'

He opened his mouth, frowning, but said nothing and just

stared at her. After what seemed an eternity, he shook his head.

'I've got history with the police. They'd never believe me. There's no way they wouldn't find some way to blame it on me. I'm not doing it. And if you tell, I'll deny it. Anyway, I didn't see nothing.'

'Anything,' she said automatically. 'You didn't see anything.'

'Shut up,' he bellowed. 'You're not my mother. Just because we talk a bit doesn't mean you know me. You don't have the right to tell me what to do and what not to do.'

'OK, OK,' she said wearily. 'Look, I won't tell, Harry. I promise.'

He moved quickly away, back towards the headland and the way he had come. Jo watched him go. He was rattled. She was rattled herself. Before this meeting she had all but convinced herself that Harry had been messing with her; now she was sure it was no game. He had seen someone.

It was an uncomfortable, half-formed but unavoidable truth and she didn't know what to do with it. She felt a drop of rain fall on her bare arm, then another. Glancing up, she saw the white clouds had turned to a steely-grey. She turned quickly and made for the steps.

*

Frank and Mari walked out of the barn together. Depending on the number of students and the topic for that week, some of the workshops were run by a pair of tutors. This week it was their turn. *Expressing Yourself in Poetry* was the course and they'd just finished their first morning together. Frank was pleased; it had gone well. The tutor pairings weren't always so felicitous but he and Mari had worked together before and complemented each other: he was in the students' faces,

127

pushing them, being controversial, making them think outside the box; Mari was soft-hearted, patient and coaxing with a real talent for choosing exactly the right word. She was annoyingly good at times. Her mild and often apologetic manner hid a shrewd brain. But she was a sweet lady - sweet with everyone, not just him - and devoted to Imogen. How Louisa could be jealous of her was beyond him.

'They're shaping up into a good group,' he remarked to Mari now. 'They might shock us with some decent poetry by the end of the week.'

'Oh definitely.' Mari smiled. It was her default expression. They moved aside as the last students let themselves out of the barn and drifted away. The afternoon was set aside for one-to-ones, tutor and student, discussing individual issues. As was the usual workshop practice, he and Mari were making themselves available on alternate afternoons. It was Mari's turn that day.

'What are your plans for the afternoon?' said Mari.

'Oh, a bit of writing,' he said dismissively. 'Louisa's gone to do a signing in Tavistock. She went off early this morning. She said she'd do some shopping on the way back.'

'I think Imogen's out too.' She glanced at her watch. 'I'd better go and grab a sandwich. Rich Taylor wants to see me at two to look at a sonnet he's written.' She pulled a face. 'At least, he thinks it's a sonnet.'

Frank grinned as she walked away, heading for the courtyard. He turned and went in the other direction, left the estate and made for the pub which stood towards the top of the village on the road out.

The George was busy with holiday makers. With the start of the school holidays the population of Petterton Mill Cove appeared to have quadrupled in one weekend. Frank stood just inside the doorway and looked round. Vincent might claim to have found God and abandoned his dissolute ways but he still drank regularly and he'd been seen having the occasional lunch at the pub. And indeed, there he was, sitting alone at a small round table the other side of a pillar. Frank queued at the bar, bought a pint and weaved his way back to Vincent's table.

'You won't mind if I join you,' he said, pulling out the only other chair and sitting down.

'Certainly not. Company is good for the soul, they say. And my soul, poor sinner that I am, needs all the help it can get.' Vincent raised his glass to his lips, watching Frank over the top of it. 'Yours too, I imagine.'

Frank took a long pull of beer, returning the cool assessment.

'Imogen tells me she's seen you prowling round the house,' he said, 'and wandering through into the private garden.'

'And why did she do that?'

'Because you've been behaving oddly and I asked her if she'd noticed it too.'

Vincent took another drink with a serene expression. 'I don't think you're in a position to call my behaviour odd. Nor indeed, is Imogen. We're all odd, dear boy, let's face it. We're writers. We live in make-believe worlds, pretending we can illuminate people's lives, when God knows - and I use the phrase advisedly - we struggle to illuminate our own.' He paused, a smirk tugging the corner of his lips. 'So, engaged, eh? You've finally taken the leap and moved on. I suppose we all assumed you'd go back to Eleanor eventually, the way you always did. Tell me, how is *la grande passion* going? I hear Louisa's latest novel has just hit the bestseller list.' He raised an eloquent hand. 'Her star is clearly rising. A shrewd move on your part, I must say.'

Frank reached across and grabbed Vincent's glass as the man had it half way to his mouth and forced it down onto the table again.

'What are you insinuating, you little weasel?'

'Poor Eleanor.' Vincent kept his gaze on Frank, steady and unflinching. 'She's not been able to hit the giddy heights recently, has she? The buying public is so fickle.'

Frank's lips curled into a slow, sardonic smile. He released the glass and watched Vincent calmly drink from it again.

'I never loved Eleanor for her money as you know very well. I loved her. I could say that Eleanor only lets you stay here and participate in the workshops at all because you're her cousin. Or maybe it's pity. But I wouldn't suggest that.'

Vincent pinched a smile too. 'It's all coming out now isn't it? And to think we were such a happy group of friends. Those were the days.'

'Friends are honest and don't go behind each other's backs.'

Vincent scoffed. 'Is that so?'

'Meaning?'

'Meaning nothing. Just curious to hear your point of view. I guess that doesn't apply to lovers then. As I recall, you were happy to go behind Eleanor's back now and then with the latest pretty face. That's why you kept breaking up isn't it?'

'You liar.' Frank clenched his fists but fought to control himself. Vincent liked to wind people up - it was a game he played - and Frank refused to give him the satisfaction. 'Is that what you've been telling Louisa?' That would account for all the insecurity and jealousy, he thought.

'No, indeed not.' Vincent took another pull of beer,

emptying the glass. 'On that, my lips are sealed.'

'That would be a miracle. But you've said something to her. I saw you, last week, in the den, all secretive.'

'Did I?' Vincent pursed his lips together, lifting his head, making a show of thinking back. 'Maybe I did. She didn't tell you what it was then? Interesting.'

'What did you say?' demanded Frank.

'I think we were just sharing our sympathy for poor Eleanor. And Jo. Must be difficult for her.'

Frank stood up. He glanced round but no-one nearby was paying any attention to them, wrapped up in their own meals and loud conversations. He leaned his fists down onto the table, pushing his face a hand's breadth from Vincent's.

'I'm warning you, Vincent. You're going to leave Louisa alone from now on, or you'll be sorry.'

Frank straightened up and Vincent blinked a couple of times, looking surprised.

'You're threatening me? How wonderful. It's like something out of one of Eleanor's novels. But perhaps you'd be better served asking Louisa what she got up to the night Eleanor fell. I saw her going to the house.'

Frank stared at him a long moment and walked away. When he glanced back, Vincent had pulled Frank's barely drunk pint towards him and was lifting it to his lips.

He walked back down the hill, barely aware of his surroundings or the cars which threatened to cut him as he rounded the last corner before the turn off for the estate. He had been woken in the early hours of the night before by Louisa, dreaming and twitching and mumbling in her sleep. As he came to, she rolled over to face him and was silent for a few minutes, her breathing deep and slow. Then it got faster, anxious.

131

'So?' she said, her voice suddenly clear. 'I know what you're doing. You see? I know. What sort of fool do you take me for?' Her voice drifted away again, mumbling, unintelligible.

For ages afterwards he'd stayed awake, even after Louisa had rolled over and fallen silent. He had often wondered if Louisa had seen that message from Eleanor the Friday afternoon that they'd arrived. He had left his phone on the bed and gone into the bathroom and she'd had an odd manner when he came back out. It wasn't the first time he'd suspected that she kept checking up on him. Not that he had replied to Eleanor's message. Had she checked that too? Either way, it was unnerving.

So what exactly did Louisa do that evening?

*

'Eleanor's gone to the physio department.'

Jo turned abruptly at the sound of the voice, taken aback. It was the Monday afternoon and she had arrived later than usual. Louisa was sitting behind the door on the only small chair in Eleanor's side ward and now stood up, looking apologetic.

'The nurse said she usually goes in the morning but they're short-staffed today and had to juggle everyone around.' Louisa smiled, hesitantly. 'I wasn't sure I should come, you know, in the circumstances, but then I didn't have any workshops this week so I thought perhaps I ought to. After all, it's not my fault, is it?' The smile was replaced with a frown. 'Or do you think it's a bad idea?'

She was talking too much and too fast, clearly nervous.

'I honestly don't know,' said Jo.

She examined Louisa suspiciously. But for the workshops

the previous summer, the woman hardly knew Eleanor. Given her recent engagement to Frank, the visit did seem out of place.

'I suppose it depends on how she reacts when she sees you,' she said. 'She's still confused.'

'Oh she will be. I had a friend once whose brother had a head injury like that and he was never the same again.' Louisa put out a hand to Jo's arm. 'Not that I meant that your aunt would be like that. I just...' Her eyes were wide with alarm. 'I'm sorry, I do have a way of saying the wrong thing.'

Jo pulled her arm away, moving to put her bag down on the bed. 'It's OK. I quite understand how this might go.' She sat in Eleanor's vacant armchair.

'Yes...of course, but I'm sure Eleanor'll be fine.'

'I'm afraid no-one can be sure of anything. Her memory might never come back.'

'No...well....' Louisa sat down again and clasped her hands together in her lap, watching them as if they might offer a safer topic of conversation. 'Sorry,' she said suddenly, getting up again. 'Did you want to sit here?'

'No, I'm fine, thanks.'

Jo found herself facing the open doorway, looking out towards the nurses' station, watching the toing and froing of staff, a porter pushing a woman in a wheelchair towards the exit, a man in a check dressing gown slouching towards the bathroom, pulling his drip stand alongside him. This was what Eleanor looked out on every day, stuck in a chair. For such an active and intellectually dynamic person, it wasn't surprising she was frustrated and difficult. Jo glanced round the room. The number of get well cards had continued to grow and a new small bouquet of pink carnations stood in a vase on the bedside cabinet.

Louisa followed her gaze. 'I brought those. I hope that's

all right. The nurse found a vase for them.'

'It's very kind of you,' Jo said politely. Eleanor didn't like carnations, especially pink. She would like them even less if she realised who had brought them.

Jo glanced at her watch. More visitors entered the ward and scattered in search of their nearest and dearest.

Louisa stood up again. 'I think I should go. I didn't realise you came in the afternoons. I don't want to trespass.'

'You're not. Don't go on my account.'

'Frank doesn't know I'm here. Please don't tell him. I came on an impulse but I realise now I probably shouldn't have.'

'Eleanor's here,' said Jo. From where she sat she could see the porter sweep Eleanor's wheelchair onto the ward. Already Eleanor's familiar bristly hair and pale face were in the doorway and a nurse was following the chair in. Eleanor was glaring at Jo.

'No,' she said, waving an indignant finger. 'My share.'

Jo got up, smiling. 'I know it's your chair, Eleanor. I was just warming it for you.'

She held back while the porter and the nurse helped Eleanor into her armchair. Her aunt stood well but seemed nervous and reluctant to do more than shuffle her feet round. She was still catheterised and the bag, on its metal stand, was put close in to the side of the chair. It wasn't until the porter had gone and the nurse was carefully tucking the cotton blanket round Eleanor's legs that Jo noticed Louisa had gone too.

Jo pulled the small chair closer and faced Eleanor.

'How did the physio go today?'

'Phuh,' said Eleanor explosively.

'That well, huh?'

'Phuh. Awgufl.'

Eleanor looked tired. She also looked distracted, glancing round and repeatedly staring out of the door as if looking for someone. Maybe she had seen Louisa after all.

The tea trolley came into view and stopped outside the door.

'Great,' said Jo, with forced enthusiasm. 'Here's the tea.'

The nurse brought a feeder beaker in with an unidentifiable milky brown liquid in it. Eleanor took it and sucked noisily on the spout, eyeing Jo up as she did so.

'Do you know who I am, Eleanor?' Her aunt was staring into her face as if learning every contour. 'I'm Jo. You remember the little brat who used to run through your flowerbeds chasing butterflies? You used to shout at me - tell me off for ruining your plants. I'm Jo, Candida's daughter. Your niece. You taught me to play chess. You play really well. I'm still rubbish.'

Still Eleanor stared at her, sucking on the beaker spout. She removed it and put it down erratically but purposefully on the table in front of her and returned her gaze to Jo.

'Can-did...' she began, then shook her head. 'No...' Again the shake of the head then a heavy sigh and a refocussing. 'No. Not Can-dida. Sheeze ma shishter.' She nodded, pleased with herself. 'Jo,' she said. 'Jo.' There was the faintest suggestion of a smile, then her eyes narrowed. 'Peeno. pee-peeno.' Eleanor shook her head again, frustrated.

Jo frowned. 'Sorry, Eleanor. I don't...oh yes, the piano. I play the piano, that's right. We used to play together.' She leaned forward. 'Do you remember your garden? You live by the sea. You've got gardens all around the house with steps down to a little private beach.' She watched her aunt's face for any sign of recognition. 'Can you remember? When the sun

135

sets it turns the sea by your home glorious shades of flaming orange and red. Beautiful.'

Eleanor was watching her intently again, focussing on her lips.

'Bootiful,' she repeated.

Her speech was definitely getting clearer. She leaned forward too, arms on the table as if waiting to hear more.

'Can you remember the terrace, Eleanor?' said Jo. 'That's where you fell.'

Eleanor opened her mouth, still looking intent, frowning. Her lips pursed forward then reshaped as if she had changed her mind about what she wanted to say. But nothing came out and she sat back again and banged a hand down crossly on the table, making the tea beaker vibrate.

'Don't worry. It'll come back.'

Eleanor pointedly turned her head away and a few minutes later her eyes fluttered closed.

Jo sat back in the chair and tipped her head back wearily. After spending all weekend fretting over what Harry had said, by the Monday morning she'd decided to tell the police and had looked at their website to see how best to contact them. There was a form to fill in. But what was she going to tell them? She had promised not to give Harry away which left her with the spurious evidence of some stones thrown down the cliff side. And even the stones only suggested that Eleanor probably fell from the terrace and not the steps. She needed something else or they'd think her a time-waster.

Jo looked back at Eleanor, wondering if she would ever remember what happened. Ironically, she'd be safer if she didn't, because remembering would make her even more of a target than before.

Chapter 10

Jo suspected everyone and suspected no-one. She found it difficult to believe that anyone would want to hurt Eleanor. Her aunt was a strong character and could be painfully forthright but she had no malice in her; she was fair and straight, supported a number of charities and wasn't given to victimising anybody. And she spent much of each day in her study alone, writing. Her work then? Had something she'd written offended someone that much? It was doubtful. Though she wrote political thrillers, she was careful not to base her characters on real people, alive or dead. It was more likely to be something personal.

In all the mystery books Jo had edited, a lot was made of motive. But Eleanor had no current lover as far as Jo knew, no-one likely to perpetrate a crime of passion. Money? She had no idea who would benefit from Eleanor's death. Maybe herself. She hadn't thought of that before but, as Eleanor's closest living relative, it was possible. The police would love that as a motive. Of course there was Vincent too. Eleanor might have put him in her will - if she had made a will. But she hadn't seen Jo in a while and she wasn't close to Vincent so the estate could have been left elsewhere. Frank? Surely not now, assuming it had been changed. And what about the rest of the 'old friends'? And Lawrence? He seemed to spend a lot of time and energy safeguarding her financial interests. Were they his interests too? In any case, if Eleanor's earnings had fallen off in recent years, how much did she have to leave? Though the value of the property itself must be immense - if it wasn't mortgaged...

Closeted in Eleanor's study on the Wednesday evening, Jo searched the drawers and file boxes but could find no sign of a will. Lawrence would undoubtedly know if one existed and where it might be kept but she couldn't ask him. Of everyone, she distrusted him the most: he had repeatedly lied to her. And if the will was being held by a solicitor, no-one would let her see it anyway.

She flopped down in Eleanor's chair and sighed heavily. Perhaps she should go to court and get whatever control she could of Eleanor's personal affairs. Then maybe she would have access to the will as well as to Eleanor's accounts. How difficult would that be to arrange? She opened her laptop and logged onto the internet. After spending ages searching different websites, it seemed she would have to apply to be a court-appointed deputy. It looked complicated and sounded like a slow process. Nothing could be done quickly unless an urgent reason were proved - like the need to access funds for care home fees. But there was no urgent reason. Lawrence had all the finances in his grip anyway. More importantly, Eleanor would have to be deemed to lack mental capacity.

Jo thought about her visit that day. Eleanor's speech was improving rapidly: words came out more clearly even when they weren't put together into coherent sentences. Odd memories seemed to be coming back too, though always scenes from the distant past, nothing recent. There was definitely growing activity in that brain of hers. Jo closed the computer. It was too soon to apply to court and she didn't want to go down that path if she could help it. By the time it was granted, Eleanor might be better. There was a look in her eyes now which hadn't been there before, a gleam of understanding and fire, a little of the old Eleanor.

But she could still be in danger from whoever had pushed her. It was unlikely that it had been a trespassing stranger. There had been a row with someone and it had happened in her private garden. It suggested that it was a person Eleanor knew, someone close. Jo picked up a ball point pen, pulled a notepad towards her and scribbled a list of names.

Lawrence
Vincent
Louisa
Frank
Imogen
Mari

Who else? Charlotte? Charlotte who argued with Eleanor daily and verbally abused her employer to her face but wouldn't let anyone else bad-mouth her? Who kept preparing Eleanor's favourite foods for Jo to take in, sure that they would tempt her employer to eat better? Who insisted on cooking and leaving food for Jo's evening meal every weekday? Not likely. In any case, Charlotte would have been long gone at that time in the evening. Still, if she was going to do this thoroughly…

Charlotte

She stared at the list, then crossed out Mari's name. Mari had been in Exeter that night, over an hour's drive away, and it was impossible to imagine her hurting a fly. She scored through Frank's name too. Once upon a time, he would have been the most likely candidate for a crime of passion but he had been with Mari in Exeter and had a new love anyway and no doubt different romantic conflicts. In any case, she had seen him argue with Eleanor back in the day. It was what they did; they had thrived on it. It had never meant anything.

Lawrence. He was obsessed with Eleanor's money and with preventing it from being spent. Maybe he needed money in the short term and knew he would inherit on her death. In that case Eleanor's survival might account for his sullenness. Or maybe there was other history between them. She had no idea.

Vincent? There had always been tension between him and Eleanor, blood relatives notwithstanding. He admitted to having discussed his play with her; it felt like there was more to that conversation than he was prepared to say. And what about that visit he had made to the garden, asking Jo for the manuscript back? Was he really making veiled threats? She hadn't taken him seriously.

As for Imogen, Jo knew of no reason why she would have issues with Eleanor, nor was she particularly steady on her feet. It seemed unlikely that she would be in a position to push anyone about. And it still felt absurd to consider Charlotte. Which left Louisa. She hardly knew Eleanor and she was the one who had 'won' Frank. It was easy to imagine Eleanor being resentful of Louisa but not the other way around. What possible motive could there be?

Jo put her fingers up to her forehead and massaged the tension in it. Somehow, she needed to find out more about these people and what they were doing that evening. They had been in and out of her life forever and yet she couldn't honestly say she knew them. She stared down at the names, then ripped the sheet of paper off the pad. After a moment's hesitation, she ripped the next sheet off with its ghost writing and fed them both through the shredder.

Matthew hung the tea towel to dry over the front bar handle of the oven and put the crockery away in the cupboards. When he was first married he used to wash dishes and leave them to dry on the sink drainer because that was what he'd done as a student. Sophie soon objected. The drying water left marks behind, she complained, and even when they had finally got a dishwasher, she still insisted on rubbing over the crockery and cutlery with a cloth to buff them up. She had been very particular about it. And now he had to do it too - because she had.

'You're a tyrant, Sophie,' he muttered, leaving the kitchen.

Harry was already in his bedroom, some godforsaken music throbbing through the floor. Matthew shouted up the stairs, telling him to turn it down. It had become a nightly ritual.

He stood in the middle of the sitting room, restless, edgy. He ought to be working on the website for the festival, adding to it, improving it, but for several nights he'd had something else on his mind which he couldn't quite bring himself to do. But the idea wouldn't leave him alone either, so maybe he should just do it and lay it to rest. In a burst of resentful energy, he crossed to the cupboard under the stairs, opened it, pulled out the vacuum cleaner and began tugging out the boxes stored behind it. Each box had a loose description of its contents written on it in felt pen from when they had moved and three of them were already spread across the sitting room floor by the time he found the one he wanted. SOPHIE'S BOOKS was scrawled on the top.

He carried it over to the hearth rug, left it there while he got a bottle of beer and took a swig, then got down on his knees and opened it.

On the top of the books piled inside were *Rebecca* by Daphne du Maurier and *Not in his Line of Work* by Eleanor Lambe. *Wuthering Heights* by Emily Bronte was visible but had been pushed down a gap at the side. After Sophie had died, he had packed all these books himself, pulling them from the bookcase, stacking them up any old how, putting them out of sight as quickly as he could. Sophie had owned a lot of books. Because she read so much she had started reading digital fiction too but still she loved her print volumes, especially her old favourites. Anything which she especially liked she would buy in a hard copy too. Matthew had taken a lot to a charity shop before they came down to Devon but he couldn't part with her favourites.

He kept pulling books out, working down the box, checking titles, piling them on the floor to each side. He found a copy of poetry by John Keats and had to pause, had to open it and flick through the pages, his stomach tightening in a knot. It was old and dog-eared, one of the first books Sophie had eulogised about to him when they were students. She had dipped into it often. Her books were like old friends. Sometimes she got so involved reading that she forgot the time, missed putting the oven on for a meal or left something to boil dry. Occasionally she would stay up after Matthew had gone to bed. 'I'll just read to the end of this chapter, then I'll be up. Don't wait for me if you're tired.' And she would be ages, would then slip silently into the bed beside him in the dark room. He remembered reaching for her, feeling the cold of her skin under his touch, wrapping her in his own sleek body warmth.

A thin, old bookmark fell out of the Keats book. It had the

name of a bookshop on it, probably long since closed. And, on the reverse, some of Sophie's crabbed handwriting, scribbled quickly in pencil.

eggs
candles
matches
chocolate buttons

A shopping list. She used to scribble them on anything to hand. A list made before Harry's birthday perhaps. Matthew replaced the bookmark carefully in the page, laid the volume to one side and took a deep breath. This was a bad idea. Really bad. He drank several more mouthfuls of beer, then took another slow controlling breath, and began again, driven on. Maybe he'd got rid of it. But no, he found it near the bottom: *Now and Then* by Frank Marwell. Several of the pages had small corners turned down and he slowly picked through them. One of the poems marked was instantly familiar. He had known it would be.

Flirting, fondling, melting, melding,
Steeps the sun in the skymeet sea.

The one Jo had quoted to him. What were the chances of her doing that? It was unsettling and yet eerily intriguing too.

He got up off the floor and sat down with the remains of his beer, closing the book but still holding it against his belly, memories scrolling through his mind. He finished the beer and sat, staring into space.

'Oh Sophie,' he murmured. 'Why?'

*

When the weather was dry, Imogen walked in the Skymeet

143

grounds every morning early, sometimes with Mari, usually alone. She would stop for a rest on the bench seat tucked under a towering fatsia japonica plant, set back from one of the winding paths through the shrubberies. Jo had seen her there before.

'It's this hip gets me out of bed in the morning,' Imogen had confided on that occasion. 'Aches like crazy sometimes. It helps to walk a bit. Stops me seizing up completely.'

On the Saturday morning, Jo made a point of walking too and of passing along the nearby path just as Imogen was easing herself down onto the seat. Her timing was impeccable. Imogen called a casual greeting and Jo walked across.

'Lovely morning,' said Imogen. 'Great suntrap here. Join me, why don't you?'

Jo did, sitting and turning her face up to the sun. It was pleasingly warm.

'Any change in your aunt?' asked Imogen.

'Not really. She's still muddled and, well, out of it really.'

'She can't remember anything?'

'Not much. The doctors aren't sure she ever will.'

'How sad. Eleanor was such a vibrant person. You will give her our best, won't you? It's not easy to get to see her as much as we'd like.'

'Of course.'

They were both silent.

'How are the workshops going?' Jo enquired.

'Fine. No problems so far. Lawrence might whinge about them but he organises it all fairly well. We get quite a lot of repeat students now.'

'Good. I'll tell Eleanor, just in case she understands.' Jo hesitated. 'Imogen? Were you here - on the estate - on the Friday evening when Eleanor fell?'

She felt Imogen stiffen beside her. 'Ye-es. Mari and I arrived mid-afternoon. To give her time to settle a bit before going off to Exeter. Why?'

'I was searching for a pad yesterday and found a note Eleanor had jotted on an odd scrap of paper. She's always doing that. It seemed to imply she had a meeting with someone - a couple of initials and a date but such a scrawl I couldn't read it. It might have been the twenty-third of the sixth. I wondered if you were here and if you'd seen anyone around, heading for the house maybe?'

'You think this unidentified person might be suspicious then? I thought the police considered Eleanor's fall an accident. Or, well, you know…'

'Yes, but I thought it was worth asking around.'

'I see. Well I didn't see anyone,' Imogen said firmly. 'The police did ask us if we'd seen any strangers hanging around. No-one had.'

'But I suppose you were inside at that time of the evening anyway.' Jo said it lightly, eyes closed again, face to the sun.

'What time was the appointment?'

'I'm not sure. Maybe seven-thirty.'

There was silence and Jo opened her eyes to find Imogen staring at her face.

'I was reading,' Imogen said abruptly. 'In our room. All evening. Except for when Mari rang.'

'What time was that?'

Imogen's eyebrows lifted. 'This feels horribly like the third degree. I trust you aren't trying to accuse us of anything.'

'I'm sorry. I never meant it that way.'

Imogen paused, expression shuttered. 'Mari gets nervous before she performs so she likes to touch base. She was due to go on around eight so a bit before that, I suppose. What were

145

these initials?'

'Either J.D. or J.P. It wasn't clear. And the date might have been the twenty-third of the eighth instead so...' Jo shrugged. 'I'm sure it's nothing.'

'Lawrence might be more helpful. He probably arranged the meeting himself.'

'Of course, he might have. Thanks.'

Afterwards, Jo reflected on what she had learnt. Not a lot. Reading all evening? Maybe. The phone call from Mari might be worth checking but she didn't truly suspect Imogen. She had intended to pump her about the other tutors and about Lawrence but Imogen had quickly put up barriers. The strategy had seemed simpler in the planning. It had been a mistake to underestimate Imogen and treat her as naïve. None of the tutors were that.

But she had managed to rule out Charlotte. The previous day, using a spurious excuse, Jo had waylaid the housekeeper as she did her weekly morning clean and linen change in Lawrence's annexe. It had been a chance to see inside his sophisticated and somewhat austere apartments too though they had afforded no real insight into the man. But, using the same fictitious note excuse, she had found out that Charlotte had gone with her daughter to the theatre in Plymouth the evening of the fall so Jo had happily struck her name from the list.

She hoped she was doing the right thing. Now Imogen knew of her suspicions, it wouldn't be long before the others knew but she had allowed for that; it was a calculated gamble. It would be interesting to see what happened next.

*

Eleanor heard the night staff at the nurses' station speaking in low tones. Somewhere further away, an old man's reedy voice was calling out, 'Nurse? Nurse? Please someone.' She was dimly aware of the sound of the double doors to the ward swishing open and now a man's voice and the metallic clang of a trolley. They had become the background sounds to her life and she barely registered them.

The girl had brought some photographs in that afternoon, pictures of a house and a garden and snaps of people. Some of those images still circulated in her head. Candida had been among them. She remembered Candida - how could she not? - larger than life and endlessly trouble. And there had been a picture of her mother too. Eleanor frowned. Her mother. Ursula Lambe, novelist. Sweeping historical romances. She remembered those, sort of. There were things coming back, pictures in her head from the past, some clear, some very fuzzy.

'You were all novelists,' Candida's daughter had said. What was that girl's name? It had gone again. 'Your mother, your sister and you too, Eleanor. You still are. Very well known. Political thrillers, that's what you write. Brilliant they are.'

Yes, Eleanor sort of knew that, not the well-known or the brilliant bits, but she knew she wrote. That was odd. How did she know that? She just did. Like she knew that she loved strawberries and hated apricots. She almost smiled. Yes, that's right. And she loved pasta but hated goat's cheese. Ha.

She turned her head towards the locker where Jo had put the photographs. Joselyn - that was it. Jo. It was too dark to see them now and she didn't have her glasses to hand anyway but she remembered the photograph of herself.

'This is like the one they use on your books, Eleanor,' Jo had said. 'Very chic, aren't you? I love your hair like that.'

147

Eleanor raised a hand to her face and ran her fingertips over it and then the hair which was growing rapidly but still felt spiky and odd. It was hard to believe she was the same person.

You know you had an accident? Yes, they kept saying that. She had grasped that but she still didn't remember it. She did know that a lot of her mind seemed to be missing. Gone. She fingered cautiously at the scar on her scalp. There was something she knew she should remember but it wouldn't come. There were many things that wouldn't come, images and words that teased and flitted at the corners of her mind but slipped away when she tried to fix on them. And there were some that scared her, even though she couldn't recall them. They seemed dark, heavy shadows deep in the recesses of her mind. Maybe she shouldn't try to raise them.

Eleanor frowned. She wanted the toilet. They'd taken that tube out earlier in the day and she was so grateful - it was a hateful thing. She fumbled about in the bed: there was a button here somewhere to press which would call the nurse. She found it and thrust her thumb down on it hard but it was too late. She felt the hot liquid seep round her legs and cried out in frustration.

Chapter 11

On the Monday morning Jo was sitting at Eleanor's desk when the study door was rapped twice and Lawrence walked in. She produced a smile, eyebrows raised enquiringly.

'Morning Lawrence.'

'Morning.' He glanced round as he always did, checking for any changes, something to pick on, then slowly drew his inscrutable gaze back to rest on her. 'I've been hearing a strange story. Perhaps you can clear the matter up?'

'Try me.'

He came to stand the other side of the desk, looking down on her.

'You found a note Eleanor had written about a meeting on the Friday she fell, is that true?'

'Yes.' Lying didn't come naturally to her but she knew how to do it. Jo had watched her mother lie to every lover she had ever known: eyebrows raised just a little, gaze steady; look accessible and easy-going.

'Can I see it?'

'The note? Erm, I think it's in my bag upstairs. Tell me, how did you hear about it?'

'Vincent. He said it was two initials and a time and you'd been asking a lot of questions about it.'

'I only remarked on it to Imogen actually. I wondered if she'd seen anyone that evening, hanging around. Did you?'

'Me?'

'Yes. Sorry, I assumed you were home that night so...'
She shrugged. '...perhaps you went out for a walk at some
point or went to get something from the car?'

'I was out.'

'In the car?'

'Yes. Your point being?'

'If you were driving in and out you might have seen
someone.'

'I would have said so before.'

'You saw no-one?' She sounded surprised.

'That's right. I saw no-one.' He leaned his knuckles down
on the desk, bending forward ominously towards her. 'And I
didn't arrange any meeting for her that night. What exactly
were the initials on the note?'

'J.D. or J.P.'

He shook his head. 'They mean nothing to me.'

'Not to worry. It was just a thought.'

His eyes narrowed. 'Don't think you can fool me, Joselyn.
It's a pathetic story. There is no note is there? It's a fabrication
to ask questions and point fingers. I object to being cross-
questioned about my movements, like a criminal.'

Jo rose to her feet, obliging him to straighten up. 'You
aren't being accused of anything, Lawrence. And anyone who
has nothing to hide has no reason to be concerned about
answering questions.'

He frowned, momentarily taken aback. Jo had never
answered him back before.

'Anyway, tell me about Vincent,' she said. 'He came to
me asking about a play he'd written based on one of Eleanor's
novels. They were working together on it, he said. I've found
the play so that much is true. Do you know anything about it?'

'No,' he said coldly. 'And she would have told me if they were working together on anything. It's impossible to imagine. Though Vincent did come to see Eleanor that Friday and he did look angry when he left.'

'What time was that?'

'I don't know: sevenish.'

'Did you tell the police?'

'I believe so. Eleanor made light of the visit but Vincent is always trying to take advantage of her.'

'Have you challenged him about it?'

'No. I leave these matters to the police; it's not amateur night. I'd advise you to do the same.' He paused. 'I assume you'll be at the festival meeting tonight. And I trust that this nonsense won't spread outside this estate?'

He raised his chin, walked briskly to the door, and left.

*

They were nearing the end of another tedious committee meeting and Matthew had surreptitiously watched Jo at intervals throughout. She had arrived at the hall slightly late, alone, yet Lawrence had been in his seat before seven-thirty and they sat well apart. Matthew had watched Lawrence too: efficient and precise but officious, he had barely glanced at Jo all evening. Matthew wondered what was going on in that house up on the headland. More than Jo was letting on for certain. She had given a report on Eleanor's progress, had ventured for the first time to suggest that it was unlikely that her aunt would be well enough to speak at the festival and that, despite the short notice, she was looking into finding a replacement speaker.

Nancy closed the meeting. Some quickly left including Lawrence, but a small group gathered near the door to go for a drink. Matthew saw Steve, one of the organisers of the festival stewarding, invite Jo to join them. She appeared to accept. The next minute he too had fallen in with the group and was wandering up the hill with them.

They went to The Mill. Sitting alongside the stream and set back from the winding road out of the village, the redundant old stone mill, converted and extended, was now a smart wine bar and restaurant with a separate function room to the rear. Matthew had only been there once before. Opening at ten each morning, it served coffee and continental pastries through the morning as well as bar drinks and meals later in the day. Gareth had described The Mill to him as 'the opposition' but Matthew didn't see it that way. It had a different ambiance: The Mill aimed for muted, chic and sophisticated; Millie's was beach-side, bright and cheerful. Unpretentious.

That evening the main bar of The Mill was a crush of people and noise. There were six of them and they looked round vainly for a vacant table. A large conservatory extension had recently been built on the side and they found space there, squeezing onto two cane sofas either side of a long low table. It wasn't comfortable and conversation was stilted. They didn't stay long, desultorily picking over the discussions of the evening, joking about Nancy's micromanaging. Jo spoke rarely unless addressed directly, giving little of herself away and even less about Eleanor.

Steve left first, pleading an early start the next day. Jo got up soon after and suddenly they were all on their feet and moving to the door. The others lived further up the hill and Matthew and Jo walked together back down towards the cove. It was nearly ten o'clock. The sun had long since set but a waxing moon cast a silvery glow over the village and bounced white light from a strip of sea in the distance. They could hear the distant sound of waves rolling onto the shore. Matthew found it both pleasing and a little eerie; he had never lived anywhere like this before.

'So what will your son be doing while you're out?' Jo asked him.

He gave a short laugh. 'The same thing he does when I'm there, I imagine: play music in his bedroom very loud. He's into rap...or hip hop. Or both. I'm afraid I don't know the difference.'

'Don't you do anything together? Watch films or something?'

He flicked her a glance, taken aback at the question. 'No, not really. We can't seem to agree on what to watch.'

They walked on several paces in silence. Her head was tilted down to watch the road and her bobbed hair fell over her face, obscuring her expression.

'What sort of film would you watch?' he asked her.

She looked up quickly, hair swinging back. 'Me? From choice? I don't know...a thriller maybe, or a classic like *A Room with a View*, or something like *The Imitation Game*. I don't watch much - whatever's on usually.' She hesitated. 'And you?'

'I like a thriller too. Or a Bond movie. I enjoyed *The Lord of the Rings*. I haven't done that in a while either.'

A car drove up the road from the coast and they both stopped and stood close to the banked hedge, out of its way. It passed and they started walking again.

'I guess teenage boys like different films,' she remarked. 'I wouldn't know what.'

'Harry wouldn't like anything I liked on principle.' It came out more bitterly than he'd intended.

Jo turned her head to stare at him. 'Why?'

'Oh, he's a teenager.' He affected a lighter tone. 'It goes with the territory.' The silence between them yawned wide. 'No...honestly...it's since his mum died. He's not been the same kid.'

'I see. I'm sorry.' Again he felt the scrutiny of her eyes in the half light. 'How long ago was that?'

'About two years.'

'It must have been difficult for you too.'

He shrugged but didn't answer, felt the familiar clenching of his jaw, the sudden inability to articulate any part of how it had been, and they walked on in silence. Now they were looking full down on the bay and the piercing moonlight reflecting off the water's surface. Matthew began trying to pick out his house among the jumble of the settlement, checking for lights, wondering if Harry had been true to his word and stayed in.

'Ow.' Jo had stopped and was reaching down to her ankle.

'What's the matter?'

'I didn't see a hole at the side of the road and I put my foot in it. My ankle went over.'

'Is it bad? Can you walk? Do you need a hand?'

She tentatively tried a step. 'It's fine. Just a bit sore.'

He put a hand to her elbow all the same and she didn't pull away, limping on beside him till they reached the turning for Skymeet. They both stopped and again there was that awkward silence.

'Would you like to come in for coffee?' she offered.

He hesitated. Was she just being polite or did she genuinely want him to come back? He wanted to. She was interesting and pretty and there was something gentle and understanding about her. Jesus, she smelt good too, some light

154

musky perfume.

'Thanks,' he heard himself say, 'but I'd better get back to Harry.'

'Of course. I understand.'

He hesitated. 'But I was thinking maybe we could go out for a drink sometime, just us, I mean?'

She didn't reply and immediately he regretted the remark: he had misread her. What an idiot.

'Sorry, I only meant something casual,' he mumbled. 'But of course, if you'd rather not...'

'No, no,' she said quickly, and smiled. 'A drink would be good.'

He produced a smile too. 'Good. I'll ring you then.' He pointed down at her ankle. 'You should put an ice-pack on that.'

'Yessir.' The suggestion of a teasing salute. 'Night, Matthew.'

He stood, watching, as she limped across the road. She stopped and looked back.

'Just checking you're OK,' he said.

She gave an embarrassed wave then turned and made slow progress up the track towards the estate gates. He walked on down the hill towards home.

'Nice girl,' Sophie told him. 'But she's not me, darling.'

'I know she's not you.'

'Do you? Good. Are you sure about that?'

'Why do you think I'm going home to Harry?'

'Because you feel guilty, Matthew.'

*

Harry stood on the shingle, idly skimming stones over the water. He was wearing earphones connected to something in a holster attached to a belt around his baggy shorts. His new phone presumably. And between bending over to pick up stones and flicking them he occasionally waved his arms in some semblance of a dance, shuffling his feet and stamping them to a beat.

He was wrapped up in his own world and he looked unusually content. Jo watched him for a couple of minutes, pleased to see him that way, reluctant to break his personal spell, jealous even of his absorption. It was ten-thirty in the morning - a fine, dry Thursday but with a chill breeze coming off the sea - and she had struggled to settle to work, her mind too full of other issues. Eventually she'd abandoned her computer and made her way outside instead and, seeing Harry on the beach, had climbed down to join him.

Now, caught in her indecision about disturbing him, she watched him raise bent arms, shift them side to side rhythmically, then do a violent pirouette, jumping his feet round and making a pumping fist movement with both hands. He was facing her and his mouth dropped open, his cheeks colouring. He immediately pulled the earphones out.

'How long've you been there?' he demanded.

'I've just arrived. I guess you didn't hear me because of the music.' She could hear the throbbing beat of it buzzing out of his earphones; it sounded like the rap music Matthew had mentioned. 'Great moves, by the way.'

'No need to be sarcastic.'

'I wasn't being sarcastic. Trust me. I can't dance for toffee.' She pointed towards his belt. 'You've got your new phone already?'

'Yeah. That was part of the deal - getting it now.' He pulled it out of its holster, looking down at it with clear satisfaction.

'At least it's safer in there than your pocket. So what did you have to do for your part of the deal?'

He shrugged. 'I'm working in the coffee shop a bit so I could get a decent phone straight away and not have to wait for my birthday. It was Gail's idea. She works there.'

'How's it going?'

'I've only done two days. It's all right. Freddie's cool. He works there too.'

'The tall guy with the ponytail?'

'Yeah.'

She bent over, picked up a stone and skimmed it out over the water. They both watched it skip four times and plop into the water; neither remarked on it.

He put the earphones back in and turned to face the sea again.

'Harry?'

He grunted, still staring at the water.

'Harry, please take those out. I want to talk.'

He pulled them out impatiently. 'What?' he demanded rudely.

'Hey, hey, c'mon. Don't be like this. I don't want to shout. I'm guessing you wouldn't have spoken to your mum like that, would you?'

His face puckered and he shook his head. 'Sorry,' he mumbled.

'Look, I just need your help. I'm trying to figure out who you might have seen that night up on the terrace with my aunt.'

Again the scowl. 'You've not told anyone what I said?'

'No. I'm doing it by myself, trying to eliminate anyone who had a reason to be somewhere else.'

'Oh.' Now he looked intrigued. 'Like a P.I. sort of thing?'

She smiled. 'Yes, something like that, only without the

157

grubby raincoat. So I need to know roughly what time it was you heard those voices. I checked and low tide that night wasn't until around half eleven. What time would you have got here?'

'I can get around when the tide's about half way out. Depends how choppy it is.'

'So, what, maybe three and a half hours before low tide?'

'Something like that.'

'Is that what you did that night?'

'I think so.'

'That would make it somewhere around eight o'clock. And how long had you been here when you heard them?'

'Dunno. Not long. Twenty minutes maybe. It was still light. The sun didn't set till late.'

She nodded and smiled. 'That's great, thanks.'

'Will you tell me what you find out?'

'If I find anything out, I will. Only you've got to promise you won't tell anyone what I'm doing.'

'And get into trouble for being here. No way.'

'Fine. See you soon.' She smiled and turned to go.

'Jo?' She looked back and he pulled the earphone lead out of his phone, allowing the music to thump and echo around the beach. 'You really should learn some moves yourself.' He raised bent arms again and shimmied his shoulders side to side, shuffling his feet. 'Come on. Try.'

She hesitated then lifted her arms and mimicked him, feeling silly but then starting to laugh, stamping her feet and shaking her shoulders to the beat. The song finished and she stopped, grinning and shaking her head.

'I've got to go.'

He grinned back. 'Nice moves yourself.'

She laughed again and made her way back up the shore

but she wasn't smiling by the time she reached the steps. There was too much going on in her head. As if finding out who had argued with Eleanor wasn't problem enough, now she had the added complication of Matthew. On closer acquaintance, he wasn't what she had expected. Coloured by Harry's descriptions, she had almost wanted to dislike him. But she didn't. So was he the difficult, angry person Harry described or the pleasant, softly spoken one she'd sat and had a drink with? Either way, wouldn't it be wiser to stay away from this all too complicated relationship?

She climbed the steps, unaware that someone had been watching her talking and dancing with Harry from high up on the cliff, pushed into a gap in the screen of bamboo.

*

Frank drew his car into the car park at the back of the pub, killed the engine and glanced at his watch. Twenty past five. He'd arrived ahead of time so there would be no rush. The pub was called the Travellers Arms and stood not far from Jo's route home from the hospital. He had suggested the rendezvous to her in a text and was a little surprised she had agreed. *Need to talk with you*, he'd said. Even to him it sounded cryptic.

He went inside. The place wasn't busy and the bar was deserted. He ordered a pint, sat at a table nearby, and waited.

Jo was ten minutes late. He was nearly half way down the pint, agitation making him drink too fast, and he got up as soon as she entered.

'Jojo. Thanks for coming at such short notice. Can I get you a drink?'

'Thanks. Ginger beer please. Ice, no lemon.'

She sat down and he came back with the bottle and a glass

with ice.

'This is very cloak and dagger,' she remarked lightly, pouring the beer over the ice and taking a sip.

He smiled. 'I suppose it does seem that way. But it's nice to have a chance to talk - away from all the pressures of that place.'

'That place?' She raised her eyebrows, replacing the glass on the coaster and fingering the condensation down its sides. 'How sad that it's come to that. "That place" used to be a refuge of calm. You told me once that you thought that way too.'

'I did.' He shook his head. 'But these last weeks have changed everything, Jo. You know that.'

'I think it changed for you a while back.'

'It did.'

'Irrevocably?'

'You know the answer. Nothing stays the same forever.'

'*Change to survive, adapt and thrive, The dodo never did.* See how I remember.'

'You always did quote my poetry back at me. It's a little unnerving.'

She smiled but her expression gave nothing away. Jo had changed it occurred to him now. As a child she had always been reserved, emotionally restrained: she had spent too much time ducking and diving her mother's moods. But with Eleanor's influence she had come out of her shell as she got older and expressed herself more, become easier to read. She was quick and well read - inevitably - and could be good company when she relaxed. But now she looked more shuttered than ever, as if intentionally holding something back. That was unnerving too.

She took another sip of her drink. 'Why did you want to

see me, Frank?'

'Tell me about Eleanor. I can't ask on the estate.'

'No? Well, she's improved but…' She gave a quick shrug. '…it's kind of superficial. She's moving better and speaking more clearly but her thoughts get very jumbled and mostly all she can remember is way in the past, like her childhood, sometimes with astonishing detail.' She glanced up at him, coyly, he thought. 'She was catheterised but they've taken that out which is creating a few issues, shall we say. She gets very frustrated at times.'

He smiled ruefully. 'She never did like not being in control.'

'Who does?' She fixed him with a look. 'Your text suggested there was more to this meeting than a polite enquiry after Eleanor's health.'

He bridled. 'Why the accusatory tone, young lady? You don't think I still care about her? We were lovers for a long time, Jo. That doesn't just go away because you break up.'

'I suppose not. I suppose it depends on why you break up.'

He studied her shrewdly. 'You sound like someone who's recently broken up yourself.'

'It's a little while now. I took your words to heart: I'm learning to adapt. I'll survive.'

'I'm sure you will. I've always been impressed by your resilience. So was it that Richard? I imagine Eleanor was relieved. But you'd been together a while. I hope he didn't hurt you too badly.'

'I'm sure you didn't ask me here to discuss my love life - or the lack of it.'

Again the cool rebuff. He smiled an acknowledgement and took another draw on his beer.

'OK. You're right. Though it is nice to be able to talk

freely with you. There's an atmosphere on the estate right now. Everyone's a bit jumpy. It makes them tetchy.' He glanced round the pub. 'This is good: old world, faded, relaxed.'

Jo said nothing but continued to watch him.

He met her gaze. 'Imogen said you were asking about some appointment that Eleanor had made, someone referred to with just a couple of initials.'

'Yes. I bumped into her and asked, just in case she'd seen anyone that night. I know you wouldn't have - I gather you and Mari were in Exeter.'

'We were. Mari gave a wonderful performance that night to much acclaim. I'm afraid it's been overshadowed with subsequent events. But, tell me, where has this come from suddenly?'

She shrugged carelessly. 'It's probably nothing. I found something hanging around on a piece of paper and I didn't pay it much attention at first, then I wondered. It might not have been an appointment though. You know how bizarre Eleanor's scrappy notes are.'

He nodded, choosing his words carefully. 'The thing is, Jojo, I'd rather you didn't pursue this with Louisa. She's pretty rattled by Eleanor's accident as it is and she's fragile at the best of times. I don't want her upset any more.'

'I see. She was here that evening though?'

'Yes, we arrived late afternoon. But what is there to say? She was very tired and had a bath, then an early night. She'd have told the police if she'd seen anyone.'

'Of course. I probably misinterpreted Eleanor's writing anyway.'

'I'm sure Lawrence would have known if she'd got an appointment with someone.'

'Even a private meeting?'

'Lawrence makes everything Eleanor does his business - or tries too.'

'True. It doesn't seem to be on his radar certainly.'

'So you won't speak to Louisa?'

'It doesn't sound like there's any point.' Jo finished the last of her ginger beer, put the glass down and stood up. 'Thanks for the drink.' She frowned, then spoke more softly. 'Are you happy with Louisa, Frank?'

'Really Jo, what a thing to ask a man who's just got engaged. Of course I'm happy.' He hesitated, reaching out to take her hand. 'Louisa isn't the reason Eleanor and I split up, you know. We simply couldn't live together. That's the way it goes sometimes, however much you love someone...' He shrugged. '...they drive you crazy.'

She smiled sadly, extracting her hand from his grip. 'I know. I hope it all works out for you this time.'

He watched her walk away. Yes, Jo had changed. There was a lot she wasn't saying. Why was that? Had he become the enemy now? The thought saddened him though he couldn't really blame her. But she hadn't promised not to speak to Louisa after all that.

Chapter 12

Inviting Jo out for a drink was a mistake. Over successive nights, Matthew fretted into the small hours, wondering if he should cancel. It wasn't that he didn't like her; he did. He loved her eyes, their vibrancy and warmth, and he liked her natural and unaffected manner; she was direct, like her aunt. And there was a stillness about her which made him feel comfortable somehow. Even the way she regularly arrived late and apologetic for meetings was endearing. But he couldn't have Jo in his life without pushing Sophie out of it and he couldn't do that. It was too soon, much too soon. Apart from anything else there was that lingering, barely acknowledged sense of guilt.

But the house felt emptier than ever and Harry more distant. It would be nice to see her again. In any case Jo had accepted his invitation and he couldn't go back on his word.

He finally made the call on the Thursday evening and suggested a drink at The George the following night, maybe a meal too. Keep it simple, he thought, casual. The Mill would suggest something more serious. She accepted and offered to meet him on the village road by the turn-off for Skymeet so they could walk up together. He was there on the dot of seven-thirty; she was late - of course - and apologised, and they walked in an awkward silence. Matthew hadn't been on a date like this since he was a student and now he was forty-two. He felt old suddenly. This was an absurd thing to be doing.

They fell into a conversation about the festival, how it felt too last minute and shambolic, how it should have been arranged sooner but, without Eleanor's guiding hand, had understandably faltered. Jo had tracked down a friend of Eleanor's, another thriller writer, who thought she might be available to speak and was happy to help out. The subject kept them safely occupied until they were in the pub.

It was busy but Matthew had rung ahead and reserved a table. They sat by the fireplace - dark and empty through the summer months - and silently studied the menu. Jo was quiet, uncomfortably so. She wasn't making this easy for him. He went to the bar and ordered.

'What made you choose to come to Petterton Mill Cove?' she asked when he returned.

He didn't want to talk about himself. He should have asked her something first.

'A fresh start. And it's a lovely place, isn't it.'

'It is. I've always liked it here.' She hesitated. 'But why here particularly?'

'I saw Millie's advertised. It was an opportunity.'

She was watching him. She was astute: she knew he wasn't telling the whole story. Perhaps because she never did herself.

'Have you settled in?' she said. 'Does your son like it here?'

'More or less. It's not been a year yet.' He gave a light shrug. 'Millie's takes up more of my time than I'd expected. Naïve, I guess. But Harry's OK. These things take time.'

She smiled, then her expression fixed and she shifted her gaze a couple of times slowly to look over his shoulder.

'Are you all right?' He automatically turned to glance

165

round.

'Yes. It's nothing. One of the workshop tutors is here. Vincent. He also happens to be my aunt's cousin, which makes him my…something cousin too, I suppose.' She was still looking across and she gave a weak smile and nod of acknowledgement to the man somewhere behind him.

'Does he bother you in some way?'

'No, he's just…' She looked back at Matthew and the smile mutated to a rueful grimace. 'I'm never sure where I am with him, that's all. I hope he doesn't come over.'

'That's the trouble with a small place like this. I found it took a bit of getting used to - everyone knowing your business. It's intrusive. When I first arrived, a couple of the local women found out I was widowed and they tried to organise me, take me out of myself, meet people. Talk about it, they said, it'll be good for you. Christ, talk about insensitive.'

He stopped suddenly. Jo was staring at him, wide-eyed with concern or maybe wariness. He could hear an echo of his voice in his own ears and the bitterness it exuded. Anger was never far away, he'd found. It sneaked up on him when he wasn't looking.

'Maybe I've seen this guy,' he said, trying to shake it off. 'Some of the tutors come down to the café. There's a woman who often comes in: loud voice, straight blonde hair and quite a bit of make-up. And that Frank Marwell, the poet you mentioned, he's been in a couple of times with her. He wasn't what I'd expected somehow.'

'In what way?'

'I don't know. You think of poets as being all other-worldly and head in the clouds. He seems fairly normal.' He laughed. 'Stupid thing to say. What's normal anyway?'

Her lips twitched into a knowing smile, as if party to a

166

secret. 'You should see Frank perform his poetry. He can sell it.'

With her gaze fixed in mid-air, she began to recite:

'I remember
When there were bees,
Great colonies of them.
I remember
Meadows and swaying swathes of colour in the breeze
And tiny whir-winged messengers, flitting
From flower to flower.
I remember
The heart-slowing drone of their wings
The sleepy day buzz of them:
Mailmen, sugar-drunk, gold-dusted.
I remember.'

Now she looked embarrassed and grinned. 'I saw him recite that once. He was mesmerising. There's more of course but I can't remember the rest by heart - all about how important the bees are and how sorry we'll be when they're gone.'

'You sell it pretty well yourself,' said Matthew. He found her mesmerising too.

Their meals arrived and the conversation stuttered. Neither of them seemed sure where it should go next and they ate, wary, exchanging nondescript remarks.

On the walk back down the hill afterwards, Matthew felt the pressure to speak. In any case there was something he needed to know. Keep it casual, he told himself.

'It must be quite difficult staying here, away from your usual life. Do you have a boyfriend back home? You said you live in Sussex normally?'

'Yes, but no boyfriend at the moment. I've just broken off

an engagement actually. We'd been together a while so it was kind of hard…' She laughed awkwardly. 'I don't have a great record in that department. Anyway, my work can be done anywhere there's an internet connection these days so being here isn't a problem. It's just, you know, difficult with Eleanor at the moment, not knowing…'

'I understand.'

He opened his mouth to add something, thinking of offering to help somehow, moral support perhaps, but closed it again. He didn't like hospitals. He had spent too much time in them with Sophie and couldn't face doing that again. That hospital smell; the sound of trolleys clanking up the corridors; the curtained beds and hushed voices and sympathetic glances from the nurses…

'I hope the festival is a success,' Jo said suddenly. 'I want it for Eleanor.'

'Is she pleased it's going ahead?'

'She doesn't know what I'm taking about when I mention it. At least I don't think so. Sometimes she just stares at me. I have no idea what she's thinking.'

They had reached the turning for the estate but there was no invitation to go in this time. That was probably his fault for refusing before or maybe for scaring her by sounding so angry.

'Thank you,' she said. 'It was nice to…' She waved a hand vaguely towards all that lay beyond the trees. '…get away from all that for a while.'

'You're welcome. I enjoyed it.' He felt clumsy. He should say something else but wasn't sure what. He had a sudden desire to hug her, just to put his arms round her and hold her for a minute, but pushed the thought away before it could take possession of him.

'Please don't tell anyone else what I said just now about

Eleanor, will you?' said Jo. 'It wouldn't be...'

'It's all right. I understand. I wouldn't say anything anyway.'

She leaned towards him suddenly and stretched up to press her lips briefly to his cheek. 'Thanks.' She started to move away. 'Night Matthew. Thanks again.'

He watched her go. 'Night Jo,' was all he managed to say and she probably didn't even hear him.

He glanced at his watch as he trudged down the hill home, Jo's musky scent still in his nostrils. He had told Harry he was meeting up at The George with someone from the committee, thinking it too soon to explain about the date since it wasn't likely to lead to anything anyway. He'd been right about that.

'Well, you didn't handle that very well, did you?' said Sophie.

*

It was raining heavily when Jo got back from the hospital on the Saturday evening. Key in her hand ready, she left the car and ran to the front door, fumbling with the lock and throwing herself inside. Holding the door open she looked back into the rain. The sound of her car being parked would often bring Sidney running to the house but he wasn't there. He was probably sheltering somewhere dry. She tried calling his name, then gave in and closed the door.

The rain didn't last. It blew through leaving the grass sparkling in the early evening sunshine. Several times, while she ate her meal in the conservatory, Jo looked out over the garden. There was no sign of Sidney. After clearing up, she went outside and wandered round the garden, occasionally calling his name.

It was good to be in the fresh air. It wasn't cold and she

lingered. The lower terrace still caught the rays of the sinking sun and she stood savouring them, hearing the sound of the surf down on the beach. She was tired and woolly-headed. Odd bits of conversation with Matthew had replayed in her head into the night. She still wasn't sure what to make of him. She liked him, much more than she had expected. He was charming and kind and he had a sensitive smile, yet being with him felt like walking along a knife edge, precarious and uncertain. That flash of temper had been revealing. She could guess at some of the pain he was still feeling but she couldn't cope with it right now; he needed patience and time and she didn't have enough of either.

It had been hard work with Eleanor again that afternoon. Jo spent ages showing her aunt photographs, trying to elicit some memory and response. Sometimes Eleanor seemed to recognise something; sometimes she tried to talk about it, but the words or thoughts didn't come the way she wanted. Names were a particular struggle for her. She would either lose interest or get cross. The photographs had been pushed ruthlessly away at one point, a number of them fluttering to the floor.

'Sorry,' Eleanor had said, a little grudgingly, still with the warning glint in her eye.

Occasionally her aunt showed flashes of the woman she had been; at other times she was another person entirely. It was like going on a series of blind dates, never sure what kind of person would turn up.

A flash of light caught Jo's eye now, something between the pavers on the terrace, glistening in the low beam of sunlight. She went closer and bent over. The mortar which had originally been pressed between the slabs had broken up in places and something metallic had got trapped among the bits which now sat in a shallow rill of rainwater. It looked like a stud earring. Odd. She picked it out and held it up to examine. Yes, it was: a solid round of gold set with a small bulbous stone, backed with a gold post. The stone looked like an agate: it was purple with bands of pale pink and grey running through it. It would need a butterfly clip to hold it in the ear though. She searched around but there was no sign of it, presumably the reason the stud had fallen out. It could have been there a while; only the rain and the late sunshine had revealed it.

She felt a warm body push against her leg. Sidney was back, yowling softly for his dinner. She went inside to feed him and took the stud with her.

Later, up in Eleanor's bedroom, Jo opened the jewellery box on the dressing table and picked along the cushion of earrings. They were all in pairs. There were a few loose earrings on the tray below and she checked those too. None matched the one she had found. She hadn't really expected them too. Eleanor didn't wear neat little studs like this: she wore bold statement earrings, large or colourful or both, pieces that hung and attracted attention, just like the hats and the clothes she wore. So this stud had been worn by someone visiting the terrace. It might have been anybody or it might have been worn by the person who argued with Eleanor that night. Beforehand, Jo had been almost convinced that it had been a man but now... How many people ever visited the terrace?

Once formed, the idea took hold and refused to be ignored. Jo went to bed that night still wondering where it led her. Perhaps she had found something concrete at last.

*

Eleanor sat with the photographs spread out on the table in

171

front of her. She had looked at them so many times that they had become familiar to her in the way the words of a poem can be familiar even when you don't understand what the poem means. There were photos of her home and her gardens; photos of friends and family; photos of Petterton Mill Cove.

It was Sunday morning; the radio had told her so. There had been a religious and current affairs programme on earlier. One of the younger nurses kept changing the station when Eleanor was out of the room but Jo had pre-set her aunt's favourites and, with the press of a button, Radio 4 was back on. Easy. Eleanor kept the radio close now - on the table or on the bed beside her chair. They might manage to get her walking down in that physiotherapy department with their help, but she couldn't risk walking on her own yet. Her legs didn't always do what she told them and too often she felt like she was walking on the deck of a pitching ship.

But there was no speech therapy or physiotherapy today because it was Sunday. Her usual physio, Steph, had told Eleanor that she was going away somewhere for the weekend. Eleanor couldn't remember where. It was annoying the way she kept losing thoughts that way. Still, it meant peace. There would be no-one exhorting her to hold this bar or move that leg or stand straighter. 'Come on, Eleanor, you can do it. Try harder.' All that eagerness and enthusiasm and downright bossiness was maddening.

No, this morning she could be still. She could read maybe. Jo had brought her a few books, which were stacked up in the locker beside her bed. No, she couldn't read. She wanted to but she had tried and the lines of text didn't register with her. She understood the individual words but, put together, they didn't mean anything to her. And sometimes they were out of focus anyway. She had thrown a book across the room the other day in frustration and Jo had got cross, upset even, and Eleanor had been a bit shocked, her anger quickly dissipating. She was sorry: she didn't want to upset the girl. But Jo didn't like books to get marked, never had. Eleanor remembered that quite clearly about her from when she was young. Always kept her things neat and tidy, Jo did; didn't like other people messing with them, putting things out of order, turning corners back to keep the page.

No, looking at photos was the best she could do. She carefully picked one up, fumbling it a little. It was a photo of Jo paddling in the sea. There was another one of her, sitting playing the piano.

'That's your piano,' Jo had pointed out. 'In your sitting room at home.'

'My piano,' Eleanor muttered now. She stretched out her free hand and wiggled the fingers up and down. Yes, she could see herself playing the piano, though she couldn't remember it. But these fingers were no more obedient at times than her legs. The harder she tried, the more errant they became.

She picked up another photo. These gardens were hers. It was a visceral reaction she got to them rather than something conscious - hard to identify, harder still to explain to Jo. Bloody hell, Jo fussed at her so. Eleanor wished she wouldn't. It was so tiring, trying to remember; sometimes Eleanor just wanted to sit and be. It felt like her head was full of water, swishing backwards and forwards, jostling the images in her brain, fragmenting them. She wanted to be still and let the water settle, then maybe the images and memories would come back together and form something she could identify.

She dropped the photo of the gardens back on the table and pushed it away with the back of her hand.

'Eleanor, don't you look better?'

A small, slight woman with short dark hair had walked into the room, smiling, a bunch of flowers in one hand, a plastic pack of grapes in the other. She dumped them both on the bed and bent over to wrap her arms around Eleanor's back in a gentle embrace. Her shoulder bag swung round and banged the chair.

'Oh sorry.' She straightened up, backing away then pulled the small upright chair over and sat down.

Eleanor stared at her. She knew her. There was a photograph of her somewhere on the table, she was sure, but the name wouldn't come. They'd been friends, hadn't they, years ago? Yes, in London, just graduated and full of the hubris of youth, talking about books and art and politics. She grinned. Ah yes, politics, one of her favourite subjects, but it had got her into trouble more often than not.

The woman was smiling back at her. She had an elfin face, kind, anxious.

'Mari,' said Eleanor suddenly and grinned again at her success. 'Mari,' she repeated.

'Yes, I'm Mari. You remembered. Oh darling, how wonderful that you're getting better. I'm so relieved.'

Mari's smile stretched from ear to ear. Yes, she remembered Mari. She had shared Eleanor's political views but had always been reluctant to argue her point home, too quick to defer to others and doubt herself. It used to drive Eleanor wild. She liked her though. Mari had married some bossy man - what was his name?

'How is he?' Eleanor enunciated slowly. 'The bossy man. Hm? So bossy.' She shook her head reprovingly.

Mari looked hunted. 'Do you mean Lenny? We split up years ago. I...well, I realised he wasn't right for me. I'm with Imogen now. You know Imogen?' Mari surveyed the

174

photographs spread out on the table separating them, half-standing, turning her head to see them the right way up. She rifled through them. 'Here, this is Imogen with me. See?' She handed Eleanor the photo.

Eleanor thought she recognised Imogen. Maybe. It wasn't as clear as when you saw someone in the flesh.

'Good,' she said, putting the picture back down. It was what she said to keep people happy and stop them chivvying her.

'Yes, we're very happy together.' Mari picked up another photo. 'Here's Candida. I know it's been years but I do still miss her. You must too. Such a special person and so full of energy.'

'Candida,' said Eleanor. 'My sister. Yes.'

'I know you didn't always get on, darling, but that's the way it is with sisters, especially creative ones like you were. It's normal.'

'I love Candida...' said Eleanor.

'Yes, we all did.'

'...but sometimes...' Eleanor leaned forward in the chair, clenching a fist. '...she's inf...infur... Tsch. She's clever but washes...no, wastes...' She nodded vigorously and released an index finger to prod inexpertly at the table top. '...wastes herself. We row - always row.'

Mari was silent for a minute, expression wary. 'You do remember what happened to Candida don't you, Eleanor? She fell, darling, remember? Fell off a boat, poor thing.' She hesitated, then put a comforting hand on top of Eleanor's. 'She drowned you know, darling.'

Eleanor took a minute to digest this. Yes, Jo had said something like this to her too.

'She drowned,' she repeated.

Drowned. Sudden and horrible. Yes, this was something Eleanor could feel, deep in the pit of her stomach and it twisted now at the thought. Candida had gone.

Mari laughed briefly, trying to lighten the atmosphere. 'It shows how much I miss her that I sometimes think I see her in the street, you know? Even after all these years. It happened quite recently, in fact, just before we came down here, I thought I saw her in a shop in London. It's odd how that happens, isn't it? A face in the crowd and suddenly you're transported back twenty years.'

Eleanor stared at her. She felt a chill run down her spine and groped suddenly, urgently, for the call button and pressed it.

'I need to pee,' she told Mari. 'Now.'

*

Jo visited Eleanor that afternoon and found her aunt quieter than usual, distracted.

'The literary festival is starting to come together,' she said, trying to capture her aunt's attention. 'The whole village is excited about it now. Matthew Croft's designed a website for the event. There's information on it about Petterton Mill Cove and the speakers and ways to get hold of tickets.' Eleanor was silent, pulling at a piece of skin on her thumb. 'Do you remember Matthew? He runs Millie's, the coffee shop. But he's a web designer and it was you who suggested he get involved with the festival.'

Eleanor looked at her blankly.

Jo pressed on. 'I've managed to find someone to fill in as a speaker for you: Penny Finn. You know Penny. She writes thrillers too. You've known each other for years. In fact you met her at a literary festival. You told me you both drank too much Pimms and felt awful the next day. Anyway, she said she'll try to get here to visit but if not, she'll see you when she comes for the festival.'

'Penny,' repeated Eleanor dully, apparently disinterested.

Jo produced the stud earring from a side pocket in her handbag and held it out on the palm of her hand.

'Eleanor, do you recognise this?'

Her aunt became more animated, stared at the stud, then bent closer. She reached out to take it but it was too small and she couldn't coordinate her fingers to pick it up. She swore and tried again, succeeding the second time and turning her hand to look at the earring from both sides. She dropped it back on Jo's palm.

'No,' she said.

'I found it on your terrace. Do you remember anyone you know wearing ear studs like this? I should return it to them.'

Eleanor slowly moved her head side to side. 'Mari came,' she said. 'She saw Candidi...Candida.' Her expression clouded. 'She said.'

Jo was stunned. 'Mari came to the terrace? When? And what do you mean about her seeing mum?'

Eleanor stared at her. 'Mari came here.' She gestured an index finger downwards. 'Today.'

'Here. I see.' Jo relaxed. She'd misunderstood again.

'She saw Candida.'

'She couldn't have, Eleanor. Mum died years ago.'

'I know.' The familiar stubborn line returned to Eleanor's mouth. 'But she saw her. She said.'

Jo reached a hand and laid it reassuringly over Eleanor's.

'No, Eleanor, your sister passed away. Look, I see her too sometimes, in my dreams. She's always with us.'

Eleanor shook her head, frowning. 'We row. We always

177

row.' She nodded meaningfully.

Jo didn't like the turn of the conversation and began talking about Sidney.

Going to bed, the stud still preoccupied her. Vincent used to wear an earring or a stud. He even went in for coloured ones sometimes to match his waistcoats. She remembered a silver charm dangling from his ear when she was a child. It had been in the shape of an open book and she had been fascinated by it. Lately she hadn't paid much attention. Did he still wear them? As for Mari and Imogen, they both wore their hair short and they both wore earrings. If she remembered correctly, Mari wore small, neat ones while Imogen's varied from the small to the flamboyant. She didn't know about Louisa. Her hair was shoulder length and hung like a curtain over her ears, usually obscuring them but the woman wore a lot of jewellery. And Lawrence didn't wear jewellery of any kind. It frustrated her to think this might rule him out.

She fell asleep in the end with the light still on and woke an hour later, her paperback fallen to one side, the bookmark on the floor. She had been dreaming about her mother again - for the first time in more than a year.

She saw her. But Mari couldn't have seen Candida. Eleanor's mind was playing tricks on her.

Chapter 13

The following Monday, one of the ward doctors spoke to Jo. He was the registrar, a serious, edgy man with a long face and eyebrows that nearly met. They were looking to get Eleanor home, he said. Eleanor didn't need much medical care now, just rehabilitation, and she would benefit from being in a more normal environment. Outpatient physiotherapy and speech therapy could be arranged for her.

Jo was shocked. She was also scared. She didn't want Eleanor home yet; she didn't know whom she could trust and, at home, Eleanor could be vulnerable to the person who had attacked her. Jo wanted more time: time for Eleanor to get her memory back and time to find out what had happened that night and to take it to the police.

'Aren't there specialised places where people go to get rehab?' she asked him. 'You know, as in residential?'

He looked surprised. 'Yes, some. I was talking to someone about this yesterday oddly. There aren't many NHS facilities and they all have waiting lists. But there's a private place up on Dartmoor which I was told is very good. They might have room if that's the way you want to go.'

'I'd need to look into it.'

'We're not talking immediately. But soon.' He smiled and turned away to speak to another doctor. It was a first warning.

On the Tuesday, Eleanor started with a head cold. By the

Wednesday, it had developed; she was streaming and coughing and slept a lot. Jo's sympathy was tempered by relief. They wouldn't discharge her while she was like this. On the Thursday she decided not to visit and spent much of the afternoon on the internet, looking into the possibilities of rehabilitation for Eleanor and checking out what she could learn about the unit up on Dartmoor. The Moorhill Centre, it was called. It offered comfortable private rooms and a range of therapies and, to judge from the photographs, had an amazing setting. It also asked some eye-watering fees.

By four o'clock, with information overload, she went for a walk through the village and up onto the cliff path. It was a bright, dry day and the path was popular. She got caught up in a stream of holidaymakers beating the same route along the clifftop. Coming back and descending the final steps to the village, she noticed Louisa go into the convenience store. It was the opportunity she had hoped for to speak to her alone. Jo stopped to look over the wall at the sea then idled along until she was a stone's throw from the shop. A few minutes later, Louisa exited the store carrying a plastic carrier bag and turned for home. Jo hurried to catch up with her and smiled a greeting. Louisa's expression was friendly if guarded.

'Hello,' said Louisa, glancing round. 'By yourself?'

'Yes. I've been for a walk. Eleanor's laid up with a bad cold so I decided to stay away and let her rest.'

'Poor Eleanor. She is in the wars.' Louisa carried on walking and Jo fell into step.

'Nice day. Busy now though.'

'Yes.'

'You're doing the workshops with Imogen this week, aren't you? How's it going? I guess it's been difficult at times, being the newcomer. All the others seem to have been doing

180

them forever.'

Louisa stopped and turned, meeting Jo's eyes, her face expressionless.

'Did you mean something by that?'

'No. In what way?'

Silence. 'I don't find it difficult,' Louisa said eventually. 'I couldn't speak for anyone else. It's such a well-oiled machine that I just go with the flow and do my bit. Anyway, I like to think I bring something fresh to the table.'

She began walking again and Jo went with her. They reached the bottom of the path that led up to the estate and started the climb in single file. The increased effort made Louisa hot and she lifted a hand to push the hair back off her face, ramming it behind her ears. Jo kept close and, as the path turned, caught the definite glint of earrings. It looked like Louisa wore two pairs.

'Louisa,' she said, 'did you stay around Skymeet the night Eleanor fell? The reason I'm…'

'I know.' Louisa interrupted her sharply and stopped again, almost making Jo walk into the back of her. She turned. 'I heard. You're fretting over some cryptic note Eleanor wrote. Really Jo, you can't truly believe there's been some sort of conspiracy? It's too horrible. Anyway don't you think you've got enough on your plate without playing super sleuth? Maybe you've edited too many murder mysteries.'

She had been waiting for the question, Jo was sure of it, had wanted it to be asked so she could dismiss it.

'I'm only making some casual enquiries to see whether it's worth handing the thing over to the police,' said Jo.

'The police? Good grief. Not them again.'

Louisa started off again. The path widened and Jo managed to move alongside.

'Let me see...' Louisa nodded thoughtfully. 'Yes, I did stay on the estate. Frank had abandoned me and dashed off to Exeter with Mari and I was tired after the travelling so I had a lazy evening. I went to the den to watch a little television.' She stopped again, breathless, and pushed some hair that had escaped back behind her ear. 'Steep isn't it? Anyway, I think I had a short walk but I didn't see any strangers hanging around. I generally draw the curtains in the evening in the apartment anyway, especially if I'm alone.' She paused, her eyes fixed on Jo's. 'Do you really think the note is important?'

'I've no idea but probably not. Eleanor's always scribbling notes to herself. They don't make much sense to anyone else.' Jo's gaze shifted slightly. 'Pretty earrings.'

Louisa was wearing neat teardrop pale sapphires, set in gold, hanging delicately from the bottom of each ear. On each side, a little higher up, was a small opal set in a gold stud.

'Thank you.' Louisa automatically put her free hand up to finger one of them. 'Frank bought them for me.' She started walking again.

'How is Frank?'

'He's gone off on one of his "musings". He says it's the only way he can compose. Just when you think you've got something planned, oh no, an urge overcomes him and he has to go off alone.' She snorted. 'It drives me mad. And then there he is, suddenly back again.' She stopped suddenly and smiled sheepishly. 'I don't know. These poets, what's to be done with them?'

'Where does he go?'

They had reached the gate and Jo keyed in the week's code to open it.

'You tell me,' said Louisa as she passed through. 'You've known him longer than me. He never says. And I daren't come

182

between the man and his muse, dare I?' She was trying to sound flippant but only succeeded in sounding petulant.

'I suppose not. But at least he has his muse. Eleanor used to say he was like a bear with a sore head when he couldn't write his poetry.'

Louisa darted her a reproachful look. 'Did she indeed. Tell me, have you been asking Vincent questions too?'

'Not yet. You think he was around?'

'I know he was. We saw him when we arrived.'

'Then I'll speak to him.'

They were back walking in single file and the conversation died. As the path spilled them out into the open ground near the house, Louisa stopped and turned.

'When you go to see Vincent, ask him what he was doing heading for the house on that Friday night. I didn't see any strangers but I did see him and he looked angry. He was drunk too; I could tell from the way he was walking. He's a pig when he's drunk. Everyone says so.'

'Did you tell the police this?'

Louisa laughed sardonically.

'He'd deny it. Or say he saw me going there for spite. No, Jo dear, I've learnt to keep my head down around here. I find it doesn't do to make waves. Like you said: I'm the newcomer. Some people resent that. But I don't like being accused of things.'

'Who's accusing you of anything?'

'Really? How disingenuous.' Louisa smiled sweetly. 'But of course, you're just asking questions. Personally, I think you're very brave.'

She raised her eyebrows and left.

Jo stood and watched her walk away. There was nothing fragile about Louisa. She was a very bitter woman and interestingly keen to implicate Vincent. She would definitely bear further investigation.

*

It was nearly eight o'clock when Frank finally returned to the apartment. Louisa was writing, sitting at the small utilitarian table against the further wall, a table lamp throwing a circle of light over her laptop and notes in stark contrast to the gloom in the rest of the room. She barely looked up as he entered.

'Hi,' he said, throwing his rucksack on the floor. 'Sorry I'm late. I got involved in something and couldn't leave it alone.'

She nodded but said nothing, her attention apparently fixed on the screen of her computer though her fingers weren't moving. She was freezing him out, making him suffer for leaving her. For all that she was a writer, Louisa didn't understand the particular energies he needed to feed off in order to write his poetry. Frank knew himself well. He couldn't write in a confined space, with other people around. He had to wander, find isolated places to sit, away from any bustle. He couldn't settle either; when he was on a writing binge, he was nomadic.

He walked up behind her and put his hands on her shoulders, massaging them.

'Had a hard day?' he asked. Her muscles were tense and hard.

'You could say that.'

'Tell me about it.'

She saved what she had been doing and snapped the lid of the laptop down, turning in her seat, shrugging his hands away.

'Shouldn't we go and eat? It's getting late.'

'You haven't eaten?' He stepped back, surprised.

184

'You mean you have? I was waiting for you.'

'Darling, I'm sorry. I never thought. I grabbed something while I was out because the time was going on. I just assumed you'd do the same.'

'You assumed. It didn't cross your mind to phone me?'

'I'm sorry, no. I was wrapped up in the words. I can't risk stopping the flow, you see. Anyway, we can go out. We can have a drink and you can get something to eat. Hell, I'll have something to keep you company. How's that?'

She stood up, mollified, he thought. He wondered where to take her. Everywhere was so busy in August.

'Perhaps we should try The Watchmaker?' he suggested. 'It's one of your favourites isn't it?'

'Were you really writing or have you been to see Eleanor again?'

That hurt. 'No. Of course not. Why do you ask?'

'Going off like that. All day. I know she still holds some fascination for you. I know she does, Frank.'

'Well you're wrong. I've told you before.' Now she was irritating him.

Louisa hadn't moved; she was standing square on to him, her expression stony and unflinching. 'I thought you said Jo was harmless.'

He laughed at the absurdity of the remark, then regretted it. Louisa wasn't joking. Her mouth was pursed up in a tight button, her eyes hard with something he couldn't identify. Fear perhaps.

'What do you mean?' he asked. 'When did you see Jo?'

'I went to the shop. She walked back with me from the village.'

He nodded slowly. 'What did you talk about?'

'All sorts. As you do.'

'And she was asking questions again?'

'She went too far, Frank. She was virtually accusing me.'

'Of what?'

'She was playing games. Very clever games.' Louisa raised a finger and waved it at him. 'You see, this is what you expose me to when you leave me here alone. Why do you keep going off like that? And today of all days when I had something I particularly wanted to tell you.'

She put the back of her hand up to brush her cheek and turned away.

'Something you wanted to tell me? What was it?'

She walked to the wardrobe and pulled a light jacket off a hanger, shrugging it round her shoulders.

'It doesn't matter. I need to get something to eat. Shall we go?'

He walked across to her and put his arms around her. After a moment the anger fell away from her and she relaxed into his embrace, resting her head against his chest.

'Oh Frank, I'm sorry. I'm being…well, I'm not sure what I am. I guess I'm just feeling kind of vulnerable right now. My silly old hormones are playing up. But I do love you so. And I was excited and then disappointed because you weren't here.'

'I'm sorry too,' he murmured, stroking her hair. 'Going off by myself like that, it's just the way I am. It's the only way I can work. I don't mean to hurt you.'

'I know. I suppose I'll get used to it.'

'I hope so. I think I'm too old to change my ways now.'

'I hope you can change them a little.' She laughed softly into his rugby shirt. 'Darling you're going to have to.'

'What do you mean?'

She pulled away from him and looked up coyly. 'I'm late coming on, Frank.'

He frowned. 'You're late?'

'Oh come on, don't be obtuse. Don't you see what I'm trying to tell you?' She smiled. 'My period's late. And I did one of those tests earlier and it showed it. I'm pregnant, darling. Isn't that amazing? I didn't think I'd have this chance now at my age. I thought it had passed me by.'

Frank said nothing, staring at her.

'Well, aren't you pleased?' she said.

'But I thought you'd been taking precautions.'

'Darling, mistakes happen. But it feels like a thing to be. We'd better not tell anyone else just yet though. It's still so early, it might be tempting providence.' She stopped, looking concerned. 'Frank darling, I thought you'd be pleased.'

He pulled her close again, staring sightlessly over the top of her head. 'Yes…yes, of course I am. That's wonderful news. I'm just a little shocked. I'm… I mean, we didn't plan it, did we? I'll need time to get used to the idea.'

*

Jo rang ahead and visited The Moorhill Centre on the Saturday afternoon. It was an old granite building which stood in rolling countryside on the northern slopes of the moor. No doubt it had been a grand house in its time but it had been altered and extended over the years. It now offered twenty en suite rooms, some recreational space and a range of rehabilitation facilities - including a pool - mostly in modern single storey satellite buildings. The buildings were pleasingly light and airy and the staff were professional but friendly, giving her an extended tour. The current 'residents' seen in the sitting room and manoeuvring around the passageways and grounds appeared happy and at ease. There was no doubt Eleanor would be safe here for a while, cared for and helped to get stronger. It solved several problems at once and Jo embraced the idea gratefully. It did mean getting Eleanor's agreement however. More problematically, it also meant persuading Lawrence to sort out the financial implications.

Arriving back at Skymeet around five o'clock, Sidney again failed to meet her. He was becoming very independent. She was both pleased and perversely disappointed. Sidney had become a comforting companion and she missed having him round the house. He didn't appear all that evening and by the time she was ready to go to bed, there was still no sign of him. She went out into the garden and walked round, calling his name, pausing, waiting, but there was no answering yowl of recognition, no sudden movement from the trees or warmth at her ankles. In the end she had to go to bed without him in the house. It felt very empty and she struggled to get to sleep. It was the first time he had ever stayed out all night.

It was out of character and that bothered her.

Chapter 14

Jo was talking, very intense and animated, but Eleanor wasn't listening. She was remembering playing a duet on the piano with her niece when the girl hadn't long come to live with her. Jo would have been maybe sixteen or seventeen. No, sixteen. But what stuck in Eleanor's mind was that Jo had laughed. They had started playing an arrangement of a Scott Joplin rag for two people - which one she couldn't remember - and had both speeded up inexorably until they were racing through it. They had got out of time, then back in again, and had somehow managed to finish together. While the final chord was still vibrating round the room, they had both burst out laughing.

It was the first time Jo had laughed since she'd arrived at Skymeet, the first time Eleanor had heard her laugh since Candida had died.

'Eleanor, did you hear me?' Jo was saying now, frowning, her lovely face all puckered and serious.

'Mm? No, no. Sorry. I wasn't listening.' She fixed the girl with a look. 'You don't laugh enough, Jo.'

'Sorry?'

'You don't laugh enough. We used to laugh, didn't we?'

Jo smiled. What a relief. Every time she came to visit she looked so severe, so concerned.

'Yes we used to laugh,' said Jo. 'What were you thinking about exactly?'

'Playing duets,' said Eleanor. She still felt a thrill of pleasure at being able to speak so clearly. Duets wasn't something she could have said not long ago.

'Yes,' agreed Jo, 'we had fun playing the piano together, didn't we? We'll do that again soon.'

'Good.'

'But you need to get all your movements back first. That's why I was just telling you about the rehabilitation centre that the doctor mentioned. You'll get a lot of physiotherapy there and it'll get you back on your feet more quickly.'

'Re-hab-il-it…it-at-ion centre,' Eleanor repeated slowly.

'It's not far from Exeter, on the edge of Dartmoor.'

'I don't like hospitals. I want to go home.'

'I know. And I want you home. But I want you better, and going to the rehab centre will help you get better more quickly. It's not like this.' Jo waved a hand to roughly indicate the ward. 'It's not a hospital. I checked it out. It's more like a big hotel but with facilities to help you get stronger and independent again. You'll have physio and speech therapy like you do here but much more intensively. Other activities too. It's private so it has to be paid for but it's much quieter than here. Nice rooms. It'd be worth it. Gets great reviews.'

'Independent,' repeated Eleanor. Odd words or sentences tended to catch her attention and stick, making all the other words drift away from her. 'I hate asking for help.'

Jo smiled again. 'I know.'

'Is there something wrong?'

The smile faded. 'Wrong. What do you mean, wrong?'

'I don't know.'

'No, there's nothing wrong. I just want you to understand what the plan is. We need to make some arrangements and then you'll be out of here and away to the edges of Dartmoor.'

190

'Dartmoor.' Eleanor nodded. 'Cold then. I'll need jumpers. And gloves.'

Jo grinned this time. Eleanor didn't know why.

'It's August, Eleanor. I don't think it'll be that cold. So you're happy to go? It's important for you.'

Eleanor frowned. There was something her niece wasn't telling her but Eleanor felt like this a lot. She was cut out of the loop; people kept making decisions for her without consulting her. Doctors would talk about her - either with each other or with a nurse - standing at the end of her bed, as if Eleanor were deaf or perhaps not there at all, just a lump of flesh in the chair. Often she was sure they talked about her at the nurses' station, just out of her earshot. She could hear them laughing sometimes. Her impotence frustrated her.

'I'm not happy,' said Eleanor, still frowning. She leaned forward in the chair - a luxury now that she had regained some balance and didn't need to be fastened in. 'I know my brain is…isn't working right yet but I'm not stupid, Jo.' She paused, making an effort to enunciate and emphasise her next words. 'Everyone treats me as if I'm stupid. I'm just…mu-muddled. I know things but when I want to say them…it sometimes comes out wrong. Bloody annoying. That…' Eleanor pointed with a wagging finger. '…that doctor with the beard. Doesn't talk to me. Keeps patting me on the hand and smiling, nodding his head…' She nodded her own head to emphasise the point. '…like…like...those…those dogs in cars. I want to slap him.'

'Don't do that, Eleanor. You'll be leaving soon. But I do understand. It's frustrating for you. You're the cleverest person I know. Not stupid at all. And it's wonderful to see you getting better, day on day. But you have to trust me on this. Going to this rehab centre just for a short time is the best thing for you.' Jo hesitated, fixing her striking eyes on Eleanor's. 'I

191

wouldn't suggest it if I didn't think it was the right thing. You know I wouldn't.'

Eleanor studied the girl's face long and hard. She sat back, a little heavily.

'Yes.'

'So I can arrange it when the doctors are happy to discharge you from here?'

'Yes.' Eleanor sniffed. 'I hope the coffee is better than this stuff.' She waved a dismissive hand vaguely towards the door where the drinks trolley usually stopped.

'Now I know you're getting better.'

She looked smug, thought Eleanor. No, she looked relieved. Why? Eleanor knew she was missing something. And it was something she felt she ought to know, something she did know perhaps but couldn't quite grasp.

*

'The doctors recommended this place to me,' Jo said.

Lawrence was sitting at his desk, staring at the website of The Moorhill Centre. It was Monday morning and Jo had sent him the link from her phone, insisting that he look at it while she stood there, waiting.

'I went there on Saturday to look round,' she said, 'and spoke to a couple of the patients. The staff call them "residents". Anyway, they were very positive about how much it had helped and said it was comfortable there.'

'I should think it is,' said Lawrence. 'Have you seen the fees?'

'You're saying Eleanor can't afford it? I don't believe that.'

'Not exactly but I've told you before: she's not made of money these days. It's not something to rush into. It's expensive.'

'Because it offers great therapy and a comfortable environment. So sell some shares.' She gestured impatiently with her hands. 'Take out a loan. Get these supposed friends doing the workshops to pay their keep since you say they don't. It must be doable. It won't be for long but Eleanor needs it now, not next year. Or are you suggesting she doesn't warrant such treatment?'

He turned in his chair then and stared at her.

'If you could hear yourself, Jo. You sound like a petulant teenager.'

'And you sound like a pompous headmaster. I've spoken to Eleanor about this place. She likes the sound of it and has agreed to go. The centre has confirmed to me that they have a place. I've downloaded the form to fill in and I'll get the doctor to fill in the necessary parts of it. All I want you to do is organise the money. I'm just giving you warning. I'll keep a check on when she's being discharged.'

He smiled thinly. 'You've already taken it out of my hands.'

'I'm anxious to do whatever is best for Eleanor. I assumed you would be too.'

'Is Eleanor in a position to make this kind of decision? Does she know she's paying for it?'

'Yes, she knows. I'm tired of you trying to save Eleanor's money. It makes me wonder why. What better use of her money is there than to make her well again? The doctor recommended it. I explained that the place was private and Eleanor agreed. As far as I'm concerned that's good enough. I don't understand why it isn't for you too. Or do you have an agenda I don't know about?'

His expression darkened. 'I won't grace that with an

193

answer.' He turned back to his computer. 'Just give me the account details when all the arrangements have been made and I'll sort it out.' He flicked her a black look. 'And you can put your instructions in writing to me too. I'm not taking responsibility for this.'

'Fine.' She didn't move. 'Have you seen Sidney?'

Lawrence dragged his eyes from the computer screen again and settled a condescending gaze on her.

'The cat? No.'

'He's disappeared.'

'I warned you he might, if you remember. Push the door to as you leave, will you?'

Jo walked out of his office, bristling with anger and frustration. She made herself a mug of tea, exchanged a few words with Charlotte and went to Eleanor's office where she sat for several minutes, staring at her blank laptop but doing nothing.

Getting Lawrence to agree to the centre had been a victory of sorts but it felt small. That she had manipulated him didn't concern her much; that she was keeping things from Eleanor did bother her. But, since the fall, Eleanor had no filter; she often repeated what was said to her, sometimes hours or even days after the conversation. And she was brutally honest. If she thought it, it came out of her mouth. Like a child who has recently learned to talk, Eleanor seemed unwilling or unable to stay silent. Jo dared tell her nothing of importance, not until her aunt could understand its significance and keep it to herself.

She booted up her computer and tried to immerse herself in her current editing brief. Normally she would have enjoyed the distraction but she struggled to concentrate. There had been no sign of Sidney since he'd left the house on the

Saturday morning. Something had happened to him, she was sure. He wouldn't stay away from choice. Repeatedly she had called him and gone out searching for him but every time she had drawn a blank. Now, after three-quarters of an hour of fruitless screen time, she got up and went outside again, checking all his favourite places. Half an hour later, she walked down to the village and wrote a card to put in the window of the convenience store, describing him and asking for information to help find him, adding her phone number. On a whim she bought a packet of four sausage rolls and headed back to the house. Stowing the rolls, an apple and a can of fizzy orange in a cotton shoulder bag, she went down to the beach.

It was deserted. Harry didn't seem to have been down for a while; she had made a point of glancing down several times recently. Of course he was working part-time at the café now. Or maybe he'd found out that she had gone out with his father. That wasn't likely to have gone down well.

She walked to the water's edge and watched the waves rolling onto the shore and sucking back, eating up the beach. The tide was coming in. She retreated to a rock higher up and sat, her thoughts running in pointless circles. She hadn't found an opportunity to speak to Vincent yet but she could already guess how that would play out. Louisa must have been out on the estate and not just at the den as she first claimed or she wouldn't have seen Vincent going to the house. So he would probably accuse Louisa of suspicious behaviour just as she had accused him. It would be one person's word against another.

Jo remembered seeing Vincent lose his temper years ago and she remembered him sounding off when he'd had too much to drink. He could be arrogant at times, opinionated certainly - politically he used to be quite right wing - but he always used to back down when challenged. He was a weak character. There again, maybe being weak made him dangerous. Weak people sometimes overreacted didn't they? And he had been angry with Eleanor earlier that night. But what was Louisa doing out prowling the estate while Frank was away? Maybe Louisa was simply trying to put up a smoke screen. The more she saw of her the more that woman bothered her: Louisa had a steely, vindictive nature. What Jo wouldn't give to see inside her jewellery box.

A scuffing noise made her turn her head. Harry had just skidded and nearly fallen down the side of a rock as he picked his way round the cliff edge. He found a surer footing and paused, not far away, looking at her.

'Afternoon,' she said. 'Those flip-flops'll break your neck one day.'

'None of your damn business.'

'Don't swear at me, Harry. No, you're right. You wear what you want. It's your neck. But don't do it here and cause me a load of hassle will you?'

He looked at her long and hard, then moved closer and sat down.

'I must have known you'd be here today,' she remarked mildly. 'I bought sausage rolls for lunch. Want one?'

His eyebrows shot up; he nearly smiled. 'Yeah.'

She delved into the bag, pulled out the packet and ripped it open, offering it to him. He took a roll and bit into it greedily. Jo took one too. She hadn't eaten a sausage roll in years; it was surprisingly good.

'How's the work going at the coffee shop?'

'OK. I was there this morning.' He chewed another mouthful, rubbing flakes of pastry from his chin. 'It's a bit boring, doing the same stuff all the time.'

'Most work's repetitive. It's how you get good at something.'

'I'm not going to get good when dad doesn't trust me to make the coffee.'

'Ah.' She changed tack. 'So what do you want to do when you finish school?'

He shrugged. 'I dunno. I like engines. Maybe something with cars. Or a drummer in a band. 'Cept I haven't got a drum kit yet.'

He finished his sausage roll. She proffered the packet and he took another.

'Thanks.'

'Doesn't your dad feed you?'

'You should know. You went out with him. Someone told me they'd seen you together. I'm sure you had great fun discussing all my faults.'

So there it was, the grudge she knew was coming.

'We didn't talk about you, Harry.' She shrugged. 'We had a meal and a chat. We had a drink. That's all there was to it.' She grinned. 'Anyway, how many faults have you got?'

'Are you going to see him again?'

'Maybe.' She finished eating her roll and reached into the packet for the last one. 'Why? Does it matter?'

There was no answer. A seagull landed nearby and sidled towards them. Jo and Harry both waved an arm at the same moment and it skittered away up the beach. Harry finished eating and brushed off his fingers, then stared out to the incoming sea.

'I wish you'd let me tell him that we've met,' said Jo. 'If I explain, he won't mind that you've been coming here.'

'Yes he will. He probably won't say anything to you but he will. Then I'll get it in the ear back home. Again. He's

197

always on my case.'

'I don't like living a lie, Harry.'

'Then don't see him.' There was a painful silence. 'I don't see how you can be friends with him and with me.' He wouldn't look at her.

She choked back a sigh of frustration, reminding herself how young he was and how hurt. She remembered her own bravado after her mother died but it had all been show, probably fooling no-one but herself, and at least she'd had Eleanor.

'Don't do this, Harry. It's playground stuff. "You can't be friends with me if you're friends with him." My date with your dad doesn't affect our friendship. It was just a date. Casual. You've had dates, haven't you? They don't always mean anything. It was simply a relaxing evening. I don't get much down time what with hospital visiting and work.'

He looked at her. 'OK. But don't tell him I come here, right? You promised, remember?' He gave her a mischievous smile. 'Anyway it's kind of neat that he doesn't know.'

'For you, maybe.'

Jo finished eating and changed the subject. 'You haven't seen my cat anywhere, have you? You know, the grey one without a tail? He hasn't been home since Saturday.'

He shook his head. 'Cats stay out sometimes don't they? Especially in the summer when it's warm.'

'I guess.'

'Have you found out anything about that night?' His tone was conspicuously casual.

'No. Have you remembered anything more about it? Like the voice you heard maybe?'

'No.'

She gave up. She couldn't force him to tell her - and

maybe he didn't know.

'I'm going away on Saturday to stay with my aunt,' he said.

'Has she got kids?'

'Yeah. Two. Adrian's thirteen and his sister Cheryl's seventeen.'

'Looking forward to it?'

He shrugged.

Climbing the steps half an hour later, Jo's thoughts shifted to Sidney again; he was never far from her mind. It struck her now that he had disappeared just two days after that conversation she'd had with Louisa. Louisa again. Was that a coincidence?

She reached the garden as her phone rang. It was Matthew.

'I was just wondering,' he said diffidently. 'Harry's going away to stay with my sister for a few days. I thought maybe you'd like to come round? On Saturday maybe? It's a chance for me to cook something other than pizza or chips.'

She hesitated.

'Don't worry if you're busy,' he said. 'It was just a thought.'

She looked back towards the beach and the lad she couldn't see. She couldn't allow Harry to dictate who she saw and what she did.

'No, I'd love to come round. What time were you thinking?'

*

It was the following Thursday the eighteenth of August when Eleanor finally left hospital. Jo took her aunt in her car along with two suitcases of clothes. The Moorhill Centre wanted

Eleanor to have clothes suitable for 'activity' and Jo had gone shopping on Eleanor's behalf, buying lightweight sportswear that she knew her aunt would never normally wear. And good luck to the staff persuading her to wear it now, Jo thought as she packed it in the cases.

Driving away from the hospital, Eleanor was quiet, unusually so. Jo glanced across, concerned.

'Are you all right?'

'Yes.'

'Good.'

Jo felt inadequate, unsure how much or how little she needed to do for her aunt. How ill was she still? Eleanor had managed to walk a few steps with her niece's help from a wheelchair to the car but it seemed like only yesterday there had been tubes sticking out of her body everywhere and she could barely move a muscle. The speed of her improvement had taken everybody by surprise.

She glanced across again. Eleanor was staring out of the window. Jo made idle remarks about the festival and the workshops, trying to fill the silence. Still there was no reaction.

'I guess it's odd to be out again after all that time in hospital.'

The suggestion of a grunt. Jo cast about. Ever since the word Dartmoor had crossed Jo's lips, temperature seemed to be a pressing issue on her aunt's mind.

'Are you warm enough?'

'Yes.' Still Eleanor stared out of the window.

A few minutes passed. They drew to a halt at traffic lights.

'Are you cross with me?' said Jo.

Eleanor turned her head, eyes wide. 'Cross? No. Why should I be cross?'

'I'm not sure. You're very quiet.'

Eleanor looked away again. 'I'm scared. This place I'm going to…' She stopped speaking suddenly.

The lights changed and they moved off again. Again Jo glanced across. Maybe she was having a relapse; maybe the excitement of leaving the hospital had been too much for her.

'I don't know what to expect,' Eleanor said suddenly.

Jo breathed more easily. 'It'll be fine. Honestly. The people there are really nice. And it won't be long till you'll be able to come home. It's just a stepping stone.'

Another brief silence. 'I'm scared of going home too.'

Jo felt her insides lurch. Perhaps Eleanor had finally remembered how she came to fall.

'What makes you scared of going home?'

'I don't know. I remember home…I think…' Again a pause. '…but it feels unreal.' A long, stretched silence. 'And there's something else.'

Jo could barely breathe, waiting, but Eleanor didn't elaborate. 'What?' she asked eventually, taut and impatient.

'I don't know,' repeated Eleanor. 'I don't know what it is.'

She said nothing more. Jo negotiated a busy roundabout and turned onto the road that would take them across the moor. It was a bright, clear day. Hopefully the views would be stunning. She became aware of Eleanor staring at her.

'Is there a reason I should be scared?' her aunt demanded, frowning.

'No.' Jo spoke too quickly. 'Of course not. What made you ask that?'

Eleanor didn't reply and they travelled much of the rest of the way in silence. Jo wondered at the speed and ease with which she had just lied - and how long she could or should keep this up.

Chapter 15

'This was stuck in the handle of the gate,' said Charlotte. 'I was just reaching to put the code in and there it was. It's addressed to you.'

Jo frowned, taking the offered envelope. It was a long, white anonymous affair with *J. Lambe* typed on the front. She felt the blood drain from her face and slipped an anxious finger under the flap of the envelope, ripping it open. It held one sheet of white A4 paper and a couple of typed lines of text:

> Your cat is shut up in the shed at the demolition site. You should be more careful. Just think of all the awful things that could happen to him otherwise.

'It's about Sidney isn't it? I knew it would be.' Charlotte was watching her face anxiously. She had fretted over the cat's disappearance almost as much as Jo had.

Jo looked up, her face pinched. 'Yes.'

She turned the sheet over but there was nothing else on it. No identifying marks, nothing. It was a typical sheet from a pack of inkjet printer paper, used by millions. It could have come from anyone - inside or outside the estate. She handed Charlotte the note.

'The demolition site?' Jo queried. 'What does that mean?'

Charlotte quickly read it. 'It'll be The Old Orchard. You must have seen it. The house there has been fenced off for ages. It's derelict. Someone bought the site to redevelop but went bust or something. There's all sorts of legal wrangling going on. I'm sure there's a shed at the back of it somewhere.' Jo was looking at her blankly. 'It's up beyond the pub, the first lane on the right and a short way along on the right again. You can see it from the main road. But who'd leave a note like that? I mean…'

'I'll go and look,' said Jo, snatching the paper back.

'It might be a trick,' Charlotte called to her retreating back. 'Be careful.'

The lane was narrow with a field on the left and a straggle of houses on the right. Jo passed a cottage and an overgrown orchard and then she was there. Charlotte was right: the place stood out. A mess of high metal fencing surrounded the gardens of an old double-fronted house with broken windows. The grass at the front was knee high and rubbish and dead leaves were piled up in drifts along the path to the door. A couple of the metal barriers had tilted and shifted, by accident or intent it was hard to tell, but it was easy to get between them. Jo glanced round uneasily. Was it a bad joke? A trap of some kind? Either way she had no choice but to check it out.

She eased between two barriers and walked up the path, calling Sidney's name. There was no answering sound. Reaching the house she turned left. There was a path of a sort here too, but barely visible. She glanced in at a grubby window - there was no furniture and no sign of life.

Around the back she came on a large square garden with the suggestions of ancient flower beds and a rusting rotary airer rammed in the middle of what had once been the lawn. And beyond the lawn was a shed, overhung by trees, its roof covered in mould and lichen, its one window intact but cloudy with dirt. Again she called Sidney's name. This time, she was sure she heard something. She walked closer and called again. Definitely, yes, a little squeaky answer. Her throat choked up and tears clouded her eyes.

'It's OK, Sidney, I've found you.'

There was a padlock looped through the hook and bar on the door but thankfully it hadn't been pushed in and locked. She was clumsy in her haste to undo it but finally pulled the door back.

Rusting garden tools were propped up against the walls and shelves held dirty plastic and terracotta pots. An ancient lawnmower stood to one side and the floor was strewn with lengths of cable, more tools, half-filled plastic compost bags and filthy pieces of cloth and canvas. There were more plant pots on the floor too and a pile of plastic and ceramic plant pot saucers had toppled over, many of them broken.

In among the dirt and mess stood Sidney, shaking, eyes wide and suspicious, watching her. He didn't move. Jo bent down and slowly put her hand towards him so he could smell her. He was filthy and painfully thin. He couldn't have had anything to eat since she had last seen him. One of the plastic saucers lay on the floor nearby. Maybe someone had put water in it for him, maybe not, but it was dry now. It looked like he had been sick. He emitted another pitiful squeak and took an unsteady step towards her. Jo gently picked him up and held him close, murmuring nonsense to him. She didn't care that he smelt or that he was dirty. She was so relieved to have found him, the tears ran down her cheeks.

'What bastard did this to you, Sidney, hm?' she murmured. 'Who was it, hey? It's OK. You're all right now.'

She took him home, cradling him in her arms. She'd got the message: she had been asking too many questions and someone had sent her a warning. And they had used a defenceless animal to do it. She was incensed.

*

Matthew took Harry to Totnes station on the Saturday morning and waited to see his train leave. The lad had money in his pocket - not as much as he would have liked but enough - and a week's worth, hopefully, of clean clothes in his huge sports bag. He also had his tablet computer and a couple of car magazines. The boy had refused to take a suitcase because it looked 'so retro'. It felt odd to see him go. Matthew had half expected to feel a sense of release, of freedom - Harry would be Karen's responsibility for a little while - but he didn't. There was just a different kind of concern.

He drove home and worked at Millie's until the lunch rush abated then spent the rest of the afternoon at the house, cleaning and tidying. At five o'clock he went upstairs again, making sure he hadn't missed anything. He hadn't bothered much with Harry's room - just a cursory tidy up since it was a lost cause anyway and Jo wouldn't see it - but the bathroom had to be right. Earlier he had found a damp towel rammed on the back of the door and a single dirty sock of Harry's behind the cupboard in the corner and never retrieved. It had been there an embarrassingly long time too: it was covered in dust. And then there was his own mess. He thought he kept the bathroom reasonably clean but, looking at it as he thought Jo might, he had noticed the scale on the washbasin, the spattering of toothpaste on the mirror over the top and the sloppiness of the cheap old soap. Sophie would have been appalled.

Now, however, the bathroom was spotless. One last look at his bedroom. The bed was carefully made, his clothes put away. Though there was no reason for Jo to see his bedroom either. It was too soon for that. What was he thinking? Of course it was too soon. He wasn't ready for that kind of relationship and God only knew what Jo would think.

He went back down to the kitchen and began preparing the meal. He was making a roasted vegetable and cheese frittata accompanied by salad and French bread. There had been some chef on the TV the other week demonstrating the recipe and it looked tasty but not too difficult. Matthew laid the table and tried to make it look nice. Sophie had always been good at that.

'Don't hate me for doing this,' he muttered to her.

It was what he used to say to her when he was about to do something he knew she disliked. 'Maybe not hate you,' she would say and smile. She had a cheeky smile sometimes, mischievous, and he had loved it.

But this time there was no answering reply in his head. Busy trying to figure out what to do next, he didn't notice.

*

Jo stood in front of the mirror, turning this way and that. The dress clung to her body, emphasising every curve. She pulled a face at her reflection. She had been invited for a casual home-cooked meal by someone she barely knew. It sent out the wrong signals; she wasn't on a mission of seduction. She wanted to keep it low key, wanted to relax and talk and keep it simple. Except that it wasn't simple, not when she was hiding the fact that she knew Harry.

She peeled the dress off and threw it on the bed in disgust. The only reason she had this dress and others like it was because Richard had liked her in figure-hugging clothes. What was it Eleanor had said that night on the phone about not trying to be something you're not just to please someone else? It was about time she did some shopping.

Twenty minutes later, wearing a pair of flared slinky trousers and a loose sleeveless top, a cotton cardigan thrown around her shoulders, she made her way down to the village and stopped at the store to buy a bottle of wine. She stared at the unimpressive choice. OK so red or white?

'Finally,' said a voice behind her.

Jo turned to find Imogen looking at her reprovingly, Mari one step back.

'We were coming to see you and saw you heading for the footpath,' said Mari. 'We've been trying to catch up.'

'You walk too fast,' Imogen accused her.

'Why did you want to see me?'

'We're going out tomorrow for the day,' said Imogen. 'There's an open air performance of *A Midsummer Night's Dream* in the grounds of Spellerton House, in Dorset...'

'And we thought you might like to come,' interrupted Mari. 'You spend so much time alone in that big house. Join us, why don't you? Frank and Louisa are coming. Vincent's going somewhere else but that means there'll be room in Imogen's car for a little one like you.'

'It's a bit of a drive,' said Imogen, 'but we're going make a trip out of it. It starts at two and tickets are on a first come, first served basis so we'll have to get there early. If we leave at nine we'll have time to stop for lunch.'

'Do say you'll come,' said Mari eagerly.

'I'd love to but I can't, I'm sorry. I'll be going to see Eleanor.'

'Oh dear, yes,' said Mari. 'Lawrence told us she'd moved to some centre. Is it a good place?'

'Yes. Very. And very private.'

'Good. But we're sorry you can't come.'

Imogen was looking at Jo speculatively.

'Buying wine?' she said meaningfully, eyebrows raised. 'Dressed up? You look as if you're going somewhere special.'

'Oh, wonderful,' said Mari. 'Someone did say that they'd seen you the other night with a man. I'm so glad.'

'Yes. Do tell, Jo.' Imogen's gaze was fixed on her, eyebrows raised. 'Who's the lucky guy?'

'I'm seeing a friend,' Jo said quickly. 'That's all.'

She grabbed a bottle of red wine, any wine, and went to the till, leaving the two women studying the bottles and arguing about what they should buy for themselves. But when she left the shop a few minutes later, Imogen was watching her.

*

The house wasn't hard to find. 'The last one in the thatched terrace,' Matthew had said and he opened the door almost before she had finished ringing the bell, welcoming her in with a cautious smile.

'I'm sorry I'm late.' She thrust the bottle at him. 'I can't vouch for the wine. The choice wasn't great.'

'Thanks, but you shouldn't have.'

They were in a narrow hall with a straight run of stairs ahead. He ushered her through a doorway to the right into a low-ceilinged sitting room with a couple of armchairs positioned around an open fireplace. A television stood on a cupboard in one corner.

'I've got some Prosecco chilled,' said Matthew. 'Would you like a glass?'

'Please.'

He slipped through a door at the back of the room into the kitchen. She could hear the sound of a fridge opening.

'Where does your sister live?' she called through.

'Gloucester. I put Harry on the train this morning. And he's arrived safely. Karen - that's my sister - texted me.'

Jo shuffled restlessly, glancing round. There was a framed snap of Harry on a cupboard against the side wall - the only photograph on view - and she crossed to look at it. The boy was on the beach, naked but for swimming trunks, posing with a cricket bat in front of two sticks rammed into the sand, his bony chest puffed up proudly, grinning happily.

'Harry was eight when that was taken,' said Matthew, reappearing and handing her a glass. 'He was big into cricket at the time.'

'Does he like staying with his aunt?'

'Yes, but not for too long. He hasn't been there for a while. He gets on OK with his cousins. She's got a boy and a girl. Karen's very organised and likes to make sure everyone else is too. Her kids are used to it but Harry isn't. We were never like that.'

Jo smiled, unsure what to say.

'Have a seat.'

'Thanks.'

Matthew drank a little wine, fidgeting in the chair, glancing at his watch.

'I hope you haven't gone to too much trouble with dinner,' Jo said and immediately wished she hadn't. So trite.

'I've enjoyed it.' An awkward pause. 'It was...just an idea I had. I...well, I don't cook much but I find I quite like it. It's very absorbing.' The words petered out. 'So...how's your aunt?'

'Improving, thanks. In fact she's been discharged. I took her to a rehab centre up on Dartmoor yesterday and called back there today. She's settling in.'

'That's a good sign. I'm glad.'

He sounded like he meant it. How good to be able to talk about her aunt with someone who had no agenda with her.

'How long is she likely to be there?' he asked.

'The doctor said three or four weeks could make a big difference to her movement.'

'And her memory?'

'The jury's still out on that one.'

Matthew nodded, thoughtful, then grinned.

'My only knowledge of rehabilitation units comes from watching Bond movies. Spies round every corner. In fact, if the therapists are as glamorous as the ones in the films, let me know - I want to go there too.'

She laughed. 'I will, but I think you might be disappointed. Still, hopefully she'll like it there. There's one thing you can be sure of with Eleanor: if she doesn't, she's bound to let me know about it.'

'I love her spirit,' said Matthew.

'So do I. Though not when she's throwing things at me.'

It was his turn to laugh. 'She throws things?'

'Not so much recently. But the head injury has, let's say, brought out her angry side.'

'Will she be well enough to come to the festival do you think?'

'I doubt it. It'll be too soon.'

'Whatever, I hope the festival goes well. She got some flak for setting the thing up so it would prove her critics wrong.'

'Flak? What sort of flak?'

'Oh, you know: people who don't like the idea of the place being taken over by "coachloads of pseudo-intellectuals".' He grinned again. 'There is just a hint of exaggeration there. No-one's expecting even one coach. Hell, how would it get down the lane?'

'And Eleanor knew about this?'

He shrugged. 'I think so. I think we discussed it at an early meeting but most people were happy about it. Though if you're not interested in books and don't have a business to run, I suppose it might feel intrusive.'

'It's only for a weekend, Matthew,' she said defensively.

'Hey, don't shoot the messenger. I'm not expressing my views.' He glanced at his watch again. 'Let's eat, shall we? We do it in the kitchen here. I hope that's all right.'

It was a plain pine table laid with brightly-coloured place settings, neatly arranged cutlery and napkins. Matthew served a golden frittata onto two plates and put a bowl of salad and a basket of sliced baguette on the table, inviting her to help herself. The atmosphere had noticeably eased. She began to relax. He offered red wine - his own - and they started to eat.

'This is good,' said Jo.

'Thanks. I'm relieved.'

'So does Harry phone you when he's away, or is he too grown up for that?'

'Only if there's a problem. I think I've mentioned before that he's not big into communication these days.'

'Were you when you were his age?'

'Probably not. But Karen took it upon herself to speak for both of us so I didn't need to.'

Jo took a sip of wine. 'Assuming she represented your views, that is.'

'Trust me, it was easier to go with the flow either way.'

'Really? I find that hard to believe. You don't strike me as someone who goes with the flow much.'

'No? So how do I strike you?'

211

She flushed. 'Oh I don't know. Forthright; strong-willed; not the sort of man to let his sister dictate to him.'

'You make me sound scary.'

'I didn't mean it that way.'

They fell silent for several minutes. Jo tried to think of a way of dropping her meetings with Harry into the conversation. But the words *you promised* kept ringing through her head. She kept eating.

Matthew finished first and picked up his wine glass. 'I looked up your mother on the internet the other day. I seem to be the only person on the committee who doesn't know much about books and writers so I thought perhaps I should.'

'You could just have asked me.'

'Yes. But Nancy said your mother died young. I thought it might be better to look her up first. I read about her accident. I am sorry. I got the impression that she was quite a character. Like Eleanor I suppose.'

'Yes and no. They were both strong personalities but had very different temperaments. Eleanor's passionate and life-loving but quite disciplined. Organised. Mum was...' She smiled sadly. '...I dunno: big-hearted and self-indulgent, kind but had no self-control. Gifted. She tasted extreme success too young and nothing quite lived up to her expectations after that.'

He frowned. 'Sounds sad. I'm sorry.'

'It was a waste and yet...' She shrugged. '...I can't imagine her growing old somehow. She hit life running and she'd never have coped with slowing down.'

'That's a nice way to think of it.' He seemed to get lost in thought.

For dessert they ate raspberries with vanilla ice-cream and talked casually about the coffee shop and how busy everywhere was. Jo told him about Sidney's incarceration but passed it off as an accident, unwilling to tell him the full contents of the note or her suspicions. What had happened to Eleanor was too tied up with Harry now.

Afterwards, with fresh glasses of wine, they returned to the sitting room. She noticed a book on the lower shelf of the coffee table and picked it up.

'Frank's poetry. I didn't know you had this.' She opened it and was pulled up short. 'Oh, sorry. It was Sophie's.'

'Yes. It's OK.'

'This book's out of print now but I've got a copy back in Sussex. Well, you know how much I love his poetry.' She began to flick through it. 'Your wife must have loved it too. She's marked so many pages.' Jo found the poem about the bees and scanned it again, her fingers automatically smoothing down the dog-eared corner. 'Was it meeting Frank that made you get this out?'

'Not really. It was you. Quoting him to me like that. I remembered that Sophie had something of his. It was…surreal to find that you liked his poetry too.' He pressed his lips together, fingers clenching. 'Please don't do that. Sophie always turned the corner over on things she wanted to go back to.'

Jo stopped, only then realising what she was doing. 'Sorry.' She carefully pressed the fold back into place, closed the book and put it back under the coffee table. She took a sip of wine, glancing across at him.

'It sounds like we'd have had a lot in common. Which other writers did she like?'

He pulled a dismissive face. 'I'm not sure. There were lots.'

'I'm the same. So many authors and so little time to read.'

213

'It's a bit of a busman's holiday for you, isn't it, reading?'

'It can be. It has to be something that really absorbs me.' She made a point of looking round the room. 'You haven't got a photo of Sophie up. I'd love to see one.'

He shook his head. 'I'm sorry. No.'

'No?'

He stared at her, frowning. 'You're doing that thing, aren't you? Trying to get me to talk about her. Why do women do this?'

Jo's eyes narrowed. 'Do what? Show an interest? Care?'

'Care? Is that what you call it?' His tone of voice had changed. He was cross and defensive.

'Yes. Of course it is. I care. Sophie is part of you so I'd like to know more about her. Is that so unreasonable? And, yes, I guess it might help you not to keep it all trapped inside. It can eat you up can't it?'

'Well it doesn't help,' he said, voice rising. 'It won't bring her back. I tried all that nonsense before, after... Karen insisted I saw a counsellor. It just brought back all the pain, mountains of it. I'm not doing that again.'

'I see.' She stared into her wine glass, swirling the red liquid round in the bottom of it. 'I'm sorry.'

When she looked up Matthew was rubbing the flesh of his thumb back and forth across the side of the wine glass.

'I know, don't tell me: I should be getting over it by now.' He flicked her a bitter, angry look. 'I've heard it a thousand times. Everyone's so full of advice but no-one knows the hell other people have to go through.'

She finished the remains of her wine and put the glass down with deliberate care.

'You're absolutely right. They don't. But you can't keep blaming everyone else for your own pain either. Or for trying

214

to help, can you? It seems to me that you can't move on with your life without coming to terms with the past. Shutting it up and throwing away the key doesn't work.' She stood up. 'I don't want to argue though. Can I use your bathroom?'

He looked up, surprised. 'Top of the stairs and to the left. There's a light switch at the bottom on the right.'

The bathroom smelt of cleaning fluid and sparkled. Jo took her time washing her hands, regrouping her thoughts. She liked Matthew. A lot. Part of her wanted to hold him and soothe away his pain. She understood pain. But another part wanted to shout at him, force him to step outside himself and see what he was doing both to himself and to his son. He felt wronged - Sophie had been stolen from him - but his resentment was shutting everyone out and a shouting match wouldn't change that.

She exited the bathroom and hesitated on the landing. There were two other doors, both a few inches open. The nearest one had a *Beware* sign on it and a picture of a skull and crossbones. She heard the armchair creak downstairs as Matthew stood up and she waited, listening. There was a clink of glasses. He had gone back into the kitchen. She pushed the nearest door back a little. It swung silently and she took a step inside. Clearly this was Harry's bedroom.

It was untidy and cluttered though the bed had been made and assorted clothes had been loosely folded and stacked up. Every wall was covered in dark, fantasy posters. To her right stood a tall chest of drawers and, right at the back, behind an abandoned baseball cap and a couple of comics was a framed photograph. She edged closer and picked it up. This was the photo Harry had mentioned. A younger version of the boy stood with a woman and the likeness between them was evident. They were laughing at something out of shot. Jo

215

examined it, sucking her lower lip. Sophie looked so young and pretty and vital and now she was gone. *No-one knows the hell other people have to go through.*

Putting the picture back she noticed Harry's broken phone, the one with all his old photos on. It had been pushed behind the photo frame out of sight and left there, gathering dust. On an impulse she picked it up, slipped it into her pocket and went back downstairs.

Matthew was still on his feet when she entered the room, standing square on, facing her.

'I'm sorry,' he said. 'I was out of line there. Completely out of line.'

'Forget it.'

'No, I am sorry. Really.' He pointed to her glass which was back on the coffee table, not quite half full. 'I divided up the last of the wine. Is that OK?'

'Thanks. But I ought to go. My cat's had a rough week. He's pretty shook up. I don't want to leave him too long.'

Matthew didn't respond, examining her face, dragging a restless hand across his cheek. No doubt it sounded like an excuse and maybe it was, partly.

'Look Jo, I know people mean well but sometimes I just can't cope with it all. It's in the past and I want to leave it there. I feel safer like that. Does that make sense? But I didn't want to offend you. You least of all.'

'I'm not offended. Look, I'd better be getting back.'

'I've frightened you away.'

'No.' She sighed. 'No, Matthew, and yes. I realise it's not me you're angry with but it is intimidating.'

'I know. I can see that.' He reached out and took her hand. 'Please say you'll give me another chance. You're right, I need to come to terms with it all. And I will, somehow. Really.' He

216

lifted her hand up to his lips and kissed it. She smiled and he kept hold of it, pulling her closer, kissing her softly on the mouth, gentle but insistent. He pulled away as suddenly as he'd started and looked down, taking a long breath, then back up into her eyes. 'Can I see you again? Please say I can. I promise I won't bite your head off next time. That was unforgiveable.'

She held his gaze. He had kind eyes, honest too. Not that she had a great record at judging men. But she could see the pain there as well; he was haunted. She looked away, uncertain. Even so, she found herself saying yes.

'Thank you.' He put his arms round her and held her tightly, rocking her gently.

Walking home a few minutes later, she suspected she was going head first down yet another rabbit hole.

Chapter 16

Sunday morning dawned fine. It was bright and fresh and still. Frank hadn't slept well and got up early, sliding out of the bed as smoothly as he could. It was an unnecessary precaution: he had never known a woman who slept as deeply as Louisa. Even the agitation of her dreams only rarely woke her. He envied her that rest.

He relieved himself and dressed in the bathroom, grabbed his notebook and pen and left the apartment. Outside he shivered lightly in the chill. It was nearly seven o'clock and sunshine already cast shadows on the ground and lit the treetops in yellows and golds. There was no-one else around, no sign of life from the other apartments and he liked it that way. The world was his for a little while, silent, expectant, welcoming.

After a moment's hesitation, he found his steps leading him towards the house. He yearned for the sanctuary of its grounds. He missed them. Or was it Eleanor he missed? So much of his life had been spent with her in and around that house. The previous summer, staying for a few weeks in one of the apartments, brave with his new freedom from their tumultuous love affair, proud of their adult attitude to the final break up, it had all been an adventure. He had met Louisa. Everything felt possible. But it had been an illusion; the cords that bind you to someone else don't break that easily. Some of

218

them are invisible, impossible to get hold of let alone to cut.

He turned left along a track through the shrubs and trees and only crossed the entrance road far from the eyes of the house. He didn't think Lawrence was an early riser but he wasn't taking any chances. If Jo was up and around, so be it; he thought she would understand. He opened the gate to the rear garden, lifting the latch carefully to avoid its metallic ring and silently passed through. Now he was in among the skirt of Eleanor's private grounds, the pittosporum bushes, the late-flowering roses, a weeping crab apple tree. This section of the garden arched up above the lower ground of Lawrence's annexe and the vegetation made the path invisible from his windows.

He paused, savouring the peace. Out of sight, birds sang mellifluously as if determined to make the summer last. A large bumble bee buzzed slowly past him like a miniature helicopter; he saw it land on the purple flower head of a buddleia bush to his right. To his left was the bench with its arch of trellis over the top where a clematis clambered. When he had first seen this garden it had been little more than a stretch of weedy lawn and some overgrown flowerbeds. The woods had been trying to reclaim the land for themselves. Eleanor had had a vision for it even then though it had taken years for it to come to fruition.

He walked on, carefully negotiating the path furthest from the house till he came out on the lower terrace. He glanced towards the rocks and bushes marking the edge and the fall beyond, then across at the steps. An image of Eleanor in her hospital bed, ashen and flaccid loomed into his mind. Jo had told them she was a little better now, talking occasionally about the past and walking short distances. Lawrence had informed them on Friday that she had gone to a rehabilitation unit. He ought to go and see her again but that was more complicated than ever now.

Frank retreated from the terrace and sat on the bench under the clematis. A red admiral butterfly fluttered past, a tortoiseshell soon after, both heading for the buddleia and its nectar-heavy flowers. He used to sit here quite often when he lived here; Eleanor knew but never bothered him when he was trying to write.

The news of Louisa's pregnancy still resonated in his head. He didn't know what to think. Many years ago, he and Eleanor had wanted children but it hadn't happened for them and, after a few tests, they found Eleanor couldn't. They might have gone down the adoption route but too many arguments and too many break-ups had intervened and they didn't pursue it. After that he'd put it out of his mind. But now Louisa had presented him with the prospect of fatherhood again and this time it was a fait accompli. He knew he should be excited but he felt too old for it now. He had changed; he was set in his ways. He was a little bit scared.

And there was suspicion too. Louisa was thrilled about the baby yet she described it as a mistake. So was it a mistake or had she chosen not to fit her cap one night...without telling him? Who was this woman he was living with exactly? Every time he thought he had a take on her, she changed, undergoing a subtle mutation.

He got his notebook and pen out of his pocket. He did it from habit, to be ready, but there hadn't been much writing lately; he couldn't concentrate. If he was honest, he hadn't written anything really special since he'd left Eleanor. He took a deep breath and closed his eyes, listening to the hum of the insects, the cries of the gulls and the soft roar of waves on the shore down below. He stayed that way for several minutes but no words came. Instead he thought about Louisa again. Increasingly he felt that he was being manipulated. She kept trying to curtail his working pattern and now this. She was already making plans for the three of them. Her plans. He needed to find a space to talk to her, clear the air maybe. If they were going to bring a child up together he had to stop drifting in this relationship and set some of his own boundaries and not constantly jig to her tune. That was simply not going to work and she needed to know that.

Then he remembered that they were going out with Mari and Imogen to see *A Midsummer Night's Dream*. Hell, he wouldn't go. If he had the whole day to himself he might actually get something done and he badly needed to do that. When he couldn't write he felt stifled, as if he couldn't breathe or would burst from trying.

He put the notebook away, left the garden and made his way back purposefully towards the apartment to tell Louisa.

*

For Jo, the morning dragged. She was tired, anxious and jumpy. It had taken hours for her to get to sleep the night before, the roller-coaster evening with Matthew circulating on a loop in her head, alternating with her hare-brained plans for the morning.

She had convinced herself that it was Louisa who had caused Eleanor's fall and when Jo had started asking too many questions, Louisa had taken Sidney and shut him away. And Frank had pointedly tried to stop her from approaching his fiancée. That was suspicious in itself. Did he know something about it? What was he hiding? With everyone going out today Jo knew it was her best opportunity to get into the woman's flat and finally find some proof.

221

It was already ten-thirty and the fine weather of the early morning had broken; clouds were scudding overhead on a brisk breeze and showers intermittently peppered the windows. Jo had acquired the spare key to Louisa's apartment from the key box under the stairs and it sat tauntingly in the pocket of her capri pants. Mari had said they would leave at nine but Jo hung around, procrastinating, glancing nervously out of the front windows. There was no movement around the apartments. Then she saw Lawrence, sports bag in hand, leaving for one of his regular gym trips. She waited another five minutes, then left the house.

Dark clouds loured and a gloom had descended; it felt more like October than August. Rain pattered rhythmically on the roofs of the apartments as she approached. They all appeared deserted and there were no lights on. She headed to number five, glancing in at the window casually as she passed then stopping, looking round the courtyard and peering in again. There was no-one there. She slipped the key in the lock, turned it and went inside, closing the door softly behind her.

Jo had been in these studio flats before. They were all much the same: a double bed, assorted laminated furniture for storage, a couple of small armchairs, a small desk with a lamp and an electric kettle with a courtesy tray for making drinks. A door led through to the bathroom. In this flat, the bed was unmade, the lower sheet badly rucked, the upper sheet - and the thin coverlet over it - thrown back wildly and trailing on the floor. A pair of ladies' house slippers had been abandoned near the wardrobe where they had been kicked off. A half-drunk mug of tea stood on the dressing table. It looked like a room that had been left in a hurry. Perhaps they had got up late.

There was no jewellery box visible. Did Louisa even have

a box with her? If she kept her jewellery in separate bags or boxes, it could take ages to check what she was missing. The dressing table had one central drawer and two on each side. Jo opened the first on the left. It contained knickers and bras. The drawer below contained socks and tights, some in packets, some screwed up in a ball. The central drawer held a box of paper tissues, a packet of wet wipes, a few small notebooks and an assortment of pens. Already she feared this was going to be a waste of time.

A noise had her nervously glancing back at the door but there was no-one there. The rain still fell and it was darker than ever. She flicked a switch to turn the wall light on over the dressing table.

There was a jewellery box after all, a small wooden one with an inlaid lid, hidden under headscarves in the top drawer on the right. Jo pulled it out and laid it on top of the dressing table. It had no lock and she flipped the lid back. The box was lined with velvet and a run of small earrings on straight posts had been pushed into a ridge along the back. She pulled the stud she had found out of her pocket but knew without checking that it didn't match any of the ones she could see. In any case, they were all in pairs. A loose tray in front of the ridge held a couple of bracelets and several pairs of large drop earrings with hooked posts. Underneath the tray lay a variety of necklaces, mostly beads, all jumbled and knotted together. There was no sign of a solo earring stud.

She straightened up, blowing out a long, frustrated breath. Perhaps this was a wild goose chase. Maybe she had been wrong and it wasn't Louisa's stud after all or maybe the woman had thrown the pair of it away. Did people do that with jewellery? Wouldn't you keep it on the off-chance and perhaps keep looking for the missing stud? Maybe not if you were scared you'd lost it somewhere incriminating. But this was gold. So perhaps Louisa had hidden the remaining stud somewhere. She abandoned the jewellery box where it lay and turned, looking round the room.

'Where would I hide a stud?' she muttered to herself. 'Among my clothes?'

Desperate to prove her theory about Louisa right, she turned back and ferreted obsessively through the remaining drawers, plunging into every corner, finding nothing. The other smaller chest of drawers contained only Frank's clothes. The wardrobe had shelves and hanging rails and most of it was filled with Louisa's things. Jo delved into pockets and felt behind sweaters. Wrapped up in her task, she didn't hear the door opening, nor the light squelch of a damp foot on the floor.

'What the hell do you think you're doing?'

The voice was male and angry. She spun round.

'Frank. Hi. I...' She didn't know what to say. There was no disguising what she was doing. She watched his gaze sweep the room. 'I thought you'd gone out with the others.'

'Clearly. Sorry to disappoint you. What are you looking for?'

Still she hesitated, searching for a plausible excuse but finding none. She had known Frank a very long time; his relationship with Louisa was a mere drop in the ocean in comparison. She could risk honesty and hope he would hear her out.

'An earring.'

His face crumpled into disbelief. 'An earring? Are you kidding me? Why are you looking in here?'

'I'm looking for the matching pair to this one.'

She took a couple of steps towards him, holding the stud out on the palm of her hand to show him, watching his face.

Frank looked down at her hand, still frowning, then back up at her.

'Why are you looking at me like that, Jo? What weird game is this you're playing?'

'I wish it were a game, Frank. I found this earring on the terrace near where Eleanor fell. You know the place. No-one else goes there much. It's Eleanor's favourite spot.'

His eyes narrowed. 'You're suggesting it has something to do with her fall? And to judge from your accusing expression, you think that the person who wore this was responsible for it?'

'It's possible.'

His expression hardened. 'And you're looking through Louisa's jewellery to prove it's hers.' It wasn't a question this time.

'I'm looking just to check. What was I supposed to do? I couldn't ask her, could I? Look at it from my point of view.'

He gave a hollow laugh. 'I'm shocked at you, Jojo. This is beneath you. Louisa has no reason to want to harm Eleanor. On the contrary, Eleanor was the one who might have felt wronged and bitter, if anyone, not Louisa.' He glanced back at the earring. 'Have you shown it to the police?'

'No. I wanted something more definite to tell them.'

'I should damn well hope so before you start accusing innocent people and destroying their reputation. And that...' He pointed at the stud. '...is meaningless. In any case, it isn't Louisa's.' He hesitated. 'It's most likely to be Eleanor's. Have you thought of that?'

'Of course. But I checked her jewellery and she doesn't own anything like this. She doesn't recognise it either.'

'If she'd lost it, maybe she threw the pair away. And the way her memory is, she wouldn't recognise it, would she?

You've no idea how long that tiny thing has been hanging around on the terrace. Really, Jo, it's about time you got a life. You're becoming neurotic and small-minded.'

'How dare you? Can you blame me for looking out for Eleanor - after all she's done for me?'

'And this helps her?' He looked round the flat, at the half open drawers and the jewellery box with the lid thrown back. 'Intruding into other people's lives, making accusations you can't possibly back up. Frankly I find your behaviour offensive. I want you to leave. Now. And don't ever abuse your position here to trespass again.'

'Frank, please just listen…'

'Now, Jo, before I lose my temper.'

Walking back to the house in the rain, the stud clutched in her hand, Jo felt alternately angry with Frank - she had hoped for better - and a fool. Maybe the earring was Eleanor's after all and maybe it had been a dumb theory. It didn't change the fact that someone had been up on the terrace with Eleanor though because Harry had heard the row. Sooner or later she was going to have to break her promise to him and tell someone. Sooner, she thought, before Eleanor comes home.

*

Louisa didn't arrive back until nearly eight o'clock. She swept into the studio flat like a summer breeze, smiling, cheerful, the argument of the morning with Frank apparently forgotten. Pregnancy clearly suited her; she looked lovelier than ever.

He was waiting for her, sitting reading, eyes glued to the page but taking little in. He looked up as she came in.

'Had a good day?' he enquired.

'Absolutely. You should have come. We had a wonderful lunch at a wayside inn nestling by a river somewhere.' She threw her bag and jacket on the bed and came across to drape herself across his knee. He put his book down and let her, putting his arms around her. 'And the play was wonderful.'

'I thought it might have been called off. We had a lot of rain here earlier.'

She leaned in and kissed him, softly, sweetly.

'We only saw one shower,' she said, pulling back, 'when we were inside having lunch.'

'Lucky.'

'Yes. Are you all right?'

'Yes. Why?'

'I don't know. You seem…' She put a finger to his nose and pressed it gently. 'What have you been up to then? Lots of brilliant composition I hope to make up for not coming with me.'

'Some. Maybe not brilliant but I had some ideas that might develop into something.'

'Oh good.' She kissed him again. 'Clever you. Do you want to go out darling?' She eased herself off his lap and stood up, turning to look back down at him. 'Why don't we wander up to The Mill?'

'But you're not drinking are you? I got some wine in for me and there's a can of cream soda for you. They're on the desk.'

'Oh.' She glanced round, noting the bottle, already open, a wine glass half full, but also a can and tumbler. 'All right then. But I quite fancied going out. And the soda won't be chilled.'

'I quite fancied staying in,' he countered, 'and talking.'

She opened her mouth to speak, then closed it again. She hesitated then moved towards the bathroom. 'I'll just freshen up a bit.'

By the time she emerged from the bathroom, Frank had topped up his glass and poured soda into the tumbler. He was sitting back in his chair, one leg crossed over the other, ankle on thigh. The only sign of his agitation was the constant twitching of his free foot which bounced rhythmically up and down.

Louisa smiled as she picked up her glass and descended gracefully into the other armchair.

'So here we are then.'

He noted the slight apprehension in her voice and took a mouthful of wine, swallowing it slowly.

'Why didn't you tell me you went to see Eleanor?' he asked, eyes fixed on his glass.

She was silent and he raised his eyes to look at her. She was round-eyed, staring at him.

'I…I did go to the hospital, it's true. I thought I ought, you know? I didn't tell you because I wasn't sure how you'd feel about it. It's an awkward situation, isn't it?'

Frank found he wanted to laugh, a raucous, mocking laugh which stuck in his throat somewhere. 'Awkward. Yes, I suppose it is. It's certainly awkward not knowing that your fiancée visited your ex-lover the same night she fell off the cliff.'

The silence was profound. Frank drank another mouthful of wine. The glass was emptying rapidly but he didn't care.

'I don't know what you're talking about.' Louisa looked at him defiantly.

Frank reached into his pocket and pulled out a small gold ear stud. He held it up between his index finger and thumb for her to see.

'This.' He tossed it to her and it bounced from her chest down onto her lap.

'What's this?' She picked it up, examining it.

'Your earring. I found it in your toiletry bag. A good place to hide it I suppose. Certainly Jo didn't find it.'

'Jo?' She looked worried now.

'I found her here earlier, searching the place. She found the pair to this on Eleanor's terrace. It's time to start telling the truth, Louisa. What were you doing there?'

She stood up, still cradling the tumbler in one hand, holding the stud in the other, and walked to the dressing table. She put the earring down with elaborate care and turned to face him.

'I went to see Eleanor. I wanted to talk, just talk, nothing else. You and she were a couple for so long, I wanted to be sure she wasn't going to try to get you back.'

'You went to warn her off.'

Louisa straightened her back, lifting her chin. 'Something like that. I was scared. You don't realise how obsessed you still are with her. I knew she'd pull you back in if I didn't do something about it.'

She stopped abruptly and drank some soda.

'And what did you do exactly?' he prompted.

'Nothing. There was no answer to the doorbell but there were lights on so I went round to the back. I'd only been there once before - that night last year when Eleanor had us all round for a final barbecue. But I did go on to that terrace, yes. I remembered it and I paused to look at the view. The clip on one of my earrings was a bit loose and it must have dropped off. I didn't notice at the time. Anyway, I never saw Eleanor. I chickened out. I didn't hurt her Frank. I suppose that's what Jo's trying to prove. But really, you of all people…' She shook her head, eyes wide and indignant. '…you must know I wouldn't do that.'

229

He stared at her, long and hard. Her expression gave nothing away.

'I don't know what to think. You lied to me. Why would you do that?'

He finished his wine and got up to refill the glass. Louisa walked across to join him by the desk. She tentatively put an arm round his waist.

'I know I was wrong, Frank. I'm sorry. I went to see her on the spur of the moment and I was too embarrassed to mention it afterwards. Then we heard about Eleanor's fall. How could I say then?'

He said nothing.

'What did you say to Jo?' she asked.

'I told her it wasn't your earring, but I knew it was.' He turned to face her and smiled sadly, raising a hand to finger her delicate ear lobe. 'You have such cute ears; I always notice your earrings. Anyway, I remembered you buying them. It wasn't until after she'd gone that I found it. I remembered that you often drop odd safety pins and all sorts into that toiletry bag. And that's where the pair was.'

She frowned at him. 'What do you think she'll do now?'

'Nothing. She's got no proof you were ever there. Unless someone saw you. Did you see anyone? Vincent perhaps?'

'Vincent did see me ringing the doorbell, but that's all. He must have seen that there was no answer. I pretended to walk away after. But he was behaving oddly too and then he disappeared. I told him he'd better not mention it or he'd be in trouble too. There was no-one else around.'

'Vincent,' said Frank thoughtfully. 'What was he doing?'

'I don't know. He was outside her house, looking up at it. He looked like he was praying. But he's always doing that.'

'Hm.' Frank drank another mouthful of wine.

'I'm appalled that Jo should break in here and go through my things,' Louisa said crossly. 'Little madam. So full of herself, so holier than thou. I hope you told her off, Frank.'

'She thought she was doing the right thing by Eleanor. But yes, I told her off. She won't bother us again.'

Louisa muttered something, turning away. Frank didn't hear it, his thoughts elsewhere.

Chapter 17

Eleanor sat in the chair by her patio doors and looked out at the gardens. It was Monday evening and Jo had just left. Already Eleanor had been at The Moorhill Centre for more than three days. It was strange how quickly it had become where she was, her room, her home.

A movement caught her attention on one of the paths. A man was walking out there, a patient she had seen sitting at a nearby table at lunch time. Except that the staff didn't call them patients, they called them residents. Resident. The word sounded too permanent. Eleanor was particular about words; when she was writing she would sometimes spend ages choosing just the right word to describe something. Words were loaded. The original meanings had often changed with years, sometimes centuries, of use, all sorts of subtle layers weighing them down. So much depended on the context or on the manner in which it was said. Odd how clearly she knew that now when not long ago she could barely pronounce a single one.

But being ill these last weeks had made Eleanor more aware of it than ever, perhaps because she felt vulnerable, or perhaps because so many people had been evasive or offered empty words of encouragement. To start with she had been happy to accept those platitudes as she swam towards what felt like a very distant shore. But now she was over that and she needed a grasp on reality. 'You're looking better today', was a common throwaway line. Better than what? Better than a half-dead corpse? 'Getting your memory back could take some time'. That meant she might never get it back, didn't it? She looked for hidden agendas; she was sure people lied to her. Were they trying to protect her from the truth? Didn't they think she would find out eventually? If only everyone wouldn't be so hearty and enthusiastic, just honest.

She watched the man walk out of sight. How she wished she could get up and go wherever she wanted like that, alone, unaided, not fussed over, though the thought of it scared her too.

'You will,' Jo had said earlier. 'That's why you're here. And you're getting better all the time.'

Even Jo told half-truths. Eleanor could see it in the girl's eyes and it worried her because Jo wasn't like that. Her niece was a naturally direct person, not garrulous but honest, so what was going on?

Jo had turned up at seven looking worn and distracted.

'How's it going?' she'd asked.

'Going? I don't know. I just do as I'm told.'

'Really?' A grin. 'I find that hard to believe. How's the coffee?'

Eleanor smiled then. 'The coffee's OK. I'll give them that.'

'Good.'

'You've just missed Lawrence.'

'Lawrence was here?'

'Yes. Is that a surprise? He brought me those grapes. Bit of a cliché but I do like grapes.'

'What did he say?'

Eleanor pulled a face. 'Nothing much. Just nosey about

where I was, I think. He asked how I felt - the usual. How was my memory? Everyone seems obsessed with my memory. Oh and he asked if I felt like writing. Worrying about the next book. Thinking about his salary no doubt.'

'No doubt.'

Jo seemed preoccupied. She always looked preoccupied these days.

'What did you tell him about your memory?'

'What do you think?' Eleanor said crossly. 'If you don't remember, you don't know you've forgotten.' She shook her head. 'No, sorry. That's not true. I do miss things. Except I'm not sure what it is I'm missing. I get vague feelings but they're just holes. And sometimes bits of memories…odd images, you know? No, of course you don't know what I'm talking about.'

'Not really. Tell me. What sort of images?'

'Oh darling they come and go. Last night I woke from a dream. Something from the past, I think. It felt very real and I was sweating but afterwards I couldn't remember it. Something to do with a party or something like that. And there was a name. I kept murmuring a name. But I don't know who it was. Or if it was anything.'

'What name?'

'I think it was Hugh… Hugh…Hugh something.' Eleanor concentrated on it for a minute but knew from experience that nothing came to her if she tried too hard. 'I can't remember.'

'So what did you say to Lawrence about your memory?'

'I don't know. I think I said it was rubbish. Because it is.'

Jo nodded, thoughtful. 'You look tired. Have they been working you hard?'

'Yes. That's why you brought me here, isn't it? Phys-i-o-ther-apy - see, I can even say it now - that's all morning. Occ-up-a-tion-al therapy and speech therapy all afternoon. I get weekends off for good behaviour, except I don't because they make you do everything yourself - dressing, eating, washing. Always at you, they are. It's exhausting.'

'Maybe I shouldn't come again until the weekend then.' Jo smiled. 'I could take you out on Saturday and we'll have lunch or something.'

Her voice tailed off. There was definitely something going on in her head. Eleanor studied the girl for a moment then it clicked and all Jo's strange behaviour began to make sense.

'You've met a man,' Eleanor declared triumphantly.

'No, what, down here? I've only been here a few weeks.'

Eleanor raised her eyebrows. 'There are men in Devon.' She waited, watching Jo pointedly. 'So come on. Who is it?'

'OK so I have been out with someone, yes. You know him in fact: Matthew Croft? I've mentioned him before. He's on the festival committee.'

'Matthew Croft.' Eleanor frowned. She closed her eyes; it sometimes helped to bring an image to mind. 'No, I don't think I do.'

'Computer guy. He took over Millie's last winter.'

Eleanor opened her eyes and smiled. 'Yes I do. Serious man. Personable but intense. Something about his wife; can't remember what. Please tell me you're not going out with a married man.'

'Of course not. His wife died before he came here - of cancer. Very sad. The trouble is, Eleanor, he still loves her.'

Eleanor snorted. 'Of course he does. What do you expect?'

'I don't know. Just...' She pulled a face and sighed. 'I'm not sure I'm in the right place at the moment to be what he needs.'

'What he needs? Is he what you need?'

'I don't know that either. It's complicated.'

'Ha. It always is, Jo. Love, sex, family. It's never simple.'

'I know.' Jo hesitated, frowning. 'You were with Frank a long time. You remember that now don't you?'

Eleanor was silent. She could see Frank clearly in her mind's eye, could even remember a host of odd unconnected memories of their time together but they were still jumbled, out of order. And she thought she remembered the final parting, not distinctly but hazily, the emotion of it more than the words.

'Yes, I remember Frank.'

'If you could do it all again, would you still choose him?'

'Oh yes,' said Eleanor distantly, still sorting through the memories.

They fell silent. Jo reached into her bag.

'You remember the literary festival I've been talking about? The programmes have come through. Here, I thought you might like to look through one.'

'Ah yes the festival. Hand me my glasses will you?' Eleanor read the front then flicked through the pages. She could read for short spells now, especially if the typeface wasn't too small. 'Can I keep this to look at?'

'Of course. I've managed to fill the last vacant speaking slots.'

'I think I'd like to come to this festival. I should be home by then, shouldn't I?'

'That's not a good idea, Eleanor. There are going to be too many people there, pushing and shoving, you might get hurt. And it'll be very tiring.'

Jo was doing it again: telling a half-truth. Maybe the preoccupation wasn't about the man after all.

'Shirley,' Eleanor said suddenly.

'What?'

'No, that's not right. It's…No, I had it there for a minute. Yes, yes, it's Shrig-ley.' She smiled with satisfaction. 'Hugh Shrigley. That was the name I was saying when I woke up.'

'Hugh Shrigley? I don't know who he is.'

'Neither do I.'

'Is it important?' said Jo, leaning forward.

'Important? I've no idea.' Eleanor leaned forward too. 'In what way might it be important?'

*

Jo sat in Eleanor's study, staring at her laptop. She had a page of information about Hugh Shrigley up on the screen in front of her. More of a half page, in fact - a tantalising glimpse of a life which apparently no-one thought merited more detail. She had lost count of the number of times she had done this. Returning home from The Moorhill Centre the night before, she had immediately searched the name on the internet and had found several articles about him but they were all short and all said identical things. And while it was mildly interesting, none of it explained why Eleanor should have been dreaming about him.

Hugh Shrigley had been a journalist and writer of political essays; he had also written a book of short stories and one full length novel. None of his writing had made a particular impact but family money had made him a wealthy man and he had been a small-time patron of the arts, occasionally sponsoring a play or an exhibition. He had also been a vocal supporter of the Labour party. Having read about him, Jo thought she dimly remembered the name though she might have been imagining it. He had died some twenty-five years previously following an accident at home. He had been only forty-four.

She minimised the page and returned to her document. It was six thirty already and she had been working all day, trying to get ahead of an editing job which should have been sent off by the previous Friday. There had been too many distractions, too many issues fighting for dominance in her brain, but at last she was writing up her final notes.

'There,' she muttered. 'Done.'

She would have a short break, check again that everything was in place, then send it off. She sat back in the chair.

It was something to do with a party. That's what Eleanor had said. Caught up in the mystery of the name, Jo had forgotten that. A party. A party as in drinks and celebration? Eleanor wasn't a big party animal though it could have been a special occasion maybe. Or perhaps a political party? If Hugh Shrigley supported Labour, maybe it was that. Eleanor used to be quite passionate about politics herself and quite the socialist when she was younger, but later she had been proud to call herself a floating voter, insisting that there was something in most of the parties she liked and a lot she hated. 'In any case all their policies shift with the wind,' she used to say. But why would she dream about a political party? Jo's eyes roamed round the room. Maybe there would be something in here about it. If Eleanor had belonged to a political party, if something had happened to upset her and make her leave, there might be some record of it here….somewhere. Could she have missed something before, something important?

She left the desk, walked across to the bureau and had just pulled the top down when her phone rang. It was on the desk. She went back, picked it up and scanned the screen.

'Hi Matthew. How…'

'We need to talk.'

His voice was cold and demanding. Her heart sank; she became defensive.

'OK but I'm in the mi…'

'I'm not asking you, Jo,' he said curtly. 'I'm telling you. We need to talk. And I'm not doing it on the phone. Can I come round?'

'Now?'

'Yes, now.'

'I suppose so. But what's this all ab…?'

'Code?'

She told him. 'Matthew?'

The call went dead and she stared at her phone in amazement.

*

Disillusionment swamped him and anger came in waves, interspersed with moments of utter dejection. Striding through the village, Matthew forced himself to pause by the wall, looking out over the beach. He watched the waves rolling in, listened to the soft roar of the surf and took some deep breaths, trying to get a grip on it all. He had been so upset when he got the note that he'd hardly been able to think straight, then anger had bubbled up inside him and he had reacted on reflex and made that phone call. But he could still just turn round and go home; he didn't need this. He'd been slowly getting his life back on an even keel, hadn't he? He had even dared to think that Jo might be someone he could care for again. Yes, he and Harry had been having some issues but what parent didn't with their adolescent offspring? They would have been OK. Then Jo had come along and… He felt sick.

He straightened up, took a step away and turned back for home. Then immediately changed his mind and set off again through the village. He had to do this now. The issue had to be addressed and it had to be done while he could face it, while his anger was still fresh and he could use it to get through. People didn't understand. His sister didn't understand. She kept telling him not to be angry, to let it go, but it was only his anger sometimes which had allowed him to cope. Without it, despair would have got the better of him. And in this case there was Harry to consider. Matthew was angry and Harry deserved his anger.

He strode on, up the footpath to the woodland gate and quickly let himself into the Skymeet estate. When he reached the house and rang the bell, Jo opened the door almost immediately.

'What's the matter?' She looked both anxious and cross.

'Can I come in?'

She said nothing and stepped back. He walked past her and, after glancing up and down the hallway to check there was no-one else about, entered the sitting room.

Evening sunshine streamed through the patio doors, filling the room with a glowing, warm light. The colourful intimacy of Eleanor's furnishings, the apparent strength of her presence in the room gave him pause. Sidney took one look at him, jumped off the sofa and immediately edged round him and out of the room.

'You've scared my cat away,' said Jo, following him into the room. The throwaway remark sounded forced.

Matthew turned to face her.

'So?' she said. 'You demanded to see me.'

'You've been seeing Harry.' There was no point hedging round the issue; in any case it consumed him. 'A woman your age with a teenager. He's not even half your age. He's fifteen,' he said bitterly. 'I could report you to the police.'

She stared at him open-mouthed. 'What on earth are you talking about?'

'Come on, don't pretend. Though I suppose you're bound to deny it. But it's all making sense to me now. It was never about me was it? You went out with me to find out more about him. You certainly asked enough questions about him. So is that how it works for you? Being with me, thinking about him - was it all a game? Are young boys what you get off on?'

She took a step towards him, pulled her right arm back and slapped him hard across the face. He put a hand to his cheek; it throbbed.

'Get out.' She pointed to the door. 'Get out now.'

'No, not until you've explained what's going on. And why? How could you do that to me?'

'Do what to you?' Her eyes narrowed; she smiled grimly. 'You don't really want me to explain, do you? You've already decided: judge and jury. But yes, I'll tell you what's going on, Matthew, since you're too wrapped up in yourself to notice. Yes, I've met Harry. I stumbled into him on Eleanor's private beach a few weeks ago. I had no idea who he was but it didn't take a degree to see that the kid was unhappy. He said he came to this beach because it was quiet. He comes round the headland when the tide is low enough to scramble round. He said he liked to be alone. Odd when he looks like one of the loneliest kids I've ever seen. We got talking. We skimmed stones. He was messing around in the sea and dropped his phone into the water and was upset because it had pictures of his mother on it. Pictures incidentally that you don't seem to care about.

'He got wet so I brought him up here to dry off and we played chess. Pretty shocking stuff, isn't it? And he told me about his mother. He also told me that you wouldn't talk about her. It eats him up, do you know that? He thinks you'd rather forget her, that maybe you're glad she's gone. So, Mr High and Mighty One, throwing out your filthy accusations, perhaps you'd like to consider what kind of father it is who makes his son feel like that?'

She stopped talking but continued to glare at him, breathing heavily.

He struggled to process it.

'That's all there is to it?' he said eventually.

'For God's sake, Matthew, why would you think anything else? Don't you know me?' She scoffed. 'Clearly that's a stupid question. But I can see you've just been looking for something like this as an excuse to mess up your first chance at a relationship since you lost Sophie. Because you're scared. Well, don't you dare blame me.' Her eyes blazed.

'So why didn't you tell me? All that time we spent together and you never mentioned meeting him. Why hide it if it's all so innocent?'

'Why? Easy. Because Harry made me promise not to say anything. He said you were always on at him and you'd tell him off for coming here. I thought, if it helps him to come and potter round this beach...' She shrugged. '...why not, he isn't doing any harm. And on the odd occasions I see him, he talks to me. I guess maybe that does him good too.'

Matthew frowned and ran a hand through his hair. He pushed his fingers into the back pocket of his chinos, pulled out a folded piece of paper and handed it to her.

'Someone pushed an envelope through the letter box while I was at work today. This was in it.'

She took it and unfolded the paper. Matthew had read it through so many times he knew it off by heart. He watched her scan the typed letter.

Are you aware that your young son is having secret meetings with Joselyn Lambe on her aunt's private beach? I've seen them. Maybe they do it other places too. You ought to check where he goes and what he does. But she's quite the little seducer and no match for him, poor child. He probably thinks a little romp in the sand makes him very grown-up. She should be stopped. The police would certainly like to know.

Jo read it twice, her face puckering with disgust. Silently, she handed it back.

'You see why I had to speak to you?' he said.

'You assumed that what the letter said was true,' she said dully. 'You didn't give me the benefit of the doubt.'

'Why would someone write that if there was no truth in it?'

'Because they like to cause trouble. Because they have a grudge. How should I know?'

'What was I supposed to think?'

'It's anonymous and cowardly. Do you normally believe anything that's said to you, especially crude printed notes pushed through your door?'

'Jo, look at it from my point of view. I had to question it.'

'No, I'll tell you my point of view. I don't understand why you refuse to talk about your wife to your own son or why you don't want any photos of her around the house. You can't let go of her and yet you can't cope with her there either. Harry needs you right now. So he talked to me because I let him talk about his mum. Stop blaming other people and get over yourself.'

'Don't tell me how to cope. You haven't been through anything like I have. You can't judge me.'

'Maybe not. But Harry can.'

She walked to the cabinet in the corner, poured a generous measure of gin into a glass and added tonic. She drank a mouthful, swallowing it slowly before turning and grudgingly holding up the bottle to him. He nodded and she poured him a drink too, walking away, leaving it on the cabinet for him to retrieve. He crossed to pick it up.

But Harry can. Her words kept echoing through his head. He didn't like them but he couldn't refute them either. He drank a long draught of gin and sighed.

'I'm sorry,' he said curtly.

'You don't sound sorry.'

'What am I supposed to do, go down on my knees and beg your forgiveness?'

'For God's sake, Matthew, you know as well as I do what sorry should sound like.'

She stepped across to the patio doors, cradling her wine glass, looking out over the garden. He came alongside her.

'I'll have to tell him that you know,' she said. 'And how. I don't want him thinking I broke my promise.'

'He's my son. I'll do the talking to him.'

'You don't know how.'

'Excuse me. And when did you become such an expert in child-rearing? A series of broken relationships behind you; an engagement you couldn't make last out till the marriage; not the remotest likelihood it seems of you having any kids of your own.'

She stretched a pained smile. 'Thanks for that, Matthew. Now I know just how low you're prepared to go. And no, I'm no child expert. But at least Harry talks to me, really talks. So I trust what he tells me.' She paused as if having an internal argument. 'And since you know about his visits now, I guess

244

it makes no difference if you know this: Harry was on the beach the night Eleanor fell. He told me. He saw someone with her and thinks whoever it was might have pushed her. That's why I've been so protective of her. I'm scared for her.'

He shook his head and gave an ironic smile.

'What? How is that funny?' she said crossly.

'You shouldn't take it so seriously. Harry lies. He's been doing it ever since Sophie fell ill.'

'I don't believe you.'

'It's true. It was just silly things at first, nothing really, attention seeking I suppose. Then when she passed away it got serious. He fell in with the wrong crowd, started taking drugs, told me a pack of lies about where he was going, what he spent money on, who he was with. His imagination is very fertile. Then he started petty stealing to finance the habit.'

She was frowning at him.

'You don't want to believe it but it's true. Eventually he was picked up by the police. Might have been the best thing to happen really. It's been a battle since but he's clean now. I think. Even so, I'm sure he tells me lies. I catch him out in it every now and then. I guess it becomes a habit - or he thinks it's cool in some way.' Matthew drained the glass, walked across to put it on the cabinet and turned. 'Before accusing me of being a bad father, you should get all the facts first. I chose this place to live in so I could get Harry away from the bad crowd and into something good and fresh. He's not a bad kid. But he lies. I try to do my best by him, I really do. You only heard his side of the story.' He threw her own words back at her. 'Do you believe anything that's said to you?'

He walked out into the hall and to the front door. Jo came quickly behind him and reached him just as he opened it.

'I do believe you try your best, Matthew - the best you

can, given that you're so unhappy yourself. But why does Harry try to escape his home all the time? I think it's because it feels empty. He yearns to talk about his mum, to keep her with him. You wouldn't talk to me about her. Are you telling me that you do talk about Sophie with him, that she's not a forbidden subject in your house? Is he lying about that?'

He paused, glaring at her, opened his mouth to speak then closed it again. He walked out but turned before she could close the door.

'I don't want you meeting Harry,' he said. 'Is that understood?'

'Why not? We're doing nothing wrong and he likes coming here.'

'You don't get it do you? He doesn't understand rules and you're encouraging him to trespass. And it seems like you're making him think the worst of me.' She started to protest. 'I haven't finished. I want you to remember that he's a kid and he lives here. He needs rumours about his relationship with you like he needs a kick in the teeth. Leave him alone.'

Matthew strode away without giving her a chance to reply, down into the woods and heading for the gate, his pulse thrumming in his head, fists clenched. He felt winded, head all over the place. It wasn't up to Jo to interfere in his relationship with his son. What did she know? They were fine - better in fact - without her.

Chapter 18

Petterton Mill Cove heaved with people. The August Bank Holiday was a few short days away and it seemed as if half the country had descended on the small seaside village. Jo had seen it busy before but had never felt so assaulted by it. There were too many people trying to drive the narrow lanes, tentatively squeezing their cars past each other, blocking roads, getting frustrated; there were too many people swarming over the beach, claiming territory, playing ball games, shouting and shrieking; there were too many people vying for places in the cafés and queueing to be served. Jo's nerves were frayed; she wished they would all go away. It felt airless as if the place and all the chattering, laughing, sweating people were closing in on her.

She didn't sleep the night after Matthew's visit. He had been unforgiveable, the way he had behaved; he had no right to speak to her like that. And to actually believe the filth written on that note... How could he? And then there'd been that jibe about her relationships. That had been cheap. Some people were luckier in love than others, everyone knew that. So he had managed to find the love of his life, had he? Well, bully for him. Would it have lasted? He would never know. There were so many things she wished she had said. How easy it was to think of clever rejoinders after the event.

But then she wished she'd said nothing at all. He was

right: she barely knew either Matthew or his son, nor did she have any understanding of their relationship or the particular strains and pressures it had experienced these last few years. And, though she had experienced loss, her family life had always been disjointed, fractured even, her relationship with her mother a complex weave of love, frustration and distaste. Yes, she could admit it to herself now, she had hated her mother's pernicious and self-destructive way of living, had even at times hated her mother for living it. Though exquisitely painful, her loss had been a very different one. She was in no position to hand Matthew family advice. And how could she even think of taunting him about Sophie and where their relationship might have gone? What had she become?

But still their argument went round and round in her head. The news of Harry's drug habit upset her. Perhaps she understood Matthew's attitude after all. On top of the loss of his wife, watching his son descend into drugs must have been another hell to endure. Did Harry still habitually lie? Had he made up the story about Eleanor's argument that night? Doubts stalked her. Perhaps she had been on a wild goose chase, looking for clues where there were none, searching for someone who had never existed.

She still had Harry's phone, a constant reminder of her rashness in taking it. What had she been thinking of and what was she going to do with it? It had now become much more complicated. On the Thursday, after two days of indecision, she picked up her phone and rang Richard's sister. It rang four times before being answered.

'Yes,' said a guarded voice.

'Annie? Hi. It's Jo. I hope you're all, you know, OK. I'm ringing to ask a favour - but not for me. And it is important. Please hear me out before you decide if you'll do it.'

There was a moment's silence. 'Go on.'

'Thanks. I'm down in Devon at the moment because my aunt isn't well. And there's a lad here who lost his mum to cancer. The thing is, he had a pile of photos of her on his phone…'

*

Frank stood outside Eleanor's door at The Moorhill Centre. It was nearly half past five on the Friday afternoon. The holiday traffic was horrendous and it had taken him twice as long as he'd expected to get there.

A care assistant had shown him to the room and now stood with him. 'Shall I show you in?' she offered.

'No, thanks, we're old friends. I'll surprise her. She is conscious and everything now?'

'Oh yes. And everything,' she replied drily.

'No locks on the doors.' He grinned. 'Aren't you afraid people might escape?'

She looked at him oddly and didn't reply. He was used to that.

He waited until the woman had walked back down the corridor and turned out of sight, then took a deep breath and knocked on the door.

'Yes?' called a voice.

He opened the door and walked in.

Eleanor was sitting in an armchair, dressed and poised. The difference in her from when he had seen her last was striking. The bruising had gone and her hair had grown into a long stubble, like a field of recently harvested wheat, sun-bleached; it was a startling golden white. She looked at him as he entered, eyes alert and questioning. Then she put a quick hand to her blouse, straightening it, and touched her hair as if checking it was in place, grimacing briefly at the feel of it. The vanity was still there, the pride. He felt a frisson of memory, a soft echo of all those years of shared intimacy, of passion, of laughter. There was regret too. A lot of it.

'You've come,' she said. 'I wondered if you would.'

'I did come once before - when you were in hospital.'

'I don't remember.'

'You weren't conscious.'

She nodded. There was an unfamiliar look of uncertainty in her eyes suddenly. Beneath the old veneer of assurance and strength, he sensed a new vulnerability. It was engaging. If she had been like that more often before, perhaps they would still have been lovers.

He pulled a bottle of gin out of the paper carrier bag he was holding. 'I wasn't sure if you were allowed this - but you can always hide it somewhere. There's tonic too. I thought you might need it.'

She smiled, that infectious smile of hers which started as a dance of the eyes, then a twitch of her upper lip and slowly spread till she was grinning. He was relieved that she could still smile like that for him. But it hurt too. He found himself wondering if they could still make it work, even now, a fleeting traitorous thought that flickered at the edges of his mind.

'I'm sure I'm not supposed to have it,' she said, 'but I'm certain I need it.'

He glanced round. 'I'll put it in the wardrobe. Can you get it there?'

'I'll manage.'

He stowed it away at the back of the wardrobe. There was an upright chair with a padded seat against the wall. He pulled it over and sat near her. For several minutes they said nothing, looking at each other.

'Jo told us how much better you were,' he said. 'She said you were walking and everything again.'

'Yes. I do all the tricks now. Well, maybe not all. How's Louisa?'

He was surprised into silence, knew it showed on his face.

'Jo told me about your engagement. She said that I knew about it before...' Eleanor waved a hand vaguely over her shoulder to indicate that past time, before her accident. 'She was anxious it didn't come as a shock to me.'

'And did it?'

She frowned. 'No, I don't think so. But I didn't remember.' She paused and an odd look crossed her face. 'It frightens me, Frank. There's so much I don't remember. It feels like I've got huge yawning holes in my brain.'

'But you remember *us*?'

She pursed up her lips, smiling sadly. 'Some, not all. Everything's... It's all snatches and odd scenes. Never whole. I hate it Frank. I feel like my life has been stolen. If I can't remember, what was it all about?'

He felt an urge to get up and hold her the way he used to.

'Other people remember,' he said quickly. 'And there are your books. They'll always be there.' He grinned. 'You can read them, fresh eyed, and see if you like them.'

'But I remember my books. How weird is that?'

'The rest will probably come back.'

She shook her head. 'I think the doctors are surprised I've remembered as much as I have. They say there'll always be holes.' She pointed to the side of her head where the scar from the craniotomy still showed. 'Brain damage, my dear.'

'You always had holes in your head anyway. Completely batty. Who'll notice the difference?'

251

He hoped she would smile again, laugh even, but she said nothing, resting her gaze on him, calm, penetrating.

'So where is Louisa?' she said. 'Did she come with you? Is she waiting in the car?'

'No. She's gone to see an old friend who recently moved to live near Exeter.' He hesitated. 'She has been to see you though.'

'Did she? I don't remember that either. Not here?'

'No. A while ago, in hospital, and she hasn't been again. She's not sure how you feel about her.'

'Oh, really, she's no need to worry. I don't feel anything about her. Not that I particularly want to see her.'

'You don't have much in common. I don't see you as great friends.'

She smiled ruefully then frowned, leaning forwards in the chair. 'Are you happy Frank?'

He laughed, uncomfortable. 'Good God, Ellie. You're not yourself, are you? You never fretted over my happiness before.'

She leaned back in the chair with a resigned expression.

'I have a feeling I used to know, without asking.'

They sat in silence again. Frank left soon afterwards and Eleanor got up and walked with him to the door. She was weak and a little unsteady but did it with her characteristic determination. He leaned over and kissed her on the cheek.

Walking back to the car, he wasn't sure he should have come. It had been a spur of the moment decision, taking advantage of Louisa's absence. But it had unsettled him badly. He stopped by the car and leaned against it. It was times like this in days gone by when he would have lit a cigarette. He missed them. He missed Eleanor too.

She clearly had no recall of Louisa going to see her, either in hospital or at the house but, given her memory, that was hardly surprising. So Louisa's story might be true, or it might not. He was still uneasy about it.

*

On the Saturday of the Bank Holiday weekend, Jo kept her promise and took Eleanor out. They drove out over the moor, pausing occasionally to enjoy the view, getting out to stretch their legs, and stopped for lunch at a pub in Princetown. Eleanor's movement had noticeably improved in the week or so that she had been at the centre, but her mood seemed flat and she was quieter than usual.

'Had any more strange dreams lately?' Jo asked over lunch.

'Nothing I can remember.'

Eleanor was silent again, concentrating on manipulating her cutlery to cut her roast beef into bite-sized pieces.

'I looked up that man you mentioned: Hugh Shrigley. He was a writer and a journalist and a bit of a sponsor of the arts. Ring any bells?'

'No.'

'Sure?'

'Jo,' said Eleanor warningly.

'OK, just asking.'

Another pause.

'Frank came to see me,' said Eleanor.

That explained the mood. 'What did he say?'

Eleanor gave her one of the withering looks she used to do so well. Jo hadn't seen one in a while.

'Usual Frank,' she said. 'Something and nothing.'

Jo studied her aunt's face. 'Was it difficult to see him?'

'A little.'

Jo changed the subject and talked about the festival the following weekend. Eleanor was determined to come home for it and refused to be swayed. She was better, she insisted; she would improve further at home. Another week in 'that place' would be more than enough. Jo bowed to the inevitable and agreed to organise it.

'I'll see if I can arrange a carer to help if I'm not there,' she said.

'No. I'll manage. I don't want anyone fussing over me. That's final.'

There was no doubt she was better.

On the Sunday Jo had a late breakfast and hung around the house, doing odd chores. She sat down to play the piano but, after two tunes, gave up and sat on the floor to play with Sidney instead.

Eleanor worried her: in a handful of days she would be back at Skymeet. Whether Harry had lied or not, Jo was still convinced that someone else had been involved in Eleanor's fall. Someone had shut Sidney up as a warning to her. Someone had sent Matthew that note. And there was an intangible but unnerving atmosphere on the estate. It was too quiet, too still, too…she wasn't sure what. It felt as if something was brewing up to happen, something over which she had no control.

Like that silence you get before a big thunderclap.

Harry's words. He'd sounded genuine.

She glanced at the clock, got up and went in search of the tide timetable. Ten minutes later, she was heading down to the private beach. The tide was ebbing and was already more than half way down the pebbles. And finally Harry was there again, sitting on his favourite rock at the side, earphones in, shades on, head bobbing to the beat of the music. She'd had an uncanny feeling he would be.

Jo walked down to the sea, bending to collect a couple of pebbles as she went. She skimmed them, then turned and walked across to where Harry sat. He hadn't moved but something in the angle of his head suggested he had been watching her. He pulled the earphones out as she came near.

'Hi,' she said.

'Hi.' The voice was expressionless. She couldn't see his eyes, couldn't judge his mood. 'Did you ever find your cat?'

'Yes, thanks. He'd got shut in a shed.'

He nodded but said nothing.

'I guess your father's told you about that letter. Does he know you're here?'

'Jesus, he went on about it for hours,' he said evasively. 'I didn't listen to most of it.'

'Someone must have seen us talking.' She glanced up towards the gardens. 'Someone with a twisted mind.' She hesitated. 'Your dad doesn't want me to see you again.'

'I know.' He paused. 'He told me not to come here.'

Jo sat down nearby. 'You should do as your dad says, Harry. I'm happy for you to be here but he's the one who's responsible for you. And you shouldn't lie to him.'

'I don't lie.'

'He says you do. He said you took drugs for a while and you lied to him then.'

'Well…yes, I did…then.' He looked at her sidelong. 'But not now. Doing drugs was kind of dumb, I know that. Mum would've flipped. And it wasn't that great anyway. But I don't lie now. Sometimes I just kind of tell him nothing so he doesn't get on my back. Like coming here. I didn't lie; I just didn't tell him.'

It was a moot point. She let it go.

'So when you told me that my aunt had had an argument with someone, you were telling the truth?'

'Of course.'

'It's important Harry. I need to know. I don't care about your street cred or how cool it might seem to pretend you've been a witness to something. It's OK if you aren't sure or if you made it up before, but I need to know the truth. Was there someone else up there arguing with Eleanor?'

'Hell, I thought you were different.' He jumped down onto the shingle, turning to face her, gesticulating angrily with his arms. 'See, even when you tell the truth, no-one believes you. You don't. Dad doesn't. I made a mistake with the drug thing, sure, but that was ages ago and now he doesn't believe me about anything. No-one does. It sucks.'

He scuffed down to the water's edge and she got up and followed him.

'I understand but I had to ask. You're telling me it's true. So I believe you.' She bent over and picked up a flat pebble, throwing it out along the water. Five skips. Average. 'But it's different for your dad. He was there, worrying about you when you were taking drugs. You lose trust in someone very quickly if you're let down; it takes a lot longer to build the trust up again. He's scared for you because he cares about you. Give him a break. He only wants what's best for you.'

He frowned at her suspiciously. 'Why are you defending him? I thought you guys had a major bust up?'

'Is that what he said?'

'Not exactly. But I kind of figured it out.'

'Well, yes, we did.'

'And he won, obviously.'

'Not exactly. I think it was a draw. Good and bad on both sides. Anyway, Harry, tell me again: this person you heard,

256

have you thought any more about it? Have you any idea at all whether it was a man or a woman? Please try and remember.'

He shook his head, kicking at the stones beneath his feet, sending some rolling down into the lapping waves.

She watched him for a few moments, hoping for an answer, then gave up. Even if he knew more he wasn't going to tell her. It wasn't a lie as far as he was concerned; it was a tactical omission.

*

Eleanor came to, heart thudding. She lay still, waiting for the thudding to subside and tentatively opened her eyes. It was still night and dark in the room but a security light somewhere outside shed an eerie glow through the curtained windows. It had been that dream again but now, strain as she might, she couldn't keep a hold on it. She never could. Wisps of figures; echoes of voices; the shadow of a narrative playing out in a deep, dark recess of her mind. She closed her eyes again, willing it to form a shape, something she could identify, but it slipped away again.

She reached across and clicked the switch on the bedside lamp. A comforting cheery light suffused the room. Eleanor eased herself up into a sitting position, turned awkwardly to adjust her pillows and leaned back. She took a couple of deep breaths. That's what the physio kept telling her to do when she was struggling to get something right: wait, take a couple of deep breaths, calm yourself, then focus again. If it worked for her motor skills, it might work for her mental powers too.

She closed her eyes and reached back into her mind, looking for something to give her a foothold, a way in. There must be something there that she could recall. It was all in there somewhere surely or why all these tantalising images?

257

Or was it all just smoke and mirrors, nothing of importance? So why did it feel so insistent and why, though the dream seemed to vary in small ways, did she have the impression that she kept replaying the same scenes in her head?

It was a party. Yes, a party - she knew she had dreamt that before. She opened her eyes and picked up the notepad and pen from the bedside cabinet. Jo had left this for her, exhorting her to write down anything she remembered from her dreams, however foolish it might seem. Eleanor had accepted, dismissing the necessity of it, just as she denied still having these 'strange dreams' as her niece put it. She was sorry for the lie but Jo probed and worried too much. If something needed working out, Eleanor preferred to do it alone. These dreams, these memories if that's what they were, resided in her head. She would tease them out and unravel them herself.

Hugh Shrigley. Yes, that was the name she had told Jo and he was definitely in there somewhere, she wasn't sure how.

She hadn't tried much writing and the pen felt small and slippery in her hand; she manipulated it painstakingly producing a crooked script. Hugh Shrigley, she wrote. Then Party. OK so what kind of party? A children's party? No. It felt like something adult. A birthday party maybe? Or a wedding reception? Perhaps it was something to do with one of her books, like a launch party. But why would she dream about that? Or any of them, come to that? But she had the feeling that some of the people there - or most of them even - were people she knew.

She closed her eyes again, willing faces to come out of the mist. Nothing happened. Her eyes snapped open and in a fit of frustration she picked up the pad and pen, throwing them across the room. 'You don't have much patience, do you?' the occupational therapist had said to her one afternoon, eyebrows raised. 'Just try again. Give yourself time.'

Eleanor sank back into the pillows. No, she didn't have much patience for things she thought she should be able to do. Never had. See, she remembered that. 'A party,' she muttered to herself. 'A party.' A few deep breaths. Her eyes drooped. 'It was a long time ago,' she murmured. Her breathing slowed; her thoughts drifted. 'Vincent came. He wasn't invited. But then he never was.'

She fell asleep, the bedside light still on. The pad lay on the floor with just three words scribbled on it. By the time she woke the next morning, she had forgotten all about Vincent at the party.

Chapter 19

The summer workshops were over and the holiday crowds began to disperse. All attention in Petterton Mill Cove now focussed on the literary festival due to start the following Friday. The village hall and the function room at The Mill had been booked from the Thursday in order to set them both up with chairs, a speaker's table and the necessary technical equipment.

The first talks started at six in the evening and Jo planned to collect Eleanor around ten on the Friday morning. That allowed time for her aunt to be comfortably installed at home and get used to being at Skymeet again. Eleanor, in typically bullish fashion, wanted to go to the whole of the festival. Jo wanted her to settle in and wait until the Saturday and the issue remained unresolved.

Jo had been exchanging emails and responding to phone calls for several days as participating speakers checked details. It was finally coming together. Brian Hunwin, the retired MP and Jenny, Eleanor's agent, were both speaking on the Saturday and had accepted Jo's invitation to stay in the main house for the weekend. Jo was relieved; she dreaded her aunt being left alone. Not that she had told Eleanor yet.

But her plans began to unravel. On the Sunday of the Bank Holiday weekend, Jenny emailed her apologies, saying something had come up and she wouldn't be able to stay over after all. She would give her talk then had to get away. 'Please give Eleanor my love and apologies; I hope she'll understand.' On the Monday morning, Brian rang to say he could only stay on the Friday night and had to be in Oxford by Saturday afternoon. 'We'll be able to catch up on the Friday evening at least. Tell Eleanor to have the Scotch ready.' That same evening Jo received an email from Patrick Digence, another speaker. There had been a death in the family and he had to pull out of the event.

Now there was a vacant slot to fill. At a push Jo could ask someone to double up and repeat a talk but that was far from ideal even if she could persuade anyone to do it. So who to ask? She had a working relationship with a lot of writers but didn't know them well enough to gauge their talents as public speakers. In any case, how many of them would be able to come down to Devon at such short notice? And there was also the issue of cost. Patrick had been doing the festival as a favour to Eleanor as were many of the others. It was an embryonic event, run on a shoe-string, uncertain of breaking even. The committee weren't going to like paying out more money, unplanned. Jo could offer one of the studio flats for a night's accommodation but couldn't promise more than travel expenses and most writers, she knew, earned little enough as it was.

Of course there was Vincent. He was could be quite the performer on his day. She remembered hearing him speak years ago and he was excellent, but what he might be like now she had no idea. And Eleanor had expressly excluded him from the line-up. He had a reputation for being unreliable. Suppose he started quoting the Bible and evangelising? He was more than capable of torpedoing the event if the whim took him, just for spite. No, it wouldn't work.

She spent the rest of the evening and all the following morning chasing her tail, contacting anyone she could think of, hoping someone would bite. No-one did. Late on the Tuesday afternoon she gave in and went in search of Vincent. He'd told Lawrence he had arranged a private tutorial with a student for the Tuesday morning and would leave on the Wednesday. He had to be around the village somewhere.

She found him eventually in The Mill wine bar with a large black coffee on the table in front of him and his nose in *The Times* newspaper. She crossed to stand by his table.

'May I join you?'

The newspaper descended and Vincent regarded her over the top of his reading glasses.

'You may. How refreshing to hear someone use the correct verb - 'may' and not 'can'. May I order you a drink, my dear? Though perhaps it's I who will need something stronger. You look as though you have bad news to impart. I hope it's not dear old Eleanor?'

She sat on the chair opposite him. 'No. Dear old Eleanor is fine, thank you.'

'And coming home, I understand. What a shame I shall miss her. I really wanted to stay to see her - we are family after all - but Lawrence suggested... To be honest, suggest is altogether too polite a word to describe his manner. He told me I had to vacate the flat since I am not needed for the festival. Apparently I am now redundant so, since I'm not wanted here...' He left the sentence hanging.

'That's why I've come to see you.'

'Indeed?' He folded the newspaper up, laid it on the table and removed his reading glasses. His thin mouth stretched into a fair imitation of a smile. 'Tell me more, do.'

'Are you available to speak at one of the sessions on

Saturday? It starts at five...for an hour. Well, the usual: speak for forty-five to fifty minutes then field questions. How would you feel about that?'

'Did this come from Eleanor?'

'No. It comes from me.'

He sucked ruminatively on the end of one of the arms of his glasses. 'Someone has let you down.'

'A family bereavement.'

'Tragic. Tell me the name and I shall pray for them.'

'You haven't answered, Vincent.'

'I'm thinking. I'm also wondering what the fee might be. I presume the previous speaker was receiving remuneration?'

'No. He was doing it as a favour to Eleanor. Just as the other tutors are - after being allowed to stay all summer I might add. You, as well as being able to stay on in the flat, rent free, for the rest of the week, would be doing her a favour too. You keep saying that blood is thicker than water.'

'Ah.' He gave another sickly smile and gestured with the glasses towards her. 'But it seems the blood flows more thickly one way than the other.'

'Perhaps it does. Though I imagine we might disagree on which way that is.'

He gave a hollow laugh. 'Well, I believe I'm capable of turning the other cheek. Still, it would be nice if Eleanor asked me herself. I have my pride to consider.'

'Eleanor's not here, nor is she in a position to do that. I am organising the speakers. If you want the job, Vincent, say so now. And deliver. Or I will ask someone else.'

'Whom you have already struggled to find, or you wouldn't be here now.' He hesitated, pursing up his lips. 'Will you do some special publicity, splash it about that I've stepped into the breach? And of course cover my plays and novels, mention my latest book? I do happen to have several copies with me.'

'Yes. Of course we'll do that.' It would mean liaising with Matthew and Lawrence but she could do that.

'Then I shall indeed be available, my dear.' He replaced the glasses on his nose and picked up the newspaper again. 'Are you sure you don't want a drink? The coffee here is really quite tolerable.'

Jo declined and left. Leaving The Mill she pulled the voice recorder out of her pocket and played the conversation back. It was all there. She didn't trust him.

*

'I'm just going to the committee meeting in the hall,' Matthew shouted up the stairs, trying to outgun the music and failing. He raised his voice still further. 'Harry?'

A shape appeared on the landing.

'What?'

'I'm going to the committee meeting in the hall. I won't be late.'

'Fine.' The shape disappeared.

Matthew let himself out and walked down to the sea front. It was only twenty past seven but the sun had nearly set and the village was bathed in an amber half-light, like a taste of the autumn to come. It was nearly the end of August already; the summer had passed in the blink of an eye.

He leant on the wall for a minute, looking out at the sea. The previous few days had been hectic in the coffee shop: the tables had been full, the queue to the counter apparently endless. If people weren't ordering drinks to sit inside and enjoy they'd been ordering takeaways. Matthew was exhausted though his staff had been brilliant, never once complaining and working with an enthusiasm and good-nature he envied. The atmosphere in the place was happy. People were on holiday; the shop buzzed with high-spirited chatter.

And Harry had helped out. He had agreed to do it in his usual, wordless way - a nod of the head and a grunt of apparently reluctant acceptance. He had worked hard too and Matthew had even spotted him laughing with Eddie a couple of times. But since the awful confrontation over his visits to Skymeet, the relationship between father and son seemed to have reached a new low.

'What on earth possessed you to trespass on a private beach when we've got a great beach on our doorstep?' Matthew had demanded. 'And you could have broken your neck, climbing round the cliff like that. To say nothing of the underhandedness of your behaviour. And visiting a woman on the sly. God, Harry, what did you think it was: some kind of game? Trying to see how much you can get away with without me finding out?'

'I didn't tell you I was going there,' Harry countered, his voice rising with angry indignation, 'because you'd have given me a load of grief about it like you're doing now, that's why. You're always on at me. I can't do anything right. And Jo listens to me. She actually listens like mum used to do. You never listen. And it's not dangerous to climb round if you know what you're doing. That's just stupid. You have to watch the tides, that's all. Any fool can do that.'

'And clearly did,' Matthew retorted. 'And don't you dare call me stupid.'

Between taking orders and making coffees, Matthew had watched his son carrying trays of drinks and sandwiches to the tables, saw him clearing dirty dishes and wiping down. There was a resignation about him, as if he had crawled even deeper inside himself like a hibernating animal retreating into its lair and shutting down till conditions outside improve.

Now Matthew turned away from the sea and began walking again, inland towards the hall. *Jo listens to me.* I'd listen too, Matthew thought bitterly, if you ever said anything to me. He took a deep breath and let it out on a long sigh. No, that wasn't strictly true. He didn't always listen. When Harry tried to talk about Sophie, Matthew cut him, just as Jo had said. It was how he got through. He had closed the door on all that - Sophie's illness, her stoic suffering, the unbearable pain of their parting... Surely it was better that way. What was the point in opening it now and reliving it all again? How would that help anyone? Yes, it meant Sophie was shut away too but that was the way it had to be. Jo simply didn't understand. How could she? She wasn't there.

He reached the hall and paused outside the doors, took a breath to compose himself, then went inside and found a seat.

Jo was late again and apologised as she always did. She slid into a seat near the door with a distracted air, as if she had lost something and didn't have any idea where to find it. He remembered her saying something about Eleanor being pushed, that her fall wasn't an accident. Too cross about her attitude to Harry, he hadn't paid it much attention since. Nor did he think it credible anyway; her imagination had been working overtime. He watched her now surreptitiously. She did look pinched. Perhaps he ought to at least ask her about it, show some concern. He had thought about her a lot over these last days and he deeply regretted saying all those things to her; he had over-reacted and ought to apologise properly. Maybe after the meeting he would invite her for a drink and try to build bridges. The thought of not sharing time with her again made him feel empty.

He became aware of Lawrence's eyes on him and shifted his own gaze to the top of the table, trying to concentrate on what Nancy was saying. She was running through the arrangements for these final days leading up to the festival, checking that everyone knew the timetable for setting up the venues and that all committee members in charge of volunteers had given them the information required. Various members reported in. There was an air of nervous anticipation.

'I believe the tickets are selling well,' she said proudly. 'There are a few left but Lawrence has arranged a piece in the local paper on Friday. That should bring some extra people to buy on the door. Any questions?'

Jo raised her hand and said that one of the speakers had pulled out because of a bereavement but that she had organised a replacement. 'It'll need a change on the programme and some new publicity material, I'm afraid.' She glanced between Matthew and Lawrence, her expression blank and unreadable. 'The new speaker's name is Vincent Pells. I'll send you everything you need.'

Matthew noticed Lawrence pull a face, looking at Jo with annoyance. She ignored him and sat down.

'That's very unfortunate,' said Nancy. 'The programmes have been so beautifully printed. I suppose we'll have to write on them. Not very professional.' She immediately delegated someone else to do it.

The meeting closed. Matthew stood up, exchanged a word with a neighbour and walked round the table towards the exit. He expected Jo to wait around but she was already leaving without a backward glance. It wasn't surprising in the circumstances. He tried to shrug his disappointment away and trudged heavily home.

Back at Skymeet Jo wasted no time in sending out the promised emails about Vincent with links to his books and further information. She asked that it be made clear that Mr Pells had kindly stepped in at the last moment. Job done. She expected grief from Lawrence but didn't care. From Matthew she had no idea what to expect nor what he wanted from her. Confused and still hurting, she refused to dwell on it; there were too many other things pressing on her mind right now.

On the Thursday she burned up and down the path to the village, dividing her time between the venues - checking how they were being set up and making suggestions - and helping Charlotte prepare the house for Eleanor's return, barking ideas and reminders into Eleanor's voice recorder which she kept in a pocket for whenever anything struck her. In the house, Charlotte was anxious and fussed over every detail. Clearly delighted that Eleanor was coming home, she was equally determined not to admit to it. Lawrence in contrast, drifted round the house without expression, watching what they were doing, saying little except occasionally to criticise.

'She's not going to like you moving the rug,' he remarked coldly as he watched them rolling the hearth rug up and carrying it out of the sitting room.

'She wouldn't like falling flat on her face either,' countered Jo, barely looking at him.

At the end of the afternoon, Jo returned to the village hall. The setting up had finished and the main door was locked but there were lights on and she could hear someone talking inside. Curious, she went round to the single door at the back. It opened to her touch and she walked into the kitchen at the rear of the stage. The door to the main hall was open and she could hear the voice clearly; it was Imogen's, practising her talk for the following evening. Jo held back, listening. Imogen spoke well but too fast, falling over her words, and stopped suddenly.

'I keep getting ahead of myself. How does it sound from there, Mari?'

'Very good, Immy,' returned Mari's fluting voice. 'It's just nerves. Remember to take a deep breath now and then to slow you down.'

'No, right. I don't think I'll do any more now. It just makes me more nervous.'

'You'll be fine. You always are once you start.'

Jo walked in on them.

'Hi. I've just come to check everything's OK in here.' She glanced round. The chairs had been laid out in rows; there was a table by the main doors and another on the platform. Several posters had been stuck to the walls. Leaflets, some advertising other literary festivals and some relating to specific speakers, were spread over the admission table.

'It's all fine.' Imogen descended the steps from the stage. 'Right Mari, shall we go? Mari's speaking up at The Mill and wants to try it out up there. Vincent was supposed to be coming down but he hasn't shown so I'll give the keys back to...what's her name?'

'Wendy Lawson,' said Jo. 'But I'll do it if you want to go on up to The Mill.'

'Thanks. OK Mari?'

But Mari lingered, watching Jo's face. 'It's going to be nice to have Eleanor back. Is she excited?'

Jo hesitated. 'I think so, yes. How are you feeling?'

'Nervous. We always are at these things.'

'Isn't everyone?' said Jo. 'That's supposed to be good, isn't it?'

'I bet Vincent's not nervous,' said Imogen bitterly. 'He's probably in training now, downing Scotch in readiness. I still can't believe you asked him to give a talk.'

'He doesn't drink as much these days,' said Jo.

Imogen laughed. 'Is that what he told you?'

'He can be brilliant,' said Mari.

'Or a disaster.'

'He used to do amazing performances at launches.' Mari smiled with an air of wonder. 'Off the top of his head. He didn't need to read from the book. He just knew it. He'd do it at parties too, impromptu. And bits of plays sometimes, speaking all the parts. Amazing.'

Imogen scoffed. 'Yes, if he wasn't drunk.'

'No, he did it when he was drunk too,' Mari replied doggedly. 'Except the words weren't always so clear.'

Imogen grunted. Jo had stopped listening at the word 'party'.

'Does the name Hugh Shrigley mean anything to either of you?' she asked.

The two women looked at each other then back at Jo.

'Yes,' said Imogen warily. 'We knew him. Why?'

'He used to give wonderful parties,' Mari said. 'But he died. It was very sad.'

'I saw a piece about him somewhere the other day.' Jo tried to sound casual. 'I'd never heard of him before. A writer and a patron of the arts, it said. He had an accident or something.'

'That's right. After one of his parties. He'd been drinking.' Mari flicked another glance at Imogen. 'He fell off his balcony. Everyone had gone and his wife was away. It must have been awful for her to hear the news.'

Jo felt something tighten in the pit of her stomach. 'He

270

fell? I didn't know. Who was there - for the party, I mean? People I'd know?'

'Yes. Well us, of course,' said Imogen, 'except that Mari was married to someone else then so we weren't together. The whole gang were there: Frank and Eleanor; Lawrence; and Vincent turned up too. He always did whether he was invited or not.'

'Yes, Vincent was there.' Mari mentioned another novelist and a couple of playwrights and some names that Jo had never heard of. 'But Vincent definitely. He and Hugh had a big row.' Her eyes grew bigger. 'It cast a shadow over the event, especially with what happened afterwards.'

'Really? Did people think the two events were linked in some way?' Jo looked from one woman to the other. Neither seemed keen to answer.

'No,' Imogen said, unconvincingly. 'Not really. But it was kind of awkward.'

'What was the row about?'

'Money,' breathed Mari. 'But I didn't hear the details because Hugh insisted on taking Vincent into his library. There were raised voices but nothing clear.' She glanced questioningly at Imogen.

'I heard nothing,' insisted Imogen. 'Anyway it's years ago. Why are you so interested, Jo? Hell, I need to pee again.'

Jo watched her limp away to the back of the hall and out into the foyer. Mari stood nearby, shifting restlessly from one foot to the other.

'She's always nervous beforehand. Makes her touchy. She'll be fine tomorrow.'

'Mari, I don't suppose Louisa was at that party, was she?'

'Louisa? No. She's too young.' Mari paused to reflect. 'Though there were a couple of younger women there, come to think of it but I don't think I spoke to them.' She hesitated. 'Your mum was there too, Jo.'

'That's probably why the name rang a bell.'

'You've been asking a lot of questions. Is something bothering you?'

'I'm just… trying to get a few things clear in my head.'

They both turned as Imogen pushed back one of the heavy doors from the foyer with a bang. She tottered back up the hall.

'Are you coming, Mari? Let's go. The keys are on the table in the kitchen, Jo.'

Mari smiled a farewell and they both left.

Jo locked up, pondering the significance of Eleanor dreaming about Hugh Shrigley's party. Maybe there was none. Or maybe Vincent was the link and Eleanor had known all along what he was like, a loose cannon, not safe to have around. And she, Jo, was the one who had just persuaded him to stay on at Skymeet.

Chapter 20

The front door was open before they had even got out of the car. Lawrence processed regally down the steps and held the car door back as Eleanor eased herself out and onto her feet.

'Eleanor. So good to have you home.'

He put a hand under her elbow, pulling on her, but she pushed it off.

'Don't fuss, Lawrence,' she said gruffly, putting a hand to the car body instead, steadying herself. 'I'm fine.'

He stepped back, looking awkward, and went round to the back of the car to help Jo with the bags.

'A parcel has arrived for you,' Eleanor heard him say to her niece. 'I signed for it.'

She didn't hear the reply, too occupied looking up at her home, trying to ground herself. She started walking cautiously towards the front steps but stopped at the bottom. There were only two but there was no rail. Suddenly Jo was by her side, silently offering an arm to hold and she took it gratefully.

Once inside she paused in the hallway, looking round again, then walked slowly into the sitting room. It all felt surreal, acutely familiar and yet alien too, as if she were still in one of her dreams. She walked to the patio doors and looked out over the garden. Her garden. She frowned.

Jo joined her, was silent a moment, giving her time.

'Lawrence has taken your bags up to your room.' She

hesitated. 'Would you rather sleep downstairs? We could make up the daybed in your study.'

Eleanor shook her head. 'No, upstairs is fine. There's a rail. I might need someone around, just to start with.'

'OK. Shall we have lunch, then you can settle in.'

'What time's the first talk?'

'Six o'clock,' said Jo. 'Plenty of time. Oh, here's Sidney.'

The cat slinked cautiously into the room. Jo crouched down and picked him up, stroking him, letting him get used to Eleanor's presence. Eleanor saw her do it but barely registered it.

'Who's doing that first talk,' she said. 'I've forgotten.'

'Brian Hunwin. And he's staying over here tonight so you can catch up. I was keeping it as a surprise. So you see you don't need to go down to the hall to see him.'

'Good. But I want to hear him speak, Jo.'

There was the distant sound of a phone ringing and Lawrence's voice, talking loudly, laying down the law to someone, something to do with parking.

'Jenny's coming later too,' Jo was saying, raising her voice to block him out. 'She's doing a talk in The Mill at seven thirty but she can't stay, I'm afraid. She sent her love in case you don't get a chance to meet up.'

'Oh.' Eleanor's brain reeled. There was too much to process: the place, the sounds, the activity, the information. She felt buffeted by it. It had been noisy and busy both in the hospital and at the centre but this was home. She had expected it to be easier, that she would slot back in, like a toy building block which had slipped out of place but was easily nudged into position.

'So you've come back to torment us then? I thought the peace was too good to last.'

274

The voice came from behind her. Eleanor turned a little too fast and had to steady herself, putting out a hand to the nearby cabinet. Charlotte was standing in the doorway, hands on hips, staring at her accusingly.

'Your lunch is ready on the table in the conservatory,' she announced crisply. 'It's going cold.'

'It's your fault; you shouldn't have been in such a hurry, you old hag,' said Eleanor, waving her away with a dismissive hand.

'I'm not at your beck and call, you know. You can eat it or leave it. But I'll have you know there's people in this country starving who'd be glad of it.'

Charlotte turned and stalked out and Eleanor smiled. Now that felt more like home.

*

The afternoon passed smoothly. Brian arrived and Jo left him and Eleanor to chat, taking the opportunity to check in with Lawrence and Nancy in case of last minute problems. By the end of the afternoon, Eleanor was still adamant that she wanted to hear Brian speak and Jo took her down to the village in the car. He had proved a big draw and the whole area swarmed with people. Jo parked in a reserved place and walked with Eleanor into the hall, stopping frequently as local people asked after Eleanor's health and expressed their pleasure at seeing her back on her feet. They found seats near the rear of the hall and settled in a few minutes before the talk started. Virtually every seat was occupied and the audience buzzed with anticipation. The stage spotlights illuminated a chair and a table with a pitcher of water and a glass. The hall lights dimmed. The audience fell silent as Nancy walked out onto the stage accompanied by Brian. She began a fulsome

275

introduction. They were up and running.

Jo listened to the first few words but took little in. She glanced round the audience who seemed rapt. In the glow of light from the stage she searched faces, unsure what she was looking for exactly. She had become paranoiac. Eleanor wasn't at risk here, among a crowd of well-wishers and strangers. Maybe Eleanor wasn't at risk at all. Here, in the mundane surroundings of the village hall, listening to Brian telling witty - and sometimes improbable - anecdotes of his time in office and hearing the laughter of the audience, the idea seemed as absurd as it ever had.

The talk came to an end. Brian fielded a few questions then Nancy gave her vote of thanks. Jo leaned across to Eleanor.

'Shall we go home now? Charlotte's left a meal for us.'

There was no immediate reply. Eleanor was staring at the programme as if struggling to take it in.

'Or did you want to see Jenny? She's not on for another half hour.'

'No. It's Louisa speaking next up at the Mill, isn't it? Have I read that right?'

'You want to hear Louisa?'

'Yes. We've got time for a drink first, haven't we?'

Jo opened her mouth to argue and closed it again. There was no point.

*

Louisa was nervous. It was obvious from the set of her shoulders and the tautness of her voice. Instead of embracing the audience with an occasional sweeping gaze, she darted nervous looks, desperate not to make eye contact, and spoke in pinched sentences.

276

She had been practising off and on all day long, flipping through the notes on her laptop, murmuring to herself, her lips sometimes moving when no sound emanated from them.

'Keep it as spontaneous as you can,' Frank had told her, part concerned, increasingly frustrated. 'It'll go down better that way.'

'Easy for you to say,' she'd snapped back, then leant in and given him an apologetic kiss in that temperamental way she had. 'Oh Frank, why can't I have your gift for speaking?'

He shrugged. 'Develop your own. Don't care so much. People want to be entertained, so entertain them. Surprise them, shock them even. Talk to them, not at them. Tell them that story you told me about seeing a woman climbing out of a bedroom window at six one morning, wearing nothing but her underwear, how it spawned the character of…whichever one it was.'

'Sylvie. But I'm not sure about that. This isn't suburbia; it's rural England. I think the people round here might be a bit strait-laced for that.'

'Nonsense. People are the same the world over. Trust me.'

Now, as he sat in The Mill function room watching her give her talk, he saw her shoulders drop, saw her smile start to assert itself and her speech become more flowing. She had worked through it. He knew she could do it.

Then he found himself wondering how genuine it had all been in the first place and the doubts which had been niggling at him began to crowd in again. He had never thought that you could - or would - fake nerves. But he had suspected for a while now that Louisa sometimes cultivated her insecurities and exaggerated them. It got her his attention; it kept him close and under her control. And sometimes when it suited her, she slipped those insecurities off as she might a dressing gown, with a shrug of the shoulders. He had watched her do it with others at parties, manipulating them, coy at times, cheeky at others. Looking at her now, wandering with assured steps up and down the stage, engaging with her audience, getting her timing just right, the transformation was remarkable. Louisa wasn't necessarily the person she seemed.

He was confused. He kept feeling cheated. When they were getting ready to come out, an hour before the talk was due to begin, Louisa had told him that she'd started her period so she couldn't be pregnant after all.

'What about the test you did?'

'It must have been a mistake, darling. I think maybe I took it too soon after missing that period. Or I did it wrong.' She looked at him doe-eyed. 'Or maybe it's my age. Terrible thought. And I'm gutted, really gutted. And for you too. I am sorry. Are you very disappointed?'

He didn't know what he was. He hadn't planned on having a child but the idea had grown on him and now… And Louisa hadn't looked as upset as her words had implied. She seemed to have taken it in her stride, brushing the news aside with less interest than she would have given an indifferent review. Now he was wondering if she had ever thought she was pregnant in the first place, if she had even done the test. Was it all a devious game she was playing to keep him on side? He sometimes caught her watching him when she thought his mind was elsewhere.

Perhaps he should leave, go for a walk and clear the agitation of his thoughts. Would Louisa notice? Did it matter if she did? He had enjoyed feeling needed but he didn't like being played.

In a flush of annoyance he got up and edged past his neighbours to the side aisle where it was dark. He planned to

278

slip out anonymously but before he could move any further, someone entered through the double doors from the bar area and for a second he saw a tall, stringy silhouette against the light, a man, slightly hunched. Frank stood, frozen, watching the man flash a pass at the attendant on the door. It was Vincent. Unmistakeable. Frank watched him search the audience then fix on one figure. Following his gaze, Frank saw that he was watching Eleanor. It was the first time Frank had registered that Eleanor was here. She was sitting on the back row with Brian Hunwin on her farther side.

Frank held back. He didn't want to get caught up with Vincent and now the man was heading for the exit again. So what was that about?

Frank looked back at Eleanor. Her gaze was fixed on the stage, her head turning a little as she followed Louisa's movements. The light from the stage wasn't bright enough to make out her expression. He had known she was back at Skymeet but he hadn't expected her to come to Louisa's talk. She was wearing one of her trademark long dresses and her head with its spiky hair had been cleverly wrapped in a scarf, turban-like. She looked as intriguing and Bohemian as she had in their youth. Compelling. He almost smiled. There was a vacant seat this side of her and he experienced a strong desire to go and sit in it and just be with her. But that wouldn't do would it, not in such a public place, and perhaps never again. Did he really want to restart that roller coaster relationship and would she even consider him if he did?

He dragged his gaze away, slipping out of one of the rear doors into the foyer and then out into the cool of the evening.

Chapter 21

On the Saturday morning, Eleanor woke but kept her eyes closed, holding on to a scene from her last dream which still flickered through her head. She had been at the party again but this time the scene has moved on, like an old home movie which kept sticking at the same place but has now corrected itself and started rolling once more. She automatically replayed it, picking over it, examining its bones. Bits of it were astonishingly clear.

The party was in Hugh Shrigley's flat and she was there with Frank, bickering as always but still in the early flush of young love. Hugh was his usual affable self, a generous host, too keen at times to top up your drink or press you to a fresh one. His wife was away, had taken a late summer holiday to Paros with her sister, and Hugh seemed a little intoxicated with his freedom. He spoke louder; he flirted innocently but ostentatiously as if pleased with himself. Eleanor too fizzed with youthful energy; she laughed at every joke; she was a little bit drunk. Sometimes she hated this sort of party but Frank had persuaded her to come and she was glad. It had a good atmosphere and everyone was happy.

Hugh made a point of joining them. He and Frank had known each other for years and though Hugh was the elder by some twelve years or more, they invariably enjoyed a boyish banter, each trying to outdo the other in clever, old-world insults. It was an idle, amusing rivalry. Frank, she knew, scoured the larger dictionaries, searching for long-forgotten terms of abuse, ready to trot them out at their next encounter. Only at gatherings populated largely by writers would such an arcane contest take place, she thought.

But this evening, Hugh seemed taut with information he was keen to share. He had another rivalry with Frank: they were both collectors of fine things and he liked to show off his latest acquisition, and he had by far the larger income with which to indulge his hobby. Before speaking, he glanced round almost theatrically and made a point of dropping his voice.

'You must come into the library...'

Still cocooned in her bedclothes, Eleanor frowned, still half-asleep, but determined, while it was fresh, to correct any inaccuracy in this dream which she was convinced was a memory. Did Hugh invite her too or just Frank? No, she was sure he had invited both of them. They had been standing together; he hadn't singled Frank out.

'...I've got something to show you,' he'd said.

But they never went into his library. Vincent had arrived, all loud voice and waving arms and indignant posturing. She remembered that bit of the dream clearly. He'd burst in, bellowing Hugh's name and calling him a mean-minded scoundrel. Hugh had agreed to back a play Vincent had written but Vincent was denouncing him for reneging on the promise when preparations had already been set in motion.

'That's not true, Vincent,' Hugh had responded. 'I never promised you that. You're drunk. We'll talk about it when you're sober - if that ever happens.'

But Vincent kept ranting and refused to back down and Hugh insisted on taking him away from the party and into his library. Ten minutes later, Vincent had gone, storming out, pushing people aside, swearing.

On the roof of Eleanor's Devon home, just above her bedroom, a seagull mewed loudly and her eyes popped open with the sudden inappropriateness of the sound. The scene in her head instantly evaporated. She was lying on her side and lay still for a moment, staring at the lamp on her bedside table and her reading glasses, returning to the present, trying to place herself back home. But she felt disjointed, incomplete. She hadn't finished remembering that dream and that made her anxious; this was important in some way.

She rolled onto her back and closed her eyes again, holding them tight shut, trying to recapture it. She wanted the images to keep moving; she needed to know what happened next. But all she kept seeing was Vincent leaving the apartment. Or maybe she just heard him go...or someone said he'd gone. Lawrence perhaps. No, Lawrence had gone into the library as soon as Vincent left, didn't he? Did he? Did Hugh come out again to speak to her and Frank? Damn it all, she couldn't remember. Damn, damn, damn. She felt her hands clenching on the bedclothes in frustration, her breathing become heavy with the concentration. The images in her head wouldn't form properly now; they were vague and insubstantial. But if she didn't get them quickly back into focus, she might never be able to raise them again. She had lost too many memories already.

It didn't matter how hard she screwed her eyes up, it wouldn't come. Maybe... Her eyes flicked open again. The idea scared her. What was she blocking out?

She worked herself up into a sitting position and made an effort to let her breathing settle. Glancing around the room, it all looked calm and unthreatening. There were her neat fitted wardrobes; there was her dressing table with her hair brush and her jewellery box and a tumbling pile of get well cards she had dumped there the previous day. Her handbag had been abandoned on the slipper chair by the door. A soft, warm light permeated the cotton curtains. The darkness was all in her head: corners that turned into fog and gloom; distant shadows from the past glimpsed through half open doors.

For the first time, she thought maybe she didn't want to remember. She should push those doors closed and start afresh - if her brain would let her.

*

Jo fed Sidney and leaned against the utility room units, watching him as he delicately cleared the dish. She had just started letting him out again. He was better, stronger and more confident; it was she who was nervous. Was he at risk still? Probably not because Eleanor was home. The risk had transferred.

There were things Jo ought to be doing - she had a string of memos on the voice recorder waiting to be replayed - but they would wait. Eleanor was upstairs in her bedroom, having a shower. Jo had gone up and listened outside her aunt's door some half hour since. She had heard the sound of the running water and had poked her head round the door to check all was well. Satisfied, she had left her to it.

'If I want help I'll ask for it,' Eleanor had insisted the day before.

Charlotte had acquired an old bulb bicycle horn from somewhere which she had given Eleanor to call for assistance if she needed it.

'Why in God's name would I carry a thing like that around, you dotty woman?' had been Eleanor's caustic response.

Undeterred, Charlotte had come into work again that Saturday morning, had told Jo that she might as well work, that she had nothing else planned. She stood now in the kitchen, cooking bacon and eggs for Brian who was sitting in the conservatory reading one of the newspapers Charlotte had brought up from the village store.

Lawrence was in his office already, fielding phone calls. Jo was avoiding him.

She pulled herself away from the units and walked through to Eleanor's study. She phoned Nancy to make sure there were no problems she hadn't heard about then glanced at her watch. The talks didn't start till eleven but the speakers wanted to get in early and check out the sound equipment. She ought to go down. And there was something else she had to do which was going to be much harder. She started picking at the sealing tape on the parcel which had arrived the day before.

Twenty minutes later, Eleanor was downstairs and installed at the table in the conservatory, eating her breakfast and chatting to Brian. He was taking her to one of the morning sessions then bringing her back for lunch. After that he would leave but Charlotte was going to be around all day. The housekeeper kept looming into view, watching her employer beadily, then disappearing again without speaking.

Jo threw on a sweat jacket and slipped out. No harm was likely to come to Eleanor while Charlotte was there.

*

Ian Hennion, one of the speakers, was having a problem with his laptop: it wouldn't recognise the projector and he had a long sequence of slide images with which to illustrate his talk. Matthew sorted it out in a few short minutes and Ian apologised for the umpteenth time. Matthew brushed the

284

apology aside.

'No problem.'

He had been at Millie's when Jo rang him to ask if he could help and he had gone straight to The Mill, leaving an unconcerned Gail and Freddie to cope. Now he waited to watch the author practise run through his opening slides then left him to it. Pleasant bloke. Wrote biographies apparently. Matthew had never heard of him but there was nothing unusual about that.

As he entered the main bistro, Jo was involved in an earnest conversation with the manager. It was ten-twenty and already half the tables were occupied with people drinking and snacking. There was a low buzz of conversation. Matthew had brought his camera and had arranged to go back and take a couple of photos of Ian Hennion to put on the website once he'd started his talk. He planned to go and arrange the same thing with Imogen Pooley over in the village hall, if she was there. But Jo had said on the phone that she wanted to see him so he stayed around, feeling conspicuous and a little apprehensive. He wandered outside.

It was a cloudy morning with a light, scudding breeze. Only a couple of the outside tables were occupied. Matthew sat at a vacant table near the door, stretching out his legs, savouring the quiet. Nathan was back from his holiday in Portugal and Harry had caught the bus into Kingsbridge, a town six miles away, to meet up with him. School started again on Tuesday. Several times Matthew had toyed with asking Harry if there was any truth in the story he had told Jo about Eleanor's fall from the cliff, but in the end he hadn't pursued it. It was a no win argument in the making.

A waitress appeared and he ordered an Americano. The coffee arrived at the same time as Jo who emerged from the interior and stopped by his table.

'Coffee?' he offered. She hesitated and he smiled. 'I'm buying.'

She met his gaze then glanced at the waitress who stood expectantly, looking both casually amused and a little bored.

'Thanks. I'll have a cappuccino please. Regular.' She sat down and slung her bag over the back of the chair. 'There's stuff I should be doing,' she said, looking harassed, 'but I guess it'll wait while I have a drink.'

'Don't worry. It'll happen whether you run around like a headless chicken or not. It's on autopilot now.'

He smiled again, struck by how pleased he was to see her. He relaxed more into his seat, seemed to breathe a little more easily. Increasingly, he realised that he had been quite stupid about Jo and Harry and probably a lot of other things too; it had set him thinking. The introspection hadn't brought forth any earth-shattering conclusions except that he knew he wanted to see her again - if she would let him.

'It wouldn't have happened this morning...' Jo was saying now. He forced himself to pay attention. '...if you hadn't sorted Ian out with his computer.'

'He'd have managed.'

'Since when did you become the guru of calm?'

'I'm turning over a new leaf.'

She studied him, eyes narrowed.

He leaned forward. 'I'm glad you said you wanted to see me. I've been trying to pluck up the courage to contact you. I wanted to apologise for the way I behaved. I mean it. I'm so sorry. I was completely in the wrong.'

'OK.' She spoke cautiously, studying his face as if to judge his sincerity. 'I said some things I shouldn't have too. Shall we just forget it?'

'Yes. Can we?' He hesitated. 'How's Eleanor doing? I saw she was down last night. People have been talking about it.' He tapped the table with a restive index finger. 'I'm sorry, I was a bit hasty, dismissing your concerns, wasn't I? But I'm sure you're worrying unnecessarily about her fall.' He stopped, sure he ought to say something else, unsure what it should be. 'Anyway, I just wanted to say that. In case you're still worrying.'

'OK,' she repeated. Again a pause. She pressed her lips together as if trapping some further comment before it could come out. 'But that wasn't why I wanted to see you.' She turned and foraged in her handbag, pulled out a small bubble-wrapped package and handed it to him. 'This belongs to Harry. It's his old phone. There's also a memory stick in there with the photographs that were on it.'

Matthew stared at her then down at the package in his hand, frowning. 'I don't understand.'

'It's the phone Harry dropped in the sea. When he couldn't get it to work, he was upset about losing all the photographs on it - lots of his mum apparently. Anyway I know someone who works with smartphones and she was able to do something about them. He doesn't know because I told him that I didn't want to ask her...' She hesitated. 'The someone is my ex's sister, you see. Anyway, I did ask her and she came up trumps. She's rescued the photos and I thought you might like to give them to him. You don't have to mention me.' She hesitated. 'I should have...'

'Wait a minute,' he said, cutting across her. 'If Harry doesn't know about it, how did you come to have his phone?'

'That's what I was about to say: I should have told you. Well, no, I should have asked you first. I'm sorry. When I went upstairs to the bathroom at your house I saw the *Beware* sign and guessed it was Harry's room. He told me he had a photo of Sophie on display and I just wanted to look at it. Then when I picked it up I saw that phone hidden behind it.' She shrugged apologetically. 'I took it. I figured he probably wouldn't notice for a while. I don't suppose he picks the photo up very often. We'd kind of fallen out hadn't we, so I didn't tell you. I did it on an impulse, you see, feeling guilty for having refused him.'

He continued to stare at her in stony silence. He could feel his heart rate quickening; his breathing felt heavy and hard. Jo's coffee arrived and even the waitress seemed to feel the glacier that had developed between them. She put the drink down and retreated wordlessly.

He fingered the package. 'So you were nosing around Harry's things behind my back?' He raised his eyes to her face. 'And now you think I should pretend I did this, not say anything, just pass it off as my own work. Is that because I'm such a useless father? Well thanks a bunch for that. Do you know how rubbish that makes me feel? What kind of man do you think I am?'

Jo leaned forward onto the table towards him.

'I'm sorry. I just wanted to help. I didn't want to do it behind your back but I wasn't sure what your reaction would be. I thought maybe if you gave them to him it might help both of you come together or something. I didn't mean anything by it. Of course you're not a useless father. I'm sorry, Matthew…' Her voice trailed away.

Matthew felt his throat thickening; his face began to crumple and tears threatened. He hadn't cried since he didn't know when and it scared him. If he started crying now he might lose it completely and the fragile world he had created could break down around him. He stood up abruptly, abandoning the package on the table, and walked away leaving his coffee untouched.

*

Up at Skymeet, Eleanor stood at the patio doors, looking out over the garden and to the sea beyond. It was half past three in the afternoon. When Brian had left, two hours since, she had fallen into a heavy sleep on the sofa and had only recently woken. Her head still felt woolly. She suspected she had been dreaming again but this time had no recall of it.

'It's good to see you back on your feet again,' said Lawrence.

She turned carefully, being sure to lift her feet the way she had been taught, to place them evenly a little apart to keep her balance. Lawrence was standing just inside the door to the room. She wondered if he had been in before, had seen her lolling on the sofa, mouth open probably, snoring or, worse still, talking in her sleep. Frank had said she sometimes did that.

'You look well,' Lawrence added and smiled. 'I've asked Charlotte to bring you some tea, now you're awake.'

So he had been in.

'Thank you. We need to do some catching up, don't we?'

Again he smiled, that slow, guarded smile of his. 'It'll wait till the weekend's over.'

Charlotte bustled in carrying a tray with the tea things on it. She set it down on the coffee table, glanced from Eleanor to Lawrence and back, then left without a word. She had put two cups and saucers on the tray. Had those been Lawrence's instructions?

'Do you want to join me?' said Eleanor.

They both heard the front door open and close and Jo walked in.

'Thanks,' said Lawrence, 'but I need to go down to the village.' He hesitated. 'Were you thinking of staying for the concert tonight? Only I think it might be rather loud and tiring for you. You'd be better off coming back here.'

'I haven't decided, Lawrence.'

He looked ready to argue the point but then didn't, nodded, glanced at Jo and left.

Eleanor turned to her niece who looked terrible: pale and fraught.

'What is it darling? Are you all right?'

'Yes, fine. It's been kind of busy - you know.' Jo smiled wanly. 'And I keep doing dumb things, Eleanor, that's all.' She glanced down at the tray. 'But tea would be good.'

'Yes. Let's have it.' Eleanor walked slowly back to sit on the sofa. 'Then I want to go and hear Vincent's talk.'

'Really? Well, there's plenty of time before that.' Jo sat beside her and reached to the tray, sorting out the cups and saucers. 'I thought you might be cross that I'd asked him.' She picked up the pot and began pouring the tea. 'You didn't want him to speak originally. I had to ask him to fill in on the last minute. Do you remember me telling you that?'

'Yes dear. He can be a bastard and he always wants money. I was probably cross with him about something - I don't know what.'

Jo handed Eleanor her cup and saucer and offered the plate of biscuits Charlotte had added to the tray. Eleanor shook her head and sat back. The front door opened and closed. Jo waited a couple of minutes, listening, then turned back to her aunt.

'Eleanor, I don't think I've ever asked you how you came to employ Lawrence all those years ago? Do you remember?'

'I do actually. Why do I remember some things and not

others?'

'What do you remember?'

'Oh...well, when I first met Lawrence we were both students. He never fitted in, even then. He could be tricky - prickly, you know. At school, he'd been a bit of a loner, creative and quite clever - which is never popular - and he didn't like sports so he got teased and picked on. It made him defensive. Then at university, he seemed to immediately alienate people. He should have gone on to be successful in his own right but he drifted from one job to another. Couldn't settle and didn't get on with his bosses. He tried his hand at writing novels on the side but didn't get anywhere with that either.

She paused and drank some tea.

'Anyway, I had some hard times early on and had fallen behind in my rent payments. I didn't want to admit it to my family and certainly not Candida. Lawrence bailed me out. A few years later, he was looking for a job again and I asked him if he'd like to be my PA. He's good at it.'

'But you don't always get on do you? He can be very domineering, likes to have his own way?'

'Yes. I can manage him though.' Eleanor shrugged.

'Does he ever lose his temper with you?'

'Lawrence? What an odd thing to ask.' She shook her head. 'Lose it, no. Well, yes and no. We've had our differences. Why?'

'I just wondered.'

Eleanor watched her niece pause, clearly wanting to say more.

'*You* don't get on with him though, do you?' Eleanor said, more statement than question.

'Not really. There's always an atmosphere when he's

around.'

Eleanor drank her tea and didn't reply.

'Don't take this the wrong way, Eleanor, but have you made a will?'

'Good God, Jo, what is this all about?'

'Can't you remember?'

'No. I might have.' She screwed her face up trying to recall. 'No, I don't know. I wish you'd tell me what this is about.'

'Nothing really. I've got all sorts of nonsense going round in my head. Nothing for you to worry about.'

'Good. So stop asking questions.'

Jo smiled. 'All right. Let's finish this tea and go down to the village.' She paused. 'Eleanor, Imogen asked me if we'd like to eat with them this evening. It'll be early - before the last talks. They've booked a table at The Mill for all of them: Imogen, Mari, Frank, Louisa, Vincent. I think Lawrence is going too. A sort of parting meal but, since you've only just come home, don't feel pressured to go. It'll be easy to make our excuses.'

Eleanor looked away, studying the floor.

'The rug's gone,' she said.

'Only till you get a bit steadier on your feet. But what about this meal, Eleanor? Shall I say we can't do it?'

'No, we'll go. I'd like to see them before they leave. Anyway, if they're going to talk about me, I'd rather they did it to my face.' She sniffed. 'I suppose we could ask Charlotte too.'

'Charlotte's daughter's coming over. She's got a meal planned then they've got tickets for the festival this evening.'

Eleanor barely heard her reply. This kept happening to her - her mind seemed to wander off at a tangent and she was

292

obliged to follow where it went. Now Lawrence was stuck in her head.

'He's very good at his work, you know. But it is true that he's changed. It's made him even more isolated.'

'Sorry?'

'Lawrence. I'm not sure being here is good for him. It makes him…unsociable. He's got worse you know. And he does like to be in control.' She handed Jo her cup. 'Can I have some more tea?'

Chapter 22

Matthew and Harry ate their evening meal early so Matthew could get back into the village for the evening sessions. Harry had spent the hour since his return from town in his bedroom and now sat, silent, squeezing ketchup onto his plate.

'Good day?' Matthew enquired casually, sitting down. 'Did Nathan have a good holiday?'

'Yeah.' Harry cut into a sausage. 'Sickening. He's dead brown.' He rammed the piece of sausage in his mouth, glancing up through his fringe. He scooped up some mashed potato on his fork and hesitated with it half way to his mouth. Another wary glance. 'He said I might be able to go with them to Portugal at Christmas. It's not hot but it's usually warm, he said. They even get to swim in the sea in December sometimes and eat outside. Sounds brilliant. Can I go?'

Matthew felt his stomach lurch; he hadn't expected that. It was hard to imagine Christmas without Harry. Images of Christmases with Sophie immediately came to mind. He would always associate Christmas with her and with their son, with absurd amounts of wrapping paper and too much pudding and all the decorations on the tree. Sophie always bought chocolate decorations too, especially for Harry to find. He became aware that Harry was still watching him, like a nervous bird, waiting for his response.

'This was always going to happen,' a voice murmured in

his head. 'Harry's growing up.' Sophie? Just a whisper now.

Matthew managed a smile. Of course she was right. He needed to get used to it. In the blink of an eye Harry would be all grown up and leaving.

'Yes, I think so,' he heard himself say. 'We'd need to check out some things first, wouldn't we? But yes, in principle.' He ran his tongue round a dry mouth. 'It sounds good.'

Harry looked at him a moment, surprised perhaps. *Jo listens. You never listen to me.* Harry thought he didn't care, that he was glad Sophie had gone. How in God's name had that happened?

They ate in silence.

'So about this evening...' said Matthew, '...you know I've got to go and hang around the events, take some pictures maybe, but I'm not going to be busy all the time. And this Frank Marwell who's giving one of the talks, he's supposed to be very entertaining. I bought a ticket for you in case you'd like to see him. I'm going to try and catch most of it myself.'

Harry rammed another forkful of mashed potato and sausage in his mouth and chewed, watching his father now in frank amazement. He gulped it down.

'But he's a poet, isn't he?' he said.

'I know, listening to a poet doesn't seem cool but the lyrics of songs are just poems, after all. It depends on how you look at them. We're not talking, oh I don't know, iambic pentameter and forty-six verse ballads here. Anyway this guy's reckoned to be quite a performer: funny and clever.' Matthew paused and found he needed to swallow. 'He was one of your mother's favourites. She had a book of some of his poems.'

'Really?' Harry stopped eating and stared at him. 'I don't

remember that.'

'We've got it here. I found it in one of the boxes.' Again Matthew managed something resembling a smile. 'She even scribbled notes in it. You should take a look.'

Still Harry stared at him but didn't speak and started shovelling food in his mouth again, flicking glances up at his father now and then.

'So do you want to go?' pressed Matthew. 'There's a concert afterwards too - well, I'm sure you've seen the posters. I don't know what it'll be like but worth a try.'

Harry shrugged. 'Maybe. I dunno.'

'I've got tickets for both anyway. I'll give you them, just in case. Sit at the back. You don't have to stay if you're not enjoying it.' With an effort of will he added, 'Jo will probably be there.'

Harry flicked him another confused look but said nothing.

They finished eating and Matthew began clearing up. After a moment's hesitation, Harry carried his plate across to the sink then stood in the kitchen doorway, hands rammed in his pockets, an intense expression on his face as if he was about to say something. In the end he didn't and drifted away upstairs.

*

It was a mild but dull evening with occasional drizzle in the air, a small foretaste of the rain that had been predicted for later in the night. The Mill was jammed with people. A handful of keen smokers sat or stood outside but every indoor table was occupied and a cluster of people stood at the bar. Imogen had booked a table for eight for their dinner and had asked the management for a place in the room to the rear of the bar which was smaller and quieter. Two tables had been pushed together for them and attractively laid. Imogen and Mari arrived first. Eleanor and Jo were last, though one chair remained empty.

'Oh good, you've made it, Eleanor,' said Mari breathily. 'How wonderful to have you back with us again for our last supper.'

'How are you, Eleanor?' said Louisa. 'You look amazing.'

Eleanor put a reflex hand up to the scarf covering her head and smiled at Louisa without conviction. 'Thank you. Though I'll be happier when my hair's grown. Otherwise, I'm doing well, despite my doctors' best efforts.'

'On the contrary,' remarked Frank, who had somehow ended up sitting opposite her, 'I'm sure your doctors made a huge effort to get you well so they could get you out of their hair. No doubt you were telling them what to do as usual.'

A ripple of laughter went round the table. Eleanor grinned but said nothing, reaching a slightly shaky hand to her glass of gin and tonic. Jo had seen the shake; she wondered if they all had.

'Isn't Lawrence coming?' Mari looked towards the vacant chair.

'It would appear not,' said Frank. 'I daresay we'll cope.'

'Oh Frank,' said Louisa.

'Your festival's gone terribly well so far, darling.' Mari was smiling at Eleanor. 'Look at all the people who've come. And after your awful fall and such an inauspicious start to the summer.' She picked up her glass of wine and held it up towards Eleanor. 'Congratulations.'

Eleanor shook her head, looking unusually flustered. 'No, congratulate Jo...and all the others. Please. It's not my festival. I don't even remember planning it.' She smiled. 'And thanks to you all for taking part. I must fall over more often. I seem to get more done that way.'

Again there was laughter. A waitress appeared and, after some hesitation, they all ordered.

'So you're enjoying the festival, Eleanor dear?' said Vincent. 'I saw you at my humble little talk. I was surprised consid…'

Jo quickly intervened. 'Your talk went down well, Vincent. Thank you for doing it at such short notice. Did you make many sales?'

'Not bad. Just as well since we aren't being paid.'

'Vincent, don't,' warned Imogen.

Eleanor frowned but said nothing. Jo was sitting next to her and glanced sideways. Her aunt had that glazed, preoccupied look in her eyes again as if an internal eye had suddenly fixed on something that no-one else could see.

'I just thought…' Vincent paused for emphasis, '…that we should be recompensed for our efforts.'

Eleanor seemed to have trouble dragging herself back to the present. She looked momentarily lost.

'The terms of everyone's performance were laid out beforehand,' said Jo. 'As you well know.'

'Vincent? Shut up,' said Frank vehemently, glaring at him. His expression softened as he turned his head to look at Eleanor. 'He's just messing with you, Ellie. Ignore him.'

Vincent snorted. 'There speaks a man who doesn't worry where his next meal's coming from.'

'Really Vincent,' protested Imogen, 'you're nothing like as poor as you make out.' She pointed at the large whisky in front of him. 'Perhaps you should stop drinking if you can't make ends meet.'

Louisa silently followed the to and fro of the exchange with watchful eyes.

'It must be awful not to be able to remember things, Eleanor,' she said. 'Poor you. Some memories can be so precious, can't they? Never to be repeated moments.' Frank gave her a baleful look. She ignored him. 'Can you even remember what you were writing? Will you be able to finish it do you think?'

'My writing might benefit from a bit of amnesia,' Imogen interposed drily. 'There are bits of it I'd certainly like to forget I wrote.'

Laughter lightened the mood and a couple of the others agreed, adding their own jaundiced perspectives on their writing. Eleanor never answered the question. Jo watched her warily.

'Has everyone else sold lots of books this weekend too then?' Louisa embraced the whole table with a triumphant smile. 'I was thrilled. And they say print books are dead. It's nonsense.'

There were grunts of agreement and dissension.

'You must have spoken well, Louisa,' said Mari, generously. 'That's what makes people buy.'

'She certainly practised enough.' Frank flicked Louisa another look. 'She was consumed with nerves earlier.'

'Really? It didn't show.' Mari shrugged apologetically. 'I'm afraid nerves got the better of me again yesterday. I couldn't get into gear. I'm really not good at this speaking business.'

'Nonsense,' said Frank. 'Everyone gets nervous. And poetry's not an easy sell but look how well you went down in Exeter. I didn't see any sign of nerves there and you absolutely stormed them.'

Jo automatically turned to Mari for her reply but Mari said nothing, diffident as ever, staring at Frank wide-eyed as if

299

desperate to believe him.

'You get nervous, Frank?' Imogen rolled her eyes. 'My God, you've shaken my whole belief system.'

'Frank recites his poetry to his busts,' declared Eleanor. 'In his study. He told me.' She leaned forward, reaching a hand across the table with a teasing smile, and put it on top of one of his. 'It's true isn't it darling?'

There was silence for a moment then more laughter.

'She means his busts of dead poets,' said Louisa crossly, colouring.

'The perfect audience.' Frank grinned, unfazed, and squeezed Eleanor's hand. 'No heckling.'

The food arrived and the conversation dwindled then meandered. Eleanor fell silent again and Jo watched her occasionally, wondering what exactly was going on in her head. And she wasn't the only one. Apart from Vincent, who appeared uncaring, everyone at the table kept an occasional and watchful eye on Eleanor.

*

Frank was the perfect end of festival speaker, able to tell jokes and stories and move seamlessly into reciting his poetry, which was sometimes deceptively simple, sometimes quite obscure. Somehow he made it accessible. He had the audience eating out of his hand.

Jo glanced round the room now and then. Louisa was sitting near the front; Imogen and Mari sat in the row behind them and Matthew was there too, sitting on the farther side of the aisle. There were other faces she recognised: committee members and people from the village. Lawrence had appeared and was standing at the back of the hall but there was no sign of Vincent.

The meal had made her uneasy again; there had been an atmosphere at that table, something tense and unspoken. She glanced sidelong at her aunt's face. Eleanor was rapt, watching the man who had been her lover off and on for the majority of her adult life. Now and then, her lips moved as if she were recalling something, murmuring it out loud to fix it. Or perhaps it was nothing, a repetition of words from one of his poems maybe, a line which struck a chord.

Frank wrapped up his talk and invited questions from the audience. There was a brief awkward silence then a hand went up.

'How long does it take you to write a poem?' said the woman.

'Sometimes ten minutes; sometimes ten months.' Frank smiled. 'Sometimes they have to be dragged out of you kicking and screaming. No seriously, it's…'

Jo stopped listening. She found herself thinking about the dinner. Something had unsettled her, a comment perhaps or a look, something which didn't quite fit, like a line of poetry that doesn't scan properly and brings you up short. It kept niggling at the back of her brain. There was a brief vote of thanks to Frank for his talk, then ringing applause. Jo came back to the present.

'The concert will begin in approximately half an hour,' said the MC. 'Please take all your belongings and leave the room while we reset it. You'll need a concert ticket to be readmitted. The bar is open next door if you want a drink while you wait.'

People began to stand up and shuffle out. There was a separate designated bar area just for the use of the function room. Jo gave Eleanor an arm to hold and they joined Imogen and Mari and managed to find a seat for Eleanor while the

301

others stood around with their drinks. Frank and Louisa passed but didn't speak; they appeared to be in the middle of an argument. Eleanor's eyes followed them.

'Am I too old to find a new lover?' she demanded suddenly.

Imogen laughed. 'Of course not. You're still in your prime. Did you have someone in mind?

'Not yet.'

'Plenty of time. Find someone who doesn't recite poetry to the busts of dead poets though, huh?'

Eleanor stared up at her, looking troubled.

'Sorry, was that a bit crass of me? I was only joking, Eleanor.'

Jo found Mari's eyes on her, her gaze steady and meaningful. She was trying to communicate something. Jo stared at her and Mari jerked her eyes sideways towards the washroom. Jo got it. She finished the last of her drink and put the glass down.

'I need to go to the bathroom,' she said, fixing Mari with a look.

'Me too,' said Mari. An announcement came through the speakers warning that the concert would start in five minutes. 'Will you and Eleanor get the seats for us, Immy?'

'Sure.' Imogen turned to Eleanor as the two women walked away. 'So, what kind of man are you looking for?'

*

In the ladies cloakroom, Mari and Jo stopped by the washbasins and faced each other.

'Did you want to say something to me?' asked Jo.

'Yes.' Mari glanced round. One of the cubicles was occupied.

302

A toilet flush sounded and a woman exited the cubicle. They moved aside and she washed her hands, tossing them both a suspicious glance. The woman left and they were alone.

'I didn't see Frank in the audience that night,' Mari blurted out.

'I'm sorry, I don't...'

'You know.' Mari looked anguished. 'Frank said he watched my performance on the Friday night in Exeter. At the poetry weekend. He keeps referring to it and how well I spoke. Well maybe he did - I mean he probably did - it's just that I didn't see him. Only the thing is, I've kept agreeing that he was there and that's what I told the police too because...well, you know, it was Frank and I'm sure he must have been. Frank's been a friend forever. I'm not trying to contradict him. It's just that I didn't actually see him and it's been bothering me. I don't like to tell lies.'

'Maybe it was the stage lighting...' suggested Jo. This didn't make sense. Frank? He lied? Jo began to feel queasy as it sank in. Not Frank, surely? It couldn't be significant. 'What about afterwards?'

'After my slot I went to the bar with another poet friend for a couple of drinks. She'd done her stint earlier so we were both free.'

'And you didn't see Frank then either?'

'No.' Mari smiled tentatively. 'He was there the next morning at breakfast though. He said he'd wanted to get some fresh air the night before and had wandered further into town for a drink. This isn't really important, is it? I didn't want to say anything in front of the others. Anyway, Imogen says I talk too much. But I wanted to set the record straight. I don't need to tell the police, do I? Tell me I don't.'

Jo said nothing, still trying to process it.

'I had a lot on my mind for my performance,' Mari added. 'I could have missed him. Easily. I could.'

'But I saw your face tonight when he said how well you spoke.' Jo paused. She hated what she was thinking. 'You don't believe him.'

Mari looked away. 'I don't know,' she said in a small, obstinate voice and disappeared into one of the cubicles.

The concert had started. The Mill function room was full and buzzing with every seat taken and people standing in the gloom at the back and sides, drinks in hand, all eyes fixed on the brightly lit stage. A five piece band had opened the programme, playing covers of well-known hits. They were late starting due to a hiccup with the sound system but already they had electrified the atmosphere, their music loud and pulsating. It felt a little surreal after the constrained and measured talking events of the rest of the weekend. Jo slipped into her seat next to Eleanor and glanced across. Her aunt was staring at the stage vacantly, a light frown puckering her forehead. It wasn't her kind of music.

'Are you tired?' Jo asked her. 'We can go if you want.'

Eleanor brushed Jo's concerns away with a shake of the head.

Jo wanted to leave; she wanted space to think about what Mari had said. The music drummed around her, number after number, none of which she heard. And now they had finished their set and there was to be a brief pause while the stage was cleared of instruments and reset. A number of people got up to refresh their drinks. Jo got up too, affecting the need to stretch her legs and back. Warily, slowly, she glanced round the room. Imogen and Mari were sitting the other side of Eleanor. Charlotte and her daughter were sitting two rows back from them; she caught Charlotte's eye and smiled. Matthew was in the audience too, over to her left, his camera on his lap and, standing right at the back, Harry was leaning against the wall, trying to look cool and succeeding in looking really awkward.

And now she could see Frank too, sitting over on the far side towards the rear, alone, talking to the man next to him. The next act were being introduced and she sat down. It was a duo: a man with a guitar and a woman who played the fiddle and they started with a fast instrumental number which quickly got the audience clapping and drumming their feet. They moved into a slower ballad, the fiddle's haunting notes harmonising with the man's singing. Jo took a minute to realise that Eleanor was speaking to her.

She leaned across. 'Sorry, Eleanor?'

'Hugh managed to find Shelley.' Her tone was pressing, urgent. She stared into Jo's face. 'He was very proud of it. It was something special. Frank had been wanting one for years.'

'Shelley? I don't understand. What do…?'

'Percy Bysshe Shelley,' hissed Eleanor.

'Ssh,' said Jo, putting a quelling hand to Eleanor's arm, sure that others would be able to hear her, maybe even Frank, but scared to look round, just in case. The song came to an end and everyone clapped. The duo introduced their next piece and started singing unaccompanied. When the man began playing a guitar accompaniment and the fiddle kicked in too, Jo leaned over again.

'Are you talking about Hugh Shrigley?' she whispered.

'Yes. He showed it to us. To Frank and me.'

'Showed you what exactly?'

'The bust of Shelley. It was special.'

'Please keep your voice down,' said Jo, squeezing her hand.

'The sculptor was famous for it,' whispered Eleanor.

'Can't remember her name. But I'm sure Hugh only bought it because he knew Frank would be jealous of it for his own collection. Hugh was like that.' She was picking hard at a piece of loose skin on her thumb, agitated and restless. 'But Frank didn't seem that bothered and we left.' She hesitated, still fidgeting her fingers. 'Yes, I'm sure we left soon after.' She shook her head and fell silent.

Jo stared unseeingly towards the stage. What Eleanor was talking about happened years ago; what significance did it have now and why was it bothering her? A bust of Shelley. Yes, given his passion for collecting poet busts, you would have expected Frank to be jealous. Then Eleanor and Frank had left the party soon afterwards. And now Frank had lied about being in Exeter. Was there a missing link here, something obvious that she was failing to grasp? Frank could easily have had time to drive back to Petterton Mill Cove to see Eleanor. But what would have made him do that and then lie about it? The music drifted over her, an instrumental number now, then another singer joined them. Instruments were changed for the final item before the interval and they struck up again.

It came to her. 'The magazine cutting,' she murmured.

That piece of paper which Eleanor had crushed into a ball and then meticulously smoothed out and kept. The image of it flashed up in Jo's head, each detail of it suddenly clear in her mind's eye. She didn't understand everything it signified yet but it was beginning to slot into place and what she was thinking chilled her. That cutting had been the trigger to this terrible chain of events. And she would bet that Frank knew it too. He also knew that Jo had seen it because she'd told him she had. He would guess that they still had it - Frank knew as well as anyone that Eleanor kept everything.

Jo glanced across. Eleanor had settled again, her fingers relaxed, one of her feet tapping softly to the rhythm of the music. But earlier that evening it had been obvious to everyone that Eleanor was starting to recall things. Look at the way she had mentioned Frank reciting to his poet busts. Put the magazine cutting in front of her now and she would probably remember a lot more. Frank would know that too. That cutting was important in some way.

The first half ended; the lights in the room went on and everyone got up. Out in the aisle as they shuffled their way towards the exit to the bar, Jo eased across to Imogen.

'Can you look after Eleanor while I nip back to the house to check on my cat? He'll be wanting to come in by now.'

'Of course.'

'You won't leave her alone, will you?'

Imogen glared. 'Really Jo. What a question.'

Jo cut right towards the main exit. She needed to see that cutting again and she wanted it in her possession before Eleanor said anything else. Here and now, in a crowded room and with friends at her side, Eleanor was safe. At the exit, Jo glanced round, seeing no-one, searching for Frank. There was no sign of him; he was probably in the bar already. She slipped out into the darkness.

A few minutes later a dark shape followed her across the car park to the lane.

Chapter 23

Jo's fingers fumbled as she tried to input the code on the woodland gate. She had hurried and was breathless, anxious too. At one point on the path she was sure she'd heard a noise behind her and stopped, straining every sense to identify what it was. Then with a rustle, a bird had suddenly swept away, wings silently flapping, and she had breathed again. Now she had to do the code a second time to get it to register and blew out a breath of relief as the lock released and she was able to swing the gate open. Cutting through the remaining fringe of trees towards the house, she forced herself to walk more slowly. She was overreacting, panicking; there was no need to rush. It would take her no time to locate the cutting and then she would be out of there and back down to The Mill long before the concert finished. Eleanor was at no risk.

Still she couldn't shake off the apprehension. Boundaries had moved, patterns of usual behaviour had been overturned.

She put the key in the lock on the front door and let herself in. The house was dark and eerily silent as if it too was holding its breath. She chided herself for letting her imagination take hold. Even so, she felt an irrational need to stay silent too, to get this done and not advertise her presence. Still using her torch, she strode the length of the hall and entered Eleanor's study.

Flashing the torch beam around the room it was almost a

surprise that it looked undisturbed, so normal and innocent. She switched on the small table lamp on top of the bureau. Its warm glow was reassuringly familiar and she went to the patio doors, opening one of them out onto the night and softly calling Sidney's name. It hadn't only been an excuse to come back; it was time he came in. She called a second time but there was still no response and she felt another pang of fear. Leaving the door open, she went back into the room.

The library steps were in the corner. She pulled them out and looked up in the dim light, trying to remember exactly where that book was. Yes, she thought she knew: five shelves up and over to her right. She shifted the steps and climbed, using her torch to check the spines. There it was: *Now and Then*, the volume of Frank's poetry. Pulling it out, still standing on the steps, she flicked through the pages. The cutting was there, folded in half. She removed it, replaced the book and returned to the floor.

Standing examining it in the light from the lamp, it was exactly as she remembered: a waist up shot of Frank in his study with his arm around Louisa. Behind them were wooden shelves most of which were filled with books, some of them clearly leather bound. One of the visible shelves held other display items: a fine brass clock; an elaborately decorated theatrical mask - the sort Jo had seen once in Venice - and a couple of bronze busts. The photographer must have been impressed by the image they created and had arranged it to make sure they were included in the shot.

Hugh managed to find Shelley. The bust of Shelley. It was special. And there it was in the photo. Jo had seen images of Shelley before and she was sure that the bust on the right portrayed him. She was equally sure it was the one that Hugh Shrigley had bought because that's what had been bothering

309

Eleanor, gnawing at her subconscious, forcing her to keep reliving that party at Hugh Shrigley's. It wasn't proof of anything yet but it was a start.

She refolded the cutting and was ramming it in the pocket of her jacket when a noise outside made her freeze. She forced herself to turn and slink towards the open patio door.

'Sidney?' she murmured. 'Is that you?'

A man's form loomed out of the darkness just a stone's throw away and Jo's heart skipped a beat.

'No, it's me.' He took a couple of steps forwards till he was standing in the doorway. The dull light from the lamp illuminated his features just enough to make them clear. Either way, she knew who it was; she would recognise that voice anywhere.

'Frank.' She tried to sound casual. 'What are you doing here?'

'I've come to see you. In fact, I've been here a little while. I saw you abandon Eleanor with Imogen and leave the Mill. Then you went off in the dark, all furtive, so I thought I'd follow you and see what you were up to. It's not like you to behave like that my dear - or perhaps I don't know you as well as I thought I did.'

'I suspect you don't know me at all.'

He pursed up his lips and stretched a smile. 'Maybe not. Anyway I've been watching you here, climbing around Eleanor's study. Again, it seems a strange thing to be doing at this time of night.'

He wandered into the room, forcing her to take a step backwards, and glanced around as if seeing it all anew.

'I got the distinct impression that you were looking for something and, indeed, that you had found it,' he remarked to the room at large. He turned back to her. 'Does that sound fair?'

Jo slid her hand into her pocket, reassuring herself that the cutting was still there. Her fingers brushed against the voice recorder. She had been carrying it around all day, just as she had for weeks. Jo slowly felt along its edge and gently pressed the power button. This machine picked up everything.

'What does it have to do with you, Frank? This isn't your home any more. It never was really. You just boarded here.'

'Ooh, feisty.' He smiled, not unkindly. 'You're wrong, you know, I think I do know you. I always guessed you had some spunk in that straight-laced little frame of yours.' He sighed heavily and wandered further into the room. 'Oh Jojo, please don't play games. We both know why I'm here, don't we, so why don't you give me that magazine page and let the whole thing go? I don't want you to be involved in this.'

'In what?'

He eyed her up, slightly sidelong. 'Come now. You're being disingenuous. Eleanor has started to remember, hasn't she? After all, if it hadn't been for her, I'm sure you wouldn't have been skulking round here in the half dark. What were you frightened of?'

'You.' She admitted it unthinkingly and paused, brought up short by its truth. 'I've tried not to believe it, Frank. I used to think the world of you. You were something like the father I never had. Volatile at times, yes, unreliable even, but kind, clever and gentle. You bothered to spend time with me and teach me things. I thought you cared about me as well as about Eleanor.'

The challenging gaze faltered; he looked away, emitting a slow sigh.

'I did care for you Jojo.' He looked back at her. 'I still do. But you're getting involved in things you don't understand.'

'You're right, I don't understand. So explain, why don't you?' She hesitated. 'It all started with that bust of Shelley didn't it? You had to have it, didn't you, so you pushed Hugh Shrigley off the balcony?' She was gambling here, guessing, determined to draw him out.

He threw his head back with an agonised expression. 'I knew Eleanor had remembered. Hell.' He thumped a hand against the wall, making a picture rattle on its hanging. 'Bloody hell.' He began to pace the room. 'I'd hoped, I'd really hoped that she'd blank the whole thing. You know...' Again a heavy sigh. '...I never intended it to work out like this.'

'And how did you think it was going to work out? Tell me. I don't understand. If Eleanor knew about the bust already, why did the cutting make any difference to her?'

'She knew about the bust because she was with me when Hugh took me into the library and showed it off. She didn't know I had it because she wasn't there later on. She just guessed what happened and she was wrong. I told her that on that Friday, that God-awful Friday.'

'What? What did you tell her?'

'That it was an accident of course.'

He stopped pacing, his expression suggesting anger and astonishment that she didn't know. He'd assumed Eleanor had remembered more than she had. He looked down at the floor then back up into Jo's face. She could sense his burning need to talk, to explain himself. He began moving again.

'She'd seen that photo in an article she'd been sent and put two and two together and made five. I don't know how she could think me capable of... After all those years together.'

He paused, facing a framed photograph of Eleanor on the wall, a picture taken years before at the launch of an early book, and continued to stare at it as he talked.

'We'd left that party, you see, but I told Eleanor I'd forgotten my cigarette case at Hugh's flat and I went back later without her. I wanted to see if I could do a deal on the Shelley. I'd been hankering after one of those busts for ages and I thought maybe I could swop it for something else I had that he wanted, or maybe pay in instalments - or both. It's not as though Hugh truly wanted it.' He gave a wry laugh. 'He only bought it to show me he could. To win. And he'd been drinking; he was tight. He didn't want to come to any arrangement and I got cross. So yes, OK, I did push him a bit but it was nothing, just a scuffle. The next thing he'd fallen and thumped his head on the corner of the stone hearth.'

Frank turned away and began pacing again. 'He'd gone, just like that. Dead. I mean, I didn't do it to him, he overbalanced, but of course I panicked...and the next thing I knew I was carrying him out onto the balcony and pushing him over the balustrade so the thump on his head would be masked by the fall. Then I got out of there as quickly as I could. Eleanor and I had been in the room earlier so it was easy to explain away my fingerprints. They were private gardens at the back and it was very late. I thought it would be a while till anyone found him.'

'You found the time to steal the bust though.'

'I just took it on the spur of the moment. He wasn't going to need it any more and he hadn't shown it to anyone else. He'd saved it to flaunt in front of me.' He ran a hand through his hair. 'You think I haven't been haunted by it? Of course I have. For years. But time went on and...' He stopped walking and looked at her. '...I couldn't face admitting what I'd done. I was scared, as simple as that. I didn't want to go to prison for a foolish argument and a tragic accident. Can you imagine me in prison? Well can you?'

Jo said nothing. He was convincing, up to a point, and she wanted to believe him but she had seen his performances too many times. He wasn't an actor but he could turn it on when he chose; his stage persona was someone else, a mask he slipped on when needed. And the story didn't ring true - surely there'd have been blood left behind from a blow to the head on stone? Yet everyone believed Hugh had simply fallen, drunk, from the balcony, including the police presumably. And then there was Eleanor's fall. A coincidence too far.

Sidney chose that moment to stroll in through the door and insinuate himself around Jo's legs, purring. Glad of the distraction, she bent to pick him up. Seeing Frank, Sidney hissed, shrinking back in her arms. It was a struggle to hold him.

'You were the one who shut Sidney in that shed, weren't you?'

'What? Don't be ridiculous.' He turned away.

She stroked Sidney, trying to calm him down. 'What did you tell Eleanor afterwards then? After you'd left Hugh's apartment?'

'Nothing much. I didn't know what to say. I told her Hugh was completely plastered and making no sense, that he'd barely let me in through the door. I hid the bust. When the news got out and the police started asking questions, I denied knowing anything about it. Eleanor believed me; they all did. No-one had seen me go in or leave. The people in the flat below said they might have heard someone else at the apartment but they were vague and unsure. I made Eleanor promise to say nothing about me going back. I said I didn't want to get involved with the police over a tragic accident which I knew nothing about. She kept her word.'

314

'Then she saw that photograph and warned you that she would have to break that promise?'

'Yes. She said she'd seen the bust and had guessed what had happened. She told me she couldn't live with what she knew, that I had to say something or that she would.'

He began pacing again. Sidney kept bristling in Jo's arms. He spat.

Frank ignored him. 'That photograph was a mistake. Eleanor hadn't been to my flat in years. It was my bolt-hole. I suppose I got blasé about it after a while. No-one else knew about the damn bust and it never crossed my mind that she would see it. I didn't think.'

'So you came over here and challenged her about it...'

His eyes narrowed. She saw his guard come up.

'Don't be absurd. I was in Exeter. We spoke on the phone. Poor Eleanor was distraught and drinking. I could tell from her voice.' He smiled grimly. 'Anyway you can't use any of this against me, Jo. It'd be your word against mine. So if you'll just give me that magazine cutting, we'll pretend none of this ever happened and leave it at that.'

'The photograph will be on record at the magazine.'

'But who else will know it has any significance?'

'Eleanor?'

'We'll have a chat about it, Ellie and I. I think we can iron it out. I honestly think we might even be able to get together again. Louisa and I are finished. Nothing's been the same since I left Eleanor. I really think we're bonded together somehow.'

He took a step towards her, stretching out his hand. She hesitated but the hard look in his eyes didn't match the light tone of his voice and she didn't trust him. He knew he had said too much.

He took another step towards her, gesturing impatiently

315

with the outstretched hand. 'Come on Jo.'

That was too much for Sidney. He spat again and jumped at Frank, yowling, angry and protective. Jo made a split second decision and dashed for the open patio door, throwing herself out into the night. Behind her she heard Frank swearing at the cat and saw Sidney streak out past her. She started to run, heart thumping. She had to get away. Frank had killed before and now he was a desperate man.

*

Jo ran over the patio, out of the arc of light from the study and down the steps to the lawn. She kept moving, on towards where the lawn fell away to the herbaceous border. Beyond that was the fence and an army of trees. It was too dark to see anything. She had her phone with her but didn't dare switch on the torch and had to trust to memory and instinct instead. She discounted heading for the woodland path to the village - Frank would expect it and she would be too easy to follow.

He was out on the patio now - she could see his silhouette against the study light - peering into the darkness left and right. Jo weighed up her options. Hiding in the trees would be risky in the dark and she would never be able to move quietly enough on the crackling undergrowth. She edged farther down the lawn. Her eyes were beginning to adjust and she could see faint shapes forming. Then her foot dropped off the lawn into the flower bed, turning slightly, and she bit back a yelp of surprise and pain. She bent over, scrabbling urgently over the soil for a small stone. She found one and straightened up, took aim and threw it towards the trees near the village side of the house. How ironic that it was Frank who had taught her how to throw properly, like a boy. The stone made a satisfying noise as it dropped and she saw Frank turn and move that way.

Immediately she started moving again, the other way, towards the eastern side of the garden. Thank God she'd decided to wear trousers and flat shoes that night.

She crept into the side gardens and among the shrubbery, stopping behind a small bay tree, straining to listen, hardly daring to breathe. He had gone the other way, she was almost certain, but it mightn't take him long to realise that he had been fooled. Where could she go? The beach? No, it was a stupid place to hide - the sea always reflected a little light. But it was low tide somewhere around now. If she kept to the rocks at the side, she would be hard to see and she could climb round like Harry did and get back to the village and safety. Difficult in the dark, yes, but what other option was there? None with Frank prowling around the grounds. He knew them as well as she did, knew all the places to hide.

She crept out from the shrubbery, straining every sense for a sign of Frank returning. Down on the lower terrace, she made for the steps and turned to go down backwards, gripping the hand rail, moving as fast as she dared. The wind was getting up. In the distance below, she could hear the sea crashing onto the shore. Perhaps the tide had turned already. Even so there would be time. She kept feeling for the next step down.

As she took the last step onto the shingle, a dark shape appeared on the terrace, looking down. It made for the steps too.

*

The sound in the cove drowned out everything. The wind was getting stronger by the minute. Jo edged away, as close in to the cliff as she could and waited, listening. Maybe Frank would have given up or chased the wrong way; maybe she

317

didn't need to go any further. But she heard shoes on the steps, descending, and she started moving again, hoping the sound from the wind and the sea would mask the crunch of the pebbles beneath her feet. She kept to the right, heading for the big rocks lining the bottom of the cliff lower down the beach, inky black and obscure but offering a more silent route, and clambered onto one, feeling more than seeing what she was doing.

She kept moving, reaching out her hands, touching the rocks, scrambling carefully, keeping as low as she could. It was slow progress but she was heading in the right direction at least, towards the sea, the headland close on her right. She was sure Frank was coming behind her but didn't dare look round, afraid she would be more noticeable if she did. She didn't know him any more; he scared her. She stopped now and then, staying very still, then moving on, flattening herself and keeping close to the cliff as she made towards the relative brightness of the sea. She prayed that Harry was right and that this would be easy.

Now she was level with the breakers crashing onto the shore. The tide had definitely turned and the weather was closing in. This wasn't the night for climbing around the headland; it was madness. Whipped up by the wind, the sea had a new energy and was beating inexorably up the beach. She stopped, listened, then cautiously looked round. For a moment she saw nothing, then she made out the shape of a man on the rocks up nearer the beach. He had been following her and now stood, facing towards her, legs apart, balancing against the wind. Could he see her? She couldn't be sure. She flattened herself even more into the rocks. Already she was bruised and cut, her fingers raw and chilled, but she barely noticed.

There was no way Frank was going to let her go. He didn't dare: he knew she would talk. But then he knew Eleanor would talk too. It was impossible to imagine her aunt being sweet-talked into keeping his secret. Jo's heart sank even further. Eleanor. Please God Imogen and Mari had stayed with her and didn't leave her back at the house alone. Eleanor would say she was fine, that she didn't need them, and Frank would be waiting.

Jo moved on. A huge wave took her by surprise and washed up over her legs but she held on grimly, gritting her teeth, desperately trying to keep her body and the jacket up out of the water. If the cutting and the recorder got wet, she would have no proof of anything. The wave receded and she reached up to the rocks above her, climbing higher, keeping moving. As she came out from the relative shelter of the cove, the full force of the wind hit her, taking her breath away. She steadied herself and moved on.

Out in the bulge of the headland, exhausted, she managed to find a shelf of rock to rest on. It looked high enough to keep her out of the sea, for a little while at least. Surely she was safe from Frank now. Either way, she had to rest; she couldn't go any further. With numb fingers, she pulled out her phone. Wonderful: it was still working. Nearly eleven thirty. She had been climbing forever. But she stared at the screen disbelievingly: there was no signal. She rested her head back against the cliff and closed her eyes, too tired even to swear.

Chapter 24

Harry wasn't there when Matthew got home which was no surprise. Matthew had left the concert before the second half had even started and his son had already disappeared. Jo appeared to have slipped out too. He had hoped to speak to her; there were things that needed saying, but she had gone and suddenly the event held no interest for him.

Now he switched on the television for distraction, opened a bottle of beer and sat on the sofa, directing the remote at the screen, flicking through the stations. Nothing impressed him much. He took a swig of beer from the bottle and settled on some dark-screened thriller. It barely held his attention but he watched the moving pictures and took another pull on the beer. Sophie hated him drinking from the bottle. For more than a year after she'd died he used to pour the beer into a glass. He remembered the first time he'd drunk from the bottle again, in a moment of mental abstraction, and the feeling of guilt. And the acute feeling of loss, twisting him inside, sucking the air out of his body. It had been like that all along: slow, excruciatingly painful steps to acceptance. Jo was wrong if she thought he hadn't moved on. He had. Just not quickly enough, and not caring enough of his son. He had been too swallowed up in his own pain. But if he hadn't moved on at all, he would never have asked her out.

He put the bottle down and stood up again, taking the

stairs two at a time up to his bedroom and the box in his wardrobe. This was the box Harry had found when they'd moved in, when Matthew had lost his temper and torn into him. He was mortified when he thought about it now. The box held Sophie's jewellery and a pile of photographs and Matthew had refused to look at any of it since, had sealed it with tape and put it away. Now he lifted the box onto the bed and sat down beside it, pulling the tape away, pushing back the cardboard flaps.

There were neat little padded ring boxes and a bigger wooden box which held Sophie's necklaces and bracelets. Another round box contained her earrings. He wasn't sure why he kept them all except that he still couldn't imagine parting with them. He took them out and laid them aside. Then he pulled out a picture frame. It held a photograph of him and Sophie together, his arm round her shoulders. The next frame held a photo of Sophie with Harry, the boy still in short trousers and a shy expression on his face. A tear rolled down Matthew's cheek and dripped onto his sweater. He managed to brush the next one away with the back of his hand.

There were other pictures - dozens of them - some in frames, most in albums or loose in envelopes. He didn't look at them. These two were enough for now. He put the box away and took the two photographs downstairs, propping them up on top of the cupboard in the sitting room.

He had just done it when he heard a key in the lock and turned and Harry rushed in looking hunted, panting, leaving the door swinging open behind him.

'What's the matter?' said Matthew, concerned. 'Are you all right?'

Harry stood, staring wildly at him, as if he had lost the power of speech and was trying to will his father to understand the problem on his own. Matthew stepped round him and pushed the door to.

'You've been smoking again,' he complained. 'I can smell it on your clothes.'

'Jo's in trouble.' Harry's words came out in a rush. He turned to face his father, clenching and unclenching his hands. 'I didn't know where else to go. I don't know what to do.'

'Jo? Slow down. What do you mean, "she's in trouble"?'

'She's being chased by this guy and she's on the headland somewhere and the tide's coming in.'

Now Matthew paid attention.

'Start from the beginning, Harry. What guy and why is he chasing her?'

'You don't believe me.'

'Yes, I do. But I don't know what you're talking about.'

'There's no time.'

'You have to explain.'

'I was outside The Mill. I was smoking. Yes, I know, I shouldn't. And I saw Jo leave. Then I saw this guy leave too and he was obviously following her, dead suspicious-looking, so I tagged on and watched what he was doing. Jo went back up to Skymeet and this guy followed. So I climbed over the fence and went after them. She went in the house and then to a room at the back. Her aunt's study I think. There was a light on and this guy was watching her through the window. Then he went in too.'

'What? He broke in?'

'No, she'd opened the patio door to call the cat in. Anyway they were talking and arguing - I couldn't hear much of it - and the next thing she ran out of the door and he chased after her. She got away and I'm sure she went down to the beach. I saw the man go down too. I waited for a while but

322

then he came up alone and left. I went down then but there was no sign of her. I think she's trying to climb round the headland like I do but the tide's rising quickly and she doesn't know what she's doing. We've got to rescue her. Dad, please?'

Matthew put his hand on Harry's shoulder and squeezed.

'It's OK Harry, we will. We'll make sure she's safe.' He struggled to get his thoughts in order. What was the best thing to do? He turned away and picked up his phone from the table. 'I'll ring the coastguard. They're the only people who'll be able to find her in the dark. Who was this man, did you see?'

'His name's Frank Marwell. I think he might be the guy I heard with Jo's aunt…you know, round about when she fell.' He hesitated. 'I was on the beach that night, Dad. I didn't like to tell you. I heard a man but I didn't know who it was. I was scared but I should have said. I'm sorry.'

'It doesn't matter.' Matthew pressed the phone to his ear and smiled at his son. 'You're telling me now.' A woman's voice answered in his ear. 'Yes, coastguard please. It's an emergency.'

*

Jo hadn't managed to move from the ledge. The only rocks that seemed to offer any purchase on her way forward were lower down and were already being lapped by the sea. In the dark it was hard to see where else she could go. Perhaps she should go back, but that looked scary now too: the water was washing the last rock she had climbed from. And, dear God, she was so tired and cold and her teeth kept chattering. It was hard to believe she could be this cold when August was barely over. She hugged herself and tried to stay tight and compact to conserve her heat.

She closed her eyes. She might have dozed a little, she

323

wasn't sure. Eleanor kept looming into her mind. She hoped Imogen and Mari were looking after her, that they had stayed with her. Of course Lawrence might be around somewhere. Frank hadn't admitted pushing Eleanor over the cliff but Jo was sure he had done it so it wasn't Lawrence after all, or Vincent or... She drifted, half asleep, different faces and snatches of conversations running through her mind. But Lawrence didn't know Eleanor was in danger. No-one else knew. Still, Imogen and Mari would stay with her wouldn't they...? She dozed again.

She came to with a start as water washed over the ledge and soaked her trousers. The sea was all around her now, choppy, frothing, buffeting the cliff. There was nowhere else to go. Another wave overran the ledge and soaked her worse than before. She tried to unfurl herself and stand up but she was stiff and weak with the cold and it took time. She stood on shaky legs.

There was a throbbing noise deep in the back of her head, filling her ears, and then it was all around her and getting louder. She turned her head. A bright light was rapidly approaching and suddenly she was flooded with it.

A helicopter, and it was scanning the cliffs. She lifted her arms and waved as hard as she could.

'I'm here,' she shouted ineffectually over the roar. 'I'm here. Here.'

The helicopter homed in and now she was sobbing with relief. It was over.

*

It was a long night. After her nerve-jangling recue by the search and rescue helicopter, Jo was taken back to the village where they landed in the village car park and were met by the

324

coastguard team on the ground. The on-board paramedic had checked her out but, other than numerous minor cuts and bruises and some mild hypothermia, she had no obvious injuries. She refused to go to hospital anyway. She was fine, she insisted; she had to get home.

Most of her clothes were sodden and she sat, wrapped in a space blanket, feeling both agitated and yet strangely numb. It was after one in the morning but, through the open door of the helicopter, she could see a small group of local people gathered in the car park to watch what was going on. A police car arrived too and the officer came over to speak to the coastguard crews. She glanced at her watch. She needed to go. She tried to stand up but her legs felt like jelly and she sat down again.

'Jo?'

'Matthew? What are you doing here?' He was standing at the entrance to the helicopter, peering in anxiously.

'Are you all right?'

'Yes, I'm fine.' She leaned forward. 'Where's Eleanor, do you know? Is there someone with her?'

'Don't worry about her. She's OK. I've spoken to Imogen. They're all back at the house.'

'Thank God. And Frank?'

'He's disappeared. I don't understand what this is all about Jo.'

A policeman appeared at Matthew's shoulder and introduced himself, then began asking questions. Matthew disappeared. Jo told her story while the officer took notes with a non-committal expression. She gave him the digital recorder.

'Frank didn't know I was recording him. I thought the water might have got to it but I've checked it and it's still working. It's a bit muffled at times but you can hear all the important parts.'

Then she gave him the magazine cutting and explained how it had been the trigger for Eleanor and also the reason she was pushed over the cliff. The paper was slightly damp but still intact and readable.

'Did Frank Marwell actually admit to pushing her?'

'No-o. He said he only spoke to her on the phone. But he did admit to being upset that she was starting to remember things. I'm sure he did it, officer. He was frustrated and desperate. It was obvious in the way he talked.'

The police officer nodded slowly, his expression giving nothing away. Jo had begun to doubt whether he believed any of it.

'I'll need to speak to your aunt too,' he said.

'Can it wait till tomorrow? She'll probably be in bed by now. She's still getting over her fall. I'm very worried about her safety. You have to find Frank Marwell.'

'We'll look into that, Miss Lambe.' The officer glanced at his watch. 'I'll come back later this morning to speak to your aunt.'

The next few minutes passed in a blur. The police officer left but the paramedic insisted on checking on her again, telling her she must stay inside, keep warm, take warm drinks to get her temperature up. Then Matthew reappeared with a bundle of dry clothes and ten minutes later she was in the passenger seat of his car, wearing a pair of Harry's joggers and a sweatshirt, a blanket draped across her. Harry sat in the back, silent, while Jo offered an increasingly rambling account of what had happened.

'That's an amazing story,' said Matthew. 'But Harry's the hero, you know.' He glanced in the rear view mirror at his son. 'He's the one who raised the alarm.'

Jo turned to look back at him. 'Thanks Harry. How on earth did you know?'

'Later,' said Matthew firmly. 'Keep that blanket over you, will you?'

She sat back. The sea and the wind still crashed in her ears but the rush of adrenaline was fading; her eyelids felt heavy and drooped.

Back at Skymeet, Imogen and Mari fussed over her, making her tea, pressing her to eat. Eleanor had insisted on staying up, waiting to see her, but the events of the night had taken their toll and she looked pale, exhausted and frayed.

'What on earth are you wearing?' she demanded, frowning at the joggers rolled up at the ankle and the sweatshirt with *doomed* printed on the front.

'They're Harry's.' Jo sat next to her aunt on the sofa and flashed Harry a grateful smile. He was sitting on a cushioned stool at a slight remove from everyone else. 'My clothes got wet.'

'People keep saying it was Frank who caused all this but I don't understand how.'

'I'll explain in the morning, Eleanor. Why don't you go to bed now? I'm fine. It'll wait.'

'No, I'm not going till you tell me.' Eleanor glared round at them all. 'Come on, what is it I'm missing? What is it I can't remember? I have to know.'

'OK, look, do you remember telling me earlier this evening about the bust of Shelley? How Hugh Shrigley had bought it and shown it both to you and Frank years ago?'

'Yes. I've been having dreams about that party but they never seemed to finish. It's been driving me mad.'

'Well, that's when the whole thing started - at that party.' Jo explained again, how Frank had gone back to see Hugh afterwards and what had happened. 'He admitted it, Eleanor,' she said. 'Frank told me all this himself.'

Eleanor searched her face, then looked away, saying nothing.

'You were sent a magazine cutting with a photograph of Frank and Louisa. They were in his study and that bust of Shelley was on a shelf behind them. You must have recognised it and put it all together. You realised Frank shouldn't have had that bust and you challenged him about it.'

Eleanor was still silent. Everyone watched her, waiting.

'Do you remember the photograph?' prompted Jo.

'No.' Eleanor shook her head, looking anguished. 'No. I don't remember anything about it.'

'Never mind. It'll come back when it's ready. Why don't you go to bed? I'll walk up with you.' Jo stood up but her legs still wobbled and she sat down again.

'No, let me walk with you,' said Mari, coming over.

Eleanor reluctantly gave in and went with Mari out into the hall. Jo waited until she heard Eleanor and Mari on the stairs, then glanced between Matthew and Imogen.

'How do we know Frank has disappeared?'

'Louisa told me,' said Imogen. 'She said she hadn't seen him since before the concert. They'd had an argument and she'd left and gone up to the pub. He'd been behaving oddly for days, she said, ever since Eleanor left hospital. She blamed Eleanor of course. Said she knew Frank had never got over her and that Eleanor encouraged him. His things have gone from the apartment apparently.'

'I wonder where he's gone,' said Jo wearily. 'The police officer's coming to speak to Eleanor tomorrow.' She looked at the clock. 'Today, that is.'

'You need to get some sleep,' said Matthew. 'Will you be

all right here?'

'We'll stay with them,' said Imogen. 'I know Mari would want to anyway. If that's all right, Jo?'

'Of course. You can have one of the spare rooms. Thank you.' She frowned. 'Does Lawrence know about all this?'

'He did appear earlier,' said Imogen, 'but when the news came through that you were all right, he just wandered off again.' She paused and pulled a face. 'That man spends too much time alone if you ask me.'

Chapter 25

Vincent and Louisa both left quietly, saying nothing to anyone. On the Monday, Mari and Imogen departed too, claiming commitments they had to get back to. Jo thanked them for their help. Still apprehensive about Frank, she was both sorry and yet relieved to see them go. She and Eleanor needed to get back onto an even keel; they needed to establish a routine of some kind and find normality if they could. It felt a little unreal, waiting for news of Frank. This was the sort of thing you read about in newspapers or saw on television reports. It didn't happen in your own life, in sleepy seaside villages.

Eleanor appeared to have taken a step backwards. The events surrounding the festival and Jo's ordeal had played heavily on her, as had the revelations about Frank. And the interview with the policeman only upset her further. She couldn't answer several of his questions and got frustrated both with him and with herself. The police officer did bring news however. One of Frank's neighbours in London was a shift-worker and, when questioned, had reported seeing him leaving his flat very early on the morning after the concert. He was carrying a suitcase and looking purposeful the neighbour said. It seemed the police had missed him by a half hour at most.

Eleanor received the information with a blank expression. Over the next days she rested too much, appearing disinterested and unwilling to engage in any activity that was suggested. Lawrence was solicitous and offered chess; she refused. Jo wanted to take her out for a drive and maybe a meal; she wouldn't go. And she wouldn't talk about Frank at all despite Jo's occasional gentle prompting. She had closed in on herself, like an injured animal does, retreating to a safe place to lick its wounds. Unsure what to do for the best, Jo cautiously offered to take her to see the doctor. Her aunt rallied sufficiently to tell her in no uncertain terms what she thought of the idea. Jo didn't pursue it.

On the Friday morning they were both in the sitting room when Jo received a call from the police. She glanced at the phone screen and immediately stood up and walked to the patio doors with her back to her aunt. The officer had news of Frank. He had been picked up at the ferry terminal in Holyhead with a ticket for Ireland in his pocket and was in the process of being transferred for questioning. It was good news but when the call ended Jo paused, still facing the patio doors, unsure if she should tell Eleanor. It might just upset her more. There was no escaping it however because Eleanor had been listening intently to Jo's half of the conversation.

'Who was that?' she demanded as soon as Jo turned round. 'You said it was good. You were relieved. Why?'

'It was the police.' Jo hesitated. 'They've found Frank. He was about to get a ferry to Ireland. He's being questioned.'

Eleanor's face puckered. 'Ireland?' She seemed to mouth something else to herself then shook her head and looked away.

Charlotte chose that moment to bustle into the room. She had been in overdrive these last days, cooking, cleaning, fussing in and out, and yet she had been either strangely silent or painfully polite. It was unnatural and felt dangerous. She was like a pressure cooker waiting to blow. She stopped short now, standing legs apart, arms crossed, and glared at Eleanor.

'Here again. Sitting on your backside. I never thought I'd see the day when you'd feel sorry for yourself woman. It's pitiful.'

'I do not feel sorry for myself,' retorted Eleanor. 'Mind your own business.'

'It is my business. Having you draped round the house, in my way... And then there's poor Jo trying her hardest to help you out and you virtually ignoring her like you're too good for us all. You're damned ungrateful, that's all I can say. If that's not feeling sorry for yourself, I don't know what is.'

'Well, I'm not.' Eleanor turned back to Jo. 'She's wrong, Jo. And I'm not ungrateful either. Not at all.' She shook her head. 'I'm just... I don't know what I am. I'm so muddled and confused. I can't seem to... I'm sorry. I am.'

'Being sorry's all well and good,' said Charlotte, 'but it's not the same as doing something about it. You should get up off that backside of yours and do something to help yourself.'

Charlotte raised her eyebrows meaningfully, glanced at Jo, then left the room. There was a long, strained silence.

'I can't believe Frank has done these things,' Eleanor said in a small voice, staring at the fireplace. 'The row with Hugh, hitting him... And chasing you like that, frightening you.' She shook her head. 'It's not the Frank I know. Or thought I knew. I mean we argued. All the time, I know that. But I never felt scared of him. I can remember us throwing things at each other. I think I hurt him more than he ever hurt me.'

'He was desperate. And we don't know how Hugh behaved or what might have provoked him.'

'And then the police officer was asking me if Frank had pushed me off the cliff.' Again, Eleanor shook her head, chin

332

jutting mulishly. 'He wouldn't do that.'

'Maybe you were arguing.'

'I can't remember.'

'Give it time.'

'I'm not sure I want to remember.' Eleanor looked at Jo, eyes taut with pain. 'I loved Frank so much, I can't tell you. It died a little. In the end it was easier not living with him. But even so...'

Silence stretched between them again.

'So...' said Jo, 'why don't we go out for coffee? I could drive us down to the car park and we could walk from there. What do you think?'

Eleanor hesitated for a long minute, then nodded.

'All right.' She almost smiled - for the first time that week. 'You just want to see Matthew.'

'The thought had crossed my mind.'

'So why haven't you been before, you silly girl?' She pulled a face. 'I suppose it's my fault; you didn't want to leave me alone. But I'm fine. You go. You don't want me along anyway.'

'Yes I do. I don't want to sit and drink coffee alone. Stop arguing. Come on, let's go out.'

*

Matthew booked a table for seven o'clock on the Saturday night at the new Italian restaurant. It stood on the edge of town and, according to Harry, already had a reputation for making 'the best pizzas ever'. Given that the meal was a small - and belated - celebration of Harry's birthday, the choice had been his. Matthew had rung Jo on the Monday, checking how she was, asking after Eleanor and any developments. He had also invited her to join them but she had prevaricated, saying she

333

didn't want to leave Eleanor alone at the moment. And he believed her, mostly. After all that she and Eleanor had been through, it was understandable. But still he couldn't help wondering if she was using Eleanor as an excuse. Maybe she simply didn't want to bother with him again and, after the way he had behaved, he couldn't blame her. One phone call to the coastguard didn't wipe the slate clean.

But then Jo had turned up at the café on the Friday with Eleanor. It was the first time he'd seen her since that awful night and she looked all right: the cuts and bruises were slowly healing and she looked happy. In fact, she fairly exuded a light-hearted energy he wasn't sure he had seen in her before. Apparently Frank had been picked up and was being held for questioning. Seizing an opportunity away from Eleanor's keen hearing, she confided that the police said Frank would be certain to face charges, the severity of which were still to be determined. It was obvious that a huge weight had been lifted from her shoulders. On the spur of the moment, he asked her out again.

'Harry would love you to be there.' He smiled apologetically. 'And I would too.'

'Carpe diem,' Sophie used to say. She had been big into not letting opportunities pass. He hoped she would approve of what he was doing; he thought she would have liked Jo.

And this time Jo said yes.

The summer was at an end and Harry was back at school. The atmosphere had lightened considerably between father and son. While they were waiting for Jo to be rescued, Matthew persuaded Harry to tell him about the night on the beach when he'd heard Eleanor arguing. It had been a painful revelation to find out just how much his son had been bottling up inside, worse still to know that he hadn't even trusted his father to take his side. Matthew apologised, chastened, and Harry did too, admitting to doing 'a lot of stuff you don't like, partly just because you don't like it.'

He had managed to convince Harry to go with him to the police and explain what he knew but the boy was still adamant that he didn't see Eleanor fall. By the time it happened he'd already set off towards the headland, he said, frightened.

'Would you recognise the voice?' the police officer asked him.

'I'm not sure. Voices sound different from below. They're distorted. I think it was this Frank guy but I couldn't honestly swear to it, you know, on a Bible or whatever. I'm sorry.'

'It doesn't matter,' Matthew said, before the policeman could comment. 'You tell it like it was. That's all anyone can ask.'

Now Matthew and Harry were sitting at the table in the restaurant, reading the menu over and over, glancing round, both trying not to look at the empty chair. Matthew had offered to pick Jo up on the way but on the last minute she had rung to say that she would make her own way there.

'She'll come,' Matthew said eventually. 'She'd have rung again if she wasn't coming.' He looked at his watch. 'We got here early. It's only just ten past.'

Then he saw Jo at the top of the room, a waitress at her shoulder pointing out the table and she was hurrying over to them, looking flustered. He could feel the smile spreading across his face.

'I'm so sorry I'm late.' She threw herself down in the vacant seat. 'I was waiting for a phone call and it came through later than expected. Have you ordered?'

'No. We were still deciding.'

'I've decided.' Harry tossed the menu aside and sat back,

looking smug. 'Pepperoni with extra cheese.'

'Pizza, I assume?' said Jo.

'What else?'

She grinned and picked up the menu.

'I'll get you a drink,' said Matthew, half rising.

'It's OK. The waitress is bringing me one.'

He sat down again. He was trying too hard.

The waitress reappeared with Jo's glass of soda and lime and took their food order. After a couple of minutes of awkward silence, Matthew prompted Harry to talk about a show they were putting on at school in which he had some backstage involvement. Then Matthew talked about the café and how Eddie's girlfriend was moving away, how Eddie had decided to go too and that he would be hard to replace.

The food came and they fell silent again.

'It was good to see Eleanor out and about,' Matthew ventured a few minutes later. 'Is there any more news? What happens next?'

'It's still up in the air. That was the call I was waiting for. I rang to find out what was happening and they were late ringing back and I didn't want to get it here…you know… Anyway, it seems Frank has admitted to the Hugh Shrigley death. He didn't have any choice, presented with the recording but he still insists it was an accident. And he says he never saw Eleanor that Friday night.'

She paused and took a drink.

'They're still questioning him so how it'll all play out, I've no idea. The police are very close about it. They say they've got "a number of avenues to investigate" but they're hoping to have him remanded in custody while they "pursue their lines of inquiry", whatever they are. Apparently the fact that he was caught trying to leave the country will work against him. That makes him a flight risk.'

'Will I have to give evidence?' said Harry.

'I don't know. These things take ages to get to court anyway. We'll have to wait and see. If Eleanor doesn't remember what happened, I guess it will be hard to prove that he had anything to do with her fall.' She shook her head and shrugged. 'There's no sign of her remembering at the moment.'

They finished eating and the plates were cleared away. They ordered dessert.

Matthew fixed Jo with a look. 'Did you bring it?'

'Yes.' She pulled her handbag round from the back of the seat, took a pouch from it and handed it to Harry. 'I'm sorry I didn't have a chance to get anything for your birthday, but…what I'm saying is that this isn't a present exactly. It's your old phone. I had that friend I mentioned look at it. I'm afraid she couldn't get it to work again but she did manage to get the photos off it. They're on a memory stick in there.'

'What? That's awesome. I didn't know you'd got this.' He pulled impatiently at the pouch and found the memory drive, holding it as if it were made of precious metal. 'Wow. Thanks Jo. You're really cool.'

She grinned. 'Am I? I've never been called cool before.'

'We'd better make some copies of those photos,' said Matthew, 'just to be on the safe side.'

Harry looked at his father in surprise, then nodded, pressing his lips together hard and looking away again. A minute later, he excused himself to go to the washroom.

'It looks like you and Harry have made up,' said Jo.

'Oh, you know, we're getting there. It could take a while.'

'Still, I'm glad.'

'I should thank you for it.'

'Nonsense. You'd have got there eventually.' She fingered her glass. 'I'm afraid I was just interfering. I'm sorry. It wasn't my business.'

'No, it was. Someone needed to kick some sense into me.' He hesitated and smiled. 'I'm glad it was you.'

She flicked him a quick look but said nothing. He wished he knew what she was thinking, how far he dare push this.

'What are your plans now?' he asked warily.

'Short term: Eleanor is keen for me to stay on a while.'

'And will you?'

'Yes. I can work here just the same and I want to make sure she's all right.'

'And long term?'

She shrugged. 'I don't know. I'm prepared to wait and see how things work out.' She took another sip of soda. 'What about you? What are your plans?'

'Not sure really. A few months ago, I was ready to pack it all up and leave but I think maybe things are settling down now. Harry's happier and I like it here. Though I'm not sure I'm cut out to run the café forever. If it weren't for Gail and Eddie I'd have been lost. I've been thinking about setting up my own website building business… Maybe.'

He paused and glanced in the direction of the washrooms. There was still no sign of Harry.

'But I'm glad you're staying. I'd like…well…' He leaned forward onto the table, steeling himself to look her directly in the eyes. 'Look Jo, I know I'm not the easiest person in the world at the moment but I am working on it. And Harry and I have been talking. We're making a few changes. What I'm saying is, can I ring you? Could we do this again, and maybe without Harry too?'

'Well…' She hesitated, then slowly grinned. 'Do you

know, I'd like that. I was hoping you'd ask.'

He sat back heavily in the chair. 'Well hell, woman, you could have said something, or at least given me a clue. Whatever happened to female empowerment?'

She was laughing when the waitress brought the desserts, just as Harry returned to the table. His dessert was a huge plate of chocolate fudge pie.

'Yessss,' he said, making a fist pump. 'Now you're talking.'

Jo smiled. Matthew caught her eye and grinned back.

'Brilliant,' Sophie murmured, the word little more than an echo on the wind.

Chapter 26

It was the following Friday when Eleanor finally steeled herself to sit in the chair at the desk in her study. She had been back home for two weeks already. That evening, Jo had gone out with Matthew. They had left early, driving to Plymouth to have a meal and go to a concert afterwards, leaving Eleanor with strict instructions to call Lawrence in the event of any 'problem'. He was home; Jo had checked in advance.

All well and good. But Eleanor had no wish to call on Lawrence, nor did she expect to. She was fine, as fine as someone can be whose memories are perforated with holes and whose body feels like a second-hand car with too many miles on the clock. But Jo kept fussing too much, continually warning Eleanor about this and that, what to do and what not to do. She didn't understand that Eleanor needed this time alone. Eleanor was scared of it, which was the reason she needed it so badly. She didn't want to be scared of being alone, on a sliding, slippery slope of fear for the rest of her life, her world shrinking. She had to face the silence.

Jo's laptop was on the desk along with a pile of notes. She had offered to move her things out, insisting she could work at the table in her bedroom just as well but Eleanor had exhorted her not to worry about it yet. She wasn't ready to start work again. The thought of writing made her nervous too. Suppose she couldn't do it any more? That would be devastating. She took a deep breath and let it out slowly, allowing her gaze to sweep the room. Her study. She remembered sitting here; she remembered writing on her own computer, her own laptop which Jo had since closed and put to the back of the large desk top.

It was odd the way the memories still came to her. Everyone seemed to expect her memory to return in a neat chronological way but, though the farther past was remarkably clear at times, there wasn't that much pattern to it. Odd scenes would flash into her head, sometimes sparked by something someone said or by something she had seen, but often for no apparent reason. It was as if her brain was sorting through them all, tossing one up every now and then, hoping she would identify it and put it back in order. Sometimes she could, sometimes not.

After the chilling events of the literary festival weekend, the party at Hugh Shrigley's had slipped back into place in her head, fully-formed, like a child playing hide and seek who suddenly pops out from a wardrobe. See? says the child. I was here all along. She remembered that conversation with Frank after they'd heard the news of Hugh's death, remembered promising not to say anything about Frank having gone back to the flat. Had she been right to do that? In retrospect, clearly not. How easy it was now to think that. How easy it is though to make promises to the people we love, lightly, blindly, convinced of the essential goodness of them, not expecting any consequences.

But the memory that kept visiting her these last days was further back than that. It's with her now. She's nineteen and has gone with Candida to an open mic event for writers in the smoky back room of a pub. It's the first time she's seen Frank. Good-looking in a gaunt, hyperactive way, he's performing

341

some of his poetry. But he's not just reciting it, he's moving and gesturing, pausing to sweep his gaze over the audience to build their attention. One minute he's murmuring intimately, the next he's roaring till you shrink back in your seat. She has never seen anything like him before; she's entranced. Then, in one of his surveys of the audience he catches her eye and smiles and time stops for her. She thought maybe her heart had stopped too. If it's possible to fall in love in one single moment, for her that was the one.

They had spent the night together, mostly talking, and afterwards Candida had teased her. She'd said it wouldn't last. Candida. Eleanor remembers now going with Jo to identify Candida's body. It's not that long ago she was convinced that her troubled and gifted sister was still alive. What a conflict of emotions that had set in play. Maybe, after all, she had simply wanted it to be true.

Eleanor got up suddenly, pushing the thought away, walking with careful but determined steps back out into the hall and along to the sitting room. It was six-thirty. She looked at the drinks cabinet, thinking fondly of a gin and tonic. 'Don't drink when you're alone,' had been one of Jo's injunctions. 'You might fall.' Annoyingly, she was right. Eleanor turned away, moving slowly round the room, taking in the photographs and the paintings on the walls, the hangings and ornaments, letting their familiarity wash into her. The piano was open; Jo had been playing it every now and then. Eleanor ran her fingers over the keys, then pressed a few notes. She hoped she could learn how to play again.

On the piano top was a large brown envelope, unsealed. She picked it up, peering inside. It contained one sheet of folded paper which she immediately recognised and promptly put the envelope down again. Jo had tracked down a copy of that poetry magazine and had cut out the article about Frank and Louisa's engagement. She had put it in front of Eleanor, wanting her to look at it again. 'This is what you received in the post that day,' she'd said. 'It might bring something back.' But Eleanor had refused. She didn't want to look at it and after a brief tense altercation, Jo had folded it and put it away in this envelope for another time.

Eleanor stood, rooted to the spot, still staring at the envelope. She picked it up again, pulled the paper out and walked back down the room with it, pausing by the patio doors. The sun was getting low and the sky burned with peach and gold. She turned on the standard lamp nearby and looked down at the cutting. It shook a little in her grip.

Her eyes lingered on Frank, then she forced herself to scan the whole thing. There was the bust of Shelley behind him. That was kind of familiar - the position of it just above Frank's left shoulder. But nothing else came to mind. There was something deep inside that felt like it was working its way out but it was too woolly and quite impossible to grasp. She looked at Louisa's sickly smile. God. She crumpled the paper up and screwed it into a ball, tossing it on the cabinet.

She stared at the ball of paper, unable to drag her eyes away. That was weird: she had done that before, had crumpled up the cutting, crushed it into a ball and thrown it across the room. That was it. Then she had picked up the paper again... She stepped forward, picked up the new cutting and carefully straightened it out and pressed it flat. She folded it in half again. But she was in the wrong place because afterwards, she remembered, she had put the cutting in a book on one of the shelves in her study.

She shook her head. It didn't matter where she was because already the images in her head were moving on. She felt almost breathless, wide-eyed at the way they were unfolding, scared but unable to do anything to stop them. She had come through here and poured herself a drink. Yes. Then another and taken it out with her on her walk.

Eleanor unlocked the patio doors and stepped outside. The dying sun cast an amber light over the garden. She was back in the moment, living it again. Earlier that day she had phoned Frank and left a message for him, something short but pointed, something he would be bound to understand. After much heart-searching, she'd decided she had to do something about what she knew but she wanted to talk to him first. Why didn't he ring back? She needed to speak to him.

Eleanor stepped warily down one step, two steps until she was on the lower terrace. This was where she was when he came upon her: Frank, unexpected and as dynamic as ever.

'Eleanor, darling.' That quizzical grin. 'What's going on? Your message was so cryptic. Something to do with a bust? I mean, really…'

He tried to embrace her but she pushed him away.

'I thought you'd gone to Exeter.'

'I came back, especially to see you. You said you wanted to talk.'

'I do.'

The memory rolled on, her challenge about what she had guessed, his explanation of Hugh's death, their raised voices, the striding up and down, the passion.

'You should tell the police,' she insisted. 'Explain to them like you have to me.'

'You've got to be joking. Why the hell would I do that? Are you trying to ruin my life? They wouldn't believe me anyway, and what would it achieve now, after all this time?'

'It's the truth. Otherwise we're both living with a lie and

344

I can't do that. You involved me. I was given no choice.' She hesitated. She hated what she was doing but she was sure she was right. 'If you don't tell them, Frank, I will.'

'But you promised me.'

'Because you lied to me. You can't hold me to a promise based on a lie.'

He took hold of her by both arms and started shaking her, telling her to see sense. She tried to pull away but couldn't shake him off and she was moving backwards, too far back, too close to the edge, and he was coming with her. Then suddenly she was free but it was too late: she heard Frank gasp as she lost her balance and the ground disappeared from beneath her feet. She was falling, rolling, tumbling, thumping on stone, seeing stars, then seeing nothing...

Eleanor came back to the present. She was shuddering. She stepped backwards away from the cliff edge, once, twice, nearly losing her balance, then turned and made her way back indoors, her head all over the place, her heart thumping. It felt as if her wrists still throbbed from his grip. An accident, yes - it must have been, surely - but Frank had started the violence. They had never fought like that before.

She didn't care about Jo's injunction now. She locked the patio doors then poured herself a large gin and tonic and sat on the nearest sofa, hands shaking, trying to let her thoughts settle. Sidney jumped up beside her, softly nudging his head against her free hand. After a moment's hesitation, she began to stroke him.

'Hello Sidney.' He walked onto her lap and she fondled his ears. 'You know, I used to think Frank and I would grow old together. We'd still have been arguing of course, but then we always did. So what went wrong, do you think? Do you know?' Sidney began to purr, settling himself into a

345

comfortable circle. 'But he lied to me. Maybe that's when it went wrong. You can't do that, can you? You can't build a relationship on a lie.'

The light in the room had thickened into a deep rosy hue. The sun was setting, turning red. Inevitably Frank's poem slipped into her mind.

It's a fury of fire and flames and passion,
Or is it rejection and a broken heart bleeds?'

She smiled tentatively down at the cat.

'I'll get over it, Sidney, you know. I'm tougher than that.' She took a mouthful of gin. 'Anyway, I've got a book to finish. It might take a while but I'll do it. He's not going to stop me doing that.'

She rested her head back on the sofa, watching the flaming light dance across the walls and slowly die.

Acknowledgements

I need no excuse to drink coffee but researching this book gave me one. I am indebted to Jackie and Paul for their patient and good-humoured help in teaching me about the coffee shop trade. I learnt far more than ever reached these pages but it was invaluable background information. Any mistakes are entirely my own.

I should also like to thank my editorial team once again for their eagle-eyed vigilance and my gratitude also goes to Rachel Lawston for producing such a wonderful cover design.

Yet again, a big thank you to my husband for his endless support and encouragement, without which none of my books would ever have been written.

That Still and Whispering Place

Kathy Shuker

Bohenna is a small Cornish village, dominated by a thriving vineyard and the Pennyman family who run it. It's an insular community, all gossip and rumour and intertwined lives. Claire knows everyone; she grew up there. She even married into the Pennyman family.

Every summer tourists swarm over the vineyard and village. So when Claire's young daughter disappears without trace, it's obvious to everyone that a visitor took her. Who else would do such a thing?

Six years later, her marriage broken, Claire still struggles to accept what happened. She's been away but she's back now - and increasingly convinced her daughter never left the village at all. But it's not wise to start asking questions. Old resentments run deep and not everyone is pleased to see Claire back in Bohenna.

Some reader reviews:

'Full of excellent imagery, page-turning tensions and brilliant characterisations.'

'A riveting read.'

'This is a beautifully written and well-structured novel.'

'What a page-turner! The author really gets under her characters' skins.'

Lightning Source UK Ltd.
Milton Keynes UK
UKHW021958080119
335206UK00003B/76/P